ELECTIVE PROCEDURES

Also by Merry Jones

The Elle Harrison Series

The Trouble with Charlie

Harper Jennings Thrillers

Outside Eden
Winter Break
Behind the Walls
Summer Session

Zoe Hayes Mysteries

The Borrowed and Blue Murders
The Deadly Neighbors
The River Killings
The Nanny Murders

Humor

America's Dumbest Dates
If She Weren't My Best Friend, I'd Kill Her
Please Don't Kiss Me at the Bus Stop
I Love Her, But…
I Love Him, But…

Nonfiction

Birthmothers:
Women Who Relinquished Babies for Adoption Tell Their Stories
Stepmothers:
Keeping It Together with Your Husband and His Kids

ELECTIVE PROCEDURES

A Novel

Merry Jones

Oceanview Publishing
Longboat Key, Florida

ISBN: 978-1-60809-116-4

Published in the United States of America by Oceanview Publishing, Longboat Key, Florida

www.oceanviewpub.com

10 9 8 7 6 5 4 3 2 1

PRINTED IN THE UNITED STATES OF AMERICA

To Robin, Baille, and Neely

Acknowledgments

Thanks to my excellent agent, Rebecca Strauss at DeFiore and Company; amazing editor Patricia Gussin at Oceanview Publishing; the terrific team at Oceanview: Bob Gussin, David Ivester, Frank Troncale, George Foster, Susan Hayes, and Emily Baar; fellow Philadelphia Liars Club members: Jonathan Maberry, Gregory Frost, Don Lafferty, Jon McGoran, Kelly Simmons, Marie Lamba, Keith Strunk, Solomon Jones, Dennis Tafoya, Keith DeCandido, Stephen Susco, Chuck Wendig, Cordelia Frances Biddle, Janice Bashman, Kathryn Craft, Karen Quinones Miller; Mexico travel mates Nancy and Dennis Delman and Robin Jones; first reader and best husband ever, Robin, and encouraging friends and family, especially Baille and Neely.

ELECTIVE PROCEDURES

December 6, Nuevo Vallarta, Mexico

Don't look down. Don't look down.

I kept repeating those three words, a singsong mantra to steady myself and get through time, pushing through seconds and minutes until it would be afterward and this nightmare would be over.

Don't look down.

But I didn't have to look; I knew what was beneath me. I could picture what was lying six stories down on the concrete beside the kidney-shaped swimming pool, near the mouth of the alligator waterslide. Under the glowing light of sunrise, I imagined a widening crimson puddle. A clump of arms and legs. A shattered bone protruding through flesh. Tangled hair matted into a cracked skull.

Don't look down, I said again, and I didn't. Instead, I aimed my eyes straight ahead, focusing not on the brick wall in front of me, but on the air surrounding my head. I stared into it, straining to see my aura, looking for stains, for splotches of darkness. Was it possible to see your own aura? Was there even such a thing? If there was, I couldn't see it, saw only inches of emptiness between me and the bricks, and, at the periphery of my vision, the railing. For the briefest moment I had a lapse. I almost turned my head, almost looked down at my hand. Don't look, I chanted. Don't look. Looking would mean moving my head. And if I moved it—if I moved anything at all, I'd disrupt my balance and slip, and then, with a thud, there would be two blobs of bones planted beside the pool.

A pelican dive-bombed past me, the rush of air nearly knocking me over. I held my breath, holding steady. I called out

again, hoping someone would wake up, but no one came. So I
told myself to stay steady and think of other things. Other times.
I stared at the wall and repeated: Don't look down don't look
down don't look down.

~

Girls' night was always on Thursday. So that meant it had to
have been a Thursday, what, sixteen days ago? A soiled paper
napkin had been fluttering along the sidewalk alongside us,
dropping to the concrete and lifting off again, escorting Becky
and me down South Street on a blustery November evening. I
smelled onions frying at Jim's Steaks and the rawness of oncom-
ing night.

Of course, I didn't dare shiver now. Didn't dare move. I kept
still, muscles aching and taut as I concentrated on keeping balanced. Balanced. It sounded like eating a diet of yogurt, vegetables, and whole grains. Maybe if I'd eaten more granola, I'd be
better balanced now. Maybe. Or maybe being balanced meant
measuring out equal parts and counterparts—like impulsiveness
and self-restraint. Sanity and craziness. Working and playing.
Sleeping and being awake. Rising and falling. Stop, I scolded
myself. Don't think about falling. Just balance.

I hung on, and there was the paper napkin again, floating
beside Becky and me on South Street. Two weeks and two days
ago. We were in no hurry. We passed tattoo parlors, coffee
shops, pizza places, shoe boutiques, and then Becky stopped beside an orange neon sign: READINGS $10. She peered through
the storefront window, then turned to me with an impish smirk.

I knew that smirk, had seen it before. It had led to singles
bars and spa days. All-night department store sales. Weekend
cruises, online dating sites. Casinos and Zumba lessons. The
smirk was like a neon sign warning: brace yourself.

"Elle, you up for this?"

No way. I was barely up for dinner, had come out only under
duress. In the months since Charlie's death, I hadn't been doing
much of anything. For a few months, I'd dragged myself to

work and managed to feign energetic cheeriness for my class of second graders, but by the end of each school day, my face had ached from smiling and my body from pretending. I'd come home content to wallow quietly within the walls of my Fairmount townhouse until, finally, I'd taken a leave of absence so I could spend my days staring at *Law and Order* reruns. My friends, however, had been relentless. They didn't understand that losing a husband, even a lying-cheating-inheritance-stealing one whom I'd been about to divorce, had taken its toll. They didn't comprehend the grieving process or how long it might take, and Jen had endearingly begun to call me DD, short for Debbie Downer. They insisted that I "move on," which included, but was not limited to, going out with them weekly for "girls' night" dinners.

That Thursday evening, Becky and I were on the way to one such girls' night with half an hour to spare. When she asked about the fortune-teller, I thought she was joking. The place looked sleazy and dark, and everyone knew that fortune-telling was a scam. But Becky started for the door.

"I've never had my fortune told, have you?"

I hadn't, no. And I wasn't about to. I was having enough trouble with the past and present, didn't need to take on the future. I hung back, but she tugged at my sleeve.

"Come on, Elle. What's the harm? It's only ten bucks. I'll treat—maybe she'll tell me if I'll meet a guy."

"Really?" Meeting guys had never been a problem for Becky. She was curvy, spunky, short, and soft, and men were drawn to her like sleepyheads to pillows. If anything, she needed help keeping men away.

"You know what I mean. Not just any guy. The Guy. A keeper. Come on. It'll be fun."

And so, reluctantly, I'd let Becky drag me through a small entryway into an overheated, dimly lit sitting area separated from the rest of a large rose-colored room by a pair of drooping crimson curtains. Crosses and images of Jesus hung on the walls.

A couple of upholstered chairs with flattened-out cushions backed against the window. Beyond them two folding chairs faced a small cloth-covered card table. The place smelled of roasting meat. Somewhere behind the curtains, a baby cried. I couldn't breathe.

I looked at Becky and stepped back toward the door. "Let's go."

But a young woman rushed through the curtains, wiping her hands on a dishtowel, yapping at someone over her shoulder in a language I couldn't understand.

"Welcome, ladies. I am Madam Therese. You'd like readings?" She smiled, glancing from Becky to me. "What kind? Tea leaves? Tarot?"

Becky shrugged. "I don't know—"

"It's okay. No problem. I can offer you choices. The cards are twenty dollars. Tea is twenty-five."

Becky pointed to the window. "But the sign says ten dollars."

Madam Therese hesitated, shoved her hair off her face with the back of her hand. "Okay, yes. The sign is for short readings. Palms. We can start with it, and then we'll see. You can upgrade. You understand? Who will be first?" She'd held her hand out for Becky's money.

Becky handed her a twenty.

"Good, this is for two."

"No—not me." I shook my head, but Madam Therese whisked the cash into her skirt pocket and disappeared behind the curtains.

"Becky, I'm not doing this—"

"Relax. It's no big deal."

"Get your change. She owes you ten dollars."

Becky put up a hand, refusing to hear more. Behind the curtains, Madam Therese spoke to someone unseen in her foreign tongue. A man grumbled and the baby's wails faded. In a moment, she returned, her hair tied back, revealing dramatic cheekbones and large bangle earrings. The bracelets on her arms jingled when she moved. The scent of jasmine mixed with that of meat.

"For ten dollars, you get a five-minute reading. After, if you want more, we'll keep going. You pay just a little more, you understand?" Madam Therese smiled and lit a candle, made the sign of the cross. She took a seat, motioned for Becky to sit across from her, reached for her hand.

I didn't know what to do, so I sat on one of the cushioned chairs, watching the woman study Becky's palm. I felt uneasy, as if I shouldn't be there.

"You will have three children close together, but not for a while yet," Madam Therese smiled. "At least one boy. I see him shining in your aura." She looked at Becky. "Your lifeline is long, healthy. And your love line is long, also. But so far, you haven't been lucky, I am right?"

Becky glanced at me, gave an embarrassed giggle.

"But see, the line gets wider here. More steady. So, not long from now, you will meet a man and fall in love. Not just in love. Deeply in love, you understand me?"

Deeply in love? I understood her. A raw hollowness gnawed my gut. Why was it that, even though he'd been dead for thirteen months, even though I'd thrown him out and had been in the middle of divorcing him, everything reminded me of Charlie? I turned away, looking out past the neon sign at South Street. And, of course, there we were, Charlie and me, strolling past shops, his arm around my shoulder. Where were we going? Out for coffee? For a drink? I saw him lean over and kiss my forehead, felt the brush of his lips. But abruptly, a delivery truck pulled up, cutting off my view. Wiping the image away.

Becky turned to me, beaming. "Elle. Did you hear that?"

Oops. No, I hadn't.

"I'm getting married soon."

Really. Should I buy a dress?

"Actually, I see many men around you. But this man—this special one you are waiting for, he is different. He is not the man you expect. Understand me? He might be—how I should say it? Someone you never thought about loving."

"Why, is he a criminal? He's not a drug dealer, is he?" She blinked. "Or wait—is he hideous?"

Madam Therese looked up. Her eyebrows were thick and black. Perfectly symmetrical. "These things I cannot tell you. Only that he is unlike the others." Her gaze returned to Becky's hand. "Also, you will travel very soon. You have plans?"

Becky shrugged. "No."

"Well, you will make some. You will go someplace warm. I see water. Maybe someplace by the sea." She released Becky's hand. "You want more reading? Because this was five minutes. For ten more dollars, I can tell you more."

Becky paused. Was she considering it?

I interrupted. "Becky, you already gave her twenty. She already has the extra ten."

"No. That's for you." Becky stood. "Your turn, Elle."

Madam Therese persisted. "Okay. But when you return from your trip, you will come back to see me again, you understand? I will tell you more." Madam Therese turned to me, gestured for me to join her.

I didn't move.

"Go on." Becky took the seat beside me.

Madam Therese bent her head. Her bracelets jangled when she crossed herself again. She looked at me with tired eyes. "Come. Sit."

I stood, took a seat at the table.

Madam Therese took my hand, stared at it. Her brows furrowed and her back stiffened. She met my eyes. Hers were dark and deep, like bottomless holes. "You want to hear the truth? All of it?"

Despite my doubts about palm reading, my heart lurched. Why was she asking me that? What did she see? "Why not? Is it bad?"

"Bad? Life isn't good or bad. It's a balance."

Yes, she'd definitely used that word. Had it been a warning? An omen? Had she said it intentionally?

I hung onto the railing, tried to stay balanced. To remember everything she'd said. I saw her dark skirt and white sweater, her black eyeliner. Her rings. I smelled the roasting meat and the jasmine. Felt her coarse fingers holding my hand.

In a jolt, she sat back. "Who has died?" She looked from Becky to me.

Becky blinked at me.

"A spirit is with us. It isn't resting."

Becky's eyes widened. "Oh God, maybe it's Charlie. Her husband died—"

"Becky, please—"

"Okay, I understand." Madam Therese touched her forehead, frowned. Concentrated again. "Okay, listen. I will tell you only some, you understand? But not all. What would be the point?"

Lord. Was it too terrible to say aloud?

"So." She looked just above my head. "Your aura—the energy that surrounds you. It is stained."

Becky whispered, "What?"

My aura was stained? How? I pictured a halo blotched with spilled wine—or with my second graders' colored markers.

"The stains are blood."

Oh. Wrong both times.

"And also darkness." Madam Therese's voice was hoarse, throaty. "I see around you a cloud. A cloud of death—yes."

What? I felt a chill, said nothing.

Becky said, "Oh God."

"This cloud means you must be cautious. The dead—their spirits are drawn to you. Some of them are harmless. But others—" she met my eyes, "surely, you already know this."

Knew what? Were dead people out to get me? I looked

around. Was Charlie there? But Charlie wouldn't hurt me. So was it some other dead person? I saw only Becky and Madam Therese. Nobody else.

"If you are wise, you will protect yourself."

From what? The dead? How could I do that?

"You are stronger than you think. This is why they come to you. You have the gift."

She let go of my hand. "So, do you have questions for me? Things you want to know?"

Questions? Seriously? I was surrounded by hostile dead people, death clouds, bloodstains and darkness. What questions could I possibly have? "No. I just came here with my friend."

"Listen, then: You will also travel, like your friend. You also will meet a man. But be aware: this cloud—the darkness goes where you go. It surrounds you. Be careful because the dead are drawn to this darkness; to them it is a beacon. They will find you. You understand this. You know this to be true." Her tone was matter-of-fact. She let out a breath. "And so, the five-minutes time is up. I am happy to go on, if you want me to."

Want her to? God no. I let out a breath. "That's okay. I'm good." I wasn't sure what else to say. "Thank you" didn't cover it.

"Okay, no problem. You will come back to me again. Another day." Madam Therese turned to the curtain, called a name. Stood.

A lanky man with gelled hair stepped out from behind the curtain. They exchanged words I couldn't understand, and he ushered us to the door in a hurry as if we were bothering him. Or as if we'd brought with us a cloud of death.

At the time, I'd dismissed the reading. It was hogwash. There was no such thing as a bloodstained aura. And it was absurd to think that the dead were drawn to me.

But two weeks and two days later, clinging to a balcony six stories above the ground, I reconsidered Madam Therese's predictions. I called out again and grasped the railing, struggled to balance and closed my eyes, reminding myself not to look down at the concrete. Picturing the lifeless body of the woman I'd just failed to save.

~

Closing my eyes wasn't the best idea. Charlie showed up again, this time in my den with my kitchen knife in his back. I saw not just Charlie in that terrible moment, but also all the other terrible moments that had ensued—the deaths and the twisted secrets came together in a montage—no, in a stark mosaic. A kaleidoscope made from shards of terrible memories.

"Elle!"

I opened my eyes. The kaleidoscope shattered, fell away. The sunrise greeted me, along with Becky, Jen, and Susan frantically reaching across the railing, jabbering and tugging at me. Had they heard me yell for help? When had they gotten there? They pawed at me, nearly knocking me over.

"Grab her thigh," Jen said.

"No, wait. I think we should take her arm."

"Her arm? I've got her thigh. You get her arm."

"Careful," I managed, but I doubt they heard me.

My legs were splayed around the brick wall between balconies. My left foot rested tentatively on the railing of ours; my right on the neighbor's. My left arm hugged the wall; my right grasped the edge of the next-door railing. Behind my t-shirt and panty-clad backside, I felt the warmth of dawn and the calm of the ocean. And the pull of open air that extended six stories down.

Another pelican whooshed by. I glimpsed huge wings, a long beak. I wobbled, dug my fingers into the cement between bricks, closed my eyes again. And saw the face of Madam Therese.

"Take Susan's hand, dammit."

"She doesn't hear us. She's pulling an Elle."

"Now? Are you kidding?"

"Elle," Susan shouted.

"I can't take your hand. I can't let go." Even talking seemed to throw me off balance.

The three of them held onto my left thigh and leg. I glanced down, disobeying my own advice, and saw a man kneeling beside the dead woman, taking her hand. He looked like Charlie. That was crazy. From up here, I had no idea what he looked like. He could have been anyone. Hotel staff gathered. Security officers. A lifeguard looked up, saw me. Pointed. People gaped up at me.

They looked very tiny.

Slowly, I tilted my head up, moving my gaze back to the sixth floor. The muscles in my legs twitched. I couldn't stay straddled much longer.

"What's her name?" I heard a man, a Mexican accent.

"Elle."

"Come on, Elle." He wore dark pants and a white short-sleeved shirt, and his beefy arms slipped under mine, around my shoulders. And lifted. I resisted, unwilling to release the railing. But he kept tugging, dragging me up and over, laying me down onto solid tiles of our balcony where I lay still, shivering, catching my breath. Hugging the floor.

Susan, Becky, and Jen hovered around me. The man knelt, put a hand on my forehead, my wrist. He spoke with Susan. She called him Roberto. A maid stood at the balcony door, bug-eyed. Becky brought a glass of orange juice. When I could stand, Roberto helped me through the sliding doors into our suite. Jen began pelting me with questions. What had I been doing out there? Was I crazy? Why had I been climbing on the balcony? Susan snapped at her, telling her to let me be. Roberto was on a cell phone or maybe a hand radio. Something. Speaking urgent Spanish.

I sank onto the living room sofa, shivering, watching. Roberto, it turned out, was a security guard. He greeted the police, introduced Sergeant José Perez and Juan Alonso, the hotel's general manager. Susan sat on one side of me. Becky covered me with a blanket and sat on the other. Jen sat on the floor at my legs like a guard dog. And then the questions began.

~

"What were you doing out there?" Sergeant Perez sat forward with the weight on his toes, as if about to take off in a sprint.

I explained that I hadn't been able to sleep. Actually, Becky had been snoring like a chainsaw, but I didn't think that was relevant, didn't mention it. At about five thirty, I'd given up and gone out on our balcony to wait for the sunrise, and I'd heard voices from the balcony adjacent to ours.

Sergeant Perez interrupted. "They were speaking English?"

Had they been? "I don't remember."

"Well, could you understand what they were saying? Do you speak Spanish?" He was brusque.

"Sergeant, please." Susan intervened. "She doesn't remember. Let her tell us what happened."

"Excuse me, señora." Perez thrust his chest out. "A woman is dead. Your friend is, at the very least, a witness—"

"At the very least? What are you implying?" Susan's back straightened.

Oh Lord. Did he think I'd been involved in the woman's death? Again, I saw Madam Therese. So far, her predictions had come true: Becky and I had both traveled. We'd gone to Mexico with Susan and Jen. We were near the water, as she'd said we'd be. And Becky had met a guy: Chichi, one of the activity directors at the hotel. They'd been virtually inseparable since we'd arrived—Becky hadn't come back to the room until after two a.m. If Madam Therese had been right about all that, maybe she'd also been right about my death cloud and the bloodstains in my aura. I thought of Charlie. Saw him wave.

Susan was nudging me on one side, Becky on the other. Everyone was staring at me. Damn. I'd missed something.

"No, she's fine." Susan insisted. "She does this. She wanders off sometimes."

In fact, my mind did wander off sometimes. My friends called it "pulling an Elle." A shrink had called it a dissociative disorder, usually triggered by stress. Which, right then, I had plenty of.

"She's fine. Elle?" Susan's elbow hit my rib. "Elle, go on."

"Maybe she's refusing to answer the questions. Maybe she'd prefer to come to the station." The sergeant stood on his toes.

Roberto raised his hands. "*Por favor*, José. We all want the same thing: To hear what happened. Why don't we listen and then ask questions afterward?"

Sergeant Perez replied harshly in Spanish, no doubt asserting his rank and authority. Roberto backed off, having made his point. The sergeant sat again, still on tiptoe.

"Go on, Elle." Susan's hand covered mine.

Where had I stopped? Never mind. I just began again. "I heard a man and a woman talking. They sounded romantic— soft giggling and cooing. After a few minutes, I heard the sliding door open and close. I thought they'd gone inside. Everything was quiet." I looked from face to face. Everyone watched me. Waiting.

"And then?" Susan prodded.

"And then a while later, the sliding door opened again. Someone was moving stuff around. It sounded like the deck furniture. There were scraping sounds and thunks. Grunts. I was embarrassed. I thought the couple had come back outside and were, you know."

Sergeant Perez stared at me. "I know?"

Apparently he didn't. "I thought they were having rough sex."

Sergeant Perez cleared his throat. His gaze faltered. "Did you hear voices this time?"

"A woman said, '*Por favor*,' and then there were just grunts. Oh, also a yip. Like this." I made a yip. It sounded shrill.

The sergeant blinked. "That's all?"

I nodded, yes, but I wasn't sure. I thought the sliding doors might have slammed shut again. That would be important, wouldn't it? It would mean someone else besides the woman had been there. But I couldn't remember. Didn't mention it.

"What happened next?"

Next? "I got up off the lounge chair to see what the ruckus was about." I'd expected to see kinky sex. A woman with a whip. A man in bondage. I felt my face get hot admitting that I'd snooped. "I stood at the wall between the balconies, leaned over the railing and peeked around. And under a pinkish-gold glow of dawn, I saw a woman, dangling from the railing."

"You saw no one else?" Sergeant Perez frowned.

"No."

"So you can't be sure who caused those bangs and scrapes you claim you heard."

"She *claims* she heard?" Susan pounced, indignant.

"Señora, yes. All we have is your friend's word that there were sounds. I want to establish if she knew who caused them. Maybe it was the dead woman herself. Or maybe someone else—perhaps a murderer."

A murderer who might have slammed the sliding doors as he fled. I tried to remember. Couldn't.

Susan sputtered.

Becky gave my arm a squeeze. "Go on, Elle."

I shivered under the blanket. The inside of my bones felt cold. Go on, Elle. "I tried to help her."

I hadn't hesitated, hadn't thought it through. My intention had been to leap from our balcony to hers and pull her back up. Good plan, except I hadn't made it. Hadn't gotten all the way across. Instead, I'd climbed onto our railing, straddled the brick wall, and, as I'd taken hold of her railing with my right hand, I'd realized I lacked the height and momentum to swing all the way across. In fact, I'd been stuck halfway, balanced precariously with one foot on each railing. Unable to get to her. Unable to get anywhere.

I didn't tell them all that. Or about how her violet eyes made contact with mine. How neither of us spoke. How we assessed the situation in silence, measuring the distance between our hands, eyeing my right arm and her left. Calculating the risks. All I told them was, "She took a hand off the railing to reach for me."

I closed my eyes, trying to avoid the image. But there she was again, reaching. And in an eye blink, swimming through air. Again, I shuddered, felt the thud. Pictured her, face down on the concrete beside the enormous kidney-shaped pool. I thought of her hand, wondered if her lifeline had stopped abruptly in the middle of her palm. Becky put her arm around my shoulder.

"Did you know this woman?"

"No."

"No?"

"How could she?" Jen bristled. "We only arrived yesterday morning."

Sergeant Perez raised his eyebrows as if surprised the guard dog could speak. "*Sí*. And what brings you here? Vacation?"

"I'm having some work done," Jen smoothed her ash-blonde ponytail. "I brought my friends along—Elle doesn't know any-one here. None of us do."

"And yet, your friend says she risked her life. She did this for a stranger?"

"Yes, Sergeant. For a stranger." Susan was on her feet, scold-ing. "And you're badgering Mrs. Harrison when you should be rewarding her for being a hero and trying to save a life."

The sergeant stood. "As I've said, señora. A woman is dead. It's a serious matter. The death could not have been an accident. It was either murder or suicide. The information I already have makes me doubtful it was suicide." He paused, eyeing each of us one by one.

I wanted to dodge his eyes but didn't dare. I needed to act normal. Wouldn't normal mean meeting his eyes? I wasn't sure. What was normal in this circumstance? The circumstance of not having saved a woman, of having let her drop six stories onto cement? Of bringing a bloodstained aura and a dark cloud of death with me to Mexico? Was her death my fault? Was I responsible? Would a person in my position meet the policeman's eyes?

Again, Charlie appeared, sitting dead on my sofa, and I heard Madam Therese's raspy voice whisper: "The dead are drawn to you. But you already know that."

I saw the woman's violet eyes, her flailing arms.

The sergeant was talking. I'd wandered again, missed part of what he'd said.

"—Phoenix, Arizona. According to hotel records Señora Madison was a guest of the clinic. Her procedures would have been completed this week, as she was due to check out today. So, she was here for plastic surgery. Maybe like you, señora?" He tilted his head at Jen. "The General Manager Juan Alonso tells me that she had a face and neck lift. And he thinks also some work on her lips, is that right, Juan?"

Juan Alonso stood tall, nodded assent.

"She told Juan Alonso and others that she felt like new. More beautiful and happy than ever."

Again, Juan Alonso nodded, said something in Spanish, perhaps her exact words?

"So. It seems that Claudia Madison was not a woman about to kill herself."

Nobody said anything.

"We also know that Señora Madison was paying for her operation and her stay here with cash—cash that she kept in her suite. If the location of this money were known, that would provide a motive."

"Well, none of us knew her or anything about her." Susan's voice was flat.

"Maybe. Maybe not." He watched me.

"Okay, Sergeant Perez." Susan's hands were on her hips. "That's enough. You'd better go before I contact the American consul. I'm a criminal defense attorney, and I know our rights as American citizens. Mrs. Harrison has given you her statement. If you bother her further or make any more insinuations about her role in this matter, I promise you, there will be severe consequences."

"Relax, señora—I have all the information I need. For now. I will be in touch. In the meantime, please surrender your passports to the hotel manager."

"What?" Susan demanded. "That's preposterous—"

"No. It's protocol. Just a formality." He stood at the door with his police officers and Roberto the security guard. They watched while the hotel manager collected our passports, whispering apologies and gracias. Before leaving, Sergeant Perez turned and looked at me. "Be assured, Señora Harrison, we will never be far away. Enjoy your vacation."

With that, Sergeant Perez nodded, and led his entourage away.

～

Only the maid remained, asking if she could clean the bedrooms. Jen said, "Fine," just as Becky said, "Not now. Come back later."

The maid stood with her cart in the open doorway, confused.

"WTF, Becky." As was her habit, Jen spoke in curse code. WTF meant "what the fuck," not as tough to crack as other of her codes. Then again, it wasn't really necessary to translate them. If Jen used initials, she was swearing. "Let her get it done."

Becky shrugged, okay, but the maid didn't come in. She was talking to someone in the hallway, nodding, sí, saying something that sounded like "*policia*," and pointing into the suite. A man stepped around her cart, through the door.

Susan was on the phone, ordering room service. She looked up, motioned him to wait.

He was tanned, sandy-haired, lean. About my height. Elegant, even in khakis. He obeyed Susan, backing up a step, but Becky asked, "Can we help you?"

The man stepped forward. "Sorry for disturbing you. I am Dr. Du Bois. Dr. Alain Du Bois."

Jen hopped to her feet, her long blonde ponytail bobbing. She extended her hand, shook his. "Oh, Dr. Du Bois! Please. Come in." She introduced herself, offered him a seat. "I wasn't expecting you to stop by." She turned to us, beaming. "Everyone, this is my plastic surgeon, the magician who's going to transform my body."

Yes, of course. We'd all heard of Dr. Alain Du Bois. We'd seen his brochures, read the testimonials. Viewed his patients' before and after photos. Jen had been raving about Alain Du Bois nonstop. He was the reason that we'd traveled here from Philadelphia, the reason that we were in this five-star resort hotel twelve miles from Puerto Vallarta, where his patients recuperated after surgery.

Jen had done her research, checked out the references and testimonials. She'd calculated that, even with three additional airfares and a larger hotel suite, the cost of having a boob job, nose job, and tummy tuck at Du Bois's medical center would still cost less than having those same procedures anywhere in the United States. So, as a Christmas present to herself, she'd scheduled the surgeries and, with just over a week's notice, she'd insisted that Becky and Susan take time off work so that we could go along with her for an all-expenses-paid week of togetherness, sun, and fun.

We had argued about it at a girls' night dinner at Porcini. "You don't need plastic surgery," Susan had been curt. "It's a stupid idea. If you have to do something, get a belly button ring."

"I have one."

"Then color your hair. Be a redhead."

"You're already gorgeous, Jen." Becky had insisted. "What's there to improve?"

"You're sweet, Becky."

"What does Norm think?" I'd asked.

"Norm doesn't know." Jen had sipped Chablis. "It's going to be a surprise."

"A surprise?" Susan had put down her fork in the middle of a pasta twirl. "You do realize that changing your body isn't like changing your draperies."

"Actually, no, I hadn't realized that, Susan. Thank you for pointing it out." Jen had stabbed her filet.

"It must cost a lot," Becky had mused. "Wouldn't it be better to spend the money on something worthwhile? Like cancer research or protecting wildlife?"

"OMG, Becky." Jen had rolled her eyes. "Norm can afford to pay for this and for saving the whales, as well."

None of us knew what Norm did or how he could afford so much. We knew only that he owned things, that Jen had a multimillion-dollar house, plenty of jewelry, a new BMW on a regular schedule, and scads of designer shoes.

"Still, Jen," Susan put her fork down. "Surgery seems drastic. Are you willing to go that far just to soothe your own vanity?"

"FU, Susan. You're such hypocrites. Every woman has at least one body part that she despises."

"Where did you get that astounding statistic? The brochure for plastic surgery?"

"No, Susan. It's a known fact. Admit it: each of you would change something if you could."

"I don't think I would." Becky shook her head. "I wouldn't have the guts."

"You don't need to change anything, Becky." Susan swallowed ravioli.

"What about the risk?" I'd asked. "Every surgery has risks—"

"Okay—FTS."

I scrambled to translate. Fuck this shit?

Jen put down her utensils and folded her hands. "You guys can effing do what you want. I'm going with or without you. I'm nipping old age in the bud."

Old age? We were in our thirties. We'd stared at her in silence.

"Fine, bitches. Let your hair go gray. Let your necks crinkle and your butts flatten and your boobs sag. I'm off to Mexico and the fabulous Dr. Alain Du Bois. And, no matter how much BS grief you give me, you know you're all coming with me." Jen had ended the discussion.

A week later, as Jen had dictated, we were in our hotel suite in Mexico. And so was the distinguished Dr. Du Bois.

Jen batted her to-die-for eyelashes at him. "I guess you're here to discuss the procedures?"

Dr. Du Bois hesitated. "Procedures?"

Jen stood still, her smile transforming into a pout.

"No need, my dear. I'm fully prepared for you. No, I've come for another reason." He paused. "I got a call from the police. About the woman next door, Claudia Madison. She was also my patient."

Jen's mouth opened, formed an O.

"I'm so sorry," Becky offered. "You must be terribly upset."

Dr. Du Bois cleared his throat, blinked rapidly. "Yes. It's tragic. But the police mentioned that one of you was there. With her when she—"

Jen and Becky looked at me. Dr. Du Bois followed their gazes. "It was you? May I ask your name?"

I told him.

"If you don't mind, Ms. Harrison—"

"Elle." Why had I said that?

He nodded. "Elle, if you don't mind. Tell me. Before she fell, did Claudia say anything?"

"No." Something in his eyes made me add, "Sorry."

He searched my face. "You saw her? How beautiful she was?"

Beautiful? I remembered desperate eyes. A mouth twisted with terror. "I wasn't with her very long."

He looked at his hands. "You see the police implied that her death might have been suicide. You were there. So, forgive me, but I need to ask." He looked at me. "Did Claudia do this to herself?"

Sergeant Perez had discounted that possibility, but I considered it. Theoretically, she could have climbed over the railing intending to jump, then changed her mind. I saw her dangling, her violet eyes locking onto mine, her hand reaching out for me.

"Elle didn't see how she got there." Susan stood beside me. Becky put a protective hand on my arm.

I looked at Dr. Du Bois. "She didn't want to fall. She tried to take my hand." That much I knew.

He nodded. Took a breath. "So, it was murder then. Did you see who did it?"

"She's told the police everything she knows." Susan tried to fend off his questions.

Again, I watched the woman fall, arms flapping. "I didn't see anyone but her."

He leaned forward, watched me for another moment. "Well, I had to ask. At least you agree it wasn't suicide. I told the police that it couldn't have been; Claudia was happy. Of course, she still had some swelling, but her neck was already smooth as silk and her jawline taut as a teenager's. And her lips—I plumped them like ripe strawberries. She looked twenty years younger, with not a wrinkle, not a line. Suicide would be impossible. Unthinkable. The woman was a living work of art. She would never harm herself."

Susan eyed him. "You seem to have known her well. Are you that close with all your patients?" She had the tone of a criminal attorney, interrogating.

"You are very astute, madam. No, not with all. Claudia had come to me repeatedly, for many procedures. Over the years, yes, we became close."

"I'm sorry." My voice sounded far away. "I couldn't save her."

He focused on me in silence. His eyes were moist. "How insensitive of me. You've been through a terrible ordeal. And here

I am, intruding, pressing you for information." He stood and stepped over to me. Put his hand on my shoulder. Looked into my eyes. "Thank you, Elle. You risked your life to save Claudia. I, like all who cared about her, am in your debt."

He removed his hand, talked briefly with Jen and, when he left a few minutes later, I was still on the sofa under the blanket. My shoulder still felt the warmth of his hand.

~

Finally, it was just the four of us. Friends since childhood. Well, not Susan—Susan was older. When we were kids, she hadn't been our friend; she'd been our babysitter, our role model. Now, the only one of us with children, she still slipped into the role of mother hen as it suited her. And when room service delivered breakfast, it suited her.

"Sit here, Elle. Jen, pass out the mimosas. Becky, don't remove the covers yet. The eggs will get cold."

Obediently, I took my seat, slightly sickened by the smell of eggs, feeling distant from the bustle of a meal being served. But Jen handed me my mimosa and raised hers in a toast. "To my BFs effing F!"

We drank.

"To Jen for hosting us." I lifted my glass.

"And to Elle for being so brave," Becky added.

"And for not falling." Susan didn't smile.

Again, I felt empty air beneath me. I drank my mimosa. Thought about teetering over a six-story drop—or was it tottering? My gut flipped, either way. I felt untethered and ungrounded, as if I might fall at any moment. I held onto the arms of my chair.

"Elle? Be honest. I won't go if you need me."

Go? Becky waited for my answer. Jen watched us, stuffing a wad of eggs Benedict into her mouth.

"You didn't hear me, did you? You're doing your Elle thing, aren't you?"

What had I missed this time?

"Chichi invited me to the Salsa Festival today." Chichi and his partner, Luis, led the hotel's recreational activities. "I told him I'd go, but I won't if you need me. Jen has her preop tests."

"No. Go. I'm fine." Becky had met Chichi within an hour of our arrival. "I'll hang out with Susan."

"You mean it? Because, honestly, Chichi would understand."

They'd spent one day together, and already Becky talked about him as if they were a couple. Was Chichi his real name?

Becky licked egg yolk off her lip. "Remember Madam Therese?" she asked. "Funny. So far, everything she predicted has come true. We traveled to a place near the water. I met a man I wouldn't expect to fall for."

"And I'm surrounded by a dark cloud of death."

"Wait," Susan poured another mimosa. "What?"

"The fortune-teller we went to. We told you about her."

"Oh, I remember," Jen nodded. "The night we ate at Gnoc-chi."

"She said Elle and I would travel and that I'd fall in love."

"And that my aura is stained with blood."

Susan shook her head. "That's bullshit."

Becky swallowed. "No, really. She said dead people were attracted to Elle. And look, our first day here, Elle meets a dead person."

"It was just a con," Susan insisted. "A lucky guess. Anybody with half a brain can see that Elle is depressed."

Really? I was depressed? Anybody could see it? "But she knew about Charlie," I said. "She knew my husband had died. She said the dead are drawn to my aura—"

"Please, stop. Don't tell me you buy that crap." Susan chewed.

"Did she actually mention Charlie by name?" Jen asked.

"Of course, she didn't." Susan didn't give me a chance to answer. "She probably asked if someone had died, am I right?"

She was.

"Pretty safe way to pull you in. Everybody knows somebody who's died. So she says that and then you guys say, yes, and you tell her about Charlie. And off she goes. It's a scam, nothing more."

Becky shook her head. "No. She asked if someone had died and then she looked right at Elle."

"She probably followed your eyes. You must have glanced at Elle and she picked up on it. Look, the woman's a pro. She read your cues. Anyone can be trained to pick up on them."

"Really. Well, how did she know I'd fall in love?" Becky crossed her arms.

"Seriously?" Susan smiled as if the answer were obvious. "Think about it. Who goes to fortune-tellers? I'll tell you who: women. Not just women. Lonely women. Women looking for love."

"That's not true." Becky's cheeks were apple red. "Elle wasn't looking for love and she went."

"I didn't go on purpose. You dragged me. And remember, she told me I'd meet a man, too."

"Standard procedure. You go in. She sees no wedding or engagement ring on your finger. She sees ripe, healthy women coming in for a reading. What are the chances she can go wrong by promising you new love?"

Becky pouted.

Jen tore off a piece of pecan roll, popped it into her mouth. Jen weighed maybe a hundred and ten, ate like a linebacker. With her mouth full, she said, "I don't know, Susan. I've been to lots of fortune-tellers. They've always been spot-on. One told me that I should break up with Joey—remember Joey? The MF was cheating on me, and she knew. And one summer at the shore, a gypsy on the boardwalk told me to be careful. Next day I fell on my roller blades and broke my arm. And here's the best one: a fortune-teller told me I'd marry the next man I dated, and the next man I dated? Norm."

"Stop." Susan was exasperated. "I can't believe that three otherwise semi-intelligent women are lending credence to any of this horse manure."

"Madam Therese said we'd travel. We did. She said I'd meet someone unusual. I met Chichi."

"First of all, you're picking and choosing, remembering the parts you want to. And you know what else? If you like her predictions, you act in a way that makes them come true. You follow the suggestions."

Jen flapped her massive eyelashes. "Excuse me? You're saying I married Norm because some fortune-teller said I would?"

"And that Elle and I came on this trip because Madam Therese said we'd travel? That I'm with Chichi just because she said I'd meet someone?"

Susan didn't answer. She just raised her eyebrows and looked slowly from one of us to the other as if the answers were obvious. Her cell phone was ringing. She pushed a lock of black hair out of her eyes, picked up her coffee cup, and went to take the call.

☙

We sat in ruffled silence, Becky sulking, Jen playing with her nail gel. Finally, I picked up the pitcher of mimosas and refilled our glasses. Clearly, Susan was right. Madam Therese was a fake. There was no such thing as a person who could see the future, let alone discern bloodstains in an aura or dark death clouds over a person's head. I felt foolish for giving her even a moment of credibility. And relieved that that moment had passed.

"How about another toast?" I lifted my glass smiling at Jen. "To successful procedures and a happy future with a flat tummy!"

"And a week of good times with good friends." Jen raised her glass, clinked it with mine, then Becky's. I reached over and clinked Becky's.

"Oh my God," Becky shrieked, yanking her glass away, glaring, splashing mimosa on the table. "Damn, Elle. You clinked with the stem!"

I what?

"That's bad luck. What's wrong with you?"

My face got hot. Becky gawked at me, shocked. Accusing.

"What the eff, Elle?" Jen looked at the ceiling, panting. "Just what I need. Bad juju. Now I'll probably scar."

Susan came back from her call, fuming, cell phone in hand. "My damned office can't get along without me. This is a Saturday. And I'm out of the freaking country." She looked from Becky to Jen. "What?"

"Elle toasted with her glass stem," Jen whined.

"Really?" Susan chugged her mimosa. "First you believe fortune-tellers, now stupid superstitions. You're frickin' pitiful."

"Sorry." I tried apologizing. "I've never heard that—"

"Oh, please. Everyone knows you have to clink with the rim."

"What does that mean, Jen?" Susan scoffed. "That Elle deliberately tried to bring bad luck? Do you hear yourself?"

"Let it go." Becky picked up her glass. "Let's have a redo. Elle's been through enough today. Cut her a break."

We toasted again, but the conversation went on without me. The three of them referred to me in the third person as if I weren't there. They did this from time to time, and I didn't mind anymore. It wasn't deliberate. We were like family. We bickered sometimes. We knew each other's weaknesses and loved each other anyway. And we each had our designated roles to fill. Mine was to be the eccentric, the odd one. The one who spaced out under stress. And most recently, the one who messed up by clinking glasses with the stem, bringing bad luck on all of our heads.

I wondered what would happen if Jen's operation went wrong. If she scarred, would she blame me and my stem clink?

But never mind. Nothing would go wrong. Jen was just nervous, having preprocedure jitters. It was normal. And it was also normal that when she was tense, she'd pick on one of us—often me. I bristled thinking about it. Did Jen ever blame herself for anything? The operations were elective. If she scarred, wasn't it her own fault? Besides, her scars would be only on the surface. Skin deep. Not the really serious kind, scars that were invisible to the eye but that disfigured the heart or the mind.

Somewhere in my head, I heard the scrape of furniture and the slam of a sliding door. I clutched the railing, felt the indifferent glow of sunrise on my back. The woman saw that I couldn't get to her, realized that I didn't dare move. But she knew that I'd tried. Hadn't that been in her eyes? Wasn't that why she'd let go of the railing, swinging her hand toward me? I closed my eyes. My bones felt the thud of her landing.

"Elle," Jen nudged me, "you have a phone call."

A phone call?

I blinked at her. Who could be calling me here? Unless—oh, damn. The police? More questions? No. I couldn't deal with them, needed a break.

"Tell them I'm resting," I whispered. "Say I can't talk."

But Becky told the caller I'd be there in a second and held out the receiver. She grinned, watching me. What was she grinning about? Did she think it was funny that I was being hounded by the Mexican police? I got up, heard Susan on her cell again in the bedroom, arguing. "But that's impossible. We can't file that fast—"

Becky handed me the phone and stood close, trying to listen in.

"I hope I'm not disturbing you, Elle. But I want to make sure you're all right."

It wasn't the police. It was Dr. Alain Du Bois. To show me his concern and to express his appreciation for my courageous efforts that morning, he wondered if he might have the honor of taking me to dinner the following night.

～

Becky went off with Chichi, and Jen was at the clinic for preop tests. Susan and I were going to go to the beach, but as we were about to leave, she got another phone call from her office. I waited. I sat. I stood. I sat again and glanced out the sliding doors, intending to look at the ocean, seeing only the balcony railing. My feet tingled, reminding me how flimsy that railing had felt when I'd stood on it. Again, Claudia's hand reached out, trying to grasp mine. I stood.

Susan was still on the phone, deep in conversation, taking notes. I couldn't wait any more, signaled that I'd meet her on the beach. She nodded and waved. And an elevator ride later, I was skirting the concrete deck by the alligator waterslide and the pool, collecting a towel from the beach hut, strolling through sand. I kept my eyes forward, didn't look at sunblock-slathered sunbathers or vendors peddling souvenirs. I concentrated on finding a quiet spot. A couple of chaise lounges under a palm tree not too far from the water but as far from other tourists as possible. I wanted to hear no voices, just the rolling of the ocean and the crash of waves. To close my eyes and feel the sun frying my body. To lie back and let time pass without thinking or re-membering.

At the edge of the hotel's property, I found the perfect spot. Spread my towel on a lounge chair and moved it out of the shade of a palm tree into the sun. Dragged another out for Susan. Slapped coconut-smelling sunblock onto my limbs and face. Lay down. Closed my eyes. Let the sun pour over me, felt its heat sucking tension out of my muscles until my body was limp, draining thoughts away until my head was empty. A breeze tickled my feet, caressed my face; the sun embraced me like a mom soothing her child.

"You alone?"

I didn't respond, assumed the question was for someone else.

"Mind if I join you?"

I opened an eye. A woman with a striped bikini and wide-brimmed sun hat stood over me, surrounded by a halo of light.

She was blocking the sun. Before I answered, she plopped down on Susan's chair.

"That's actually for my friend—" I began.

"That's okay. I'll leave when he gets here."

"It's a she." I don't know why I told her that.

"I just want to look like I'm not by myself. Someone's following me."

I opened the other eye and sat up.

"Don't look around. Act like we're just chatting, okay?"

She was young. Maybe twenty-five. Skinny. Blunt features dotted with freckles.

"What's going on?" I watched her settle onto Susan's chair, removing her hat, releasing long dark hair. Lying back.

"His name's Luis. He's creeping me out."

Luis? As in Chichi and Luis? "You mean the guy from the hotel?"

"Don't look around. He was just following me. He's probably standing by the bar, watching me."

I couldn't help it. I looked toward the bar. Saw a cluster of people there. Waiters, patrons.

"You must know who he is. He's one of the activity directors."

"I know Chichi."

"Right. Chichi's the other one." She watched me as I looked at the bar. "You see him? He's wearing a hotel shirt and khaki shorts. He's about five foot eight or nine."

I didn't see him, shook my head. Scanned the area around us. Saw no Luis.

Finally, she sat up, looked up and down the beach. "Thank God. I didn't think I'd ever get rid of him." She faced me. "I'm Melanie Crane, by the way. Here with Grandma Crane, who's recovering from her third facelift." She smiled, stuck out a bony hand.

"Elle Harrison." We shook. I searched the beach, hoping to see Susan.

"I'm from Montreal. You?"

I told her, Philadelphia.

"Just for fun? Or are you having work done?"

Why did she think it was her business? "Just visiting." I lay back, closing my eyes, indicating that I didn't want to talk. That she could leave. But she didn't get the message.

"At first, I was flattered. He flirted with me, and he's cute. So I had a few drinks with him one night. Now, it's creepy. He won't leave me alone. He shows up everywhere I go. I hate to say it, but it's like he's stalking me."

I thought of Chichi and Becky. "Maybe he sees you here, a single woman on her own, and he thinks it's part of his job to keep you entertained. I bet he flirts with a new woman every week."

"No." Melanie was adamant. "This is more. It's no passing flirtation. He's persistent. It's really creepy."

I glanced at her. She was on Susan's lounge chair, lying on her side, facing me. "Maybe you should go to the hotel manager. Complain that he's making you uncomfortable."

She sat up. "Maybe I will. If he doesn't stop." She picked up her hat and looked at the ocean. "The waves look good. Up for a boogie board?"

What? We were buddies now? Hanging out and riding waves? "I don't think so. I'm waiting for my friend."

She stood, heading off. "Okay, later then. We should get a drink sometime."

As quickly as she'd arrived, Melanie Crane was gone. I propped myself on an elbow, looking for Luis. Or Susan. Seeing neither, I plopped back down and baked.

~

Susan didn't show up. After an hour or so, I checked on her, found her sputtering at her laptop at a desk in the lobby. When I asked how long she'd be, she glared at me so fiercely that I backed away and left her growling about judges and clients and prosecutors and partners.

I spent the rest of the morning alone on the beach, losing

track of time. Whenever I opened my eyes, vendors would lug their wares to me across the hot sand—sundresses, coconut shell masks, animal woodcarvings, silver jewelry, sunglasses, hats. They carried heavy loads of goods all day, hoping for a tourist like me to buy. But I kept replaying Claudia's death; my mind wasn't on shopping.

At some point, I got up and wandered over to the pool. Becky was there, playing water volleyball. Chichi refereed, offering tequila shots for each point scored, and Luis cheered and announced the plays over a loudspeaker. I studied Luis as he followed the game. He was engrossed in the moment, his voice rich and enthusiastic. He seemed happy, fun loving. Was it just a guise? Were stalkers happy and fun loving?

"Elle!" Becky spotted me. "Come play. We need you."

I waved and smiled, shook my head, no. Not me. And noticed Melanie, preparing to serve for the opposing team. Luis watched her from the announcer's platform.

"All right," he stretched the long vowel sound into three syllables. "Punch it!"

The ball flew into the net. Melanie dunked under the water, came up glistening, smoothed her hair. The ball came back to her and she held it up, ready to serve again, but hesitated, glancing at Luis.

"Come on! You can do it! Go for it!" His voice blared.

Melanie punched the ball and it soared over to Becky's side. Someone hit it back, but a tall guy on Melanie's team smashed it over. Point: Melanie's side.

"Seven-Five," Chichi called as he passed the tequila around to Melanie's team.

People who weren't playing lay around the pool, eating, reading, listening to music. A guy flew out of the alligator's mouth into the deep end of the pool. A couple strolled over to the spot where Claudia Madison had landed just hours before. It had been hosed down so there were no stains. No sign that she'd ever fallen. I looked up six floors at the balcony. Saw her again, dangling there. Saw myself stuck halfway across the wall. Felt the railing under my feet, the cool morning breeze. Closed my eyes, heard a thud.

"Señora?" The woman's eyes were sad, her skin dark and wrinkled. She held an array of floral dresses. "Which one you like? I have something special for you."

Salsa music pumped. Chichi and Luis cheered and the players yelled.

"No, gracias." I backed away from her. Passing the recreation hut, I grabbed a boogie board and hurried into the ocean, paddling away from shore until I couldn't hear music or voices, only the motion and splashing of water. For a while, I floated, bobbing up and down, rocking on the board. Then I rode the waves, letting the ocean lift and carry me, tossing me onto the sand. More than once, as my body slapped down against the beach, I closed my eyes and felt Claudia's thud. I wondered if she'd felt it. Or if, hitting the ground so hard, she'd had time to feel anything at all.

∿

Around lunchtime, I went to the hotel lobby again to check on Susan. She wasn't there. I called the room.

"What?" She sounded pissed.

"Are you coming down?"

"If I could, Elle, don't you think I would?" Not just pissed; sarcastic.

"Anything I can help you with?"

"Are you suddenly a lawyer?"

Okay. I'd tried.

"My brilliant colleagues screwed up a filing, and I seem to be the only one capable of fixing it. Sorry. Gotta go." She hung up.

On the way back to the beach, I saw Chichi and Becky among other couples at the beach bar, their heads leaning together. Becky was smiling, whispering into his ear. His arm was around her waist. I closed my eyes, imagined myself there with Charlie. Smelled the salty ocean on his skin. Felt his body heat beside me. He was wearing a Hawaiian shirt over his bathing trunks, and we were sipping margaritas. Dammit. I opened my eyes. Why was I always thinking about Charlie? Even if he hadn't died, we wouldn't have been drinking together. By now, we'd have been divorced for months. Even so, the air beside me felt empty, as if marking his absence. Probably it wasn't Charlie I was missing; it was being part of a couple. Having somebody to sit with at the bar. Somebody to whisper to. I looked out at the ocean, and there he was again, standing in the froth. Charlie was everywhere I looked, present in everything I did. Pathetic. Why was I so stuck? Was I still raw from his death? Or had Claudia's brought it all back?

I kept walking, moving. The sky was cloudless, the sun relentless. Even the breeze was hot. I stayed at the water's edge, where the sand was wet and my toes dug in. Where the warm waves washed my feet and backed away. I walked past rows of couples on beach chairs and under umbrellas, past guys offering to take me parasailing, past women wanting to braid my hair. And with every step, every heartbeat, no matter what, I missed Charlie.

Stop it, I told myself. I picked up a seashell, examined it. Dropped it. Kept on going, moving to a silent drumbeat, pounded by the sun.

I went beyond the line of waterfront condos and resort hotels to an undeveloped stretch where the beach was narrow, lined by untended dense foliage. Even then, I didn't turn back. I kept going, feeling alone. Not just alone. The kind of alone that was isolating and deep. The kind that had begun when Charlie died and the whole world shifted. The kind where even my best friends seemed altered—not quite tangible, as if they, like Charlie, had drifted out of reach. The kind where everything around me seemed different. Even colors—hues of red and yellow—lost their vibrancy and faded.

I moved into the water, wading ahead ankle deep. Watching the shimmering waves, wondering at the gray-blue water, if it looked brighter to others. Aware of each splashy step. Each breath.

For months, I'd been wandering this altered world, trying to adjust. Becky, Susan, and Jen had been concerned when I'd taken a leave of absence from teaching. They'd asked what I would do with my days. The question had stymied me; I didn't want to do anything. Even so, for a while I'd read travel brochures, imagining dining in Paris. Going on safari in Africa. In the end, I'd stayed put. The place I'd wanted to go wasn't listed in any brochure or pictured on a website. It wasn't a distance of miles. It was a distance of time. I'd wanted to go back to my former life—to be with Charlie before life had fallen apart, to get a second chance. I'd had no desire to be anywhere else. So I'd stayed in my house, watching time pass, wondering if red would ever be red again, or yellow, yellow.

When Jen had called, announcing that she was taking Susan, Becky, and me with her to Mexico, that she had booked a two-bedroom suite for the second week of December, I'd been hopeful. Maybe the change of scenery and traveling with my friends would jolt me out of my post-Charlie darkness. I'd tried to convince myself that a new place might mean a new beginning. And to believe that when I went away, I could somehow leave myself behind.

~

But here I was splashing alone through unknown waters, feeling lost, still missing my past. I needed to focus on other things. The sound of the ocean slapping the sand. Jen's surgeries, how they'd go. How different she'd look afterwards. And her doctor, Alain Du Bois. Lord. He'd asked me to dinner. My mind moved in sync with my steps, thinking in staccato, and eventually, I came to another development. A row of gleaming white hotels along a sandy beach.

Up ahead, a woman was standing in the sand, wearing a strapless sundress and a scarf over her hair. The breeze blew the scarf, covering her face. As I got closer, the breeze shifted, and the scarf moved away. I stopped, shuddering, eyes riveted. Where her face should have been was a flat crimson mess. Her features—lips, cheeks, chin—seemed a scrambled, indistinguishable mass of flesh. I slowed down, staring. Told myself to avert my gaze. Made myself walk on and look at the water.

Maybe I wasn't seeing things right. The bright sunlight must be causing distortions. Of course—that was it. What looked like raw wounds were probably sun glare and tricks of the light, not real. I kept walking, not looking at her. Got closer. Glanced her way.

Even with the scarf and the glare, I recognized her.

I looked away, out at the ocean. My breathing was shallow, my mouth dry. I was probably dehydrated. I'd walked too far, had had too much sun, hadn't recovered from the shock of the day before. And my dissociative disorder must have kicked in, distorting my thoughts. I was reacting to the trauma of Claudia's death and my failure to save her, reviving her in my mind. When I'd look back, she wouldn't be there. I counted: one, two three. On three, I turned back.

Claudia Madison stood at water's edge, just up the beach. Her scarf again blew over her face, hiding the disfigurements. But, obviously, she wasn't actually Claudia Madison. She hadn't fallen six stories onto her face. Her wounds had been caused some other way. Don't stare, I told myself. If she's real, she'll be sensitive about her appearance. She won't want people gawking. I moved my gaze past her, toward the hotel. A man was there, stepping through a gate, approaching her. Maybe her husband?

Or no. Not her husband.

My husband.

Charlie.

I stopped walking, stopped breathing. I was hallucinating,

had to be. The man looked just like him. He had Charlie's shape and height. Charlie's loose and confident gait. I blinked, but he didn't disappear. I squinted into the distance, and with the glare of the sun, had trouble seeing his features. I felt off balance, needed to turn around and head back. I'd gone too far from the hotel, too far from reality. The man stopped beside the woman and turned toward me, raised a hand. Oh God, was he waving? Was Charlie emerging from the dead and just casually saying, "Hi"? Or wait—was his raised hand a warning, signaling me to stay back and come no closer? I hugged myself, unable to move, and watched as the man put his arm around the woman, kissed the side of her head, and led her across the sand into the trees, toward the road.

I stood on the beach for a moment, deciding that I'd imagined the resemblances. Then, I turned and headed back, running most of the way.

~

I might not have recognized our hotel, might have kept running all the way into Puerto Vallarta if not for Melanie Crane. She accosted me as I ran along the beach.

"Elle—" She called from the water's edge as if she'd been expecting me and took hold of my arm. I slowed to a stop, panting. "Thank God. I was hoping to find you. I don't know what to do."

I bent forward, trying to catch my breath. Unbearably thirsty.

"He's been tailing me all day. I went to my room, just to get away. Grandma said that someone had sent flowers. Guess who? I went online to check my e-mail. Guess who tried to friend me on Facebook? What am I supposed to do?"

My breathing was slower, my heart calming down. "Tell him to back off?"

"Don't you think I have? I've said I've got a boyfriend back home. That I'm not interested. He doesn't listen. Before I was sitting on a lounge chair. He sent me a mojito. So I moved chairs. A while later, what do you know? Another mojito."

A mojito sounded heavenly. I was parched, dehydrated. I looked toward the bar, craving anything liquid. Took a step in that direction. Melanie matched my step, stayed with me, too close. I smelled pool chlorine and sunblock. How had I acquired this woman? Why did she think her unwanted suitor was my problem? "Go to management. Complain."

"Then he'd lose his job. I can't do that to him."

"Why? If he's a lunatic stalker, he probably shouldn't have that job."

"You're right. I just don't feel right getting him fired. And if he found out I was the reason, I'd be afraid of what he might do."

"Are you really afraid? Do you think he's dangerous?" I saw him up ahead on the platform above the pool, doing a salsa dance demo for an elderly couple. Grinning and wagging his hips.

Melanie pouted, thinking. "I honestly don't know."

"Well, if you do, don't mess with him. I saw you playing volleyball before. Just keep away from him. Don't give him a message he might misinterpret."

"Wait, you think he thinks that if I play volleyball, it's because of him?"

How dense was this woman? "Yes, Melanie. If he's looking for encouragement, he'll probably find it in anything you do that involves him."

She was wearing a scanty bikini and huge sunglasses and was so thin that her ribs stuck out. She kept so close to me as we walked that my arms brushed her skin, and she practically stumbled over my feet. As we neared the bar and its promise of water and ice, I quickened my pace. Thought of sangria. Grapefruit juice. Beer—anything wet.

As soon as we got there, I hopped onto a stool, welcoming the shade of the bar's thatched roof. "*Por favor—*" I called out. "*Agua?* Can I have some water?" My voice was ragged.

Melanie perched on the stool beside mine, twisting a wisp of hair, whining. "What should I do, Elle?"

Ice water came. I grabbed it, chugged it. Felt it slither down my gullet, quenching and relieving. And blinding me with its frigid cold. I sat for a moment, letting the freeze fade.

Melanie was still talking. "But you're right. I'll tell him one more time, and if he doesn't back off, I'll go to his boss."

She squeezed my arm as she left. I ordered a mojito on the rocks and was halfway through it before I realized that I'd pretty much brushed Melanie off. Hadn't taken her seriously because she was so cloying. But maybe I should have. After all, a woman had died there the night before. Again, I saw Claudia fall, heard her land on the concrete. Someone at the resort had likely murdered her. What if that someone now had his eyes on Melanie? What if the killer was Luis? How would I feel if, tomorrow, Melanie's body was found lying by the pool?

I looked around for Melanie, didn't see her. Well, I'd told her to go to management. That was the best I could do, wasn't it? I gulped my mojito, ordered another. Thought about Charlie kissing Claudia Madison on the beach, right in front of me. Except that it hadn't been him. My mind had been playing tricks again, nothing more. The mojitos were delicious. I kept drinking, stopping only when I saw Charlie sitting at the other end of the bar.

∼

Because of her surgery, Jen couldn't eat after midnight. So Susan prepared a mini-fiesta to celebrate Jen's last night with her natural God-given body. As she sliced onions and peppers for kabobs, the rest of us sat at the table beside the kitchenette, drinking room-service sangria.

"It's not too late, Jen," Susan stopped chopping to push a lock of hair behind her ear. "You can still change your mind."

Jen rolled her eyes, turned away. Dipped a tortilla chip in Susan's fresh guacamole. "You got burned today, Elle. Does it hurt?"

"I'm okay."

"You need to use sunscreen," Becky scolded. She'd taken leave of Chichi long enough to join us for dinner.

"Are you effing kidding?" Jen stopped chewing, gaped at Becky. "She didn't use sunscreen?"

Becky shrugged. "I gave her some. Number thirty."

"Well, did she put it on?"

Again, they talked about me as if I weren't there.

"I used the sunscreen," I told them. But in fact, I was toasted. Too much sun, too many mojitos.

"You'll get wrinkles," Jen double dipped her tortilla chip.

"Forget wrinkles, you can get skin cancer." Susan's knife punctuated her words. Chop. Chop. "Don't mess with the sun, Elle."

Why was I the focus of conversation? Becky was sunburned, too. "So, Jen," I changed the subject, "you ready for tomorrow?"

"WTF?" she snapped. "Why wouldn't I be?"

"Because," Susan answered from the kitchen, "somewhere in your dim but already beautiful head, you must know that you are about to take unnecessary risks for no good reason—"

"Will you stop, Susan?"

"—because all surgery is risky. And it's obviously foolish for someone as full-out gorgeous as you are to undergo potentially life-threatening procedures to alter what is already a naturally strikingly beautiful body." As she spoke, her vegetable slicing became hacking.

"Susan, back the fuck off." Jen's jaw tightened. She poured more sangria, took a drink. The only sound was the knife slamming the cutting board. It cut onions, but not tension.

"Susan's only saying that because she loves you, Jen." Becky put a hand on Jen's arm.

"That, and because Jen's a superficial, impulsive idiot," Susan said.

"This was not impulsive. I did research. I thought it through.

You're just pissed because you had to work all day. Don't take it out on me."

I scooped a wad of guacamole onto a chip. Took a bite. Man, it was good. Fresh avocado, garlic, cilantro, lime. Creamy texture. I thought about avocado. No other food resembled it in texture or flavor. Or color. The argument went on around me like the chirping of birds or the hum of traffic. White noise, isn't that what they called it? Comforting and familiar background sounds, the bickering of old friends.

I couldn't imagine what Jen would look like after the surgery. Would her belly skin stretch taut and her breasts stand up even when she lay on her back? Would her nose be too small for her face? I'd seen some terrible nose jobs. Noses molded to a triangular point, or to an upward curve at the tip. Noses that seemed plugged into the wrong faces. I looked at Jen, her exotic features. Of all of us, she was by far the most glamorous. Slender, busty, blonde. Long, dense eyelashes, extreme cheekbones. Why would she want to mess with what she already had? Maybe it wasn't about appearances, but about something deeper. Maybe self-esteem.

"So, Jen, you think a flatter tummy will make you feel better about yourself?"

Silence. Three faces stared at me.

Oh Lord. I'd blurted out the question. Should have listened first, waited for an appropriate time. Instead, I'd jumped into the middle of their conversation. Probably they'd say I'd pulled an Elle again.

"Actually, that's a good question, Elle." Susan skewered chunks of chicken.

Jen sank back against the sofa, wide-eyed and pale. Had I hit a nerve?

"I'm just asking. Because I think you're perfect the way you are. So it doesn't make sense that you'd change anything. Unless, deep down, you don't like yourself—"

"Don't be ridiculous, Elle," Jen cut me off. "I like myself just fine."

"Then why do you want to change—"

"You know what I think?" Susan interrupted. "I think you kids are getting close to forty. And Jen's scared about getting old."

"OM effing G," Jen slammed her drink onto the coffee table. "Will you get off my case?"

"It's just that we love you," Becky offered.

"Okay. Here's the effing deal. I like myself just fine. But I'd like myself even better with a flatter tummy. Can any of you say that you wouldn't like to change something? Becky, you arrive places a full minute after your boobs. Tell me you wouldn't want to reduce them? And Susan, you've had three fucking kids. You must want a tighter—"

"What I want isn't the issue. I'm not the one risking my life to make superficial cosmetic changes instead of looking deep within myself and confronting what's really bothering me."

"What the fuck are you talking about?" Jen sat up straight. "Go on, say what you mean."

"You know damned well what I mean, Jen. Your biological clock is ticking. You're afraid time is running out but you're focusing on the surface instead of facing what's really bothering you: Norm's issues about having kids."

"Okay, whoa—" Becky raised her hands. "Let's take a breather."

"This is not about kids, Susan," Jen hissed.

"Okay. Whatever you say."

"It's not about kids." She crossed her arms, glaring.

"Fine." Susan flipped kabobs in the broiler. "Except I'm pretty sure it is."

"Okay, that's it." Jen was on her feet. "I invited you guys to come down here so we could have some fun while I got my work done. I didn't invite your opinions. But since you feel free to judge me and label me superficial and impulsive, let me say, in the spirit of friendship and fellowship: Shut the fuck up. Leave me the fuck alone. Go ahead, Susan. Age gracefully. Get as wrinkled and shriveled as you want. But I am not going that route. I'm going to fight every step of the way. For as long as I can, I'm going to look the way I did when Norm married me— no, I'm going to look even better than that. He deserves it."

"Wait, so now it's not about you anymore? You're doing this for Norm?" I swallowed sangria.

"If you're doing it for Norm, you might be smart," Becky chirped. "Think about it—lots of guys like Norm ditch their middle-aged wives and trade them in for young trophies."

"Seriously, Becky?" Jen was sputtering, her bejeweled hands on her hips. "You're going there? Norm would never—"

"No," Susan cut her off. "He wouldn't. That was stupid, Becky."

Becky's mouth opened. She looked slapped.

"Anyway," I tried to ease the mood, "the point is that we all love you, Jen. We're just worried about you going under the knife."

"That's right." Becky stood beside Jen and hugged her. "You're already stunning. And the most beautiful part about you is something that no surgeon can change. It's not the beauty that shows on the outside; it's the beauty that comes from within. That's what we love most about you. That's what Norm loves, too."

Becky's eyes were moist. She'd made up for her trophy wife comment.

"Becky's right." Susan came out of the kitchenette with a platter of skewered chicken and vegetables. She placed it on the table beside a bowl of beans and rice, put her hands on the back of a chair. "Look. We're all a bit on edge about tomorrow. After all, we're far from home."

Jen opened her mouth to respond, but Susan put a hand up. "Hold on, Jen. Let me finish. See, even though these procedures aren't my choice for you—bottom line? It's your body, your life.

If surgery is what you want, then we're all with you. Right?" She looked at Becky, then me.

We nodded obediently.

As she sat down, Susan added, "Besides, if the surgery goes south, I don't want to remember our last night together as a fight."

Before anyone could react, I lifted a glass. "To our friendship and Jen's recovery."

Everyone toasted, and then we ate, avoiding anything related to beauty, age, reproduction, or cosmetic surgery.

~

I opened my eyes in pitch darkness. Had someone touched me? Talked to me? Wait, this wasn't my bedroom. Where was I? Oh, right. The hotel, in Mexico. I lay still, alert, watching for movement. Seeing none.

"Becky?"

No answer. Of course she didn't answer. Becky wasn't in our room; she was off with Chichi.

I reached out and turned on the lamp. Saw the dresser, the television. Becky's empty bed. No one.

"Susan? Jen?" Maybe one of them had come into the room, hoping I'd be awake.

But no one answered. Susan and Jen had gone to bed early to be rested for Jen's surgery. Susan was planning to go with her and stay at the hospital.

So what had awakened me?

I sat up, unsettled. The ceiling fan whirred overhead. An indifferent, inanimate sound. Nothing that would have startled me. I got out of bed, stepped into the living room. Shadows draped the furniture. Jen's hospital bag sat packed and ready on the sofa. Susan's computer on the kitchenette counter. Dishes on the rack by the sink. Everything as we'd left it. Undisturbed.

Probably I'd been roused by an uneasy dream. I got back into bed, but couldn't get comfortable. The pillows were too thick; I punched one, trying to make a dent, but the filling was dense, refused to give way. Who would make such fat, firm pillows? Could people really sleep on them? Never mind. I shoved the pillows aside, lay flat on the mattress. But that was no good either. Finally, I piled them into a stack, reclining in a half-lying half-sitting position, but it was no use. I couldn't fall asleep. Couldn't shake the sense that it hadn't been a dream, that something else had interrupted my sleep. I half-lay half-sat in bed, leaning on sore, sunburned shoulders and watched the ceiling fan, trying to hypnotize myself into slumber. Empty your mind, I told myself. Watch the blades spin. Do not think.

Of course, the more I tried not to think, the more I thought. Images twirled through my head, doing tortured pirouettes. I pictured Jen wrapped mummy-like in bandages. Becky salsa dancing with Chichi. Susan typing angrily on her computer. Claudia Madison reaching for my hand.

And falling.

Stop, I told myself. Watch the blades go around. I watched, and then I was in the ocean, bobbing on a boogie board. Rocking with the water, beginning to relax. Except then that annoying Melanie swam over with her hollow cheeks and bony frame, glomming onto me. Who was she? Was Luis really stalking her? Why had she picked me to come to with her problems? Damn, I was thinking again. I closed my eyes, and Melanie faded, became a woman hidden behind a scarf. A breeze lifted it, revealed her swollen ravaged face—and then Charlie led her away. Oh Lord. Charlie? Really?

Oh God. Was it Charlie who'd awakened me?

"Charlie?" I said his name. "Are you here?"

The hairs stood up on my arms, but that was the only response. The blades of the fan whirred quietly. The room was still. Of course, it was. I was talking to air.

Enough. I needed to turn my mind off.

I got out of bed again, went to the balcony door, and stared at the darkness, the star-dotted sky. The unsettled black ocean.

Damn. Why had I seen Charlie on the beach? At first, after

his murder, I'd seen him everywhere. I'd smelled his aftershave, talked to him, kept him alive in my mind. The shrink had called it a "coping mechanism," my way of dealing with the loss. But I hadn't seen or imagined Charlie for almost a year, not since his murder had been solved.

So why had he appeared that morning?

Madam Therese popped to mind, bringing fragrances of jasmine and roasting meat. "I told you why," she smiled, jangling her bracelets. "The dead are drawn to you."

"Bullshit." I answered her out loud.

I did not attract the dead—no one did. The dead were dead. They didn't go on vacations to Mexico or walk on beaches. So why had I seen Charlie there? Why had my mind brought him back—and paired him with the ghastly image of Claudia Madison? What did Charlie have to do with her?

Nothing.

Except that they were both dead. And both their deaths had involved me.

Gooseflesh rippled on my neck. I wished Susan or Jen would wake up and keep me company. But they didn't, so I went to the kitchen and downed a shot of tequila. Brought another with me and drank it after I'd climbed into bed. Turned the lamp off. Watched shadows for the rest of the night, but saw no sign of anyone, even Charlie.

~

My plan had been to get to the beach early, before most of the lounge chairs had been claimed, but as I walked across the lobby, Juan Alonzo, the hotel manager, gestured to me from the front desk and hurried to meet me. Damn. I didn't want to talk to him. I just wanted to sit by the ocean. But I was trapped. Probably he just wanted to make sure I was all right. Just a formality. A matter of professionalism. Hell, maybe he'd comp a few drinks.

"Señora," his tone was hushed as he approached. "*Buenos dias*. I hope you are recovered from your experience?"

"Thank you." I didn't engage. I was holding a beach bag and a hat, kept moving slowly toward the door to the water.

"Señora, please. I am sorry to bother you. But I have a small request to make of you. It will take just a moment of your time."

Wait. He wasn't giving me free drinks. He wanted me to do something for him? "I really just want to relax this morning."

"I understand. Of course. It is my wish for you to relax as well. And you will have all morning to relax. But Sergeant Perez is in my office now with the family of Claudia Madison."

Oh God. I gazed out the door at the sunshine. Felt trapped.

"And they have asked to talk with you."

"With me?"

"As you were the last person to see her alive."

I saw her again, reaching for me. Her eyes. I looked at the door, wanted to run.

"I was just about to call your room, but I saw you in the lobby—"

"Of course." I let him lead me across the lobby, away from the air and the water into a small windowless conference room behind the front desk.

~

Inside, the walls were dotted with framed photographs of Mayan ruins. Sergeant Perez introduced me to Claudia Madison's two sisters, who sat red-eyed, holding hands. They looked alike, solid women with thin lips and long, narrow noses, didn't resemble Claudia much. But then, they wouldn't; Claudia had had plastic surgery.

Juan Alonzo sat me across the table from them. Emily and Rose. They each wore crumpled pastel clothing and wedding bands; had come as soon as they'd heard. Had taken two flights each and hadn't slept. They wanted to find out what had happened to Claudia. What she'd said. They watched me, four urgent eyes, starving for answers.

I wanted to help them. I didn't know how.

Sergeant Perez helped me along, guided me through the

events of the night.

"Señora Harrison is the hero I told you about," he told them. "She is the woman who tried to save your sister and risked her own life."

They thanked me, rushed over, and hugged me, as if grabbing onto a remnant of their sister. Finally, we all sat down.

"Did she say anything?" Rose asked.

"Before she fell?" Emily completed her question.

I saw Claudia clinging to the railing, felt unsteady. "No. She just tried to hang on."

"But how did she get out there?"

"We don't understand what happened."

I looked at Sergeant Perez. How was I supposed to deal with these questions, this grief? I felt set up. Cornered. Perez watched me, said nothing. Was he testing to see if I knew more than I'd told him? Should I call Susan?

"I don't know what happened." I clutched my beach bag, took a deep breath. The air felt thick. "When I first saw her, she was already hanging onto the railing."

"But didn't you see anyone with her?" Rose leaned closer, sounded bereft.

"You didn't hear anything?" Emily sounded doubtful.

"As I've told Sergeant Perez," I looked at him again, "I'd heard voices earlier. A man and a woman. But I don't know what they were saying or who the man was. Really, I'm sorry. I wish I could have saved her. It's a terrible tragedy, but I have no idea how it happened." I thought about how to excuse myself and escape. What should I say? Certainly not, "nice to meet you." Or "enjoy your stay." What should I say? Why couldn't I think of anything?

And then I'd lost my chance. Emily started talking again. "You see," she went on, "you're our only link. You saw her last."

"Our sister wasn't like us," Rose explained. "Emily and I got married young and had families."

"You were young. I was twenty-four."

"That's young."

"You were only twenty. That's young."

"There's not that much difference."

"Anyhow, we both live normal lives."

"Boring lives." Rose nodded.

"But Claudia was different."

"She was the strong one. A risk taker."

"She traveled all over the world. She had romances." Emily smiled.

Rose laughed. "Lots of romances."

"She got these operations to increase her appeal."

"As if she needed to."

They reflected for a moment.

I didn't know what to say. Said nothing.

"The point is that Sergeant Perez asked if our sister might have harmed herself. We know that she never, ever would have," Emily said.

"Not ever."

"We know that she didn't go over that railing on her own."

"No. Claudia loved her life." Rose dabbed her nose.

"She loved herself." Emily's chin quivered.

"She wasn't the depressed type, but if she'd have been depressed—"

"She'd have called us."

"That's right. No question."

"She was our baby sister."

"We were always close."

"So we're positive. Whatever happened to Claudia—"

"It wasn't suicide."

"No. Someone killed her."

They faced me with twin expressions of painful certainty mixed with suspicion. I told them I was sorry but I had no more information. Sergeant Perez watched as I wished them well, took their hands in mine, and repeated my condolences. Then, I nodded at Juan Alonzo, gave Sergeant Perez a long hard look, and skedaddled out of that small close room, not stopping until ocean air flew into my lungs and sunlight hit my face.

∿

I went all the way to the edge of the property, finding a secluded spot under a thatched umbrella. Rose and Emily were on my mind. I spread out my towel, slapped on sunscreen, stretched out, closed my eyes, and listened to the water, trying to fall asleep, but their questions—their sadness clung to me. And I had some questions of my own. Such as, why hadn't Sergeant Perez warned me of the meeting? Did he have some hidden agenda? Was he hoping to implicate me in Claudia's death?

No, he couldn't—I'd had no motive. Still, I should talk to Susan about it. But Susan was busy at the clinic with Jen; it could wait until later. After all, it wasn't anything urgent. The talk with the sisters had most likely been just a courtesy to the bereaved. Nothing more.

I closed my eyes, but their faces haunted me, their questions persisted, and I kept revisiting the railing, the last moments of Claudia's life. I turned over, made myself think instead about something else. Like Jen and her surgeries.

The morning had been frenzied. Jen had been anxious to get to the clinic, had made Susan leave a full hour before her scheduled appointment. Jen had fidgeted and complained while Susan had dashed around the suite, searching for her phone, tossing her computer, a banana, a granola bar, a notebook into her bag. We'd exchanged hurried hugs, and they'd gone, returning only seconds later because Susan had forgotten her room key. I'd offered again to go along, but Susan had again turned me down, insisting that she'd be working and I'd be of no use.

I'd said that I wanted to go anyway, to be there for moral support, but Jen had cut me off.

"J fucking C, Elle," she'd tsked. "Cut the drama, would you? It's not like I'm having heart surgery. It's no big deal, okay? I'll be back tomorrow morning. Just go to the damned beach or something."

I hadn't moved. Had felt a pang.

She'd rolled her eyes, then reached out and hugged me. Her eyelashes had tickled my cheek. "I don't mean to be a bitch. I fucking love you, okay?" She pulled back, looked at me. "Don't worry. I'll be fine."

When they'd gone, I wandered the suite, my mind thick and addled, sleepless for two nights. I made instant coffee, ventured outside onto the balcony to drink it. Down at the pool, the staff was busy, preparing for the day. At seven a.m., they were testing the water, trimming hedges, hosing down the deck, restocking fresh towels and glassware. Beyond them, across the fence, the ocean glowed with golden light, offering peace and comfort. Come down, it seemed to say. I'll soothe you to sleep.

And so, I'd gotten into my bathing suit, grabbed my hat and beach bag, and headed for the elevator. Which had opened to reveal Becky.

"Elle?" she'd stepped out, looked me over. "You're going to the beach? Where's Jen?"

I'd told her.

"They left so early? Why didn't anybody call me?"

I'd had no answer. It hadn't occurred to me to call.

"Damn. I wanted to wish her luck." Her hands had been on her hips. She'd glared at me, looking rumpled. Her hair had been mussed, and she'd been wearing last night's clothes. "You should have let me know they were leaving early. How was I supposed to know?"

The elevator doors had closed; the car whirred away.

I'd felt bad. "Sorry. They just got up and went."

Becky had pouted. "You're mad, aren't you?" She'd looked at me. "Because of Chichi."

What?

"Because I'm off with him instead of spending time with you guys. That's why you didn't call me, isn't it?"

I'd sighed, shaken my head. "I'm not mad at you. Nobody is."

"Try to understand, Elle. This isn't just a fling. Chichi's different. I know it's sudden and you'll think I'm crazy, but I think he might be the real thing."

I'd looked at her, thought she was crazy.

"You think I'm being impulsive. I know you do. You think I fall in love every six minutes."

No. More like every three.

"But this isn't like that. It's like Chichi and me—like we've known each other forever. Like we're connected."

Probably Chichi connected to a new woman every week. "Great, Becky. I wish you the best." I'd pushed the elevator button again.

"Was Jen upset I wasn't here? Did she say anything?"

Had she even noticed? "She understood."

"I'll send some flowers over later."

"Good idea."

"I'll write a note, saying I was here, but missed her because she left early." Becky had always been a little cowed by Jen's temper. Tried not to irritate her.

"That'll be great."

I'd asked her to come to the beach, but she'd had plans for breakfast with Chichi. And then planned to join him at the pool for water polo—or had it been water putting? Water something. She'd invited me to join them.

The elevator doors had opened then, and I'd waved to her as the doors had closed.

And then, on my way out to the beach, Juan Alonzo had stopped me.

~

Again, I saw Emily and Rose. They could have been twins.

I lay back, warmed by the soft tickle of an ocean breeze, the sun reflecting off the sand. Images of the sisters faded. Tension in my shoulders eased. Thoughts floated out of reach. Voices murmured in the distance, and the gentle rhythm of waves lulled me until I let go and drifted.

But I jolted upright in alarm the moment I realized that the insistent repetitive sound I was hearing wasn't the white noise of the ocean or distant voices: It was my name.

~

The face was blank, backlit by the sun. Even blinking and squinting, though, I knew who it was.

Damn it. "Melanie?"

She had hold of my left shoulder, seemed surprised at my reaction.

"Oh, sorry. Were you sleeping?"

Seriously?

"How was I supposed to know?" She finally removed her hand.

"Because my eyes were closed?"

"Elle, everyone closes their eyes when they lay out in the sun."

She offered no apology.

I lay back down, closed my eyes, hoped she'd leave.

She didn't. She sat on the foot of my lounge chair, cowering next to my legs. "He's still doing it," she lowered her voice. "Elle, I'm beyond freaked out."

I opened one eye. "What's he doing?"

"He's just everywhere I go. He follows me. Watches me. I'm totally weirded out. See? I'm shaking."

I looked at her outstretched hands. The fingers trembled.

"So, can I hang out with you? Honestly, I'm scared to be by myself." Her sunglasses made her look bug-eyed. And her skinny frame hunkered almost in a fetal position, revealing her spine. I wondered if she had an eating disorder.

Not my business. I didn't know her, didn't feel like changing that. Couldn't think up an excuse.

"I'm actually kind of tired, Melanie. I was hoping to catch some sleep."

"Go ahead. I'll just hang here."

"I mean, I'm not real talkative—"

"No problem. I have a magazine."

What could I say? Go away? She was afraid and turning to me for comfort. Whether I liked it or not. I couldn't turn Melanie away.

I motioned to a nearby beach chair. "Have at it."

"Thanks, Elle." She dragged the lounge chair over, pushed it up right up to mine. "You're great. You won't believe it, but at first, I was worried I'd be imposing."

Really? Imposing? "Don't be silly."

"But as soon as I met you, I felt comfortable with you. Like we were old friends. You know what I mean?"

I was trapped. I gazed up the beach, into the distance. A woman waded ankle-deep in water, her face shielded by a scarf. Oh God. I closed my eyes.

Melanie jabbered on.

"Buenos dias, señoras, look what I have for you," I heard a vendor approach, looked up to see a man dressed in white, carrying heavy cases of silver. "A bracelet, maybe, señora? A ring?"

We shook our heads, no, gracias. He trudged away, back down the beach.

I looked the other way, saw no sign of the woman with the scarf. Not in the water, not on the sand. Melanie was talking.

"—that he sends them over. He pays them to check on me— look." She nodded toward the vendor. Sure enough, he'd made his way to the snack shack, was talking to some men; Luis was one of them.

Melanie turned away. "I don't want Luis to see me looking at him," she said. "He'll take it as encouragement. Is he looking this way? Don't stare. Just be casual."

I'd already been staring, so I looked away. "He's looking around, up and down the beach."

"I can't take it."

"Tell his boss."

"I have no proof. What can I say? He follows me? I'd sound crazy."

I glanced back at Luis. He was looking our way. "He's looking at you."

"Son of a bitch," she said. "What am I going to do? I've got to shake him." She grabbed my hand. "Let's go in the water."

She was on her feet, dragging me. How the hell had I acquired this woman? Well, there was no point arguing with her. Besides, it was hot; the water would feel good. We grabbed boards from the rack and splashed into the water, rode waves. Laughed. Occasionally, I thought of Jen and Susan, wondered how the operation was going. But mostly, I didn't think about anything except timing, waiting for a good wave, feeling the exact moment to let the ocean grab me. The sun got higher in the sky. Other than that, I lost all sense of time until my stomach demanded food.

Back on the beach, drying off, I looked around for a waiter to order lunch on the beach. Melanie was there, watching out for Luis again, talking. I tuned her out, thinking about shrimp salad and lemonade. Then I saw the woman again.

She was going into the hotel bar, a flowered scarf shielding her face.

And behind her, Charlie was holding the door.

~

I sat down, reasoned that the man wasn't Charlie. And the woman wasn't Claudia Madison, back from the dead. Not everyone was a ghost. People resembled others; it was that simple.

Even so, I didn't feel comfortable out in the open any more. Instead of ordering lunch on the beach, I decided to eat on my balcony.

"Want company?" Melanie looked stricken that I was leaving.

"Thanks, but I don't think so. I mean, I'd have to check with my roommates."

"I thought your roommate was having surgery." Her tone was sharp, accusatory.

I stiffened. "I have three roommates. One of them is working. She needs to concentrate." It wasn't a lie. Susan was working. I hadn't actually said she was doing it in our suite.

Melanie eyed me, doubtful.

Why did I feel I had to explain myself? "Besides, I'm going to nap."

She tossed her towel over her shoulder. "No problem, Elle. I'll be fine. Catch you later." She strutted across the sand.

I told myself that Melanie was a big girl. And she wasn't my responsibility. Still, as I grabbed my stuff and made my way across the sand, I felt as if I'd done something wrong.

Music pounded through the pool area. Every lounge chair was occupied; the water was crowded. Becky did lunges on the platform, demonstrating exercise steps with Chichi. Luis had the microphone, announced the directions, scanning the crowd.

"Left and up, and reach, and down. Again. Left and up—" I watched him, wondering if he was looking around for Melanie. Finally, I went inside.

I called Susan from the lobby. Found out that Jen was still in surgery. Susan was abrupt, absorbed in work. I offered to come over. She said there was no need. So I went upstairs to the room, looking forward to time alone. But when I opened the door, I realized I wasn't. Someone was in the living room. I froze, let out an involuntary gasp.

And startled a maid.

"Oh, sorry," I explained. "I didn't expect to see anyone. You surprised me."

I doubt she understood a word I was saying. She bowed her head deferentially, excused herself, and scurried toward the door.

"No, it's fine," I went on. "You don't have to rush off."

She kept her head down. "I come back later, señora. *No es una problema.*" And she was gone.

I ordered room service, hopped into the shower, and realized as the water pounded my skin, that I'd missed some spots with the sunscreen. The backs of my shoulders were scorched. Damn.

I wrapped myself in a towel, smothered my burns in aloe, took some Motrin, ate shrimp salad on the balcony. In the pool below, exercise class had ended; the music had stopped. I looked around, spotted Melanie at the poolside bar. Luis was close by, talking to a silver-haired lady wearing high heels and a bathing suit. A pelican swooped past my railing. I felt the whoosh of his outstretched wings gliding toward the ocean. Settled back on a lounge chair in the shade. Closed my eyes.

Susan shook me. Saying something urgent.

I blinked at her. Tried to make sense out of her words. Oh God. I sat up. "Is it Jen? Is she okay?"

"She's fine. Dr. Du Bois said everything went perfectly."

"Good. So should I go see her?"

She tilted her head as if my question made no sense. "No. She's groggy. She'll be back in the morning. Elle, don't you need to get dressed?"

Dressed? I looked down. I was wearing a towel.

"What time is it?"

"I just told you. It's almost seven. You better hustle."

I looked around. The pool and beach were almost empty. The sun had moved over to the mountains. Lord, how long had I slept?

"Almost seven?" I tried to understand what that meant.

"Aren't you having dinner with Dr. Du Bois?"

Dinner? What? Oh Lord, I was supposed to meet Alain Du Bois in the lobby in four minutes.

Still half asleep, I scurried around, grabbing random articles of clothes, putting some on, dropping others. Susan's phone rang. When I left, she was still on the phone, running her hand through her hair, arguing with one of her daughters. "He's your father, Lisa. I know he's clueless, but you have to listen to him anyway. Yes, I mean it. Because he's your father." She looked at me and waved. "Have fun," then shook her head. "No, not you. I was talking to Elle. She's going to dinner. No. Not until you apologize to Daddy." She raised her voice, angry. "Lisa. I mean it. Look, I'm in Mexico, for God's sakes. Can't you guys get along for one week?"

I heard her yelling all the way to the elevator.

～

We ate outside, a few miles from the hotel. A small restaurant on the beach, connected to the owner's home, not frequented by tourists. The owner was chubby and mustached, greeted Dr. Du Bois with a tight embrace, talked with him in Spanish. Dr. Du Bois introduced me in English, and Emilio took my hand and seated us on a veranda, the closest table to the water. Across the patio, a couple leaned their heads together, deep in conversation. Only one other table was occupied: an old man, seated alone. Emilio stood straight and formal, promised that, if we'd let him choose our menu, he would be delighted to create our meal.

Dr. Du Bois met my eyes, checking with me, making sure it was okay. Already, I noticed that he communicated a lot through his eyes. A blink or a spark. A twinkle. His eyes were his best feature. Or maybe not—his jaw was nice, too. And his nose—it was straight and not too small or shy. It was an elegant, proud thing. But I needed to stop staring at it. Needed not to pull an Elle and wander. Made myself smile and pay attention to Emilio as he described our dinner.

Actually, I still wasn't quite awake. Twenty minutes ago, I'd been sound asleep on the balcony, and then I'd grabbed a strapped sundress, twisted my hair into a bun and tossed some makeup onto my face while dashing out the door. Dr. Du Bois had been polite, hadn't seemed bothered that I'd been fifteen minutes late or that I'd arrived in the lobby flustered and breathless, hair already coming loose and skin cream clotted on my red-hot shoulders. He'd been gracious, had said I looked lovely as he escorted me to his BMW convertible, where he'd asked if I'd wanted him to raise the roof. I hadn't. I'd been grateful for the wind; it had been loud, limiting the need for conversation. And giving me an excuse for mussed-up hair.

Emilio's wife was squat and fair skinned. She lit candles for us, scolding that it had been too long since Dr. Du Bois had been there, that he worked too hard. She brought a pitcher of home-made lemonade, and Emilio brought a bottle of tequila with two glasses.

Dr. Du Bois offered to make me a drink, mixing the two. "It's their specialty drink." He poured tequila into the pitcher, stirred. "I've been coming here for years. I thought you'd like a chance to get away from the tourist spots. It's charming, don't you think?"

Was it? I looked around. Where was I? And why? Who was this slender, sun-tanned man across the table? I must have answered. Might have even asked a question because he went on.

"I met Emilio years back at the clinic. His kids are all grown now, moved away. But his son was burned in an oven fire when he was about sixteen. He was one of my first patients here, and I was able to help repair his scars. Emilio and I became friends, and I've been eating here ever since."

We looked at each other across the table. Candlelight flickered, emphasizing his cheekbones. He picked up his glass with steady hands. Hands which, hours before, had sliced up Jen's stomach and breasts, rearranged her nose. I cleared my throat. Tasted tequila lemonade.

"Here," he lifted the tequila bottle. "I think it needs a little more."

Oh dear. I nodded; he poured.

"So, everything went well with Jen today?"

He smirked. "Even though you're friends, we have strict privacy policies. I can't discuss her case with you. But I have no doubt that she'll be happy with her results."

Oh. I'd said something stupid. Was glad that sunburn and dusk would hide my blush.

"And besides, my work isn't why we're here. You tried to save Claudia Madison, a woman I valued not just as a longtime patient, but also as a dear friend." He held up a glass. "Here's to a brave woman. No, sorry—to a beautiful, intriguing, brave woman—Elle Harrison." He clinked my glass. At the rim.

I blushed again.

"That's sweet of you, but anyone would have done—"

"Not true. You risked your life to save a stranger. Don't try to minimize it. You're clearly an unusual woman. Are you always that daring? That selfless? Tell me: Who is Elle Harrison?"

Really? I swallowed more tequila and lemonade. And I braced myself for get-to-know-you time, the inevitable part of a first date, filled with questions and answers, flirtations, and lies. But I didn't want to talk about myself to this man. Even though he was Jen's doctor, I really didn't know him. More than that, I didn't want to say I was a widow—hadn't said that word out loud yet. Certainly not to a man who was taking me to dinner. I hated the word. Especially when combined with my profession: I was a widow who was on a leave of absence from teaching second grade. How pitiful and boring was that? Much better to stick with "intriguing" and "brave." Before he could ask more questions, I turned it around.

"I'd rather talk about you. Tell me what brought you to Mexico. Why do you practice here?" Nicely done.

"Is that really what you want to talk about?" His eyes glittered, teased.

My face heated up yet again. "It's a start."

He smiled. Told me about his practice, how he and an American colleague had opened a practice here to provide services at lower costs than in the U.S.

"In the U.S., insurance doesn't cover elective procedures like cosmetic surgery. In many cases, they are prohibitively expensive; here, we can charge less."

"So people come here to save money?" I thought of Jen.

"Mostly, yes. Sometimes they come because American doctors have turned them down."

Turned them down? "Why?"

He sighed. "You really want to talk about this?" He looked

cornered, continued only after I assured him that, yes, I did. "Okay. For some patients, one operation is enough. They correct thin lips or tiny breasts. But for others, nothing is enough."

I pictured breasts being made larger and larger, until they tipped the woman over.

"For some patients," he went on, "cosmetic surgery becomes a habit. In a way, they're surgery addicts. They undergo procedure after procedure—liposuction and rhinoplasty. Breast enhancement or reduction—they keep coming back. Maybe they want attention from the medical staff, or maybe they want to look perfect. Who knows? I'm not a psychiatrist, so I don't have to understand why. But often, American doctors turn these patients away. So they come here."

"And you'll do it? Even if you think a patient is addicted to surgery?" I was appalled.

Dr. Du Bois shrugged, took a drink. "Of course I will. As long as the procedure isn't too great a risk to their health. If a patient wants it, we will do the work."

I stiffened, looked off toward the ocean. Obviously, he'd work on anyone who could pay him. He'd operated on Jen even though she hadn't needed anything done.

"What's wrong? I've upset you?"

"Dr. Du Bois, why—"

"Alain," he corrected. "Please."

I met his eyes. They twinkled. "Alain." I took a breath, tried not to sound judgmental. "Why would you perform unnecessary surgery? Especially on patients with a surgery addiction?"

He met my eyes. "Seriously? On such a beautiful night? You want to talk about my surgical practice?" He sighed.

I sat straight, attentive. Tried to look impartial.

"All right, if you insist. Elle, quite simply, each of us is given a body. It is my belief that, as long as we don't hurt anyone else, we should have control over that body. If a man wants to change his appearance, why should anyone be able to tell him that he can't?"

Emilio's wife came over with chips, guacamole, and salsa. "I made these myself. The best." She stood behind Alain, her hands on his shoulders. "This man is my hero. Be nice to him. I love him as my own."

He took her hand and kissed it, released it as she walked away, ample hips swaying.

I drank more tequila-laced lemonade. Wondered if Dr. Du Bois thought I should fix my appearance. Did he think my nose was too crooked? My lips too thin?

"So you'll do whatever a patient wants, no matter what?"

He chuckled. "Does that bother you?" He dipped a chip into the guacamole. Took a bite. Closed his eyes, savoring. "This is exceptional."

"Anything at all? No limits?"

He chewed. Handed me a chip. "Have some."

I scooped salsa onto it.

"Of course, there are limits—"

My cough interrupted him. The salsa was fresh. And bursting with hot peppers.

"Are you all right? Sorry. I should have warned you about the salsa."

I said I was fine, asked him to go on. Dabbed tears from my eyes. Dipped a chip into guacamole, cooled my tongue with avocado. Drank tequila-lemonade. Tried to catch up with Alain's conversation.

"—if a patient's health rules out surgery because of, for example, a heart condition or other complications, such as advanced age. And sometimes, when patients have deeper issues." He looked away. "But, that's enough about my work. Let's talk about you."

"What kind of issues?"

He sighed. Leaned on his elbows. "You know, this isn't really dinner table conversation."

I leaned on my elbows, countering him. Watched the candle

flame reflected in his eyes. Why was I persisting? I wasn't sure. After all, Alain Du Bois was no one to me. Just a dinner companion. I pressed him nonetheless. "Fine. But dinner's not here yet."

He paused. Assessed me. Must have realized I wouldn't back down. "Okay. Here's an example. Occasionally, a patient will exhibit a condition called body dysmorphic disorder. These patients see themselves differently than they actually are—the image they perceive is distorted."

I thought of Jen who thought she'd needed a flatter stomach and bigger breasts. When she looked in the mirror, had she seen a bloated belly and flat chest? Was she suffering from this disorder? How would anyone find out if they had it? If you saw your nose as big, how would you know if you were wrong?

Alain was still talking. "—enough to maim themselves. One of my current patients, in fact, is so offended by her leg—finds it so hideous, that she has actually attempted to cut it off above the knee. She failed, of course. So now, she wants me to remove it."

I must have missed something. Or heard him wrong. I squinted, concentrated on his words.

"—suffers from a condition called apotemnophilia. It's an overwhelming inexplicable desire to remove a limb—sometimes more than one. Often, these patients are sexually stimulated by amputation. They might feel, for example, that only by being an amputee can they become sexually aroused."

I shook my head. "Wait. Back up. Your patient wants her perfectly healthy leg cut off?" He had to be making it up. "For sex?"

"I told you it wasn't for the dinner table. But you asked if I have limits." He poured straight tequila into his empty glass. "For me, this amputation is a limit. I've refused to do it. She needs a psychiatrist. My partner thinks I'm wrong, though. He thinks apotemnophilia is as legitimate a cause for amputation as, say, crushed bones or gangrene. We've had several serious arguments over it."

Emilio's wife arrived with bowls of rice and black beans. Emilio brought platters of fish, which he proceeded to bone at our table. "*Pescado en verde*," he announced, his knife penetrating the skin, severing the head. Fish eyes regarded me dully in the dim light, and I looked away, out at the mass of black that was the ocean, saw Madam Therese's dark eyes with their promises of bloodstained auras and death.

"Elle?" Alain's eyes glowed. "Would you like some wine?"

Wine? Emilio chatted as he finished filleting our dinner, recommending which would go best with his sauce of garlic, cilantro, chiles, other herbs I hadn't heard of.

It wasn't until he went for the wine and Alain offered me the bowl of rice that I became aware of my hands. They were under the table, clenched in a death grip on my leg just above the knee.

∿

We didn't mention anything related to medicine for the rest of the evening. Somehow my teaching career and my work with second graders seemed like wonderful topics for conversation. I rattled on with anecdotes.

"Trust me, I know whose dad had hair transplants, whose parents smoke marijuana, which dads sleep naked, which moms torture their kids by kissing them at the bus stop."

Alain laughed. Seemed interested. Asked questions about the school, the kids. He moved on to me. Resumed the first-date Q and A. Where had I grown up? In Philadelphia. Did I have a big family? No, but Jen, Becky, and Susan were like family. How was it that a woman as attractive as I was still single?

Boom. There it was: the dreaded inevitable question. I took a breath, looked down at my ringless finger. Heard Charlie call me the love of his life. Blurted out an answer: I'd been married. But my husband had died. I stumbled on the last part. My throat was tight.

Alain reached across the table, wrapped his hand around mine. His fingers were firm and soft. And lacked a wedding ring.

"What about you?" I diverted attention onto him.

His gaze shifted, turned inward. "Well, in a way, my wife is also gone."

He had a wife? I slid my hand out of his. Cursed myself. Stupid Elle—of course he had a wife. Why had I thought otherwise? Alain was in his forties, painfully handsome, accomplished, successful. Men like Alain had wives. They had families. But wait—none of that should matter to me. I wasn't out with him because he wanted to date me; we were having dinner because he appreciated my attempt to save his patient. Once again, I'd lost touch with reality, letting tequila, wine, ocean air, and candlelight carry me off, letting myself imagine that his interest in me was more than mere kindness. I was too needy. Had been alone too long. Felt my face burn.

"—so even though I'm married, it's as if I'm single."

What?

"Inez will never recover. Her condition is permanent. I've finally come to accept that. Unlike your husband, Inez is alive, but as far as having a life? She's gone. It's limbo."

Clearly, I'd missed a key piece of information.

I tried to reconstruct what I'd missed. But I'd been drifting. Hadn't heard. "I'm sorry."

"Thank you." He straightened up, inhaled. "It's life. Accidents happen."

So his wife had been in an accident? What? In the car? A fall? A fire?

"Anyway, it seems that both of us have lost our spouses." His eyes were steady and somber. "I suppose that makes us simpatico."

I remembered Charlie in his casket, his cheeks too pink from the rouge.

"But you're at least free to move on. In my case, I'm still tied to Inez. People tell me to get a divorce. I suppose I should. It's not easy here, but we were married back home in Canada. I can get one there. The trouble is—the accident was my fault. I am responsible for her condition, so I can't walk away from her."

This time, my hand went out to his. He looked up, nodded. We sat like that for a moment.

Emilio collected our plates, accepted lavish praise for his cooking. He brought espresso and bananas flambé. We sat without talking, oddly comfortable with silence.

As we walked to his car, Alain asked if he could see me again. An image flashed to mind—I'd come home early, found Charlie in the shower lathering suds onto a woman's back. Why was I thinking of that? Alain was asking to see me again, not to have an affair. And even if he were, what was the problem? Charlie was dead. Alain's wife was an invalid. We still needed companionship. Needed to survive.

Of course, I told him. I would love to see him again.

After all, I was only going to be there for five more days. Not time enough for anything serious to develop. What would be the harm?

~

Susan was sprawled out on the sofa, snoring, her neck bent at a sharp angle to her body, her computer on her lap. Probably, she was exhausted from spending the day with Jen. Otherwise, she wouldn't have been able to sleep. The hotel was having a fiesta with Mariachi bands playing on the pool deck. I debated waking her. If I didn't, she'd get a crook in her neck—or was it a crick? Neither name made any sense. But sleeping with her neck at that angle would definitely give her one of those.

On the other hand, if I woke her, she'd ask me about my dinner with Alain. Which I didn't want to talk about—not that there was anything about it to hide. Except maybe that he was married. And that, even so, I'd agreed to see him again. And that, as we'd said good night, he'd leaned over with a kiss so tender that I'd actually stopped breathing, so light that minutes later my lips still tingled. So arousing that, when I tried to thank him for dinner, I couldn't find my voice for a moment, and when I finally did, it came out a few octaves lower than normal.

Anyway, I didn't want to talk about it. I hadn't been attracted to a man in a year. I wanted to think about it, savor it. Privately.

So, finally, instead of waking her, I lifted Susan's head and put a pillow underneath, moved her computer to the table, covered her with a blanket. She didn't stir.

I went onto the balcony, looked down at the party, found Becky and Chichi near the bar, Chichi's arm around Becky's waist. I looked for Luis, didn't see him. But Melanie was there, sitting with a table of middle-aged women—maybe her grandmother's friends. Good, I thought. As long as she was with them, Luis wouldn't be bothering her.

I stretched out on a lounge chair, listening to the band, the chatter. Replaying the evening. Feeling mellow. And then I heard the argument.

~

At first, I thought I was hearing a television show. Or that the voices were coming from someplace below. They were soft, and the fiesta music almost drowned them out. But when the band stopped, the voices didn't. There was no mistake: people were arguing on the other side of the brick wall. On Claudia Madison's balcony.

But they couldn't be. That suite was empty, wasn't it? Claudia Madison had died there just two days ago, and her death hadn't been an accident. Wasn't the hotel keeping the suite empty pending investigation? Wasn't it a crime scene? And if it was, who could be out on her balcony?

I moved closer to the wall, straining to listen. A man was talking, his voice low and rumbling.

"—to resist you? I am only human." He had a Mexican accent. "Please, *bonita*. I have missed you. Let me be with you. I want to kiss you—"

"No. Leave me alone." Her voice broke. Was she crying?

"Why do you push me away, *mi amada?*"

"Stop pawing me."

I leaned forward, trying to see around the wall, but I couldn't lean too far without being seen. Or falling. When I peeked, I saw only a table with a phone and a wineglass, not people. But I heard the woman sniffling.

"Why do you cry? *Bonita,* you are the most beautiful, most desirable woman—"

"Stop the crap. Stop lying to me. Just stop. Take your hands off—"

"*Cara,* why do you push me away? Why hurt me this way? I need you—"

"I'm not one of your horny, desperate, lonely, old tourists. Understand? Your bullshit doesn't work on me. I know the truth about my looks. I know why you're here. Stop lying. Stop trying to seduce me. It won't get you anywhere."

Silence. Then she sniffed, blew her nose. "Just go away."

"Please. Let me dry your tears."

"I said, go away."

A chair scraped. "Okay. I'll go if it's what you want. But I won't give up. I'll be back. I can't stay away from you, *mi amada*. I cannot help it."

I leaned against the brick wall, heard the sliding door open, close. The woman sniffled again.

Downstairs, the fiesta was breaking up. People wandered back into the hotel.

I backed away from the railing and went back to my lounge chair, wondering about the woman next door. When had she moved in? What was her relationship with the man? When he'd said she was beautiful, why had the woman accused him of lying? Was she somehow deformed, here for corrective plastic surgery? It was none of my business, but I couldn't help it. I wanted to lean over the railing and look at her. Maybe I could pretend I didn't know anyone was there and act surprised to see her sitting there. I could say something like—"Oh, you scared me. I thought that suite was empty."

I told myself to keep out of it. To leave the poor crying woman alone. So I did.

Until I heard her speak again.

~

"It's me." Her voice was raspy, curt. Demanding. "What do you think? I'm sitting here, waiting for you."

No one responded. But I'd seen a phone on the table—she must have made a call.

"Don't make excuses. I want to see you."

A pause, and then she said, "The door's unlocked. Stop talking. Just get here."

Wow. Her voice sounded entirely different than it had earlier. It was stern, gruff. The tears were gone. What had happened?

Never mind. Not my business. I was way too nosy. I got up, went into our suite. Susan was still snoring. In the kitchenette, I found some cheese and crackers. Poured some leftover wine. Went back outside with my snack, wondering once more why the suite had been occupied so soon after Claudia's death. I sat at the table, sipped wine. Looked out at the black ocean. Pictured Claudia, reaching out for me. Losing her grip. Falling. I shuddered at the thud, closed my eyes. Saw the woman on the beach, her scarf rippling over her face, hiding its features. Charlie appeared, leading her away.

"It wasn't your fault."

I stiffened, put down my glass. Who'd said that? I looked around, even though I knew that no one was there. I must have thought the words, imagined the voice. Even so, I went to the railing and looked down, half expecting to see Claudia face down on the concrete, calling up to me. But of course she wasn't. Instead, I saw hotel staff, scurrying to clean up from the party, preparing for the next morning's activities. Nothing indicated that Claudia had ever plunged onto the pool deck in a corona of blood. I leaned forward, glanced at the railing on which I'd found her. Was her spirit still there, clinging to it? Did her terror remain? Had Claudia just spoken to me?

Of course not. I'd imagined the voice. I returned to my seat, ate crackers with cheese. Drank wine. Lay down on the lounge chair. Refused to think about Claudia or the man who looked like Charlie or my new neighbor. Thought instead about Alain, his kiss. About seeing him again. And dozed.

Drifting off, though, I heard a woman's ghostly voice. "Be careful," it whispered. "Or the one who killed me will also kill you."

The voice was crisp and clear. And close—I smelled floral perfume.

I opened my eyes, sat up, and looked around, but no one was there. I thought the sweet scent lingered, but I must have been mistaken. Or maybe it drifted over from the balcony next door.

After that, I was wide awake. I went inside. Thought again about waking Susan, decided not to. What would I say to her? That a disembodied voice had warned me of danger? That for months after Charlie died, I'd heard his voice, and that now, I was hearing Claudia's? I worried my hands, shivered. Did laps around the living room.

Stop this, I said aloud. I hadn't heard Charlie's voice after his murder; I'd imagined it. Just as I had now imagined Claudia's. The voices were symptoms of my psychological disorder— I tended to wander in my mind and confuse thoughts with reality. The voice—the warning hadn't been real. No one was trying to kill me.

I sat in the chair opposite the sofa, assuring myself that I was safe, watching Susan sleep. Hearing the voice repeating itself. "The one who killed me will also kill you." The words weren't Claudia's. They'd come from my own mind. But why would my mind have said that I was in danger?

I looked back at the balcony, searching for Claudia's ghost. Saw my wineglass on the table with the rest of the crackers. I leaned back, closed my eyes. Madam Therese smiled patiently, repeating, "The dead are drawn to you. You already know that."

No. I opened my eyes, stood, repeating the obvious: The dead weren't drawn to me or anyone else. The dead were dead. I shouldn't be rattled. I'd fallen asleep and the voice had been a dream. Nothing more. Just a dream.

I went into my bedroom, put on a nightgown, brushed my teeth. Got into bed. Lay there, wide awake, unable to shake the sense that sleep would bring more dread and warnings. Or that, if I weren't watchful, whoever had killed Claudia might come after me.

∿

Eventually, sleepless, with nowhere else to go, I wandered back onto the balcony, refilled my wineglass, took a seat. Heard a man talking on the other side of the wall. Not the man from before, a different voice.

A familiar one.

"Why don't you believe me? Why would I lie?"

I sat, listening, telling myself that I was mistaken. Certain that I wasn't.

"Why? Because you're a man. Because men lie. Because you want to control me."

"I can't defend all men. All I can do is assure you: You are beautiful—"

"I'm hideous. Look at me."

A rustle of fabric. A soft moan. Was Alain kissing her? I pictured it, recalled his lips brushing mine.

"Do you believe me now?" Alain's voice was throaty.

"I'm begging you, Alain. Please. Help me. Make me whole."

"You are already whole. You are perfect as you are—"

"I'm not. I want to feel sexy. I want to have appeal. Why won't you do this for me?" The woman wailed. "I'll pay whatever you want. It would be no trouble for you."

"Greta. No. I can't do it. What you need is beyond my capability. Your face is perfection; your body is exquisite. The work we've done has made you a goddess. I can't remember ever seeing a more desirable woman."

Really? I felt a stab, winced. Blushed, recalling his kiss. Alain was quite a player.

"Desirable?" I pictured Greta's pout. "I'm repulsive."

"Greta, please."

"If I'm so desirable, how can you manage to resist me?"

Oh God. Furniture scraped again. She moaned. He grunted. I was frozen. Horrified, yet unable to leave. Tempted to lean around the brick wall and look. Was Alain really making love to her? To his patient? I listened, picturing the actions that went with each sound. Her groan would signify his hand sliding down from her hair to her shoulder to her breast, working its way inside her robe. If she was wearing a robe. Maybe it was a nightgown. Or nothing?

"Greta. I'm sorry."

"What's wrong?"

"I can't do it." Alain's voice was low and breathy. "I have to go."

"No—" Greta sounded stunned. Betrayed. "Why? You don't have to go. That's a lie. You find me repulsive, don't you? You lied to me."

"You are anything but repulsive. But I can't keep doing this. We've discussed it. You knew that when you called me. I can't help you anymore. It's best that I go."

The sliding door opened.

"Heartless, self-serving bastard! If you won't help me—I'll take care of it another way. I swear I will."

"I hope you don't mean that, Greta. You know what happened last time."

"Stay with me, Alain. Or else—"

"I'll put a list together for you. I'll give you several names, all qualified. Take care of yourself, Greta."

The door slid closed.

The woman let out a moan, dissolved into sobs. I couldn't

help it. I leaned over the balcony and peeked around the brick wall, saw her doubled over, crying. Alain was gone. In the bedroom behind Greta, the lights were on. A maid was there, turning down the bed.

I sat on the lounge chair, gazing at the dark sky and the ocean, trying to make sense of what I'd heard. And then Greta spoke again.

"I'm glad you picked up." She sniffled. "Listen, about before? I was cranky. Sorry. Come back. Yes, now. I'll make it up to you."

She was on the phone because no one replied and from then on, there was silence. After a few minutes, having finished my wine, I went inside and fell first into bed, then into a restless sleep filled with troubled dreams of Charlie. In one, I was supposed to call him, but couldn't remember his number. In another, he was by the pool, surrounded by a bevy of faceless large-breasted women. He waved at me as I went for a swim, and I noticed that the water was the wrong color. I was backstroking in blood.

∾

Jen came back the next morning. Her nose was hidden under a wad of gauze, and she walked bent over like a crone, moving slowly and stiffly, cursing with every step.

Susan hovered, trying to help. "Should she go to bed?" she asked the aide. "Or would she be better out on the balcony in the fresh air?"

"Ask be, dot her," Jen barked. "I'b goi'g the fuck to bed." She sounded like her nose was stuffed. Maybe it was swollen? Or packed with more gauze?

"Jen," I greeted her. "Welcome back—"

"Go to hell," she snarled. She gripped the aide's arm.

"She has medications," the aide explained. "They make her say things she does not mean to say."

"That's a lie." Jen growled. "They fucked be up." She had made it to the bedroom door. "This isn't dorbal. I deed the doctor."

"Dr. Du Bois will be here," the aide assured her. "Nothing went wrong. It's the drugs. You're confused, it's okay."

"She's one of theb." Jen insisted from inside the bedroom. "Elle. Susad. Help be. Are you guys just goi'g to fuckigg stad there ad let her kill be?"

"No one's trying to kill you, Jen. This lady—"

"Maria," the aide said.

"Maria is here to help you. You have drugs in your system, so you're confused."

I looked into the room, saw Maria help Jen into bed. Jen swore at Maria; Susan scolded Jen. On their dresser, Jen's phone rang. I went to answer it. Saw that it was Norm.

"WTF!" Jen shouted. "It's Dorb. Do't adswer."

The phone kept ringing.

Susan and I exchanged worried looks.

"Do't tell hib. He doesn't dow—Tell I'b at the gyb—"

"Norm still doesn't know?" Susan gaped at her. "You really didn't tell him about the surgery?"

"Ouch! Dab it," Jen barked at Maria. "Get away from be. That's by husbad od the phode. Whed he sees what you've dud to be, he'll cub after you—all of you—" Her voice was weaker; she lay back on her pillows, fading.

I picked up the phone, went into the living room. "Hi, Norm." I told him we were having a fabulous time. That Jen was out somewhere. That she'd call him back when she could.

I ended the call and went out onto the balcony, watching a pelican glide around. I gazed at the ocean, the alligator slide, the pool. I don't know exactly what drew me to look at the balcony next door. Maybe I hoped I could get a glimpse of our new neighbor, find out what Alain's idea of exquisite looked like. I stepped over to the brick dividing wall, held onto the railing and leaned over. Probably, she wouldn't be out there; it was a silly idea. But I planted a smile on my face, a friendly greeting just in case.

Spindly bare legs sprawled across the tiles. The image didn't register until I saw the clotted dark puddle. I twisted to see around the wall.

And somewhere close by, someone screamed.

~

The woman's name was Greta Mosley. Her face had been slashed to ribbons. Sergeant Perez wouldn't tell us much more, just that her face had been unrecognizable. And that she'd been stabbed so many times that it was impossible to tell which wound or wounds had caused her death.

"Did either of you hear anything unusual in the night?" Sergeant Perez looked at Susan, then at me.

Susan shook her head. "I fell asleep early."

I took a breath. Said that I'd heard a woman out on her balcony, talking to two different men. Didn't mention that one of them was Alain Du Bois. "But I heard both of the men leave. And when I went to bed around midnight, she was still alive."

"How do you know that?"

"I heard her talking. I think she was on the phone."

"We checked her phone," Perez remarked. "She did make some calls. Did you hear that last conversation?"

I felt Susan's eyes. Couldn't read her expression. Puzzled? Worried? Did she want me to stop talking?

"I heard her tell someone to come over."

"Uh-huh." Perez nodded. "So the last person she called might be our killer."

"Not necessarily," Susan, the defense attorney, corrected him. "We don't know that the person actually came over. And we certainly don't know that this person killed her."

"*Gracias, señora.*" Perez's tone was condescending. "I believe I said this person 'might' be our killer."

"All I'm saying is—"

"That will do, señora." Perez turned from Susan to me. "Is there anything else you remember?"

I thought back. Recalled the ghost of Claudia Madison warning that her killer would come after me. But that hadn't been real, wasn't relevant.

"She was crying," I said. "She told one of the men that she thought she was hideous."

Perez stroked his chin. Watched me. Waited.

I pictured Alain with her. Heard him kissing her. Then refusing her, leaving her in tears. And I remembered leaning over the balcony. Seeing Greta cry.

"She was alone when I went to bed."

"And how do you know that? You couldn't see her."

"Well, actually I could." I bit my lip. "I leaned over the balcony."

"You what?" Susan blinked at me, appalled.

"She was sobbing—I was concerned about her." And curious about her relationship with Alain.

"And when you looked around the wall," Perez demanded, "you saw only her. No one else."

"Yes. No one was there." I shrugged. "Well, except for a maid, turning down her bed."

"A maid." Perez echoed.

I nodded. "Maybe the maid saw someone."

"What did she look like?"

I thought back, had no idea. Remembered only her uniform. "I didn't see her face."

He nodded. "Well, the hotel will know who was working. If you think of anything else, let me know." He stood, ready to go. "As you can see, two deaths have occurred in the same room right next to yours in a short period of time." He paused, as if he'd said something profound.

"What are you trying to say, Sergeant?" Susan pressed.

"Only that I urge you to be vigilant." Sergeant Perez looked at each of us, registering his point. "If you see or hear anything suspicious, contact the police."

Becky rushed in while he was still speaking. "Guys," she pointed out the door, "there's police tape all over the hall. What hap—"

When she saw Sergeant Perez, she stopped, breathless, and looked at me. "Elle? Oh God. Did someone else die?" She asked me, not the others. As if I was the one who'd know. As if death were somehow my area of expertise.

∾

Alain arrived, black bag in hand, right after Becky. Sergeant Perez took him aside, conferred quietly at the door. Telling him the news? Alain's face turned gray and he staggered. I thought he might faint, but he didn't. He lowered his head and put a hand over his eyes. Perez continued talking.

I sat on the sofa, trying not to stare at Alain. Trying to block out Susan's voice and tune into Perez's, eavesdropping. Not having much luck.

"Wow. I can't believe another woman died." Becky was wearing one of Chichi's t-shirts. It said, "Cha-cha with Chichi" on the front and "Limbo with Luis" on the back. "Maybe we should ask to change rooms. There's too much bad juju here."

"Well, why would that concern you?" Susan scowled, crossed her arms. "You're not exactly staying here."

Becky's eyes widened. "What?"

"You pop in, not knowing anything that's happened. You weren't here for Jen. You drop by when it suits you and expect us to update you."

"Susan," I tried to intervene. "None of this is Becky's fault."

Susan's phone began ringing. "Damn." She glared at it. "What would they do if I just didn't answer?" But she did answer and, gesturing emphatically with her free hand, she wandered onto the balcony, arguing with someone in her office.

"She's tired," I told Becky. "She spent the whole day with Jen, and her office is sending her work, and now this."

"No. It's not just that. Susan never takes me seriously. She thinks my life is a party, or a joke. She doesn't believe I can really be serious about a guy. Or that my relationships matter. Only hers."

"That's not true." Except, probably it was. "She's just stressed." I looked over Becky's shoulder at Alain. He looked steadier, but was still engrossed in conversation with Sergeant Perez. Was he talking about his visit to Greta Mosley last night? I watched his lips, tried to read them. Couldn't.

Becky was chattering, saying something about how hard it was to choose between her lover and her friends, especially when time with Chichi was so finite. How it wasn't her fault people kept dying next door. How she shouldn't be blamed for wanting to live her life and make her own choices.

The room hummed with voices. Susan's, Becky's, Alain's, and Sergeant Perez's. They blended into nervous fuzz. I pictured the woman next door, her face cut into spaghetti strands. Who would slash someone's face? And why? The face was personal, the part of the body that was unique, that distinguished one person from another. Stabbing it—destroying it seemed much more hateful than stabbing a chest or a stomach. Especially, in a suite reserved for patients of cosmetic surgery.

But was Greta actually a patient? The night before, I'd heard Alain turning her down, telling Greta that he couldn't do what she wanted. He'd also told her that she was already beautiful, that her face was perfect. That her body was like a goddess. I heard his voice assure her that he couldn't "remember seeing a more desirable woman."

Really? Recalling his words, I felt a pang. Lord, was I jealous? Of a dead woman? And anyway, what did I care what Alain had said to her? We'd had one dinner. He was no one to me. And he was married. No, wait, I was losing the point. What was the point again? I tried to remember. Oh, right. The point was that the murderer hadn't been happy just to kill Greta, but had needed to destroy her face, demolishing her beauty.

I was onto something. An idea began to form, something

about beauty and the killer's motive or identity. But before it took on definition, a piercing scream shattered it to shards.

~

It came from Susan and Jen's room. "SUBBODY!"

Oh God—Jen! Was she being attacked? I was on my feet. Everyone was. We stampeded, all four of us, tripping over each other to get through the doorway.

"Where the hell's everbody bid?" Even with her bandages, I could see Jen's indignant pout. "I've bid calligg for half ad hour."

Becky put up a defensive hand. "Hold on, I just got here."

"Dr. Du Bois." Jen ignored her. "You fucked be up. By doze is stuffed."

"It's packing," his voice was thick. His eyes looked glassy. "It'll come out soon."

"Those goddabbed pills dote work—I deed subthigg that works. I'b id terrible paid. I deed drugs. Ad I think I have ad id-fectiod—"

"Let me take a look." Alain snapped into his professional role, opened his black bag, and pulled out tools: a stethoscope, a thermometer.

"And dabbit, Susad. Get off the phode. You said you'd get be subthigg to eat ad hour ago."

Apparently, neither pain nor infection had dulled her appetite. Susan, still on her cell, waved at Jen and headed for the kitchenette, Becky trailing behind her.

Jen turned her glare to me. "Well? Is adybody goigg to help be get to the toilet? Or do you want be to fuckigg pee id bed?"

Alain stuck a thermometer into her mouth, stifling her. When he removed it, I helped her out of bed and guided her to the bathroom. He didn't say anything to me nor did I to him, but I felt his heavy gaze on my back as I led Jen away.

~

I sat on the balcony while Alain conducted Jen's post-op check-up. Becky made coffee and poured juice while Susan simultaneously scrambled eggs and scrapped with someone at her law office.

Down at the pool, Chichi and Luis were setting up equipment for water basketball. A barrel-bellied man rode down the alligator slide, splashing into the pool. People carrying towels staked claims to lounge chairs or walked to the beach to the rhythm of piped-in salsa music.

Two women were dead, both staying in the suite next door. And I had been there both times, had seen or heard both of them just before they'd died. I thought about the night before. About the men with Greta. The maid turning down her bed. Had there been a maid in Claudia's room too? I tried to remember, pictured her on the railing. Couldn't see into the room.

"The one who killed me," I heard her warn, "will come for you."

Claudia's death had most likely been a murder, like Greta's. But why would her killer care about, let alone come after me? I didn't know either of the victims. Had no incriminating information about their killers. What would be the reason for targeting me?

There was none. No reason.

"Just be careful," Claudia said. Or was it Greta this time?

I would be careful. Yes.

"That's good to know," Alain answered.

I spun around. Oh God. Had I said that out loud? He was standing behind me. How long had he been there? What else had I said?

"Are you all right, Elle?"

I nodded. Asked if he was.

He looked gaunt. His tan had a yellow hue. "I'm a bit shaken up."

Silence. He took a breath, folded his arms. Watched me.

What was I supposed to say? That I was sorry about his patient? That I'd heard him with her on her terrace? That I'd heard him kissing her, but hadn't mentioned him to the police?

"You have a few minutes?" I needed to talk to him. "Can we get some coffee?"

Before he could answer, I took his arm, escorting him through the suite. Jen's television was on, blaring happily in Spanish. Susan had apparently served Jen's breakfast and was pacing the living room with her phone against her ear, looking trapped and exasperated.

I told her we were going for coffee and I'd be back soon. I looked for Becky, didn't see her. Heard the shower running. Well, never mind. Becky had plans with Chichi, wouldn't care where I'd gone. I led Alain out the door, down a corridor draped with crime tape, past Greta's open door. Her suite still bustled with police. Alain picked up his pace, walking briskly to the elevators. A housekeeping cart partially blocked our way, but we shoved it aside. The maid using it was nowhere to be seen.

∿

We sat under an umbrella outside the Starbucks down the street. A man with two big dogs sat to our left; two women dressed for the beach to our right.

Alain bought my tall soy milk latte. Sipped his double espresso. Held his hands out. Stretched his elegant, sun-darkened fingers.

"I never tremble." He watched his hands. They didn't shake. "No matter what. I can be upset or frightened half to death. My emotional state has no effect on them."

Was he frightened half to death?

"Two of my patients are dead, Elle. Two women I cared about. One of them was brutally murdered. Not just murdered. Greta—her face was shredded like old bank statements." He looked at me as if I would have something to say.

I looked away. At the dogs. At the street. At my cup. Unlike Alain's, my hands were shaking. I gripped my latte with both, afraid I'd spill if I lifted it with just one. I took a careful sip.

"I go over it again and again. What happened? Who did this? Was Claudia's death also a murder? Was it the same killer? Why did he single out these two particular women?"

I saw Claudia's hand reach out for mine, tried not to wobble.

"I'm sorry." Alain put his cup down, put a hand on my arm. "I'm being selfish. You must be upset, too. How are you doing, Elle?"

I wasn't sure.

"Sergeant Perez said that you were one of the last people to see Greta."

"Well, mostly, I heard her."

He raised an eyebrow. Leaned closer. "You heard her?"

"From my balcony."

"You were on your balcony?" He hesitated. "What did you hear?"

I faced him directly, waited a beat. "I think you know."

His eyes saddened, and he removed his hand from my arm, leaned back in his chair. Let out a breath. Flared his nostrils. Bit his lip. Leaned forward again. We were about the same height. His eyes were level with mine.

"So. I suppose that you heard me there."

He watched me for confirmation. I gave none. Said nothing.

"Elle, this woman was my patient. I was checking on her."

I didn't move.

"Why do I have to explain myself to you?" Again he leaned back and let out a breath, raising his hands as if conceding defeat. "Never mind. The fact is that I want to explain myself. Because even in this short time, you matter to me. I want you to understand."

The women at the next table stopped talking. I felt them eyeing us.

"Look," Alain must have also noticed them. He leaned toward me yet again and lowered his voice almost to a whisper. "I told you about Greta at dinner. I just didn't mention her name. She'd been my patient for years, a surgery addict. We did liposuction. Breast reduction. Neck lift. Eyelids. Cheekbones. A little off here, a little on there. She was never happy. No matter how beautiful I made her—no matter how I molded and sculpted and carefully shaped her features, she still thought she was ugly."

I remembered the condition—what had he called it? "She had that disorder?"

"Body dysmorphic disorder. Yes. No matter what procedure she had done, she still had a distorted image of herself. She didn't see her own beauty. In fact, her body repulsed her. I kept trying to help her, until after some years and several surgeries, she finally let me know how severe her problem was." He paused, his body tensed.

I clutched my latte and braced myself, not knowing why.

"About a year ago, she told me what she really wanted. To take off her leg."

Okay, I knew why.

"Greta's procedures didn't satisfy her. In fact, they couldn't. Because her underlying condition was apotemnophilia. I explained it to you at dinner. She thought her legs were abominations. Especially the left one. She believed that she was deformed, sexually repulsive, and that she could only be her true, whole, real, perfect self by getting rid of them."

I shook my head, didn't get it.

"It's a rare condition, but not rare enough. Over the years, I've treated a few patients who've wanted me to remove body parts. Generally, I refuse and refer them for psychological help. But Greta wouldn't accept my refusal. She kept insisting that I help her, threatening that, if I wouldn't, she'd do it herself. Apparently, a couple of months ago, she tried. She passed out and nearly bled to death, trying to cut her leg off."

What?

"She showed me the wounds yesterday. They weren't entirely healed. I told this to the police. They'd already noticed the damage above the knee."

I recalled Greta's moaning and the rustling of fabric. Would she have moaned while Alain examined her leg? "So you were there to talk about her condition?"

He watched me. Wondering how much I'd heard? How honest to be? He took a sip of coffee, gazed at the dogs. "I think that one's a Samoyed," he nodded at the big fluffy one.

Good. He knew his breeds. Clearly, he was trying to change the subject. Avoiding the truth.

"Look, Alain, you don't have to explain. I didn't tell the police that you were there."

"Elle, I have nothing to hide from the police."

The women sat stiffly, leaning our way, poised to listen.

This time I whispered. "Alain. I heard you with Greta. Don't pretend you were there about her leg."

"But I was." His steady fingers enclosed my wrist. His eyes hung onto mine. "Here's the truth, Elle—"

I watched him, saw Charlie. Heard Charlie's excuses and explanations. But that wasn't fair. Just because Charlie lied to me didn't mean Alain would, too. I made myself listen.

"—hope you'll not judge me. At one point, Greta and I were—involved. I'd worked on her eyelids, nose, and lips, but suddenly, after I reshaped her jaw, she became beautiful. Truly exquisite. I was captivated. It was wrong, based on superficial physical attraction, but I had an ethical slip. And then, when I realized how needy she was—how really emotionally ill—I ended it. Last night, I was there solely for professional reasons. I went to tell her I couldn't help her."

I looked away, saw Charlie in the shower, soaping a woman's butt. "You didn't have to go to her hotel room to tell her that." My tone was sharp, intended for Charlie.

Alain reddened. "No. I suppose I didn't. In hindsight, that seems clear. But I thought it would be kinder to tell her in person. We had a history. And she'd come all this way."

My face got hot. Why was I making him explain himself?

Alain and I weren't in a relationship. What he had done or hadn't done in Greta's suite wasn't my business.

Unless he'd killed her.

"I want to be open with you, Elle. I did have an affair with Greta Mosley. But not last night. Not for a year. Last night, I turned her down. And not just for the operation."

He pried my fingers off my latte cup, took my hand.

"I turned her down because of her mental condition and because I'd been ethically wrong by being with her. But those weren't the only reasons. The fact is I couldn't consider being intimate with her because someone else was on my mind. And she has been since I first met her." His hands were solid and warm. And graceful enough to be a woman's except for the ginger hairs on their backs. I looked up; his eyes sparkled.

Charlie didn't notice me. He was still engrossed in lathering the woman's backside, and I watched him from the doorway even as I heard Greta telephoning someone in the night, telling him to come to her room. Some time must have passed because when I looked around, I noticed that the ladies at the next table had resumed their conversation, and the guy with the dogs was gone.

But Alain still sat there, watching me, holding my hand.

❦

My face began to feel awkward. Alain was watching it closely, a man who'd sculpted perfect lips, shaped flawless noses. What did he see when he looked at me? A to-do list? Was he imagining how I'd look with a little plumping here, a little straightening there? I turned away, self-conscious.

"I've scared you." He didn't let go of my hand.

Scared wasn't quite the right word. But it wasn't quite wrong.

"I don't mean to. I mean to be honest, that's all. I find myself drawn to you, Elle. Under the circumstances, what's the point of hiding that?"

Which circumstances did he mean? The circumstance that I'd be in town for just a short time? That I'd overheard him with a woman just before she'd been killed? That he was a player in need of a new conquest?

I removed my hand. "You're a married man."

"I am." He looked away, his jaw muscles rippling.

For an uncomfortable time, neither of us spoke.

"We should get going—" I began, just as he said, "Please try to understand."

What was there to understand?

"My wife is—has been in no condition to be intimate. Or even to be a companion. I hinted at this at dinner. But the situation is that I am married in name only. Divorce isn't an option, though, because she depends on me."

"Look, Alain, your marriage is really not my business. I'm here on vacation, for a week."

"Plans can change."

What was he saying? "We really don't know each other."

"That can change, too. I want to get to know you."

"Why?"

Again, he met my eyes. His were steady. Kind of sad. Their color had changed, taking on a golden tone that matched his yellow shirt.

"Because I'm lonely. And looking to change my circumstances." He said it that simply. "You interest me. Not many people do."

Silence. Birds swooped onto the concrete floor, pecking up crumbs under the tables. People strolled by. He leaned back in his chair, but still watched me. My face began to itch.

"What happened to your wife?"

The question must have surprised him. He abruptly turned away. "An accident. She never recovered."

"A car accident?"

He winced.

"You were driving?"

He shifted in his chair. Played with a coffee stirrer. "It was my fault. Her condition is all because of me."

Oh. I had no response.

A bus stopped at the corner. Alain watched people get off, climb on. The bus pulled away.

"She was always a delicate woman. The accident shattered her life. And our marriage. And, in some ways, me." His eyes were pained, gazing inward. Was he seeing his memories? His sorrow?

I looked at Alain, saw my own loss. Charlie, in the coffin I'd picked out, wearing the pinstripe I'd selected. Charlie in my den, my kitchen knife in his back. Charlie charming me over the years, offering me a glass of Shiraz, melting me with a wink even when I knew what a scoundrel he was. "You're the love of my life, Elf," I heard his low whisper, felt the familiar ache.

Oh yes, I knew what it was to lose a spouse. I knew about being lonely.

Alain bit his upper lip. Lord. Who was this dashingly hand-some, sun-tanned man? What was I doing with him at a Star-bucks in Mexico, discussing his invalid wife, his guilt, his loneliness, his pain?

And why was I taking his hand, assuring him that life would get better? That, for the next few days, I'd try to prove that to him?

Whatever the answers, by the time we headed back to the hotel, I'd convinced myself that there was nothing wrong with having a few dinners with Alain. It wasn't as if I'd agreed to an affair. I wouldn't be in town long enough to get involved. And, given the murders of women who'd been staying in the suite next door, it would be good to have a man around. I had a list of respectable rationalizations.

But when we said good-bye, Alain pulled me behind a palm tree. His arms wrapped around me as he leaned forward and gave me a kiss like soft butter. As I watched him walk off, I lifted my hand to my lips, not sure of his sincerity. Not sure that I could move.

∿

The maid was in my bedroom, so I grabbed my bathing suit and went to Jen and Susan's to change.

"He's calling back any minute." Susan's hands were on her hips. "You're going to have to talk to him sooner or later—"

"WTF, Susad. You doh I ca't. Everythigg fuckigg hurts. Where's Dr. fuckigg Du Bois? I've called his office eleved tibes—" Jen saw me at the door, began screeching at me. "There you are. Where've you bid? Susad said you were off with by doctor. Is that why he could't take by calls? What are you doigg, screwigg by fucking doctor?"

"Calm down, Jen," Susan rolled her eyes. She stood beside the bed, holding Jen's cell phone.

"Are you kiddigg? How can I calb down? Why don't you understad, Susad? I'b sick. I'b in pain. I ca't boove without it killigg be." The packing in her nose made her anger sound almost comical. "I probably have a blood idfectiod—and by dab doctor ca't be bothered because he's too busy fuckigg my fred—"

"Cut it out, Jen." I tried to be patient. She was in pain. And loopy on meds. "We went for coffee because Alain was upset."

"Alaid?" Jen shouted. "Alaid? You're od a fuckigg first dabe basis with hib?"

"What difference does it make?" Susan scolded. "Norm is going to call back. Jen, your husband is worried to death about you. He's already called three times today. I can't keep putting him off. You have to decide what you're going to tell him."

"Uh-uh. I ca't deal with Dorb."

"Well, I'm not making excuses for you anymore. I have work to do." Susan put the phone on Jen's bed.

Jen pouted, held up her phone. "Elle, please. Call Dr. Du Bois for be? Obviously, he'll take your calls—"

"Can I help you?" Susan faced the door.

The maid was standing just outside the bedroom, facing away. Listening? "Señoras. I finished those rooms. I come back for this one later, okay?"

Yes, of course. No problem. Susan thanked her and headed into the living room for her computer.

I peeled off my clothes, pulled on my bathing suit.

Jen sulked. "I'b serious, Elle. Call hib? I'b biserable."

I thought of Alain's kiss. Didn't want to call him. But Jen was suffering. I could call on her behalf, leave another message. I picked up her phone, but before I could punch in a number, it rang.

Jen stiffened. As I handed it to her, I saw that the screen said, "Norm."

"I ca't take it." Jen shimmied into her pillows.

"Are you going to let it ring?"

"Doh, you adswer it."

I held it out.

She snarled at me.

It kept ringing.

She stopped snarling and stared at the phone, her eyes wide. She looked terrified.

I took pity and answered. "Hi, Norm," I said cheerily, and handed the phone to Jen.

∿

I slathered myself with sunblock, especially my burned shoulders. Did sunblock work if the skin was already burned? Was skin like burned meat, just getting more and more charred? I pictured myself as a steak on the grill, turning black and drying out, becoming hard like coal. Never mind. The air was gentle, and the water rolled steadily up and back, slapping the sand. I lay back, felt the sun's caress.

When I'd left the suite, Jen had been telling Norm that her nose was stuffed because she'd come down with a terrible cold. That she'd been sleeping when he'd called, that Susan hadn't wanted to wake her because she'd been up with a fever all night. I wondered what Norm would say when he found out the truth. Pictured him gaping, stunned, unable to grasp what Jen had done. But Norm wasn't my problem. Jen would handle him on her own.

I'd headed out. Found my spot near the edge of the property, away from the other tourists. Stretched out on a lounge. Closed my eyes. Saw warm red light.

And the shredded face of a dead woman.

I opened my eyes. Vendors wandered the sand with their wares. Pelicans rode air pockets above the palms. My hands were shaking again.

Susan had noticed. "You all right?" She'd looked up from her work, stopping me as I'd gone out.

I'd shrugged. "You?"

She'd shaken her head. "Not the vacation I'd had in mind."

I'd agreed, sighed. Asked about her work, but she'd ignored the question. "Don't put on an act, Elle. These deaths—I know you're upset."

No point pretending otherwise. I'd nodded.

"You want to talk?"

I'd thanked her. Said that, for now, I just wanted to sit by the ocean.

She'd sighed. "I should be done with this filing today. After that, maybe we can get away from here. There's a big celebration in Puerto Vallarta. It's twelve-days long in honor of the Virgin of Guadalupe. People come from all over the country. We should go one day. If you're up for it."

"Yes," I'd agreed. "We should."

But I couldn't imagine going to a big celebration. Were there carnival rides? Sideshows? Fortune-tellers like Madam Therese?

I lay back, plopped my hat over my face to block out the sun's red light. Concentrated on relaxing, beginning with my toes, moving up to my ankles, my shins, my knees. Pushing tension out with every breath, inhaling freshness and strength. Trying to be at one with the water, the breeze. I was up to my shoulders, letting their tightness ease, clearing my mind when someone grabbed my arm.

"Thank God, Elle. You have to help me." Melanie was breathless.

I moved my arm away, squinted up at her. "What happened?"

"What do you think? Luis. When I got to my room last night, I could tell he'd been there."

"How?"

"My clothes were rearranged and underwear was missing. Later, he sent a bottle of wine to my room. And he kept calling. Should I go on?"

I lay back, listless. I wanted to be a slug, didn't want to hear about Melanie's drama.

"Melanie. I'm wiped out. A woman was murdered last night. I found her body—"

"I know, I heard about it. It must have been awful. But, Elle, I need your help."

Was she really that self-absorbed? I shook my head. No. I wasn't available.

"Please, Elle—when Luis called last night, he threatened me."

I closed my eyes. Wasn't interested.

"I'm not kidding, Elle. When I turned him down, he said I was making a mistake and I'd be sorry. A half hour later, he tried to get into my room."

Really?

"I had the bolt on, thank God. Who knows what he'd have done if he'd gotten in. He's completely obsessed with me."

I shaded the glare of the sun with my hand, squinted up at Melanie's big beach bag, her skinny stick-frame body, her oversize sunglasses. And saw Greta's face, cut to ribbons. "Melanie. You need to go to hotel management. He's gone too far."

"No." She tugged at me again. "It's just my word against

his. I need proof. He took my stuff. I'm going to get it back.
You're my witness. Come on."

I didn't move. Had no energy. My eyes burned, body ached.
And Melanie had no business foisting her problems onto me.
Foisting? Really? What part of my brain had that word come
from? Had I even used it right? Melanie kept tugging my hand.

"It won't take long. Promise."

"Melanie," my voice was a pathetic whine, "I've had a hell-
ish night. I need to rest."

"You'll rest afterward. We have to go now, while he's dis-
tracted."

I rolled over onto my side, turning away from her. She
walked around the lounge chair to face me again.

"Elle, I don't have anyone else to turn to. You have to help
me."

I did? "Sorry." I wasn't.

"Please."

Melanie wasn't going away. I took a breath. "Help you how?"

"It'll just take five minutes."

That wasn't an answer. But five minutes? After that, would
she leave me alone? "Okay. Five minutes. That's all. Then you're
on your own."

"You're the best, Elle."

I sat up, grumbling. Got to my feet, pulled on my cover-up.
Winced when the cloth scraped my shoulders.

"Hurry." She repositioned her bag on her shoulder, dragged
me toward the hotel.

"Where are we going?"

"There." She indicated a wing of the hotel.

"To do what?" I had trouble keeping up with her; my toes
dug into the sand.

"All you have to do is stand outside and let me know if anyone's coming."

Wait, was she planning some kind of heist? With me as the
lookout?

We passed a path to the pool. Salsa music blared. Families splashed. Chichi and Luis, muscles glistening, were on duty, setting up a net for the next water game. I didn't see Becky. Melanie led me to a narrow path in the back of the building, turned up a stark alleyway bare of lush landscaping and lavish décor.

"This is staff housing," she panted. "That's Luis's room." She pointed to a half-opened window on the first floor. Curtains dangled unevenly inside.

It was? "How do you know?"

"Sources."

Oh Lord. I couldn't see her eyes behind her sunglasses, but I sensed a beam of satisfaction. I stopped walking. Looked around at the stucco walls, the empty alley.

"What are we doing here?"

"Just wait here." She tapped my arm, took a deep breath, started toward Luis's window.

"Wait. You're not going in there."

"I'll be right back." She sped away.

"Are you crazy?" I called after her. " That's illegal."

She kept going.

"I'm not part of this, Melanie," I yelled. "I'm going back."

"Shush," she hissed as she pushed the window up. "Hang on a minute." She tossed her bag in, jumped onto the sill, and before I could say anything else, disappeared inside.

∿

So there I was. Abetting a crime. But the window had been open. Was jumping into an open window as illegal as actually breaking it to get in? Maybe not. Maybe Melanie was just trespassing. And maybe Mexican law was different. Maybe watching someone trespass wasn't even a crime here. Maybe I wouldn't be held responsible for whatever Melanie was doing. I wondered what that was. Was she rifling through Luis's stuff, stealing his underwear to get even? Never mind. I didn't want to think about it. And no matter what the law was, I shouldn't be there. I pictured Sergeant Perez and a band of armed police

surrounding us, blocking the path back to the beach. I saw myself locked in a Mexican jail, Susan arguing via a translator for
my freedom while I studied a fat cockroach lumbering up a de-
caying concrete wall.

No, I wasn't going to stay there, was not going to be part of
whatever Melanie Crane was up to. I hardly even knew Melanie
Crane. She'd rejected my advice that she go to management.
Why should I be made responsible for her safety? If she ran into
trouble while seeking revenge against a stalker, it was her own
fault.

I turned around, started down the isolated alleyway back toward the narrow path. Felt a twinge. Stopped. Looked back at
the window. Saw Claudia reaching out to me, falling. Landing
face-first six floors below. I shut my eyes, heard Greta sobbing
and saw her shredded flesh.

I hadn't helped either of them.

Never mind, I told myself. Melanie had nothing to do with
them. They had been alone in their hotel suites, minding their
own business. Melanie, on the other hand, was prowling, causing trouble. Instigating it.

Maybe I was being too harsh. Melanie was annoying, but
she was still a victim. Luis had been harassing her, scaring her,
pushing her to the brink. And she was no match for him. She
was a stranger here, helping her grandmother, whereas Luis was
home on his own turf, able to speak the language. And he probably weighed twice what she did. No, whether she had the right
to go into his room or not, Melanie was trying to protect herself
from a predator, and she'd asked for my help. How could I refuse?

I stood halfway down the alley, watching the window. Hearing nothing. Seeing nothing move. What was taking so long?
What if Luis had a roommate? Or someone had found her
sneaking around? I pictured ninety-pound Melanie overpow-
ered, unable to call for help. Unconscious. Her face being cut to

shreds. And I didn't wait another second. I ran back, past the lookout spot, all the way to Luis's window.

~

A leg popped out just as I got there. Then a hip. When Melanie saw me, she frowned. "What are you doing here?"

I backed up so she could climb out the window. "Are you all right?"

She grinned. "Oh, yes. I'm fine." She reached into her bag, pulled out a wad of lace panties.

"Those are yours?"

"Luis is going to think twice before he messes with me again. I left him a message." She strutted down the alleyway, wagging her wraithlike hips.

A message?

I hesitated to press her. Pictured broken mirrors. Graffiti-covered walls. Worse. Whatever she'd done, it was better if I didn't know. We passed the path to the pool. People hooted and wailed as a basketball sunk into the hoop. Luis announced, "Seven-Five. Team Tiburon is winning!" Chichi passed a bottle of tequila among the scorers.

"Want to stop at the café? Get something to eat?" Melanie bounced as she walked, cheerful.

I didn't, no. "Go ahead. I'm fine." I wanted to shed her.

"That's okay. I'll order something on the beach."

We passed clusters of empty lounge chairs. She didn't take one. She stayed with me, heading to mine.

"Well, I'm off. See you later." I tried to leave her at a thatched umbrella.

"What do you mean? I'll come sit with you." Melanie didn't take hints.

Fine. I'd be blunt. "I told you before. I need to chill."

"No problem. I'll be quiet. You won't know I'm there." She zipped her lips.

I was seething. We crossed the sand, heading to my lounge

chair. Melanie stuck to me like an unneeded, unwanted, unattractive, annoying body part. I was pretty sure that this was how Greta Mosley had felt about her leg. Still, it baffled me how she'd actually taken a sharp object to her thigh. Had she used a saw? A cleaver? Hadn't she realized that she'd pass out, if not from pain, then from loss of blood? Had she really thought she could amputate her own limb?

Melanie broke her promise and kept talking. "Señor," she shouted to a waiter. "*Por favor*, can you bring me a menu? Over there?" She pointed to my chair. She tossed her bag of underpants onto the sand and dragged a second lounge chair over to mine.

"Melanie," I began, "the fact is, I really want to—"

"Sleep. I get it. It's cool."

I looked out at the ocean, deciding what to say. That I wanted solitude? That she was on my nerves? She planted her chair inches from mine, and I realized that it didn't matter what I said. Melanie would hear what she wanted to hear.

"Actually," I told her, "I'm going up to my room. I'll take a nap there."

Her mouth opened. For a moment, I thought she would cry. But her lips twisted, stretched themselves into a big toothy grin. "Fine, Elle, I'll wait here. When you wake up, come get me. I'll have boogie boards ready."

Enough. I didn't answer. I picked up my towel and bag, started back toward the hotel.

"Wait, Elle?"

I froze. "What!" I whirled around, nostrils flaring, fists tight.

"Thanks for helping me out today. You're a pal." She flopped back on the lounge chair, lifted a twiglike arm, and waved.

∿

Jen had emerged from the bedroom and sprawled on the living room sofa. Her robe hung open, exposing the taut elastic bandages on her belly and over her breasts. The bruises around her eyes had blackened, so that, with her hair knotted on top of her head and the splint on her nose, she looked half mummy, half exotic bird.

"I'b dying," she moaned. Her nose was still stuffed. "I'b biserable." She swung her arm up and around in a grand gesture.

Susan didn't look up; she was typing on her keyboard. "Back so soon?" She nodded at the bathroom. "Becky's here."

She was?

"Trouble in paradise." Susan kept typing.

"She didn't stop to ask how I'b feeling," Jen complained.

Who? Me? Or Becky? Either way. "How are you feeling?"

"How do you thikk? Like shit. Worse dad shit. Shit would be ad ipprovebett. Ad look at be. I'b totally ugly."

"Poor dear. It's a shame you had to go through all this," Susan shook her head, smirking.

"Shove it, Susad. FU."

"Take your pills and go to sleep, Jen." Susan glanced up at me. "How was the beach?"

"Elle, cad you get be bore ice?"

Susan frowned. "I just gave you ice—"

"For my dose. That was for by tubby."

Susan sighed, typed on. I got ice, crushed it, put it into a plastic bag. I was wrapping it in a hand towel when Becky came out of the bathroom. Her eyes were red and puffy. I brought the ice to Jen, who blanketed her face with it.

"Chichi's a cheat." Becky's chin wobbled.

"No!" Susan cried. "What a shock."

"What happened?" I scowled at Susan, took a seat on an easy chair.

"He flirts with other women right in front of me." Becky sat beside me, wiped away a tear.

"It bight dot bead adythigg." A voice emerged from under the hand towel. "He's Latid—Flirtigg's id his blood."

"I saw him touching them. He had his arm around one."

"What did you expect, Becky?" Susan's eyebrows furrowed. "Are you that naïve?"

"Susan—" I tried to interrupt, but she kept on.

"Flirting is what these resort guys do. What do you think they're here for? To run basketball games? Please. They're here to screw lonely tourists."

Even with her sunburn, blotches appeared on Becky's neck. She opened her mouth, sputtering. "You don't even know him, Susan—"

"Oh, please. I don't have to. He's a hot guy in a resort where divorcees come for romance and homely women come for plastic surgery."

"What did you say?" Jen sat up, knocking the ice packs onto the floor. "Did she just call be hobely?"

"You have no idea, Susan." Becky stood, no longer crying. "Chichi isn't like that. He has four sisters. He respects women. And he loves me."

"Whatever you say." Susan rolled her eyes, went back to typing.

"Seriously, Susad. You have doe busidess talkigg about other people's looks. You could stadd to have subb work dud yourself."

Susan ignored her.

Becky strutted over to Susan. "What's wrong with you, Susan? You're being such a bitch. I'm upset and you say, 'Well, it's your own fault.' Easy for you to say. You're married. You've got a husband and kids. Your life is just peachy—"

I watched silently, heard them swipe at each other. Susan jabbing at Jen for whining about her decision to have cosmetic surgery, at Becky for her choice of men. They attacked her condescending attitude and her smug indifference to their pain. I sat in the easy chair, feeling the heat, the rhythm of the exchange. The words flew fast, overlapped. I closed my eyes, floated up, looked down from the ceiling and saw us, barbs flying, bouncing from heart to heart. Pain spurting with each accusation, each barb. It wasn't like us to actually fight. Usually, we razzed each other and made snide comments, but underneath remained steadfastly loyal to each other. Like family. So what was happening? Why was everyone so bitter, not holding back?

"—pulling an Elle?"

"She's dot with us, as usual."

Oh God. My turn? They were talking about me.

"Well, who can blame her for zoning out? You're both being bitches." Becky stood up for me.

"You call this bitchy? You have no idea how bitchy I can be when I want to," Susan blurted. "Excuse me if I'm a little stressed out. Unlike you and Elle who can romp on the beach, I haven't had a break. I've had to fix some junior partner's legal mistakes and serve the endless demands of Princess Jen over there."

I tried to wander off again. But I had never been able to will my mind to go away. Jen barked at Susan, and Susan at Becky. Round and round until, slowly, the energy faded. The pace slowed. Jen moaned softly.

Susan apologized.

Becky hugged her, slumped into the chair, sniffling. "I suppose you're right. I shouldn't have trusted him. I guess I was too eager to believe Madam Therese."

"So what happedd?" Jen asked.

Becky let out a breath. "I saw him with his arm around a woman at the bar."

"Maybe he was just being friendly. It's his job to make sure everyone has fun," Susan interrupted. "She might have seemed lonely."

"That's bull. Face it. Guys like hib have a dew chick every week," Jen retrieved the ice packs from the floor, positioned them on her breasts.

"So I'm just a dumb chump?" Becky covered her face with her hands. "He was just using me? I feel so stupid."

"Don't beat yourself up," Susan said. "I'm sure Chichi was quite convincing."

"Well, he should be. I'b sure he gets a lot of practice."

Becky wailed.

"Maybe you're better off, Becky." I tried to soothe her. "You don't really know much about him."

Everyone gaped at me. Jen even lifted the ice pack off her face. "She's back."

"I was here all the time."

"No, you weren't. You did an Elle."

"Susad's right. You were out in lala ladd."

I didn't want to debate my mental state. "The point is, Becky, you haven't had a chance to really get to know Chichi. He might not be who he seems."

She shrugged, blew her nose. "I thought I knew him. I still feel like I do."

"Look, I don't want to scare you—or to equate the two men. But I met a woman on the beach who says Luis is stalking her. She's terrified of him."

"What? Who's Luis?" Susan set her laptop aside.

"Luis is stalking someone?" Becky raised her eyebrows. "Doesn't surprise me."

"Who are you talkigg about?" Jen rested her head against the back of the sofa, replaced the towel.

"Chichi's coworker. The other activities director." Becky shook her head. "No, Chichi isn't like Luis. Look, I know some of the guys who work here make time with tourists. Luis does. But not Chichi. He stays away from it. He calls Luis '*cabronazo*.'"

"What the hell's that?"

"I think it means bastard," Susan reached for her laptop. "How do you spell it? I'll Google it."

"It means slimeball," Becky said. "But that's not the point. The point is that Luis and Chichi work together, but that's all. They're not friends."

"So, wait. Luis is like a gigolo?" I didn't get it. If other women were chasing after him, why was he bothering Melanie?

"Kind of. Except the women don't hire him. They don't even know he's being paid. A couple of the doctors hire him to pay attention to their patients so they'll feel attractive."

"What?" Jen was appalled. "That's sick."

"It's actually pretty clever." Susan said. "I bet a lot of cosmetic surgery patients have low self esteem and feel unappealing. Having hunky guys come after them would be good for business."

I thought of Greta, sobbing that she was ugly. Asking Alain to help her.

"What bakes you say they have low self-esteeb?" Jen bristled. "I dever thought I was uddattractive."

"I didn't mean you."

Becky continued. "The doctors asked Chichi to do it, too, but he turned them down. He thought it was degrading."

At least, that's what he'd told Becky.

"I'm not surprised about Luis bothering someone, though." Becky talked about Luis' temper. She said that one of the women he'd been assigned to had belittled him and he'd slapped her, knocking a tooth out.

What? I took a breath.

"That's got to be a crock," Jen said. "He'd have beed fired."

"And in jail," Susan added.

"No. Because the woman didn't complain. She didn't want a scandal. But Chichi knows what happened. He's the one who had to make sure Luis stayed away from her."

"And now this Luis guy is stalking your friend?" Susan asked.

Well, she wasn't exactly my friend. But I nodded.

"He sounds dangerous. She should complain to hotel management before she gets hurt. If even that story is half true, he shouldn't be working here." Susan stood, went into the kitchenette. "Anybody want food? I'm ordering."

Becky wasn't interested; Susan got her a frittata anyway. Jen ordered a cheese omelet, tortilla soup, and a banana milkshake. I asked for shrimp salad and tried not to think about Greta and the man I'd heard her send away. He'd had a Mexican accent, but that didn't mean he'd been Luis, hired to make her feel attractive. Or that he'd felt belittled by her rejection. Or that, when she'd called and told him to come back, she'd faced his uncontrolled rage.

I tried not to think about any of that. Or about the humiliation Luis would feel when he realized that Melanie had been in his room, taken back her stolen underwear, and taunted him by leaving some kind of message.

I sat on the easy chair, considering the kind of rage that might drive someone to violence. What it would feel like to smash a fist full force into someone's jaw? Or press a knife through a person's skin, tissues, muscles. Again, I saw the remnants of Greta's face. Each ribbon of flesh had required its own cutting. Like a roast beef or London broil—one deep slice hadn't been enough. Whoever had killed Greta had spent time with her, destroying the parts that were uniquely Greta. Not just ending her life, but obliterating her identity. Was Luis capable of that kind of fury?

And what about Claudia? Had she also spurned Luis? Had he killed her, too?

Maybe not. But maybe.

And if Luis was that violent, then what did that mean for Melanie?

"Earth to Elle." Susan shook my arm. She pointed to silver trays on the dining table. Jen was using a soup ladle to pour milkshake into her mouth.

"Where's Becky?" I didn't see her.

"Gone. Chichi called to apologize, and all's been forgiven."

I went to the table. Sat. Before I'd taken a bite of my shrimp salad, someone knocked at the door. I thought it might be Becky, angry with Chichi again. Or a nurse to check on Jen. Or a maid. But when Susan opened the door, Sergeant Perez stepped in.

Oh Lord. What now?

I put my fork down, not hungry anymore.

~

"We interviewed every maid who was working the night of the murder. It didn't take long, as the night-shift housekeeping staff is small. There were only three on duty." He sat at the table, across from me, and glared. "Señora Harrison, none of the maids were in the suite next door at the time you claim to have seen one."

He watched me, his gaze challenging, as if he thought I'd lied. What motive would I have? What was he thinking? I recalled the night of the murder, leaning over the railing after Alain left, seeing the woman sobbing on the terrace and in the room behind her, a maid. Susan stepped over to me, stood behind me.

"You still insist that you saw a maid in the room?"

Insist? I glanced at Susan.

"Mrs. Harrison has already told you what she saw, Sergeant." Susan's hand was on my shoulder. "Is there anything else we can do for you?"

"I only looked for a few seconds," I said. "But I saw a maid in the room, turning down the bed."

Sergeant Perez leaned toward me, squinting. "Well, if that's the case, señora, what reason would the maid have to deny it? She would be conducting her normal duties."

"Are you asking Mrs. Harrison to read a maid's mind?" Susan snapped. "How is she to know why? Maybe the maid is afraid to get involved. Maybe she saw something she doesn't want to admit to. Maybe she thinks she'll lose her job."

"Your suggestions are very creative, Señora Cummings. But none of them is possible. All of the maids were accounted for during the hours surrounding the murder. Two were assisting in the Presidential Suite after a mishap with the plumbing. And the third was stocking carts for the morning—in the presence of her supervisor."

Perez's eyes moved from me to Susan, back to me. He pro-
duced a small envelope, removed a few photographs. Spread
them on the table in front of me.

"Do you recognize any of these women?"

I looked. They were dark-haired, dark-eyed women.
Youngish. Maybe in their twenties. Had I seen any of them? I
wasn't sure.

"Don't worry, Elle," Susan told me. "It's okay if you don't."

"Señora," Perez cautioned her, "do not interfere with my
questions."

I studied the photos, had no idea if I'd seen any of the
women. Said so.

"Are those the maids?" I asked.

"Only four are maids. The others work at the police station."

"What the hell?" Jen asked. Her mouth was full of omelet.

Susan spoke at the same time, irate. "Are you trying to dis-
credit Elle? Why? She told you she didn't see the maid's face."

"Elle's dot a liar. She saw what she says she saw."

"I am not implying that anyone is lying, señora." Perez
didn't look at Jen; his eyes remained fixed on me. "I am merely
checking to make certain that the facts are indeed as reported."
He gathered up the photos. Looked at me. "Anything you wish
to change, señora?"

I shook my head. There was nothing to change. I pictured
the night and shivered, recalling Claudia's warning, "The one
who killed me will kill you." But that hadn't been real, wasn't
important. The important parts were Greta, her phone calls,
Alain's visit, the other man. Had he definitely been Luis? Should
I mention Luis to Perez?

Perez was getting up. Curtly apologizing for his intrusion.
Still eyeing me as if I'd done something wrong.

Had I? Should I tell him about Luis? I had no solid proof that
Luis had been there. He probably wasn't the only guy entertain-

ing female tourists. And even if he had been, I had no proof that he'd killed Greta. Implicating him would get him fired, not to mention arrested. Did I want to be responsible for that?

But if he were guilty, how were the police to find out when the only witness withheld what she knew?

I wrestled with my thoughts, argued with myself. Tried to rehear the man's voice, which was useless since I couldn't compare it to Luis's. Had only heard his through a microphone announcing volleyball scores. The visitor had had a Mexican accent, but that didn't necessarily identify anyone. We were, after all, in Mexico.

Still, Becky had said that doctors were paying Luis to keep company with their patients. It made sense that her visitor was, at least might have been, Luis. I had to tell Perez. I wouldn't name Luis. I'd merely suggest that one of the men visiting Greta might have been a hotel staff member with a tendency to court cosmetic surgery patients. Perez could follow that lead.

"There is something else," I began. But Sergeant Perez wasn't there.

"You say something?" Susan chewed, her attention in some magazine.

"Elle, be ad effigg sweetheart," Jen's arm extended in a grand gesture. "Brigg be by pills? I'b dyigg."

Damn. I'd missed yet another chunk of time. While I'd been drifting, Sergeant Perez had gone.

∿

Jen was napping and Susan on the phone giving instructions to her husband when I ventured back to the beach. I wore a wide sun hat and shades, skulked from palm tree to palm tree, trying not to run into Melanie. I looked for Luis. Didn't see him. Took a seat at the bar near the supply hut.

Susan had told me to steer clear of Luis. When I'd told her that he might have been with Greta the night she'd died, she'd scolded me.

"Stay out of it."

Had she really said that? "But what if Luis is the guy who came to see Greta? We know he has a temper. What if—"

"Elle." She'd raised her hand, stopping me. "The police will check the hotel's phone records. They'll see what numbers Greta called and they'll follow up. You've done your part. They're aware of Luis's past."

Susan had gone on, lawyerlike, advising me not to jump to conclusions, not to offer more information than I needed to. Not to get more involved than I already was. "We aren't in our own country, Elle. Keep your head down."

Maybe she'd been right. Still, as I sat at the bar, I pictured Greta waiting for Luis on her terrace. She'd been irritable when she'd called, maybe because she'd been needy enough to have him come back—and humiliated that he'd made her wait for him. Maybe she'd complained. "What took you so long? Did you have to break away from some lonely old woman?" Maybe she'd smelled someone else's perfume on him. Or maybe she'd just been cantankerous, picking on him for misusing an English word, like saying, "I feel great affliction for you" instead of affection. Something like that. And when she'd mocked him, maybe he'd lost his temper.

"Señora?" the bartender was waiting for my order.

"Bloody Mary, *por favor*." I smiled, tried to seem normal. Looked around again for Luis. Saw Melanie approaching. Damn.

She took the seat next to me. "It didn't work," she greeted me. "He didn't take the hint."

I looked at her. Behind her sunglasses, I saw strain in her eyes. Her jaw was tight, her bony body tight. I hadn't taken Melanie seriously, had thought she was an annoying clinging kook. But knowing what I did about Luis, I reconsidered.

"He's threatening me. I got a note." She fumbled around in her beach bag, pulled it out. Handed it to me.

"You'll be sorry, bitch." The writing was in big block letters.

"You have to show this to the police."

"I have no proof that it's from Luis. Besides, my grandmother is better. We're leaving in a couple of days."

I thought of Greta and Claudia. "Even so. Do not be alone with him. In fact, don't go anywhere near him. And double lock your door at night."

She nodded. "You're right. It's so creepy. All morning, he's been pretending not to look at me, leading water aerobics and volleyball. But he's been watching me the whole time. I can feel it." She rubbed gooseflesh off her arms.

My Bloody Mary came. I reached for it, but saw the puddle of blood around Claudia's head. The blob that had been Greta's face. Why had I ordered this grotesque drink? I signed the tab and climbed off my barstool.

"Where are you going?" Melanie sounded panicky.

I had no idea. The beach? "I'm not really thirsty. You can have it."

She assessed it. It was fancy, with a celery stalk, olives, and a hunk of lime. "Are you sure?"

"Enjoy." I backed away.

"But, Elle, I'm freaked out. Honestly, I don't want to be alone. Will you be on the beach? Save me a seat?"

I took a breath. Felt trapped. But Luis was not to be taken lightly. And two women had already died. Yes, I assured her. I would save her a seat.

～

Halfway down the path to the beach, I saw Charlie. He was stretched out on a lounge chair, a towel over his face, but I knew who he was. Knew every inch of his body. The swell of his chest. The tuft of soft hair just below his belly button. I stopped, stared. Was he really there? Could other people see him? No, I had to be hallucinating.

"What are you doing here?" I said this aloud. "What do you want?"

He didn't look up. But I heard him, as surely as I'd heard my own voice. "You tell me why I'm here, Elle. You brought me here."

What? No, I hadn't. Unless I'd unintentionally conjured him up, in which case he wasn't really there at all. Well, of course he wasn't. Charlie was dead. I was standing on the beach, talking to a man who wasn't there.

And yet, I saw him, sprawled out on the lounge, his face under the towel. Madam Therese's voice echoed in my head, "The dead are drawn to you."

He wasn't there. Wasn't real. I was under too much stress, wandering away from reality too much. Dissociating. Losing touch—That was it: touch. I'd touch the guy. If he was real, I'd be able to feel him. I reached a hand out, extended it toward his foot. It was familiar; the second toe longer than the big one. I'd massaged those feet so many times, pressing on the soles, squeezing, pushing toes back and forth, hearing Charlie purr. I knew them well. But ghosts' feet wouldn't be solid. If the feet were Charlie's, my hand would pass right through them. I hesitated, my hand inches from his left arch.

"Señora?"

I spun around, withdrew my hand as if I'd been caught pick-pocketing.

A mustached vendor smiled hopefully, held out a case of silver jewelry. "Some earrings for you today, señora? Maybe a beautiful pendant? A bracelet?"

"No, gracias," I breathed, backing away.

"No? Maybe tomorrow, then." He moved on down the beach.

I glanced at the man who might be Charlie, lying perfectly still, sprawled on a lounge chair, the towel over his head, and I kept moving, heading back toward the hotel. I didn't stop until

I got to the cabanas, and then I looked back. The man was still there, but he'd been joined by a woman. Her face was draped with a scarf.

∾

Clearly, the man wasn't Charlie. He was just a guy with similar toes and the same kind of build. As usual, I was inventing things. It was to be expected, wasn't it? My dissociative disorder was worse when I was under stress. And I was under plenty.

I stood beside the cabanas at the back of the pool, taking deep, cleansing breaths. The usual salsa music pumped through the speakers. People swam and splashed in the water, rode the alligator slide, lazed on chairs reading books, sipped drinks. None of them seemed bothered by murders or disturbed by a sinister undercurrent. No one else was plagued by images of a shredded next-door neighbor and dead almost-ex-husband. I needed to exercise and work off my stress. Take a swim. Or go down the waterslide. But I was too on edge to decide. My senses were on high alert, my body ready to spring into action.

I might have walked to the ocean except that, at that moment, Luis came out of a cabana and strutted right by me in his Speedo, displaying his six-pack, his rippled back. Without hesitation or thought, I took off after him.

"Luis." I grabbed his arm. And as I did, it occurred to me that I didn't know what I was going to say. I hadn't thought it through.

He turned, checking me out. Beaming a knowing grin. "Yes, señora? How can I help you?"

"We need to talk." I dragged him back to the cabanas, deciding to be direct.

"What can I do for you, señora?" His eyes traveled up and down, paused at my thighs. My breasts.

I felt invaded, resented his open leering. Had the urge to smack him. Instead, I took him to a shady spot under a palm, beside a cabana tent. It was secluded. No one could hear us.

"Have we met, señora? I do not recall your name."

"We haven't met. But I have to talk to you."

"Of course, I understand." He leaned close, spoke in a husky voice. "You know, señora, you are a very attractive woman. I've noticed you and thought I would like to get to know you better. How come you never play games in the pool?"

What? He stood too close, breathed onto my neck. "That's not what I want to—"

"I understand if you don't want me to know your name. It's okay. I will call you Bonita, how is that? A special name just for you." He took my hand. "Sadly, Bonita, I must go to an appointment now. Perhaps we can arrange to meet privately later?"

Privately? Oh God. Luis and his outlandish ego assumed I wanted his romantic services. My face sizzled. Did I look that lonely? That desperate? I bristled. No, I steamed.

"No, Luis. Let's talk now." I pulled my hand away, asked straight out if he knew Greta Mosley or Claudia Madison.

"Who?" He put his hands on my arms, began stroking.

I removed his hands, repeating their names, reminding him of their suite number.

His eyes didn't waver. "Why is this important to you? Bonita, you and I can find more to talk about than other women—"

"They're both dead, Luis. I'm asking if you knew them." What was he doing? Why wouldn't he take his hands off me? He was much younger than I was and not my type. What made him think he could touch me?

I removed his hands, but they returned to me, persistent and mosquitolike. One went to my face, the other to my hand. "No, I didn't know them."

"Really?" I swatted his fingers off my cheek, angry now. "Don't lie to me. I know that you were with Greta Mosley the night she died."

His eyes narrowed. He glanced over his shoulder, back to my chest. "Okay. What is this about?"

"So you admit you were with her?"

"What does it matter to you?"

"Do the police know this?"

He sighed. "Señora, everybody knows it. Some of the women who come here are lonely. It's part of my job to lift their spirits. I help the doctors by making their patients feel beautiful after their procedures. The women have a good time with me. Look, they didn't assign you to me, but tell you what—this afternoon, after the volleyball game—we can meet for a drink." His eyes traveled my body. Down and up again.

Really?

"Luis," I kept dogging him, couldn't stop myself. "This is important. Do you know anything about what happened to them?"

Luis's eyebrows lifted. "Me?" He pointed to his chest, crossed himself, mumbled something about Jesus. "Where did you get this idea, señora? Why are you asking me these things? I am all about love, señora. Only about love."

"So you didn't hurt them?" I heard my question as if from far away. What right did I have to corner Luis? Where was all my anger coming from? And why was it aimed at him?

"Hurt them? Are you crazy? I told you. I shared love with them. I made them happy, that's all." He started to walk away.

"The same way you make Melanie happy?"

He stopped. Frowned. "Who?"

"Melanie. The woman you've been stalking."

"Stalking?" He took a step back, eyes narrowing. "What?"

"I know you've been calling her and following her. I know you tried to break into her room."

He took a step back. "You're crazy, señora. I don't know anyone named Melanie. And besides, what's it to you? Why are you asking me all these questions? You know what—Forget the drink. Stay away from me, señora." He turned to go.

"Wait." I couldn't stop myself. I tapped his shoulder, pointed to the bar. Melanie was finishing the Bloody Mary. "That's Melanie. With the big sunglasses and the ponytail."

He squinted toward the bar. "The skinny one? In the red bikini?"

"Why have you been bothering her?"

He shook his head. "Señora, I haven't bothered anyone. I don't even know her."

He seemed sincere. But of course he would. Luis was a practiced liar, paid to profess adoration to women, to praise their beauty no matter what they looked like.

"If you lie to me again, Luis," I squinted at him, "I can involve your manager—"

"Okay, wait. Looking closer, I recognize her from the activities. She plays basketball or volleyball with us. Maybe also salsa class. But I haven't bothered with her. Why would I? She's not a patient of the doctors, so they wouldn't pay me, and she's too young to tip well."

He was blatantly lying. "Luis, stop denying it. I know you threatened her and snuck into her suite. I know you stole her underwear."

"I what?" He recoiled. "You're crazy."

"I was there, Luis. I saw her come out of your room with her fists full of panties."

He didn't say anything. He just stood, staring at me, eyes burning. Then he stepped toward me. "Say that again?"

I didn't back away. I stood my ground, righteous and indignant. "I said I know for a fact that you had Melanie's underwear in your room because I saw her take it out."

"You know about this, señora? You were there when someone broke into my room?"

Oh. I hadn't thought of it that way. Damn. I'd said too much.

He leaned close to me, pointing a finger toward the bar. "Is that who did it? That woman—your friend, Melanie? And you were there, too?"

I felt his breath on my face. The heat of his eyes. "No, I was outside."

"Really? You know what she did in there?"

"Yes." I met his eyes, trying not to be intimidated. But no. I had no idea. "She took back the things you stole."

"What things? I took nothing of hers. I don't even know her. But someone—that *persona loca* destroyed my room. She ripped my clothing. And worse. Like an animal, she used my floor like a bathroom."

What?

"I thought it was some *vagabundo*, so I did nothing, but now—" He stopped, ran a hand over his head, looked around, took deep breaths. Finally, he glared at me. "Señora, I don't know you. You came up to me, a stranger, and asked me if I had something to do with two murders. And then you accused me of stalking someone who in fact has defiled my property. Tell me: What is this about? Why do you want to make trouble for me?"

I had no answer, so said nothing. My surge of aggressiveness was fizzling out. I couldn't stop thinking about Melanie peeing on his floor.

His finger aimed at my chest. "Forget it. I have to go now. But, first, I am warning you, señora. Stay away from me. You and your *amiga lunática*. I mean it." He stomped off.

I stood still for a moment, replaying what he'd said. Trying to make sense of it. Melanie had ripped up his clothes? Had that been her "message"?

Not possible. Luis had to be lying. He was twisting the facts, blaming the victim, making Melanie seem guilty. I wasn't going to let him.

"Luis," I hurried after him, hooked my hand through his arm. "How's this? If you stay away from Melanie, we'll stay away from you. Otherwise, she's going to the police."

He took my hand from his arm and squeezed it tight. "No, Bonita. No police." His eyes drilled into mine as he crushed my fingers. "You know something? You're a good-looking woman.

Take some advice. Be careful who you mess with." He smiled, leaned over and kissed me tenderly before releasing my strangled hand and rushing off toward the pool.

⁓

I stayed there, cradling my fingers, watching Luis disappear among tourists in brightly colored wraps and bathing suits. What had I been thinking, cornering him that way? Revealing what I knew about him? The man was dangerous. My hand— the way he'd squeezed it? And kissed me at the same time that he hurt me? I shuddered. He'd enjoyed hurting me, had mocked my pain with his kiss. Why had I meddled with him? The problem had been Melanie's—it hadn't even involved me. Until I'd stepped into the middle of it. Damn.

I looked around the pool, didn't see him. I simmered. Thought of reporting him to management. But what was I thinking? He'd accuse me of helping Melanie break into his room and vandalizing his things. Oh God. Had he been telling the truth about Melanie? I pictured her ripping sleeves off his shirts, tossing his drawers. Squatting on the floor.

Oh Lord. Yuck. But had that been her "message"? If so, the message hadn't done much good; Luis hadn't understood what it meant, let alone who'd sent it.

Until I'd told him.

"So, did you have a good time, Elle?" Melanie appeared out of nowhere. She smiled, stood so close that her body brushed my arm.

I didn't know what to say. "A good time?"

"Just now. With Luis. I saw you together. I didn't know you were friends." Her voice was lilting, oddly cheerful. "But I saw how he parted from you. Such a sweet kiss."

What was she thinking? "I was just talking to him." And telling him that you'd vandalized his room.

"Of course, you were." She rolled her eyes. "I understand—"

"Oh, please, Melanie. It wasn't like that."

She lost the smile. "Don't even deny it, Elle. I saw you together. Look, I know how it is with Luis. He's charming and sexy."

"Seriously? Come on, Melanie—"

"Be careful, Elle. You have no idea what you've gotten into."

Oh God. I stood tall, matching her height, and I waited a beat before speaking. "Melanie. I haven't gotten into anything—"

"I thought I could trust you, Elle," she interrupted, her hands on her bony hips, her voice angry and loud. A couple of retirees stared as they walked by, but she was unfazed. "How could you? After everything I've confided to you?"

I shook my head. "Nothing happened. We talked." Why was I defending myself?

"Don't lie to my face. I saw you."

"You saw me telling him to leave you alone."

"Really. That's why you kissed him good-bye?"

"I didn't kiss him."

"How can you lie like that? I saw it."

Okay. Enough. I was done. I turned to walk away.

Melanie kept after me. "Just explain it to me, Elle—"

"No." I spun around, fed up. "You explain, Melanie. Explain what you did to Luis's room."

She stopped mid-sentence. Stood still. Licked her lips. "His room?" Her voice was sweet and cloying.

"Luis told me." I crossed my arms. Waited.

She smirked. "Good. I made an impression. He got the message."

"I doubt it. He said he didn't even know you."

For a moment, I thought she'd cry. Instead, she laughed. "And you believed him? Like he's going to admit being obsessed with me? Stalking me? Sneaking into my room? Threatening me? Of course he denied it."

Music pounded from the pool area. We had to shout to hear each other.

"You should both just stay away from each other."

Melanie smiled. "You know what, Elle? I don't need your

advice about Luis. Forget I ever said anything." She turned and sashayed back toward the pool, hips swaying in rhythm to the music.

Chichi was on the platform, demonstrating lunges for a water exercise class. I looked around, but didn't see Luis.

~

I walked along the fence near the pool, angry with myself for getting involved with Melanie's problems. How could she for one minute think that I'd be interested in—let alone involved— with Luis? Especially when I knew about his stalking and threats? Then again, she didn't know me very well, couldn't know my taste in men. And I didn't know her either. I remembered her climbing into Luis's window. Pictured her enraged, ransacking his drawers. Heard the ripping of cloth, felt the splitting of fabric. Imagined her repeating the act again and again, shirt by shirt, seam by seam.

Like Greta's face, being sliced one ribbon at a time.

I held onto the fence, trying to comprehend so much rage. Had I ever been that angry? I thought back, remembering a drained trust fund, cheating, lies, secrets, betrayals. But, even at my most incensed moments, had I ever been angry enough to rip Charlie's shirts to tatters? To use his floor as a toilet?

Honestly? I'd been angry enough to consider doing far worse. I'd fantasized a hundred ways to exact revenge. Maxing out his credit cards. Reporting him to the IRS. Poisoning him. Slowly.

But Charlie had been my husband. And, though I'd fantasized plenty, I hadn't actually done any of those things. Luis, on the other hand had, at most, had a brief fling with Melanie and harassed her for a few days. Why had her reaction been so over the top?

I scanned the people lying around the pool. Found Melanie as she finished covering her arms and legs with sunblock. Watched as she adjusted the back of the lounge chair and reclined, her oversized sunglasses concealing her gaze. Was she looking at me? No, more likely, for Luis. Posing poolside to taunt him. Daring him to mess with her again.

In the water, people of all shapes and ages stretched and crunched to the beat of the music. Becky sat on the end of the platform, eyes on Chichi as he flexed and extended, his oiled muscles glistening in the sun. The music pulsed, explosive.

I needed to get away from this place and all its angry melodrama and murder. I looked at the ocean, saw it shine. Went to the supply hut, grabbed a boogie board, and headed out.

~

I floated, resting on the board. Rotating, bobbing. I paddled out far enough to find peace. From where I was, the pool and the people on shore seemed tiny and far away. I was in a different world than they were, buoyed by swelling water. A smattering of people hung onto boards nearby, waiting for the right wave to rush up and grab them.

I waited, too, but not for the ocean to grab me. I waited for peace. I rested on the surface, rolling with the water, letting its coolness soothe my still tender shoulders. Feeling the vastness of the ocean, the fact of my own smallness. I clung to my boogie board, comforted by the moment, the motion, the combined bath of hot sunlight and cool saltwater, and I closed my eyes, rocking, paddling, relaxing, letting myself drift farther from the shore.

Which is when that perfect wave came. I wasn't watching for it, wasn't prepared to ride it. It reached down under my board and lifted me up, tossed me high onto its crest, swirled over around under me, and cast me forward, flinging me off the board into water that was deeper than I expected. Something smacked my head as I went down. Water swirled around me as I tried to surface, but I was disoriented, not sure which way was up. The wave must have stirred up the bottom; the water was murky, sandy, dark, and it grabbed me, tugging me down. Or up? I didn't know, couldn't tell. I needed to breathe. I thrashed with my arms and kicked with my legs. Wouldn't the water nat-

urally lift me up? I thought it should. Unless there was an undertow. Was that what it was called? An undertow? A current
towing you under? But wait—water currents didn't grab your
legs, did they? So what was grabbing mine? Was something
there? Yanking me?

I pictured a shark. Damn. Was I being eaten? My chest
burned, needed air. I needed to rise to the surface, but couldn't
get free. Maybe it wasn't a shark. Maybe someone else had been
knocked off their board and was panicking, grabbing onto me.
Damn. He'd drown us both. I twirled, shoved at the water, saw
a shadow. Was it a human form? I couldn't tell. The water was
too cloudy. My lungs screamed for air. I kicked randomly.
Reached my arms out, searching the water. A clump of seaweed
entangled my head, covered my eyes. I swatted at it, yanking it
off as my raging lungs threatened to explode, and I saw a long,
dark blob surrounded by tangled seaweed tufts—a shark? Some
kind of sea monster? I tried to push my way past it, but it floated
away, beyond my reach, then surged back at me. I waited for
its jaws to open and its teeth to rip me apart. But Madam
Therese whispered, "It's not a creature of the sea, Elle. It's a
vengeful spirit. One of the dead."

Never mind. It didn't matter what it was; whatever it was
had me by my legs again. I felt its teeth on my flesh. I tried to
kick but couldn't free myself. Couldn't move. My lungs gave
way, bursting, and water rushed into my nose, my throat.
Flooded my chest. Unable to escape, I saw darkness and bubbles—or not bubbles. Eyes. Big, round ones, staring at me. And
dark appendages that shoved me down. Finally, I understood: I
would never breathe air again. I was drowning. Trapped underwater by a sea monster or a vengeful spirit. Either way, my arms
were too heavy to resist, my legs too exhausted to flail. The
shadowy blob held onto me and, as I faded in dark water, I saw
its bubble eyes, half hidden by clumps of seaweed. Or maybe
by tresses of long hair.

∾

Charlie wore tennis whites and his arms reached out for me. He smiled. Light poured onto his shoulders. Onto his face. It surrounded him. I didn't have to walk. I simply moved toward him effortlessly, as if just thinking about being in his arms put me there. And then I was there, with Charlie. Leaning into his chest. Except wait—this wasn't right. I tried to remember why. Shards of memories sprinkled my mind—Charlie in the shower with a woman, surprised. I looked at him, pushed him away.

We're not together anymore. I didn't need to speak. Thoughts came out on their own.

We're soul mates, Elf. We'll always be together. He drew me close again, and his embrace felt safe and familiar. *Have you missed me?*

More than you can know. I didn't intend to admit it. Again, the words simply appeared. I wasn't sorry, though. I was relieved to admit it. Glad that he knew.

Good. Lean on me, Elf. And rest.

I did. I let go of every feeling except love, and I rested in his arms.

But something still nagged at me. Something wasn't right. I needed to ask him a question. Was it about the beach? About seeing him there with a woman? I tried to remember, but another image interrupted, distracting me: Charlie's face, cheeks dabbled with rouge, eyes shut, and perfectly still. I stiffened, tried think clearly, couldn't fit fragments together.

Charlie—wait. Aren't you dead?

A kiss brushed my forehead. *I'm here with you now, Elf.*

Elf. His pet name for me. I stopped trying to figure things out. Whatever he'd done to make me angry was in the past. Charlie had come back to me. We were together again. Besides, I was tired. Could sleep in Charlie's arms. I closed my eyes and lay down beside him, smelling his faint Old Spice, accepting that everything was okay. We wouldn't need to get divorced. We were starting over. Light poured onto us. I nuzzled against him, having forgotten—no, having tried to forget—how snugly our bodies fit together. Charlie kissed my neck, my lips. He whispered something I couldn't hear, and then he drifted away.

Where are you going?

Nowhere. I'm right here beside you.

But he wasn't. I reached out but couldn't touch him. Could barely see him.

Charlie!

Be careful, Elf.

"Charlie—" I coughed. Opened my eyes. Saw a double chin above me. Turned to see a hairy belly. A red bikini top, breasts spilling out. Where was Charlie?

"Charlie—" I tried to say again. Coughed again. Tasted saltwater and something else. Blood?

People surrounded me. "She's breathing!" someone shouted.

Breathing? Who was breathing? I looked around. A ring of faces stared down at me. Luis was there. Oh God. Why was Luis there? Where was I? I was lying down. On sand. Oh, wait, did they mean me? Was I the one who was breathing? I thought back. Felt the soreness of my lungs. Tasted salt. Remembered water flooding my chest—Charlie?

I tried to sit up. Had to find Charlie. But the man with the hairy belly clutched my leg. Pressed down on it. "Wait, darlin'." He had a Southern accent. "Don't you move." The sun made a halo around his head.

"But my husband—" A fit of coughing interrupted me. I tried to sit up and look for him.

A chorus erupted. "She shouldn't talk." "Tell her to lie back down." "Don't try to talk, darlin'." "Keep pressure on her leg."

My leg?

I squinted to block out the sun. My chest felt scraped, raw. Breathing was ragged and painful, and I was shivering. Someone draped towels over me. Said I must be in shock. But I knew better. I was shivering because Charlie had gone; his body had been warming me.

I turned my head, saw Luis. Our eyes met. He turned, walked away.

Men came with a stretcher. They wore bright, gleaming white, asked questions. Messed with me, touching and poking.

"Who found her?" one of them asked.

"I did."

The voice was beside my head. I turned toward it. Saw skinny legs and thighs. A red bikini. Melanie?

Melanie had saved me? My mind must not have been working. I heard fragments. "—unconscious—cut her leg—some guy's board slammed her head—saw her empty boogie board—swam down—pulled her out—"

They wrapped something on my leg, lifted the stretcher, and carried me across the beach. People stared. When we passed the pool, I saw Luis at the fence, watching, arms folded against his chest. Then Becky was walking alongside me, asking questions.

"Elle? My God, what happened? Are you all right?"

I tried to answer her, began coughing again.

Becky kept close to the stretcher. Talking to me. Melanie was there, too, her hair loose and sopping. Telling Becky how limp I'd been. How, when she'd pulled me from the water, she'd thought I was dead.

～

The cosmetic surgeons had a small office in the hotel. Mostly, they used it as a place to do paperwork. But it was also used for the occasional fall, heart attack, or choking incident. Emergencies at the hotel.

Later, I remembered bits and pieces. Being lifted off the stretcher onto a bed. Missing Charlie. Wondering how I'd seen him, where he'd gone. The woman with the stethoscope smelling like jasmine. The rawness of my chest. The relentless, razor-sharp coughing. Framed pictures on the wall—giant plants with big fronds, blood-red flowers. Something pinching my finger. A doctor—not Alain—speaking Spanish to the nurse, ex-

amining my leg. Which was throbbing. And Becky. Becky staying with me the whole time.

"Dear God, Elle. What happened?" she asked over and over.
I couldn't answer. Could only cough.

"You almost drowned. Jesus God. Elle, you're such a strong
swimmer. How could that happen? Did you go too far out? Get
a cramp?"

I remembered a force pulling me down, mouthed the word,
"Undertow."

"What did you say?" She frowned, reformed my lip move-
ments. "Andoo. Doe." Thought for a moment. "Undertow?"
She asked the nurse if there had been an undertow.

"Undertow?" The nurse turned to the doctor who was messing with my leg. "*Que es* 'undertow'?"

He didn't look up. "*Es una resaca.*"

The nurse said something back to him, took gauze out of a
cabinet. "No, señora, there was no undertow. Nobody swims if
the water is like that. They tell you. You can only go to the edge."

No undertow? But she was wrong, there had been. I'd felt it
pulling me down, holding me under the shadowy water. I closed
my eyes, recalled a dark shape. And big round eyes. Oh God—
that shape. Had it been a shark? Had it bitten me? I opened my
eyes, looked at Becky. And for a moment, saw a human form,
seaweedlike hair. Damn. Maybe it hadn't been a shark. Maybe
someone had held me under the water, tried to drown me. But
why? Madam Therese offered an answer. "Your aura is stained
with blood." I blinked her away and told myself to think back
to the beginning, to the wave picking me up. I'd banged my head
on something and gone underwater, disoriented. Something had
caught onto my legs, and I'd tried to kick myself free, but I'd
gotten stuck on something and I'd struggled until my lungs
couldn't hold on anymore. And then?

And then Charlie had shown up. But that made no sense.
Unless, had I—even for a few minutes—actually died? Had he

come to welcome me to the other side? Was there another side?

No. Of course not. The encounter had been my imagination. A product of panic. A defense mechanism to comfort myself in the face of death.

But if I hadn't seen Charlie, how had I smelled his scent? Or felt his arms around me, his body next to mine. His kisses on my neck. His voice, calling me Elf. I hadn't imagined all that. Couldn't have.

And yet, if he'd shown up—if I'd really been with him—why had he been wearing his tennis clothes? Had he been on his way to a match? Did they have tennis after death?

Something sharp jabbed my leg. I twitched.

"You'll be numb in a moment, señora. This way you won't feel the stitches."

Stitches?

"Thank God that woman pulled her out."

"Sí. Your friend is very lucky."

Becky and the nurse were talking. I'd missed most of the conversation. The nurse prepared a curved needle and thread for the doctor. What had happened to my leg?

"I can't stop thinking about what would have happened if she hadn't been there.

"Thank the Virgin of Guadalupe. She's the reason your friend has survived. It's her festival now, so she blessed your friend. She guided the woman who saved her."

Really?

"Elle will want to thank her. I didn't even get her name."

"It's Melanie," the nurse said.

Melanie. I'd seen her when I'd awakened on the beach. Her red bikini. I didn't remember her pulling me out. But I did remember hair floating into my face, and a dim form in dark water, holding me under. Had that form been Melanie? But Melanie weighed maybe a hundred pounds. She wouldn't have been strong enough. Besides, why would Melanie want to hold me down? Again, I thought back to being trapped, trying to escape. Something jabbing my leg as I tried to kick. I remembered flailing, fighting a shadow. And thinking that some dark spirit was drowning me.

But now it made sense: In my panic, I'd been confused. Melanie had been holding onto me to pull me up, not drag me down. I'd resisted my rescuer, in the process slicing my leg and nearly drowning us both.

The doctor had soft brown eyes and brown skin. He checked my heart again, asked how I was feeling. I shrugged, struggling to pay attention, missing a lot of what he said. What I understood was that I'd survived. I would feel better soon, my oxygen levels were already good, but my pulse was still elevated. My lungs were irritated but didn't seem to have serious edema. My coughing should ease gradually. I might develop a low-grade fever and should rest, drink warm tea, and speak only a little. As soon as he finished suturing the gash in my leg, I could go rest in my own room, unless I wanted to be admitted to the medical center.

I mouthed. "My room." And, "*Gracias.*"

"What did you do to your leg?" He kept talking as he turned back to my wound, not expecting an answer. "The injury is smooth, not torn or jagged. Hard to believe you cut it on a shell." He motioned to the nurse that he was ready. "Seriously. This looks more like a knife wound."

She leaned over, nodded in agreement.

But it wasn't a knife wound. Couldn't have been. I leaned back on the bed, feeling dull punctures as he sewed and tied thirteen individual stitches. I tried not to think about the needle penetrating my skin, the thread snaking through, the gaping flesh being reconnected. Instead, I thought about Charlie, how real and tangible he'd been. How comforting. How I missed him. Except that he hadn't really been Charlie; he'd been an illusion, a creation of my almost dying mind.

Even so, I felt shakier and more alone without his embrace. How could an imagined hug have warmed me?

It was irrelevant because Charlie was dead. Gone. I had to accept it. I closed my eyes, felt the poke, the tingle of movement in my leg. Saw cloudy water and a shadowy figure grabbing me. Tried to shove it away. Had never imagined it was Melanie.

Lord, I'd misjudged her. I'd avoided her, trying to get away from her, but she must have trailed after me like a pesky kid sister. Underwater, I'd punched at her and kicked her, but she hadn't let me go. Melanie had risked her own life, trying to save mine. When I was able to speak, I'd have to thank her.

And ask her if, when the big wave struck, she'd seen Luis anywhere near me in the water.

~

The first thing I saw when I woke up was Susan's frown. She was on the easy chair beside the sofa, apparently watching me sleep.

"You're up? Feel any better?" Her hand went to my forehead. "Still warm."

"The doctor told us she might have a fever." Becky sat on the loveseat across the room, her feet on the coffee table. "It's from the body trauma, I guess."

"Hey, what's going on?" Jen emerged from her bedroom, holding her stomach, looking like a gazelle, her eyes outlined in purple rings, her legs spindly, her hair feathery, her nose splint resembling a long white beak. "Susan, WTF? It's time for my pill—"

"How did you get out of bed?" Becky gawked.

"Obviously, I had to manage by myself. No one was there to help me."

"Dr. Du Bois said you need to walk around," Susan's voice was flat. She didn't jump to get Jen's pain medication. "Your pills are on the kitchen counter."

"Susan, I'm dying here. Why the hell did you take them all

the way in there?" Jen's nose didn't sound stuffed anymore. Had the swelling gone down already? Or had Alain come by and taken out the packing? How long had I slept?

Becky went to Jen, offered an arm for support. "Here, let me help you."

"Becky, careful. I think I have an infection. The stitches are coming apart—"

"They're not. The nurse checked them this morning. You're fine."

"Oh my God, I am so not fine. Every single part of me hurts!" Jen waved an arm to shoo Becky, took a step forward, wobbled dramatically, grabbed the doorjamb.

"You're not the only one with problems, Jen." Susan ignored her histrionics.

Jen glared at her, then at me. "Damn. What the fuck happened to Elle? She looks worse than I do."

I did? I hadn't seen myself. I touched my face. The skin felt sandy. And pain pulsed dully in my leg.

"No, she doesn't." Becky defended me.

"Excuse me?" Jen put a hand over her belly. Her voice broke. "You're saying I look that godawful?" She motioned toward me.

"I'm saying Elle looks pretty good, considering that she nearly died."

"What? What happened?"

They went on talking about me. It felt normal. I listened from a distance as Becky recapped the accident. The rescue. The stitches.

Jen gaped at me. "Damn. I don't get it. Elle would never drown."

Indeed. I'd been captain of our high school swim team. Regional champ in breaststroke. But none of that had helped me that morning. I hadn't been able to surface. Hadn't known where the surface was. I clutched the sofa cushion, recalling the panic, the disorientation. I took a breath, my lungs hurt, raw and swollen.

Susan was chiding Jen. "Unlike some people, Elle didn't choose to get hurt."

"Oh, here we go again." Jen let go of the doorjamb, wobbled toward the kitchen. "Why did I ever think it was a good idea to bring you down here? You bitches have no sympathy. Just because I chose to take action against—" She stopped, gasping, grabbing her midriff. She looked into the air. Took a breath.

"You all right?" Becky was at her side.

Jen didn't answer, just held still. Breathing.

Susan watched her for a moment, then got up and went into the kitchenette, gave Jen a pill and water. Began making tea without comment.

I sat up, moving my bandaged leg. Felt a sharp jab. Maybe I could have one of those pills?

"So you're all right?" Jen looked at me. "How'd you cut your leg?"

"We don't know." Becky answered for me.

"Didn't anybody ask her?"

"She can't talk. She gets coughing spasms. Her chest is inflamed."

"So no one knows what happened?"

"The woman who saved her said a big wave picked Elle up and some guy was too close, so he and his board crashed onto her head, and she went under. She might have been knocked out."

Had that happened? I had no memory of a guy being too close. I remembered the wave surprising me. And then struggling in deep water. But I must have forgotten what happened in between. I'd read somewhere that people often didn't remember accidents, that our brains don't have time to record sudden events like car crashes, gunshots, explosions. Maybe mine hadn't recorded the impact of a boogie board.

Jen stiffly took a seat at the table. Sat rigid while Susan

brought out tea. Taking a mug, I looked at my hand, saw my fingernails caked with grit. My pores were filled with salt and sand. I put the mug on the table, touched my head. Felt a grainy layer of crust on my scalp. Without thinking, I stood up, putting too much weight on my leg, wincing at the jolt. Three voices simultaneously yelped: Sit down. What's she doing? Elle, what the eff?

But I waved at them, signaling that I was all right and kept going, slowly, carefully into the bedroom. Becky was on my tail, yammering, holding onto my arm as I continued into the bathroom, bent over, and ran the tub.

"She's taking a bath!" Becky shouted over her shoulder.

"Wait. She can't get her leg wet—" Susan rushed in and out and back in with a plastic laundry bag.

"Hold on," Jen tottered in with a cosmetic bag and pulled out a packet.

By the time she dumped in the bubbles, I'd shed my bikini and, sitting on the side of the tub, swung my uninjured leg into the tub. Susan and Becky hovered. Jen tottered to the door and supervised. I lowered myself into steamy bubbling water, resting my bandaged limb on the side of the tub where Susan wrapped it to keep it dry. Without my asking, Becky began to wash my hair. I lay back in suds, one friend gently cradling my foot, the other massaging my head. The phone rang. Jen said she'd answer it. I closed my eyes.

When I said, "Thank you," tears welled behind my lids, and I didn't cough.

∿

They didn't leave. They refreshed the cooling bath water with more hot, brought a bottle and glasses, and joined me, Jen on a straight back chair, Becky and Susan on the floor, chatting. My bath was a social event. A wine and cheese party without the cheese.

"Who was on the phone?"

"Norm. I'll call him back."

"Have you told him yet?"

"Relax, Susan. I'll tell him."

I drifted, lulled by the rhythm of their voices. Warm bubbly water embraced me with its stillness, the opposite of the ocean water, which had held me down and shoved its way into my lungs. Finally, I grasped what had happened: I'd almost died. My lungs and throat still burned from saltwater. I could still taste it, could still recall the calmness of giving up and accepting my death. And then I'd seen Charlie.

I'd seen him, touched him. We'd talked. He'd held me, kissed me. I must have blacked out, hallucinated.

I reached for my glass. Sweet, fruity wine rinsed away the taste of salt. Susan was ranting about her firm. Her case. How she'd almost straightened things out, but was planning to dismember certain people when she got back.

I slid down deeper into bubbles. Charlie had seemed real. I'd heard his voice, smelled his Old Spice. How could that have happened if I'd just imagined him? And we hadn't been underwater. We'd been—I wasn't sure where we'd been, but it had been dry. And comfortable. But it couldn't have happened. It was impossible.

"Elle? Are you all right?"

What? Why would they ask me that?

"Are you in pain?" Becky leaned close, put a hand on my forehead.

"Why?"

"Well, you're making faces." She mimicked me, made a grimace.

I was?

They were all watching me. Waiting for me to say I was okay. Or that I was in pain. But I didn't. What I said was, "I saw Charlie."

Nobody said anything. They sat, three blank faces, watching.

"When I was in the water. He was there with me."

Nothing. No comment. They thought I was crazy.

"I'm serious. I touched him. He was rock solid. Totally real."

"Okay," Becky rearranged herself, sat Indian-style. "Well, there has to be a rational explanation. After all, Elle, you nearly drowned. Your brain ran out of oxygen. So maybe you had hallucinations—"

"No," Jen gestured with her wineglass. "She had a fucking near-death experience. You've heard about those. People who are actually dead for a few minutes and come back."

"Elle didn't die," Susan commented.

"How do we know? She wasn't breathing when she got pulled out. That woman who pulled her out said she thought Elle was dead. And they had to do CPR. Maybe she was crossing over and Charlie greeted her, but then they brought her back."

"I don't think so, Jen. People who've had near-death experiences say they saw a beam of white light. Or a bright tunnel." Becky's eyebrows furrowed.

"Yes, but sometimes they see their relatives, like their parents or grandparents or whoever they know who's already died." Jen spoke with authority.

"Jen, are you supposed to be drinking while you're taking pain pills?" Susan poured herself another glass.

"One glass won't hurt." Jen sipped.

"It might."

"I'm fine."

"Really? Because you're talking nonsense."

"Don't be so close minded, Susan. Shit. It's fucking obvious. Elle saw Charlie because she had a near-death experience. She visited the other side."

"The other side? Spare me." Susan shook her head, rearranged her legs.

"It's possible," Becky insisted. "Madam Therese said Elle's aura attracts dead people."

"Don't start with Madam Therese again. Come on, get real, you guys."

"Why can't you accept it, Susan? Maybe Charlie's spirit came to her because she was close to the line."

"The line?"

"Between life and death."

Oh, that line.

"What did he say, Elle?" Becky said. "What did you see?"

What had I seen? I'd seen Charlie. Just Charlie. Nothing else. "I don't know. We were together. Charlie seemed alive. He kissed me. He said we were soul mates."

Susan groaned.

"Whatever, Susan. I touched him. He was as solid as this bathtub. We spoke." Well, not exactly. We'd communicated, but we hadn't actually needed to utter words.

Susan ran a hand through her hair. "Look. I'm sure it seemed real. But scientists say that all that stuff—the lights, the family members greeting you—it's all just the brain reacting to impending death. The brain's shutting down. Its neurons are firing, making you see things." Susan sounded adamant. "Charlie wasn't there. Your brain just soothed you by making you think he was with you. Though God knows why seeing Charlie would soothe you."

"Which makes my fucking point, Susan," Jen smirked. "Because if Elle's brain wanted to resurrect someone to comfort her, it wouldn't choose that bastard Charlie."

For a moment, nobody said anything.

"So you guys believe in an afterlife?" Susan asked.

"Don't you?" Becky's eyes widened.

"I think life is here and now. And that's it." Susan leaned back against the wall.

"I don't frickin' know," Jen shook her head. "Maybe there's something, like a soul or a spirit that lives on after we die."

I thought of Claudia crashing onto concrete. Of Greta's dead, mangled face. Had they seen a loved one as they were dying? Had someone guided them across the line? Had their souls survived? Were they still here, watching us? I looked around, didn't see them, but sunk lower into the bubbles. Heard Charlie whisper that we'd be together forever, that we were soul mates.

"Living on after we die?" Susan considered it. She finished her wine. "I don't know, you guys. To me, dead is dead. But I got to admit, it must be sweet to think otherwise."

We sat silently for another moment. After a while, Susan picked up the empty bottle and stood. She asked if I was ready to get out of the tub.

I nodded. My skin was puckered, and the water had cooled, giving me a chill. I stepped out into a towel, wondering again why Charlie had been dressed for tennis.

~

I dozed on the terrace all afternoon, dazed and sore, my mind hazy and unsettled. I'd forgotten about my plans with Alain. When I woke up and limped into the suite, though, Susan told me that they'd talked when he'd come by to check on Jen.

"He's coming by at eight. But don't get dressed up. You're not going out. He'll just cook at his place."

She said that Alain had been with patients all day, hadn't heard about my accident until she'd told him. And that he'd looked in on me while I'd slept.

He had? Had I been sleeping that soundly? And, oh God, had I been drooling? Or snoring?

"He seemed very concerned. It's obvious that he likes you, Elle. And it's very thoughtful of him, taking you to his place."

Jen had wandered in, carrying a box of crackers. Munching, she lowered herself onto a chair. "Whose place?"

"Alain's. Elle's having dinner with him." Susan poured a diet soda.

"Alain?" Jen stopped chewing. "As in my doctor, Alain? That Alain?"

"The very one," Susan nodded.

"You're fucking kidding me." Jen turned to me, blanching. "You're seriously dating my surgeon?"

I began to explain, but Susan interrupted. "You knew they'd seen each other—"

"Fuck I did. I thought they had coffee or something—"

"Well, why shouldn't she date him?" Susan took out some avocados and a knife.

"Why? Are you serious?"

"What's your problem, Jen?" I asked.

"My problem? Okay. My problem, Elle, is that you are like a sister to me, and that he's *my* damn doctor. My relationship with him is personal and private."

"But he's your doctor, not your date," Susan sliced avocado.

"Mine is the only relationship that *any* of us should be having with him."

I didn't say anything.

"Really? Dinner at his place?" She went on. "I arranged this whole trip for you, and in gratitude, out of all the available guys down here, you have to pick my doctor? I mean, shit—are you fucking kidding me?"

My face was burning, but I didn't understand her anger. I kept silent, refusing to be bullied. Or to apologize.

But Susan wasn't silent. "What's wrong with you?" She stopped slicing, waved her knife at Jen. "First of all, if you keep eating junk food like that, you'll need another tummy tuck."

"I can't help it if I'm hungry." She looked at her belly.

"And, secondly, leave Elle alone. It's not personal between you. You're Dr. Du Bois's patient, not his squeeze. And Elle's single."

"Yes, she is. But he's not. Dr. Du Bois is married."

Susan raised an eyebrow, turned to me, the knife dangling from her fingers. "Did you know that?"

"Both of you. Stop." I took a breath, tried to not to cough. "I'm just having dinner with him."

"While his wife, what? Eats alone?" Susan frowned. She was sensitive to the idea of husbands having dinner with single women. I tried to picture her portly husband, Tim, at a candlelit dinner with a woman other than Susan. Couldn't. Didn't want to.

"His wife's an invalid." I spoke softly, managing more words than I had all day. "They don't have much of a marriage anymore. Besides, I'll be here only a few days. It's no big deal." Why did I have to explain?

"That's not the point," Jen fumed behind her nose splint. "The point is that you're overstepping. The man is my doctor. My turf. You're trespassing on my territory."

Really? Jen was claiming Alain as her personal property?

Susan and I both blinked at her.

"Stop pretending you don't know what I'm talking about. We're friends, but we each have separate lives and our own individual relationships in our own separate worlds. Norm is in mine. And so is Dr. Du Bois. You don't just fucking step into someone's world and start dating people there."

I blinked. She was declaring Alain a citizen of her personal planet? "I wasn't aware of this rule, Jen. Or of your deed to Alain's person." I coughed.

"Good God, stop it, both of you." Susan used her mom tone. She came into the living room, plopped onto an easy chair, and pushed hair out of her eyes. "You know what? Ever since we got here, all we do is bicker."

"Not true," Jen said. "I've been too miserable to bicker."

"See? You're even bickering about bickering."

She was right.

"This was supposed to be fun." Jen pouted. Or I thought she did. It was hard to see behind the splint. "But Dr. Du Bois— or should I say Elle's beau—failed to tell me how much pain I'd be in. Or how many complications I could get."

I didn't comment. Didn't mention that Jen's problems weren't the only ones we'd encountered.

But Susan did. "Oh, cut the pity party, Jen. Get over yourself. Elle nearly drowned today. Two women next door died. I've had to do a month's work in three days. Becky's fallen for some gigolo con artist. But you don't notice any of this. All you do is moan about your tender tummy and poor purple boobs, which, by the way, you asked for."

She finished with bluster, as if resting her case.

Jen's mouth opened. "My boobs are purple?" She looked down, opened her robe to check.

I couldn't help it, I laughed.

Jen glared at me. "What. You think that's funny? How would you like purple boobs?" She considered her question, let out a giggle.

"Maybe you'll start a trend," Susan remarked. "Green. Mauve. Chartreuse."

We were laughing, all three of us. Nothing we'd said had been funny enough to merit real hearty laughter, but we laughed heartily anyway, and our laughter made us laugh more and harder. It mounted until we were roaring, shedding tears, holding our sides, releasing pent-up tension. Laughing irritated my chest, so my laughter was mixed with coughing fits. Jen's with moans. But never mind, we kept laughing, expelling whatever ills we'd been holding in.

Our trip wasn't going well. But even with our nerves frayed, our bodies sore, our patience strained, and our moods sour, we were in harmony again, reunited. Old friends.

∾

When Sergeant Perez knocked, we were still laughing. Jen held her sore stomach, repeating, "I can't laugh. It hurts. Oh, shit, stop. I can't laugh. My stitches. Stop."

I was alternately laughing and hacking.

Susan answered the door, wiping tears. "Oh, Sergeant Perez," she said. For some reason, his presence struck her funny. She burst into another round of belly laughs, which reignited Jen and me. "Please," she chortled, "come in." She snorted, breaking up again.

Sergeant Perez stepped into the suite, standing stiffly at attention, regarding each of us sternly. His glares seemed cartoonish, made us laugh harder. What was wrong with us? Why couldn't we stop?

"I'm glad to see you are enjoying yourselves." His tone contradicted his words.

"Sorry, Sergeant," Susan bit her lip, struggling to make herself stop. "We were just discussing our love lives." She straightened up, attempting to adopt a professional demeanor.

His gaze traveled from one to the other of us.

"What can we do for you?" Smoothing her hair, she realized she was still clutching the avocado knife and tossed it onto the kitchenette counter, wiped her hand on her pants.

I composed myself, taking deep slow breaths.

Jen moaned and hugged herself, cradling her aggravated wounds.

Sergeant Perez stepped into the center of the room, eyeing my bandaged leg. "I have heard about your injury, señora. I would like to hear the details."

The details? Was the hotel afraid I'd sue them? "It's okay. I'll be fine—" I began to cough.

"Please, señora."

"It's hard for me to talk." My throat and chest were raw from laughing.

"Maybe I can help," Susan said. She reviewed the event, told him that I'd been boogie boarding. That a witness said someone's board had crashed into my head and that I'd been pulled under the water, probably unconscious. Somehow, I must have cut my leg on a shell or metal fragment in the water.

"Is this accurate, señora?" He watched me.

"I don't remember being hit. I remember the wave picking me up, then something pulling me down under the water. I thought it was an undertow." I stopped to cough. "And someone grabbed me. Someone with long hair." I left out the part about Charlie.

Sergeant Perez frowned, took a seat on an easy chair. "I will be frank, señora. This story troubles me for a number of reasons. First, while it's possible that you were hit on the head and knocked out in a collision, what happened to the man who bumped into you? No one saw him after the incident. Was he also hurt? Knocked off his board? We don't know. Because witnesses never saw him emerge from the water. Even the person who claims she saw the accident lost sight of him."

Odd. But so what?

"We have only her word that the collision occurred, or if it did, that it was an accident."

"I don't understand," Susan said. "What are you implying?"

"Let me finish, señora. It's not just the collision that I question; it's the wound to your friend's leg. You see, the ocean here is pristine. The bottom is not cluttered with sharp objects. The seashells and stones are rounded by the water, not razor sharp. If you were to scrape yourself on one, the wound would be just that: a scrape. Not likely to require thirteen stitches."

Wait, he knew how many I'd had? He'd talked to the doctor?

"So, what are you saying?" Jen asked. "That what happened wasn't an accident?"

"Yes, Sergeant. Please explain," Susan stepped over, put a hand on my shoulder.

"Señora," he leaned forward, "two women have died in close proximity to you. You are a witness in both cases. You were present at the death of the first woman and you discovered the body of the second. In both cases, you possess critical, possibly incriminating information."

I did? "But I've told you everything. I don't have any other information."

"Someone may think you know more than you do, *señora*. But whether you do or not, I am concerned that you have come close to death yourself, nearly drowning in calm water and sustaining a serious wound. A wound that the doctor who treated you believed was caused not by a shell but by a knife."

A knife?

I sunk in murky water, disoriented. Seaweed—or was it hair?—swirled around me, swept across my face. Something entangled my legs, held onto them. My lungs burned and raged, and I fought someone. Maybe Melanie as she wrestled to rescue me. I didn't remember getting hit on the head or cut or knocked out. I remembered Charlie.

"You think Elle's in danger?" Susan pressed him. "How are you going to protect her?"

"I cannot offer a bodyguard, señora." He turned to me. "But it would be wise for you not to go anywhere alone. And to inform me of anything else you remember. Anyone who seems odd to you."

Really? That would be a long list. But I thought of Luis, standing on the beach, watching them revive me.

Sergeant Perez urged all of us, especially me, to be cautious and to keep in touch. Susan walked him to the door. After he'd gone, we looked at each other in silence. The air had changed, felt heavier. Our laughter had not only stopped, but been pulverized.

After a minute or two, Susan went back into the kitchenette. "Well, no point sitting around," she said. "Nothing ever came of that."

A moment later, I heard her knife, emphatically striking the cutting board, dicing an offending onion or some unrepentant cilantro.

～

Alain made fish. Turbot with a sauce of mango and orange juice, onions, peppers, honey, and garlic. We had rice and beans. We had wine. We ate poolside at sunset at his white stucco villa-style home near a golf course. The house had a red tiled roof, arched rounded windows, and an inner courtyard with a fountain. It felt open and light, decorated in festive reds, blues, greens, and yellows. I assumed the tones would look brighter to a normal person; to me, they were softly muted.

I wondered if his wife had designed it, if she swam in the pool.

I wondered where she was.

Alain poured wine, asked about my leg, my lungs.

"I'm fine," I told him, but my voice was raspy.

He frowned. "Can we be honest, Elle?"

Uh-oh. I stopped chewing. People asked that question only when they had something awful to say. It was their way of preparing you for something unspeakable. What would he say? Oh God, had another woman died? Or was his wife coming home?

"Of course," I forced a smile, braced myself.

He paused, his eyes riveted on mine. "Elle, I think that what happened to you today wasn't an accident." Another pause. "I think you were attacked."

Oh. Was that all? Relieved, I looked at my half-eaten fish, put down my fork, began to reassure him. "Alain, really, I'm—" I began, but he interrupted.

"I talked to the doctor who stitched you up. He has no doubt that the gash in your leg was made by a knife and deliberately inflicted." Alain reached across the table, put his hand on mine. "In fact, he's convinced that whoever cut you would have killed you if you hadn't fought so hard. He thinks you probably diverted the knife, might even have kicked it out of the attacker's hand."

Again, I saw murky water swirling. Seaweed. And Charlie reaching for me.

Alain was still talking. "Especially, after what happened to Claudia and Greta. You were connected to both of their deaths. What happened to you can't be a coincidence."

He was still holding my hand.

"But if someone wanted to kill me, why didn't they just drown me? Why use a knife?"

Alain's voice was soft, patient. "You very nearly did drown.

But you resisted your attacker harder than expected. Maybe the knife was a backup plan. Either way, you were nearly killed. And I believe you're still in danger."

He sounded exactly like Sergeant Perez.

I thanked him, promised I'd be careful. His grip on my hand tightened.

"This week has been a nightmare, Elle. Two women who were close to me are dead. You've been attacked. Honestly, I couldn't stand it if—" He stopped in the middle. Cleared his throat. "We haven't known each other long. But you're already important to me. I care about you." He released my hand, took a gulp of wine.

His skin glowed in the candlelight; his eyes reflected the flames. I remembered the urgent pressure of his lips.

"Sorry," he picked up his fork. "I shouldn't have said that last bit."

"It's all right, Alain. Really." My voice had turned husky. Wait. If my voice had been raspy and turned husky, did that mean the rasp had turned to husk? What was husk? Why was I avoiding the situation by drifting into wordplay?

Alain watched me, waiting, wary.

I made myself stay in the moment. I concentrated, looked at Alain, his fiery eyes. "I care about you, too." I felt myself flush. It wasn't a lie, but I wasn't sure it was quite the truth. It depended on what "care" meant. It could mean a lot of things. I cared about tons of people. My students, for example. Each one of them—I missed them, wondered if little Ellen was still writing her *Es* backward. If Steve and Nicky were giving the substitute a hard time.

"You don't have to say that. It's not tit for tat." He drank the rest of his wine. Refilled it. Topped off my glass. Looked at me. Sighed. "I've interrupted our dinner. And I've alarmed you. But I had to speak up and warn you."

For a moment we were silent, looking at each other.

"Elle, please. Let's eat."

I wasn't hungry any more, but Alain began eating so I did, too. The flavors were sweet and tangy, peppery, intriguing, but I didn't care. I was thinking about danger, about nearly being killed. About being the third woman to die.

"Trouble is I blame myself. I should have seen it coming." Alain swallowed a mouthful of rice.

"How could you? You didn't know I'd even be in the water."

His eyebrows furrowed, confused. "Sorry. I meant Greta."

Oh. Greta. His patient whose face had been cut to fringe. The one he'd had an affair with, whom I'd heard him kissing the night she'd died. The glow around Alain dimmed. Something behind him moved in the shadows, rustling a bush. Maybe a raccoon?

Alain didn't seem to notice it. "I shouldn't have let her stay alone. She was a suicide risk."

The night had darkened; the only light came from four spindly candles. Alain's face reflected golden flickers.

"She didn't kill herself, Alain. People don't slash themselves in the face."

He gazed at his wine. "They do if they hate their bodies enough. Greta suffered body dysmorphic disorder. Her thigh was ringed with scars from her dogged attempts to remove her leg."

I tried to imagine it. Couldn't.

"She was incredibly beautiful, yet she believed she was an abomination." He shook his head. "I've seen patients who've succeeded in cutting off a foot. Genitals. An ear. A thumb. But not a leg."

Neither of us spoke. Darkness slithered down my back. I pictured detached body parts, wondered how people disposed of the unwanted foot, thumb, penis, or ear. I swallowed wine, tried to think of something else. Saw dark water and tendrils of hair. Felt the needle stitching my leg. Across the patio, a shadow again disturbed the bushes. Had there been a breeze? Did Alain have a cat?

"Greta was in a bad state that night. She felt hideous, deformed. Unable to look in a mirror. I shouldn't have left her alone."

"Alain, you can't blame yourself."

He made a clucking sound. "No, you're right. I'm not to blame. And yet, people close to me keep coming to harm." His eyes penetrated the darkness, riveted on me.

"But you couldn't have prevented any of it."

"Greta wanted her leg off. She begged me—"

"But her leg wasn't what got cut."

"I knew she was suicidal."

"But it wasn't suicide."

"Maybe not." He paused. "But you'd be surprised, Elle, what passion can lead people to do."

I didn't move, couldn't. My lungs were raw and sore. Someone had tried to murder me, and darkness whirled in my mind. When I looked up, Alain was there, reaching for my hand, guiding me to my feet, leaning down. Kissing me.

Pain shot up my leg. I leaned against him to take weight off it. Or maybe just to lean against him. His body wasn't much taller than mine, lean, solid. Strong arms slid around me. The candles quivered and the bushes rattled with something unseen, and I accompanied Alain into the stucco house with red, blue, green, and yellow décor.

But as he led me toward his bedroom, Charlie whispered that he loved me, that we were soul mates. I held back, smelling Charlie's Old Spice, recalling how real he'd seemed that morning. How happy I'd been with him.

"Are you okay?" Alain kissed my cheek, my neck.

I put a hand up, pressed it against his chest, a stop signal. "You're married," I breathed. It made more sense than the truth.

He straightened, bit his lip. "Yes. But I've told you. It's not a marriage. My wife—she's not my wife any more. She's too damaged." He took a breath. "But if you're uncomfortable, I understand." His arm was still around me, but only to help support my weight. Not to possess me.

Charlie persisted, insisting that we'd be together forever. Calling me "Elf." A dead man was in my head, claiming me.

"Shall I take you back to the hotel?" Alain waited.

Charlie made puppy dog eyes and pleaded. Yes. Go to the hotel.

I ignored him. Remembered his bare butt in our shower with a babe. Dead or alive, he had no right to ask me to be faithful. I reached up, touched Alain's face, guided it to mine and planted a kiss on his lips. Yes, he was married, even if in name only. But I'd nearly died that day. And selfishly, I needed to be held by someone other than Charlie. I needed to find comfort in the arms of a man who was actually alive.

∾

I didn't spend the night. In fact, we didn't even make love. I'd planned to and we would have, but Alain's phone rang before his shirt was even off. He ignored the call and, finally, it stopped ringing, but began again immediately. He apologized that it was probably the clinic, some problem with a patient. He said he'd just be a moment and answered the call, speaking Spanish but, by the urgency in his tone, I knew something serious had arisen. By the time the call ended, I'd replaced my garments in their original positions and slipped into my sandals, ready to go.

On the way to the hotel, Alain apologized repeatedly, explaining that he had to attend to an emergency. He held my hand as he drove, asking if I'd see him again the next night. Promising that there would be no more interruptions.

I didn't commit, suggested that we speak in the morning. I was ambivalent and more than a little embarrassed about being so easily seduced. After all, I didn't really know Alain. I knew some things about him—his profession, his height, smooth skin, straight nose, and strong bones. His kisses. But nothing else, really. So why had I slid my hand under his shirt and unfastened his belt?

And why had I almost hopped into bed with him? Was I pathetically desperate? Lonely? Seduced by the Mexican moonlight? All of the above? Yes, maybe. But, in my defense, I'd also been shaken by Claudia's and Greta's deaths, topped by my own injuries. And by the suggestion that I'd been attacked and might still be in danger. I was just plain vulnerable and needy. And Alain had not missed the opportunity to take advantage of that. After all, he had a history of womanizing. I'd heard him on the balcony with Greta. He'd admitted having an affair with her and indicated one with Claudia. And they hadn't been the only ones.

Still, his kisses tingled on my lips. And I felt chilled without his arms around me.

Even so, I was going back to my room, alone, and that was for the best. Alain had moved too fast. All his talk about death and danger—had it been out of concern for me? Or had it been a ploy to frighten and lure me into his bed? Either way, by the time I got back to the hotel suite, I felt both foolish and relieved, as if the emergency call had rescued me from my own impulsive behavior.

When I came in, Becky was playing Scrabble with Susan and Jen, who sprawled on the sofa.

"Becky?" I was surprised to see her.

"How was dinner?" Jen didn't look up.

"Fourteen points," Susan wrote down her score.

"How was that fourteen?" Becky frowned.

Susan moved a tile aside. "Double word score."

"Damn."

"You're not with Chichi tonight?" I took a wineglass from the kitchenette, poured some of what they were drinking.

"He's got a private fiesta."

"Becky thinks he's got a hot date." Jen reached for a bag of tortilla chips.

"No, I do not. He's calling when he's done."

"Which might be late if she pays him by the hour."

"Shut up, Jen." Becky threw a handful of tiles at her.

Jen chuckled. Winced. "Oh fuck. Laughing hurts."

"Good. You deserve to hurt. Talking like that about Chichi." Becky retrieved her tiles. "Elle, tell us about dinner."

"I hope you had a frickin' awful terrible boring time," Jen munched a chip.

Becky looked at me. "Why is she so nasty? Just because she hurts?"

"Seriously? Jen's always nasty," I sipped wine.

"No. I'm nasty because Elle is dating my effing doctor."

Susan picked new letters. "Damn. No vowels. Not a single bleeping one."

"She's winning," Jen explained. "She's actually killing us, but she's whining anyway."

"Well, my letters stink."

"So what did you have? Is he a good cook?"

"Grilled fish."

"Jen, 'coulk' is not a word."

"Hell if it isn't. Like when you coulk your bathroom tiles."

"That's c-a-u-l-k."

"No, it's c-o-u-l-k."

"Where's your computer? Google it."

I sat on an easy chair, leaned back, and sipped wine. Their voices flittered around the suite like chamber music. Tightness eased out of my shoulders, thoughts out of my mind. I felt safe, protected by familiar faces. Very tired. And glad to be home.

~

And, then, minutes later, Alain knocked on the door. I sunk into the chair. What did he want? Hadn't we said good night?

Susan let him and his black bag in.

"I'm on my way home, but first I thought I'd check on my patient." He walked in without being invited, as if he had a right to be there.

Well, I realized, he did. The suite was part of his surgery package.

"How are you feeling, Jen?"

"Miserable." She began to rattle off complaints. The pills

weren't killing the pain. She felt tender here and swollen there. She still had a fever. She was afraid she was scarring.

He went to the sofa, his gaze skimming over Becky, twinkling as it passed me. "Hi, ladies," he smiled, taking Jen's hand and leading her into the bedroom even as she continued her list of grievances.

We heard muffled voices; Jen's whining, his comforting.

"Elle, play Jen's letters." Susan waved me over to the table.

I didn't want to move, but obeyed automatically. Looked at her letters.

"It's your turn," Becky said.

I looked at the board. Checked the letters. A-L-R-R-C-U-T. Terrible letters. Useless. I searched for spare E or S to tag letters onto. I wasn't good at Scrabble. Didn't have the patience or the concentration. My letters could form cat. Cult. Cut. But I needed a link.

"Elle?" Susan urged.

"Are you with us?" Becky asked. "Maybe she's pulling another Elle."

"I'm fine." I added C-A-L to another L. Formed CALL.

"Six points." Susan wrote it down.

Not a great word, but at least they'd leave me alone. Fortunately, Jen and Alain emerged from the bedroom before Jen's next turn.

"Well?" Susan asked.

"Apparently, I'm doing great," Jen grumbled.

"So we can cancel the funeral arrangements?"

Alain chuckled. "Well, at least you can postpone them. The patient is recovering very well."

I got up, made room for Jen to spread out on the sofa. "Everything all right with your emergency?"

His smile disappeared. "Very strange. It was a mistake. Nobody from the clinic called. The nurse who gave her name isn't even on duty."

"You mean someone faked it?"

He shrugged. "Maybe. But what would be the purpose?"

I didn't know. I remembered being in his arms, unbuttoning his shirt. The roughness of his whiskers on my neck. The phone ringing. Had someone wanted him to get out of his house? To rob him?

His eyes met mine, laughing. "If I didn't know better, I might think someone was trying to ruin my evening." He turned to Jen and handed her a vial of pills. "Take these as needed. One every six to eight hours. They will reduce swelling and pain. You'll sleep better."

Then, he looked at us one by one, "Ladies, I bid you good night." As he headed for the door, he said, "I'll call in the morning." His eyes held mine for a moment, and he left.

As the door closed, two phones rang simultaneously. Norm was calling for Jen, Chichi for Becky. Susan picked up her phone to call Tim.

I sat watching my wineglass for a while. Then, abandoned, I wandered onto the balcony and stood at the railing, alone.

·~·

Something tickled my face—a mosquito? I swatted at it, refusing to wake up. Smelling hyacinth. Odd. Probably a scent from outside. The door to the terrace was open, the breeze blowing the slats of the vertical blinds. Their flapping was soft, soothing. I turned my head, wishing the pillow wasn't so thick and my shoulders weren't so burned, and sank back into sleep.

But something tickled my cheek again. This time, as I slapped at it, I opened my eyes, annoyed. Ready to hunt down the bug even if it meant waking up.

But the tickle hadn't been caused by a bug. Someone was there, in my room, standing beside my bed.

I don't know which came first, my shriek or my jump. The shadowy form didn't move. It stood perfectly still for the immeasurable duration of time it took for me to surface from the depths of sleep, struggling to identify it. Was it Susan? Jen? Becky? No, Becky was with Chichi. So, was it Alain? No. I couldn't tell; it had no face. A ghost then? Certainly not Charlie. Was it Greta or Claudia, paying me a visit? These thoughts flashed simultaneously as I gawked at the shadowy form, which seemed to be facelessly gawking back at me. Maybe it wasn't real. Maybe I was still asleep, dreaming. I closed my eyes, lying stiff on the mattress.

Smelling hyacinth.

Were there smells in dreams? I opened my eyes again. Saw the open terrace door, the vertical blinds swaying in the breeze. Moonlight beaming through the slats, lighting the form of a woman in a long loose robe. Her face was wrapped, hidden behind a veil.

A veil? Oh God. Was this the woman Charlie had been with—the one on the beach? Why was she in my room, beside my bed? How had she gotten in? Who was she? I tried to ask, but couldn't make a sound. Tried to get up, but couldn't move.

Of course I couldn't. It was a nightmare. In nightmares, you couldn't move or make sounds. But the good news was that, if the woman was in a nightmare, she wasn't real. I was safe, asleep. Except that I didn't feel safe or asleep. I felt paralyzed, helpless, at the mercy of a shadowy veiled stranger. Madam Therese surfaced, "I told you: you draw the dead." Her tone was impatient, tired of reminding me. Was the veiled woman dead? What did she want? I tried again to speak, but like the rest of me, my voice was still. Only my heart moved, thrusting itself against my ribs.

Stop it, I scolded myself. You're just asleep. She's a dream. Dreams can't hurt you. In fact, if you concentrate hard enough, you can take charge and force the dream to change.

So I did. I concentrated on making the woman disappear. On changing the content of the dream altogether—making it be about something benign and pleasant—puppies, for example. I shut my eyes and imagined a new puppy with floppy ears, a soft, downy coat, a waggy tail, and eyes filled with wonder. What would I name him? Charlie? Very good, naming a dog after Charlie. Yes. I smiled at the thought. Calmer, I opened my eyes again.

The woman was leaning over me, her eyes ablaze. Her veil tickled my cheek.

I skittered away, yelping.

"*La venganza*," she hissed.

I had no idea what she was saying. I huddled against the headboard.

"*Conseguir la venganza.*" She raised her fist. Lord. Something glittered in her hand. A knife?

I crawled backward, away from her, bumping into the nightstand, knocking the lamp over. The woman swung her fists, repeating her syllables. I shielded my head with my arms, bracing for an onslaught of punches or the slashing of blades. But neither came. In fact, except for the flapping of the slats against the sliding door, the room was harshly silent. Cautiously, slowly, I peeked through my arms. Didn't see her. I pushed my hair off my face, sat up, looked around.

No one was there.

I shivered. Had she really been there? Had she been a dream? I hugged a thick pillow, trying to stop trembling. It had to have been a nightmare. Not surprising, given all the dreadful things that had happened that week. I pulled up the blanket, leaned back against the headboard, slowed my breathing. Steadied my hands. I touched my face where the veil had tickled it, imagined the scent of hyacinth. It had been so vivid. The slats kept rapping against the glass, sounding ominous now. Moonlight cast shadows, the shadows took on menacing shapes.

I should get up, have a snack. Turn on the television. Reconnect with normal and tangible. I pondered it, but my body didn't want to move. My head was thick with sleep, my legs ached. So I stayed in bed, neither awake nor asleep, my head covered and my eyes closed. I was thinking about getting a puppy when, in Jen and Susan's room, someone let out a bone-rattling scream.

≀

The blanket tangled around my legs. I kicked to throw it off, but it resisted, wrapping around my bandage, clinging to it. I yanked at it, ignoring the pulse of pain as I aggravated my wound. Ripping and pulling, I finally managed to get free and hop to my feet.

Another scream. "Fuck!"

Running in the dark, I banged into Becky's empty bed, grabbed onto the dresser, propelled myself out the bedroom door.

"Jen!" I yelled. "Susan?" I sped across the expanse of living room, seeing Claudia's fall and Greta's spaghetti face, and finally thrust open the door to Jen's and Susan's room. Dreading what I'd see, I flicked on the lights.

Susan sat calmly on the side of Jen's bed, her hand on Jen's forehead. "It's nothing, Elle. Just a nightmare."

A nightmare? Apparently, they were going around.

"It was *not* a nightmare." Jen was trembling. The bandages around her chest hung loose and ragged, unraveled. "It was a fucking ghost." She pointed at me. "It's you and your damned spirit aura."

"Don't be an ass, Jen," Susan removed her hand. "It's not Elle's fault. There's no such thing as a ghost."

"WTF, Susan. I know what I saw."

"You had a nightmare. You're taking weird medicines. And you still have a fever."

"No, seriously. Maybe Elle attracts bad juju, like that gypsy said."

"She wasn't a gypsy," I said, even though I had no idea. Madam Therese might indeed have been a gypsy. She'd sounded like she'd come from South Philly. Or maybe the Bronx. And she'd never said anything about juju. All she said was that I had a stained aura and attracted the dead.

Jen was still ranting. "—ever since we got here. Women dying next door. Elle nearly drowning. And now a fucking ghost attacking me."

"Nobody attacked you," Susan said. "Nobody was here. I would have seen them."

"What did she look like?"

Susan glared at me. "Elle, I just said nobody was here."

"She was a ghost," Jen ignored her. "So that's what she looked like. Like fucking Casper, only black."

I pictured the dark veil draped over me, felt its tickle.

"That proves it was a dream," Susan smirked. "No self-respecting ghost would dress that way."

"You think it's funny? It's not effing funny, Susan." Jen huffed.

I sat on the foot of the bed, across from Susan. Put a hand on Jen's arm. Even with her face hidden by the splint on her nose, Jen's fear showed. Her eyes bulged. Blue veins pulsed in her forehead.

"I'm calling the clinic," Susan eyed the mess of gauze on Jen's chest as she picked up her cell. "Someone needs to come wrap you up again."

Jen picked up a length of gauze, looked at me. "Elle, if that ghost wasn't real, then I must have done this myself. How could I do this? In my sleep? I'd have had to pick up my nightgown and pull off my own fricking bandages. That makes sense to you?"

It didn't, no. But I was pretty sure that the ghost hadn't been a ghost, that she had been very real. "Jen, listen. I believe you."

"Maybe I'm a sleepwalker." She stared at the strips of gauze on the bed. Bruised purplish flesh bulged over the top of the layers still wrapped around her. "I've heard that sleepwalkers do crazy stuff in their sleep. Some of them get up and eat their entire refrigerator full of food. Or they drive cars. I read about a guy who murdered his mother-in-law and they let him off because he did it in his sleep."

"You're not a sleepwalker, Jen. Listen to me, will you? What you saw was real." But she wasn't listening, didn't even hear me. She was yammering, hysterical.

"Maybe it's not you. Maybe it's being here in this strange place so far from Norm. The climate. Those damned pelicans. Maybe they carry germs that make people hallucinate. Or it's this damned fever. Maybe my medicine is causing a reaction. Or my infection—maybe it's causing delusions. Shit. What if I'm worse off than Dr. Du Bois is letting on? Oh damn, Elle." She looked at me, as if remembering that I was there. "Do you think I'm seriously fucking sick? Am I going to frickin' die here?"

"No, Jen. You're not going to die." I squeezed her arm, hoping none of us would.

"How the hell can you say that? You don't know. Oh, fuck, what ever made me decide to get this fucking work done?" She clutched her stomach, groaned. "What was I thinking? For the sake of a double-D cup and a tight tummy, I risked my whole goddamn life? If I die, Elle, tell Norm—" Her eyebrows puckered. "What should you tell him?"

"Nothing. Tell him yourself. You're going to be fine."

Susan was in the living room, talking to the on-call doctor, explaining that Jen had had a nightmare and demolished her bandages.

Jen's eyes drifted, stared at air. "The thing is, she seemed so fucking real." She turned to me. "Maybe I was ripping at myself. But I'd swear to God, I was being attacked by an intruder."

I nodded. "And she looked like a ghost."

"Yes. I swear. She was slashing at my chest. I didn't rip off my bandages. I was fighting her off."

"I believe you. I saw her, too."

Jen still didn't seem to hear. She kept talking, recalling the attack. "Oh, and she talked to me. In Spanish. That's fucking weird. How could I have a nightmare in Spanish? I barely even speak it."

"It's your subconscious." Susan was off the phone. "Your mind knows more than you think it does."

"What did she say?" I bit my lip, waiting.

"What difference does it make?" Susan frowned. "It was a nightmare."

"I don't think so," I said. "I told you I saw her, too."

"You did?" Jen finally heard me, but instead of feeling validated, she turned to Susan, pointing at me. "See? It's Elle's bad juju, like I said."

"Stop it, both of you. There are no ghosts, and that stuff about juju is nonsense. No one was here. The door was locked. Nothing in the suite is disturbed except Jen's bandages. And I was right here in the room. I didn't hear anything except Jen screaming."

"No fucking surprise," Jen said. "You were snoring so loud I'm surprised you even heard that."

"Susan, someone was here. In my room, too."

Susan bristled. "There is absolutely no evidence to back that up, Elle. You both had bad dreams. I'd have known if someone came into my bedroom. I'm a mother. I sleep with one eye and both ears open. No one was here."

Why was she refusing to believe us? "Susan," I began, but she put a hand up, shaking her head.

"Don't push it, Elle. Jen's scared enough. Don't make it worse. Anyway, someone's coming to repair the bandage damage. Meantime, I think we all could use a drink." She went to the kitchenette.

I turned to Jen. She was fingering her frayed bandages. "What did the woman say?" I kept my voice low so Susan wouldn't hear.

She tilted her head. "You really saw her?"

I nodded. "I did. Tell me."

Her forehead wrinkled. "I'm not sure. Something about revenge."

"Revenge?"

Jen nodded. "*La venganza.*"

Oh. So that's what it had meant. My skin erupted in goose-flesh.

Susan came back with three glasses and lime sections. "I wish we had scotch," she sighed. "Tequila will have to do."

Jen reached for a glass. She looked battered, and her hand was shaking even more than mine.

∼

The doctor who stitched my leg was the one who came to rewrap Jen. He was impressed.

"You did this yourself, señora?" he asked. "In your sleep?"

Jen looked at me. "I guess I had a nightmare. I thought I was fighting someone."

He regarded the torn gauze strips. "Well, señora, you would make a formidable opponent. Remind me never to get into combat with you."

Susan and I stepped out to give Jen privacy. I took the tequila along, refilled our glasses, took another shot. And looked at Susan.

"What." Susan took a seat at the table, drank. "Go on. Say it."

I sat opposite her, deciding how to phrase it.

Susan poured more tequila.

"I started to before, but you didn't want to hear it."

She sighed, pushed hair out of her eyes. "Okay, Elle. You think someone was here. That someone came into the suite, tiptoed around your room, came into ours, stole nothing. Hurt nobody. Just unwrapped Jen's bandages? Really?"

I leaned forward, met her eyes. "Yes. Exactly."

Susan sat back, shook her head. "That's nuts."

"Susan. Jen and I both saw the woman. She was in my room first—"

"Someone was in your room and you just lay there? You didn't scream? Or chase her? You didn't call out to us? You simply chilled and waited until she attacked Jen?" She crossed her arms, not believing me.

"I was asleep. At first, I thought I was dreaming. Or that my mind was playing tricks on me, like after Charlie died. I was trying to figure out what was happening when Jen screamed."

"You know what, Elle? Maybe nothing happened except you both had nightmares. It's no surprise, what with everything that's been—"

"You really believe that both of us had nightmares at the same time."

"It's possible."

"About the same person?"

"A similar person."

"Saying the same words?"

She stopped nodding. "What words?"

"*La venganza.*"

Susan blinked at me. Took her third shot.

"I don't know how she got in or who she was or what she wanted," I said, "but someone was here."

My glass was empty. I looked at Susan, then at the bottle. It seemed to sway as I poured. After another tequila shot—or was it two? I went back to bed. The doctor had gone and given Jen a shot to calm her down. Susan and I hadn't figured out what had happened, but we'd had enough tequila that we had trouble discussing it and it didn't seem to matter much anymore.

~

Alain had called before I woke up; my cell showed two missed calls from him. Not that I could read his name very easily with the letters blurred.

The rest of the world was also off. The sunlight fried my eyeballs. My skull was filled with sand. No—with rocks. Sharp, jagged ones. How much had Susan and I had to drink? When had I gone to bed? What time was it?

So many questions. Too many.

I closed my eyes, letting the walls steady themselves. When I felt that the floor would hold still and support me, I got out of bed carefully. Slowly went into the bathroom, saw a hag in the mirror. Hair disheveled, eyes red, shoulders and forehead covered with dead peeling skin.

"Elle," Susan knocked on the door before cracking it open, "Dr. Du Bois is here."

"What?"

"He checked on Jen and he wants to see you."

"What?" It seemed to be my only word. I turned to face her.

"Wow." She gaped at me. "You look horrific."

I nodded, agreeing.

"I'll give him coffee."

"I can't see him—"

"Fix yourself."

"How? I can't—"

The door closed, and I heard Susan declare that Elle would be a couple of minutes. I turned back to the mirror. Oh God. No one would want to see a face like that. But Alain was sitting outside, waiting. I filled the sink with cold water, sunk my face into it, held my breath, felt a wave of panic as I remembered almost drowning. Kept my face in the water anyway, hoping my eyelids would unswell.

Finally, I picked my head up and patted my face dry, assessing myself. Nothing had really changed. My eyelids were still massive, my eyes bloodshot. My lips were cracked from sunburn. On good days, I wasn't a knockout. And this wasn't a good day.

But Alain Du Bois, who treated—no—who created some of the most symmetrically exquisitely captivatingly beautiful women in the world, was waiting to see me. Me.

I met my eyes in the mirror. Why would Dr. Alain Du Bois, who had habitually pursued stunning women, whose hands had molded perfect female chins and noses and breasts and butts and God knew what other parts, who was a master in the aesthetics of feminine form and who had devoted his life and career to enhancing beauty—why would that same Dr. Alain Du Bois be waiting in the living room to see me?

What did he want?

I thought of our dinner. Had it been only the night before? It seemed long ago, indistinct. Had it even happened? Had Alain really asked me to spend the night? Had I wanted to? Something welled up below my ribs, answering that, yes, I had. And probably still did. I pictured Alain's hands, fingers. The strong angle of his jaw. The soft curve of his lips. The chest I'd almost exposed— good God. I told myself to stop swooning. To get in the shower.

Water streamed over me, rinsing away my hangover, but thoughts began to surface. I remembered Jen's bandages. The woman who'd somehow gotten into our suite. The feeling of paralysis I'd had when her veil had tickled my face. Uneasiness washed over me with shampoo suds.

And ten minutes later when I hastily threw on Capris and a t-shirt and came into the living room with my hair wet and hanging loose, I was still uneasy. I greeted Alain with a friendly hug as if he'd never helped me slip out of my dress. I smiled confidently as if I had lush full lips and a perkily perfect nose. I took a seat as if we were two regular people on a regular morning. But, all the time I was hearing sirens of red alert. When Alain asked if I would join him for dinner and I accepted, I was still seeing warning lights, wondering why the man was inviting me. What he could possibly, really want.

～

Sergeant Perez arrived just as Alain was leaving.

Jen came out of her room. Alain had removed her splint, replacing it with a small strip that molded to her nose so she no longer resembled a heron. "Oh, shit," she looked at Perez. "Who died now?"

"No one." Susan kept her voice low. "We had an intruder. So I called the police."

Jen's eyes widened. "But you didn't believe me. You said it was just a dream."

"We talked," I explained. But I'd had no idea that Susan had called anyone.

"Señoras," Sergeant Perez nodded to us one at a time. "Can we sit?"

We sat. I heard myself describe the figure I'd seen in my room, aware that I sounded incredible. After all, who would awaken to see a fist-waving stranger leaning over them and do nothing? Not utter a peep. Not get into a brawl. Not run screaming out of the room. Nothing. It wouldn't help to explain that I'd been told by a professional that my aura attracted spirits of the dead, so that, when I'd first seen the figure, I'd assumed it was simply one of those. No, I couldn't say that. Nor could I reveal that I'd seen my dead husband with a possibly dead woman on the beach and that I'd suspected the woman of being our intruder. I held back all this information and stuck to the most basic of facts.

I watched Sergeant Perez and he watched me, and I was sure he had concluded that something about me was off. After all, I'd been clinging to the balcony when Claudia fell. I'd found Greta's carved-up corpse. I'd half drowned and my leg had been sliced. I'd probably had more police contact in three days than most people have in their lifetimes. And now I sounded as if, when I'd been awakened by a raving stranger leaning over me, I'd simply turned over and gone back to sleep.

When I finished, he waited a moment before speaking. "Señora," his tone was surprisingly gentle, "you have been through a lot this week. So I ask you to think carefully: Did you recognize this person? The voice? The mannerisms?"

I shook my head, no.

"How tall was she? Was she heavy? Thin?"

Not tall. Not short. Not heavy or thin. "Her clothes were loose. It was hard to tell."

He stroked his mustache, sighing.

"And you?" He turned to Jen. "You saw the same figure?"

Jen gave her account, described the attack and the woman crying out in Spanish, calling for vengeance.

"You speak Spanish?"

"*Un poco.*"

"But you understand *la venganza*? It's not a common term."

Jen shrugged. She looked better without the splint even though her nose was swollen and not quite her own.

"What's your point, Sergeant?" Susan asked.

"Why would someone break in here, seeking vengeance?" he asked. "What have either of you done to arouse that kind of passion?"

The three of us sat bug-eyed, silent. Perplexed.

"Nothing," Susan's voice was flat. "We've only been here a few days, and we don't know anyone here. It makes no sense."

"And yet someone attacked one of you in the ocean and another of you in the dark of night, calling for vengeance."

Silence. My hands were cold. And my shoulders. And the rest of me.

"Do you think it's connected to the deaths next door?" Susan suggested. "Those women—"

"More importantly, señora, do you think it is?"

More silence.

Sergeant Perez stood, asked to be shown where the figure had been. We walked him around the suite, and he examined doors, carpet, remnants of ripped gauze.

"The door was locked?" he asked.

"I locked it myself," Susan insisted.

"Bolted?"

Susan's face reddened. "No. Our other roommate was out. I didn't bolt it in case she wanted to come in."

"And where is this roommate now?"

Jen, Susan, and I exchanged glances.

"She spent the night out."

"Where?"

"With a friend—"

"But you said you have no friends here. You told me you know no one."

Aha! He had us. He stood tall and thrust his chest out, as if he'd proved something significant.

Susan straightened and crossed her arms. "She just met him, Sergeant. He's Chichi, one of the activities directors."

Perez pursed his lips, nodding slowly.

"Wait, you think our intruder is connected to Chichi?" I didn't understand. "Why would someone want revenge against us because Chichi is seeing Becky?"

Susan flashed a scowl at me. As a lawyer, she wanted all communication with the police to go through her.

Perez didn't answer. He went to the front door. Studied the lock. "Were the doors to the balcony open?"

I thought of the slats slapping in the breeze.

"You think she climbed in from the balcony?" Jen asked.

"No, her clothes were loose and long." I reminded him. "They'd have gotten tangled on the railing—"

"Sí, señora." Perez's eyes drilled into me. "You would know about such things."

My face blazed.

He folded his hands, thumped his thumbs together. "Okay. The intruder wouldn't have been able to climb in through the balcony. But the lock on the front door is intact. It shows no sign of tampering."

So? What did that mean? Did he doubt that there had been an intruder?

"But Jen and I both saw her—" I began; Susan fired another scowl.

"I need to speak with your other roommate and find out who had access to her key."

Of course. The intruder must have had a key.

"And I want to take another look at the hotel staff. We never identified the maid you stated that you'd seen next door. But a maid or anyone on the room service staff—even front desk personnel—these people have easy access to the rooms."

In other words, our intruder might have been anyone who worked at the hotel.

"Do you think she'll come back?" Jen asked.

"Señoras," Sergeant Perez stepped beside the sofa, "before I came here today, I inquired as to the availability of another suite. I thought it would be wise to take a precaution and move you to another location. Unfortunately, the only comparable suite available is the one next door."

"So that was a 'yes'?"

"It was a maybe. I don't know. But I think you would be wise to bolt your door at night. And to stay together or with large groups until we have this figured out. It seems that, for whatever reason, you are surrounded by *el peligro*." He turned to Jen. "You understand, señora?"

Jen bit her lip, didn't answer.

I didn't speak Spanish, didn't know his meaning, but I pictured Madam Therese cross herself and heard her warn that danger was around us, and that my aura was a beacon, drawing harmful spirits close.

Not that I believed in spirits.

After Sergeant Perez left, Susan got on the phone with Becky, explaining what had happened and arranging for her to speak with the police.

Jen followed doctor's orders to get up and move and began walking laps around the living room.

I went to the bathroom mirror, examining the space around my head, trying to see a shadow or an ominous dark halo. I squinted. I stared. I discovered nothing about my aura. But realized I had lots of split ends.

~

When I came out, Susan was on the phone again, pacing. "Lisa, I'm a continent away. You'll have to settle it yourselves—Yes, but you also have a father—Well, explain it to him—He's not clueless if you explain—So wait until he gets home—Look, you're old enough to work things out—Lisa, I'm gone. I'm not there—You have to talk to each other."

I stepped back into the living room. Susan closed her eyes, ran a hand through her hair. "Why are you telling me? Tell Julie . . . How will you manage when I'm dead?"

Jen was still walking. "Nine more to go." She huffed, hiking the periphery of the room, skirting the sofa on each lap.

I went onto the balcony and looked down. The pool was crowded. Luis was there, setting up his next sporting event—something with golf clubs. Vendors were setting up a minimarketplace on the deck—tables covered with wooden carvings and silver jewelry. Racks of clothing swayed in the breeze. Becky was sitting near the alligator slide, talking to Sergeant Perez.

The door behind me slid open. "I've had it. I'm done." Susan stormed out, slamming the door behind her.

"Trouble at home?"

"Of course, there's trouble at home. There's always trouble at home. Three daughters, each spoiled, each wanting her own way all the time. Each resenting the other for using her hairbrush or borrowing her t-shirt or leaving her towel on the bathroom floor. Tim is oblivious. Last night, he called to ask how long to boil the water for pasta. I'm not kidding. Elle, sorry. I need to scream. I just do."

I waited. She didn't scream. She stood at the railing, leaned against it, seething.

"I came on this trip to get a break from the grind. A rest. A vacation. But ever since we arrived—forget the break-in and the deaths, they're just icing on my cake. I've been working nonstop to meet a filing deadline on a messy case that's up for appeal—something that should have been done by someone else before we even came down here. And when I haven't been working on the case, I've been fixing Jen's meals, washing her hair, rubbing her feet, listening to her whine, being her goddamn mommy."

She was right. "Sorry. I should have helped."

"No. You shouldn't have. None of us should have. Look, if Jen can afford all these surgeries, then she can afford to hire help. I should have told her so, but I'm a chump."

I didn't answer. Becky, Jen, and I all relied on Susan more than we should, a habit leftover from childhood when Susan had been our babysitter. She had always been the most stable of us, our rock. Probably it had never occurred to Jen to have anyone but Susan take care of her as she recovered.

Familiar salsa music started up below us; Chichi announced a contest of water putting. I looked down. Sergeant Perez stood alone near the waterslide. Becky wasn't with him.

"I have to get out of here, Elle." Her voice was low, like rumbling thunder. "If I don't, I swear, I'll hurt somebody. I'll break dishes. I'll throw furniture. I'm claustrophobic. I've been inside for three days. I haven't even been to the beach." She stared out at the shimmering water, the rolling waves.

I felt terrible. Susan was right. I'd been completely self-absorbed and insensitive. "Susan, I'm so sorry. I should at least have given you breaks and stayed with Jen."

"Never mind. Becky didn't offer either. She's caught up in the love affair of the millennium. No, it's my own fault, Elle. I didn't say anything. I was martyr Susan, taking care of everyone else and boiling inside."

"But now, you've finished working on your case."

"Yes. And Jen's up and walking." She looked out at the ocean. "So from now on, for these next few days, I'm going to have fun. Tomorrow, I'm finally going to the festival I told you about. The Virgin of Guadalupe. It's the last day. Come with me if you want. Right now, I'm heading for the beach." She turned to me. "Join me?"

"My leg," I reminded her. "I can't go in the water yet."

"Right. Sand probably wouldn't be good for it either." She opened the sliding door to go inside, but Becky came rushing out.

"You guys," she panted, "what the hell's going on? That policeman wanted to know who had my room key. I told him nobody. I had it the whole time. He seemed to think I had something to do with your break-in. He can't think that, can he?"

"Hi, Becky," Susan moved around her and went inside. "I'll be at the beach."

"Wait, Susan, I'm serious. Does he suspect me?"

"Don't be ridiculous, Becky. No one would ever suspect you of anything that didn't involve a man. Elle, I'm taking your sunblock." She went inside.

Becky was on her tail. "Wait. You're going to the beach? Alone? The sergeant told me we shouldn't go anywhere alone."

"It's broad daylight. Besides, I won't be alone." She pulled off her t-shirt, passing Jen on the way to the bedroom. "There are dozens of people by the water. And lots of sharks and jellyfish to keep me company."

"I'm serious," Becky kept after her.

Susan wheeled around, her eyes flashing at each of us in turn. "Listen, all of you. I'm going to the beach. And I'm going now. You guys do what you want, but I'm strongly advising you: Do not try to stop me." With that, she unhooked her bra and stepped into the bedroom to change.

Becky looked at me wide eyed and baffled. "What's with her?"

Jen passed us, beads of sweat swelling on her forehead. "Just two laps left." She was breathing hard. "Damn. How long is Susan going to be gone? When I'm done, I'll need someone to help me with my bath."

Becky mumbled something about needing to get back to the pool, but she stayed where she was, looking trapped. I sunk onto the sofa, elevating my leg. Like it or not, we'd inherited bath duty.

~

I didn't understand how Susan had managed alone. Bathing Jen was at least a two-person operation. She was able to sit in a tub of shallow water, but her belly and breasts were supposed to stay dry. She needed help washing the rest of her, especially her back and hair. Becky knelt on the floor and scrubbed toes. I sat on the side of the tub by her head and shampooed.

"Never do this," Jen moaned. "Nothing is worth being this sore and helpless. I don't know what the fuck I was thinking."

Becky fixated on Jen's feet. "You need a pedicure. Your nails are a mess."

"I know. Susan made me an appointment. Someone's coming up to do it tomorrow. Ouch. Elle, don't rub so hard!"

My leg throbbed. I had to put weight on it to balance as I leaned over her. I took my hands off her hair and straightened up, resting it, repositioning.

"Why'd you stop, Elle?"

Becky looked at me, shook her head, no, advising me not to say anything.

Jen craned her neck, looking at me with her bandaged nose and purple breasts. "I'm covered with shampoo. Aren't you going to rinse me?"

Was I? I wasn't sure of anything except the urge to drown her.

"I'll do it," Becky stepped over, pulling me away from the side of the tub. Taking my place.

Jen sat back, closing her eyes, allowing Becky to massage her scalp.

"I feel like I haven't seen you guys all week," Becky said. "And I keep thinking it's my fault Elle nearly drowned. If I'd been there, it wouldn't have happened."

"That's bull. The police say someone attacked her. If you'd have been there, they'd have attacked you, too."

"No. If Elle hadn't been alone, they wouldn't have come near her."

Maybe she was right.

"On the other hand, Chichi says we're lucky it happened this week, during the festival."

"What festival?" Jen rubbed a wad of suds off her forehead.

"The Virgin of Guadalupe." I said it with authority, as if it was common knowledge.

"What the fuck is that?"

I knew only what Susan had told me. Mostly, that she didn't want to miss it.

"It's a big thing down here," Becky explained. "People come from villages and cities all over, carrying candles. They walk for miles to get to Puerto Vallarta. Last night Chichi and I saw people walking on the highway, holding their candles."

"What is it? Something about Christmas?"

"No, it's for the Virgin Mary. Chichi says she picked this location as a holy site. She appeared on a hill around here early in December—I don't know exactly when. Hundreds of years ago."

"What did she do? Announce herself? I mean, how did they know it was her?"

"Only one guy saw her at first. A peasant. She was surrounded by light. That's how he knew who she was." She poured a cup of water onto Jen's hair, rinsing it. "She told him that she wanted a church built there to honor her."

"Careful, it's in my eyes." Jen closed her eyes, reached out of the tub. "I need a towel."

I handed her a washcloth. She held it to her face and lay back again.

"So that's it?" I asked. "They built the church and celebrate the anniversary?" It didn't seem like much of a story.

"Well, first they made her prove that she really was the Virgin Mary. She did some miracles, like healing a sick person and making flowers grow in bad soil. But then she made her image magically appear on the peasant's cloak. There are icons of that in the church." She rubbed conditioner onto Jen's scalp. "So, anyhow, they built the church to honor her and every year people come to celebrate the anniversary of her appearance. It's a big party that lasts for days. It ends tomorrow, December 12. Chichi says that during the festival, the Virgin Mary blesses and protects the people who come to visit her special site. Which is why Elle came back to us."

"What do you mean 'came back'?" I asked.

Becky froze for a minisecond, then refilled the cup with water. "Nothing. Just that the Virgin Mary blessed you."

"She means you were fucking dead and they revived you."

"What?"

"You weren't breathing," Jen said from behind the washcloth. "You had no heartbeat. You got CPR."

I'd known that, but hadn't labeled it as actually being dead. I'd thought of it as near death. Close to the line, not across it.

"The devil didn't want you, so he sent your ass back to us." Jen wiped suds out of her ear. "Thank God I wasn't there. I'd have had a heart attack and needed CPR, too."

"Trust me, Jen, if you had a heart attack, CPR wouldn't work; the devil would not let you go." Becky rinsed out the conditioner.

"Don't be bitchy, Becky. It doesn't go with your body type."

I took a seat on the toilet lid. Wow. I'd been dead. Why hadn't I comprehended that? After all, CPR is only given to people without a heartbeat, which means they're pretty much dead. How long had my heart been still? Melanie had said I'd looked dead when she pulled me out of the water. So, probably a few minutes? And Charlie. I'd seen Charlie. I'd been with him. Talked with him. Held him.

That must have been while I was dead.

"Elle?"

Becky's hands reached out to me. Oh, for a towel? I handed one to her, and she went on chattering as she helped Jen stand up.

"So, anyway, we're both miserable about how fast the week is going. I can't believe that a week ago, Chichi and I didn't even know each other. We're talking about him coming up to Philly in January."

Not a surprise, really.

"Becky, don't be an ass," Jen wrapped herself in the towel. "You don't believe me, but guys down here are always prowling for rich American—"

"Really, Jen? You're going to criticize Chichi while I have your hair in my hands?" She was twisting it, making a turban out of a towel.

"I'm just saying. Don't be fucking stupid."

"You don't understand. We love each other, Jen. He's not like that."

"He's a man, isn't he? They're all like that. Ouch, Becky!" Her eyes opened. "What the fuck was that?"

"Sorry," Becky smirked, "my fingers got caught."

Jen pushed Becky's hands away, and I wondered if she was right. Maybe all men were like that. Charlie had been. And Alain was married but having affairs. But surely, Susan's pudgy Tim could be trusted. But how about Norm? He was slick. He owned businesses and athletic teams. Real estate. Did Jen trust him?

"What about Norm?" I asked.

"I'm sorry?" She gaped at me. "Norm?"

Oh. Again, I'd missed part of the conversation. They weren't talking about men anymore.

"Well, what you said about men. Norm's a man," I said. "Is he the same?"

"Don't be fucking ridiculous. Norm's Norm."

Oh. "So you trust him?"

"What kind of question is that? He's my goddamn husband, Elle. Of course I trust him."

Really? "So you've told him about your surgeries?"

Jen turned away. "I'm thirsty. Do we still have lemonade?"

"You haven't told him?"

"You're so damned annoying, Elle."

I was damned annoying? Really? I took a stance, ready to

tell her what she was, but Becky put up a hand and led Jen out of the bathroom. I stayed, wondering about Norm, and drained the tub. Then I looked in the mirror, trying to remember those lost minutes. Imagining myself dead.

What if I hadn't come back? I thought of my second graders. When my leave of absence was over, someone would replace me and take over my classes. Probably, the substitute who was covering for me now. I saw her at my blackboard, demonstrating an addition problem. Would my death have changed anything? Would it have caused even a tiny a ripple in the universe?

I didn't think so. The world would be perfectly fine, unchanged without me. My three best friends would talk about me now and then. The kids in my class would grow up. Life would go on.

"Don't tear yourself down," Charlie scolded. "You're important. To me, you're everything. You're the love of my life."

"Go away," I told him. "You're not here."

"No?" He kissed the back of my neck, raising goosebumps.

"Stop it!" I swatted the spot he'd kissed, startling myself. "Get lost, Charlie. You had your chance and blew it."

I had to get a grip; was talking to an empty room. I splashed water onto my face. Took deep breaths.

When I came into the living room, Becky was still going on about Chichi, how romantic he was. How musical his voice, how sensitive his nature, how fascinating his thoughts, how chiseled his abs. How she loved to watch him dance. How she could watch his hips all night. She mimicked his moves. I wanted to shake her and scream: shut up. Enough! Could she not go ten minutes without talking about Chichi? Could she not spare us the elaborate details about his body parts? His kissing techniques? His passion? I wanted to slap her. I pictured it, the pinkness in her cheek. The sting of my palm.

Charlie whispered in my ear. "You're jealous, Elf. Don't be. You have me."

I was jealous? Of Becky? No. I refused to think so. I was just tired of her being so absorbed in her love life. And I was tired of Jen, too. Her constant whining about being uncomfortable. Good God, she'd had surgery. What did she expect? No, I was fed up with both of them. Didn't they realize that two women had died there? Hell—apparently, three—*I'd* died there, too. But they went on as if none of that had happened. I couldn't bear to hear them, the lilt of their voices. My nerves were frayed. I went to the kitchenette, got them each a glass of lemonade. Then I hurried to change into my bathing suit. Even if I couldn't get my leg wet, I could still sit by the pool. Or at the bar. Anywhere but near Becky and Jen.

I grabbed my sun hat, my beach bag and felt a wave of guilt. Why was I so angry? What was wrong with me?

I stopped, remembering what Susan had said. Before fleeing to the beach, she'd said she'd wanted to hurt somebody. To break dishes and throw furniture. Susan had expressed the same welling hostility that I felt.

I sat on my bed, trying to sort out what was happening. Normally, the four of us got along effortlessly. We teased each other about our quirks. We laughed about our differences. We tolerated and balanced each other—hell, we *liked* each other. So what was happening to us? We'd been fine until we'd taken this trip. Until we'd checked into the suite. Oh God.

Could the hotel be toxic? Could it be haunted by hostile spirits, ghosts who enjoyed messing up the living?

Really? Was I seriously considering that? I didn't believe in ghosts, not even Charlie. He was a product of my emotions, part of my grieving process. But ghosts? No such thing. Madam Therese surfaced in my mind, shaking her head, insisting, "Spirits are drawn to you. You know this to be true."

No. I didn't know about spirits. But I did know that if I stayed in the suite much longer, I'd do something drastic. Maybe I'd be overcome with an irresistible urge to break things like Susan. Or cut my leg off like Greta. Or fall off the balcony like Claudia. I called out that I'd be down at the pool and hurried out the door like a condemned person escaping execution. Limping, I hopped down the hall in such a fury that I almost crashed into a maid and apologized without stopping.

She didn't seem to notice. As I passed, she looked the other way.

~

I burst out of the hotel, into the sunlight, and kept moving. I didn't look for Susan. Didn't look around. Hiding behind sunglasses and under my sun hat, I didn't stop until I got to the far end of the pool, and lugged a lounge chair away from the cluster to a quiet spot under a palm tree, facing the ocean. I wasn't alone; people surrounded me. But if I closed my eyes to the wandering vendors and ignored the blaring music, I could pretend I had a smidgeon of solitude.

Until someone landed beside me on the lounge. I jumped, startled.

"Señora," Luis's butt touched my thigh.

"Luis?" I moved my legs away.

"I startled you?" His eyes sparkled. "I only want to tell you how glad I am to see you here. I was there, señora. I saw you and your friend boogie boarding. And then I saw you, lying so still, I would have sworn you were lost to us." He took my hand, placed a gentle kiss on my palm. "It is a miracle that you survived. People are saying that the Virgin of Guadalupe herself saved you. I believe it."

I pulled my hand away, felt the tingle of his lips.

"When we last spoke, I was harsh." He leaned over me, speaking softly.

Yes, he had been. But so had I.

"When I saw you lying there on the beach, lifeless, I felt a terrible loss and sorrow. It made me want to clear the air between us." He smiled shyly, his head bent, eyes timid. Timid didn't fit Luis, he looked uncomfortable, like his clothes were too small.

"Thank you." I didn't know what else to say. My shoulders tensed. I felt trapped.

"Are you feeling all right?" He looked at my leg.

"My lungs are still sore." Why was I telling him that? What did he want? Was he still stalking Melanie? Was I next?

"And your leg?" His hand landed on my knee, gently massaged it.

In a whoosh, I saw a face blurred by water. Felt something pulling me under, tugging me down. Heard Sergeant Perez declare that my wound hadn't been accidental, that someone had stabbed me.

And now, Luis was reminding me that he had been there. Oh God. The attack had happened right after I'd confronted him. Had he been afraid I'd get him in trouble? That he'd lose his job? Had he attacked me—tried to kill me? Was he here now not to wish me well, but to see if I'd recognized him in the struggle?

My mind raced. Luis's hand was still on my knee. I removed it. Tried to tune in to what he was saying.

"No hard feelings between us. We all make mistakes."

Was he apologizing? Admitting that he'd attacked me? He was too close, invading my space. Trying to intimidate me. If I edged farther away, I'd fall off the lounge chair. I was cornered by his body, couldn't get up unless he moved. I put a hand on his chest, pushing him away. He wrapped his hand on mine as if embracing it, but squeezing it tight.

"What do you want, Luis?" I wriggled my hand, trying to free it. "Let go."

He tightened his grip.

I stopped fighting him, wincing. "Did you stab me? Was it you?"

"Me?"

"In the water—was it you?"

"Señora, how can you ask that? I came over here to wish you well." He looked into my eyes. Dropped my hand. "Look, I don't want trouble. Not with you or your *amiga loca*. I am trying to make peace." His eyes blazed.

By strangling my hand and cornering me? Anger bubbled in my belly. I wanted to slug him. "Go away, Luis."

He held my eyes another moment, then he reached over, lifted my hat, and planted a kiss on my forehead. "Be careful, señora," he whispered. "I would hate to see you come to more harm."

He replaced my hat, stood and, as he walked away, I realized that my hands were gripping the side of the chair. When I relaxed them, my fingers trembled, not in fear but in anger. I felt steam hissing from my ears, fire blazing in my blood. Aching for a fight, I got up and hobbled around, dragging my chair away from the palm tree into the sunlight. Maybe the sun would bake my brain, burning away the hostility that swirled inside me. Maybe it would turn my rage to ashes.

~

I looked around, unable to settle down. People frolicked in the pool or lay on lounge chairs, tanning and reading. Some sat at the bar, drinking and noshing under the thatched roof. Others wandered out to the ocean. I could see a bit of it beyond the fence. Light sparkled on the water. Swimmers dotted the surface. A blanket of clouds draped the horizon, but along the shore, the sun was hot and relentless. Susan had my sunblock. Damn. Never mind. I closed my eyes, felt anger pulsing through me, untargeted and generalized.

I'd been angry when I'd left the suite. And then Luis had agitated me more: The tightness of his grip on my hand, the intrusion of his lips on my forehead—his breath on my face. I should tell Sergeant Perez about him, have him investigated. But for what? Being at the beach when I'd been pulled out of the water? Bothering a woman who'd vandalized his room? Or maybe for squeezing my hand and kissing my forehead?

Actually, everything Luis had said had been completely benign. He hadn't threatened me. Quite the contrary, he'd expressed good wishes and concern. But there had been unspoken threats, hadn't there? The edge in his voice, the flash in his eyes. I wasn't sure. Maybe I was in such a hostile mood that I was projecting my own anger onto others. Maybe Luis had simply meant to wish me well. He was a rascal, not a killer. Besides, he'd had no motive for attacking me. If he'd wanted to attack someone, wouldn't it have been Melanie?

Unless he was obsessed with her and saw me as an interference.

I had to stop. Had to think peaceful thoughts. Serene thoughts. Like going to the festival. I imagined people celebrating, seeing banners of greens, reds, and yellows so bright that they vibrated. The sun baked my chest. I tried to exhale tension, inhale peace. Exhale negative energy, inhale healing. But voices around me grated like squawking crows. Music pounded my skull. My muscles tightened and, finally, I stopped trying to control my mood. I allowed myself to be as ornery and belligerent as I wanted. I closed my eyes, saw a woman with scrawny fists, heard her call for vengeance. Maybe she was me. After a while, maybe I slept.

"Something beautiful for you, señora?"

I opened my eyes, saw a human form haloed by a golden corona. An angel?

"I have rings, bracelets. Have a look."

Oh, not an angel. A vendor standing in sunlight.

"No, gracias."

"Oh, go ahead," a woman stepped out of his halo. Melanie. "Buy something."

"Melanie. Oh, wait." I moved my legs, started to stand up. "I don't know how to thank you. You got me out of the water. You saved my life." I stumbled on my sore leg, but managed to reach out and hug her. She was my height; our breasts crushed in the embrace. I felt how bony she was. Not an ounce of flab.

The vendor watched, gave up hope, moved on.

"I honestly thought you were gone, Elle." She ended the hug, studied my face.

Apparently, I had been.

"You were limp in my arms. Deadweight."

I remembered fighting, trying to swim away. When had I gone limp?

"You had no heartbeat. It was totally scary." She looked me over, head to toe. "So, you're feeling better?" She pulled a lounge chair over to join me. Plopped onto it. "Tell me, what do you remember?"

What did I remember? "What do you mean?"

"Like, do you remember getting hit in the head? Or being under water? Were you scared?"

My lungs started aching. I remembered them burning, ripping, exploding. I remembered flailing. I remembered Charlie.

"It must have been awful," she went on. "I can't imagine what you went through."

"Well, it's over." I didn't want to talk about it. "I was lucky you were around."

"That's what friends are for, right?" She turned to face me. "You got better really quickly."

I had? "I don't know. My lungs are still sore. And my leg— it'll take some time."

"I mean emotionally." She paused. "I saw you just now. With Luis. Right there." She pointed to the palm tree. "You two looked pretty intense. It was touching."

Oh Lord. I didn't want to revisit Melanie's issues. "He was just wishing me well."

Her lips curled. "He was practically on top of you."

With all that had happened in the last day, I hadn't thought about Melanie and Luis. Or how she'd reacted the last time she'd seen me talking to him. But now that I remembered, I didn't have the patience to deal with her issues. Hell, I didn't have the patience to deal with my own.

"Melanie." I lay back on my lounge chair. Anger welled up in my chest. "Drop it. There's nothing going on—"

"You don't need to cover it up, Elle. You're welcome to him.

I just don't get it though. After everything you know about him—how can you be attracted to him?"

"Melanie, just stop." My voice was steely. "We have nothing to talk about."

She tilted her head. "Whatever. But be warned: Luis is bad news. As long as he's in your life, you never know what will happen."

It occurred to me that, despite my warning, he might have done something else to her. After all, the world hadn't stopped when I'd gotten hurt. "Is he still bothering you?"

She readjusted her sunglasses. "He's lying low. Now that he's got you to distract him."

"He does not have me."

"He still watches me, but he's more careful. I think he got my message."

Right. Her message. Destroyed clothes and a soiled room. I recalled Luis's grip on my hand, the threat in his eyes.

"You really think Luis is dangerous?" I asked her.

"Hello? Elle? What have I been telling you? The guy's a psycho. He comes off all charming, but he broke into my room. He threatened me. I've told you all—"

"Melanie. He was there. On the beach."

She tilted her head. "What?"

"When you pulled me out."

"Well, you drew a crowd. Lots of people were there."

I sat up and faced her. "Melanie, listen. What happened to me wasn't an accident."

She rolled her eyes. "That's ridiculous."

"No. It's true."

"You're saying some guy on a boogie board crashed into you on purpose?"

"I'm saying somebody tried to drown me. That didn't work though. I fought too hard, so the guy tried to stab me—maybe he wanted to cut my throat. The only reason he got my leg was that I managed to kick him away."

Her jaw hung open. "You're making this stuff up. It wasn't like that. It's crazy."

"Listen. It's not crazy. The attack happened right after I cornered Luis and told him to leave you alone. Remember? You saw me with him. I was telling him that I knew what he'd been up to, and that if he didn't leave you alone, I'd go to his boss."

Her mouth remained open, a gaping hole.

"And then, an hour later, when you pulled me out of the water, he was there. On the beach. What a coincidence, right? When is Luis ever on the beach? He's always up here by the pool."

Melanie's hand covered her mouth. She watched me with wide eyes.

"I have no proof. But, seriously, Melanie, you said he's bad news, but how bad? Do you think it could have been him?"

"Oh my God," she said again. And then again. Her hand came away from her face. "You're accusing Luis?"

"I'm just asking what you think."

"What the hell's wrong with you, Elle? One minute, you're practically screwing the guy in public, and the next, you're accusing him of trying to kill you."

I hadn't done either. "I wasn't practically screwing Luis."

"Really?" She scoffed. Her back straightened. "Because I saw you myself."

"No, you didn't."

"Are you seriously going to deny it? I know what I saw."

I didn't answer, wasn't going to engage further with her; it was pointless.

"I can't deal with this." She stood, grabbed her bag. "You brought it on yourself. I warned you about Luis, didn't I? I told you about him. How obsessed he gets. What he's done to me. But you got involved with him anyway. And now you're asking if I think he's dangerous? Now? As if I haven't said a word all week?" She leaned over my chair, backlit by the sun. Her face was a blob of darkness. "One more time. Here's what I think,

Elle, I think that if you're smart, you'll get far from Luis as fast as you can, before it's too late."

She strutted off toward the deep end of the pool, disappearing into a crowd of swimmers lining up for water basketball. I covered my face with my hat and lay back, trying to make sense of what had just happened. Deciding that, even if she'd saved my life, Melanie was exasperating and that I should avoid her. Luis, though, troubled me. After I'd cornered him about Melanie, he'd been afraid that I'd report him to management and he'd be fired. But had that made him mad enough to kill me?

I peeked under the brim of my hat and saw him with Chichi, dividing the swimmers into teams. Handing out red-and-yellow jerseys. Joking with a matronly orange-haired woman, touching her shoulder. He seemed untroubled, normal—even happy. But psychos had no consciences. They could seem happy no matter what they'd done.

Melanie sat across the pool from the teams, dangling her spindly legs in the water, lifting her tanned face to the sun.

I lay back again and closed my eyes. My thoughts buzzed hornetlike. Insistent. Threatening to sting. I tried to sort them out. To find connections between a veiled intruder and an underwater attacker. Between those two and Claudia. Between Claudia and Greta. But I linked up nothing. My mind was tangled, my lungs raw and tender, and my stitches itched and ached in the heat. I listened to basketball players shouting in the water. Vendors offering wares. Waiters taking orders for sandwiches and drinks. People surrounded me, but I was alone behind my eyelids where a shadow kept reaching for me in dark water. And Charlie kept showing up with open arms, bursting with light.

≈

By the time Alain came to get me for dinner, I'd been desperate to get away from the hotel. I'd spent the afternoon spinning my thoughts into fist-size knots. When I'd come back to the suite, I'd wanted to talk about my encounters at the pool. Instead, I'd been ambushed by a dizzying flurry of Susan. Restored by her day of freedom and the beach, she'd gone to the market and bought ingredients for chicken quesadillas, guacamole, salsa verde, and flan. She'd danced around the kitchenette, humming, pouring fresh sangria, toasting our trip and our friendships, clattering dishes, chopping peppers. Susan had been on a high. By contrast, Becky had paced like a caged animal after her few hours with Jen. After chugging a glass of sangria, she'd dashed off to meet Chichi.

Jen's dour mood permeated the suite, thickening the air, snuffing out light. I'd felt equal parts guilt for abandoning Susan and relief to get away.

"Go," she'd insisted. "It's fine. I'm fine. I even got some tan today. See? She pulled down her tank top, displayed the color of her chest.

"Sure, go. Have a great fucking time." Jen had sulked, gulping sangria. "You and my damned quack of a doctor. Just forget about me and how miserable I am and how I can't feel anything around my nipples and haven't been outside of this damned hotel in days."

"Remember, Elle, tomorrow we're going to the festival." Susan danced to some melody in her head.

"Really? A festival? I don't believe you ungrateful leeches. While you're off doing the samba, I'll probably die of complications."

"You don't have complications." Susan mashed avocado.

"The fuck I don't—I have fever and scars and bulbous purple lumps—"

"I've said it before: you chose to do this to yourself." Susan shrugged, poured herself another drink. "It's your party, you can cry if you want to." She hummed the song, refusing to let Jen interfere with her mood.

"Why don't you go outside, Jen," I'd suggested. "Sit by the pool. Lots of patients are out there with those things on their noses."

"On their noses. But what about the rest of me? Don't you

get it, Elle? I can't wear clothes. I'm too sore. Am I supposed to go out bare assed?"

Susan and I'd exchanged glances. Jen had wardrobe choices: a robe. A beach cover-up. A loose sundress. The fact was that she didn't want any of those because she refused to appear in public. Jen wouldn't let anyone, even strangers, see her at anything less than her best.

Susan sang and cooked. Jen sulked and complained. And, as I showered with my leg wrapped in plastic and got dressed for dinner, I tried to forget about death and threats and knife attacks by focusing on Alain. His resonant voice. His posture—it made him seem taller than he was. His twinkling eyes. But focusing on him made my hands jittery. My chest fluttered, lips tingled. Damn. What was I doing, getting attracted to him? What was the point? I was going to be there for only three more days. Why was I even bothering to spend time with him? Clearly, we had no future.

Forget the future, I told myself. Wasn't it enough to enjoy the present? After all, I'd already died once. Who knew when I'd die again? Meantime, shouldn't I live every minute to the fullest?

Stop rationalizing, I argued. This situation has nothing to do with life or death or time. It has to do with: You think he's hot. When you're around him, you want to touch him. Something about the aristocratic way he crosses his legs. The ease of his gait. The slope of his back. The surprising softness of his kiss.

I had to stop. Or no. I had to prepare. What would I do if he wanted me to stay the night? Would I? My insides did somersaults as I considered possibilities, pictured his home. The carved wooden door. The bright décor. For better or worse, for tonight, I would push aside Jen's gloom, Melanie's warnings, Sergeant Perez's concerns. I would reject all thoughts of intruders, attackers and murderers, and give my attention to Alain. On being with Alain. And who knew? With Alain's help, I might even fend off spirits of the dead and quell the dread simmering in my belly. At least for the evening.

~

He met me in the lobby, greeted me by closing his arms around me and kissing my lips. And then we were in his car, the top down again. The wind too noisy for conversation.

The restaurant was stucco, and we sat in a courtyard under the open sky. The host greeted Alain, exchanging embraces, speaking in Spanish. Alain was known there. He introduced me; the host was polite but not attentive. To him, I was merely Alain's dinner date du jour.

Maybe so. But this was my jour. And Alain was someone I could talk to. As soon as the host left us, I began. "I'm so glad to be here, Alain. I needed to get away from the hotel."

He raised an eyebrow. "What happened now?"

Oh dear. Was I whining? Because his tone implied that I was. It was the tone a man uses when his wife complains about the kids acting up or the dryer breaking down.

"Nothing in particular." I put on a smile, stopped talking. Made myself extra cheery. "It's just nice to have a change of scene."

The waitress came by with a wine list. Alain ordered something. I didn't know what it was, red or white. I didn't care. Still, I wondered why he hadn't asked my preference. When she left with his order, he folded his hands. Seemed oddly distant.

"Is there any word about your intruder?"

"No. They think it's someone who has access to keys. Maybe a maid."

"Yes, that's what Jen said."

I nodded, said nothing. I knew that the topic of Jen was off limits, so I didn't mention her mood. Didn't suggest that he prescribe doses of fresh air and walks outside. Didn't say a word. I looked at my hands.

"You seem preoccupied."

Did I? Funny, because I thought the same about him. I

shrugged, felt him assessing me. "It's been a troubling few days."

"Indeed." He leaned back in his chair, casual. Crossed his legs. "It occurs to me that you said you saw a maid in Greta's suite when she died."

Had I told him that? "Yes."

"Perhaps that maid is the same person who entered your suite. What do you think?"

I didn't know. Why would a maid want to hurt me or anyone else? "Perhaps." Perhaps? What an odd, old-fashioned word. I never used it. But Alain had, so I did, too. I shifted in my seat, less comfortable than I'd expected to be. Sensing reserve in Alain's demeanor. Demeanor. Also an odd word for me. But there it was. I kind of liked it. Thought about it as I avoided Alain's unwavering eyes.

"How's your leg?"

"Better."

"And your breathing? The edema?"

"Better."

His questions were quick, impersonal. It seemed I was a patient, and he was examining me.

The wine came. Red. Good. Not Syrah, but still it was red. He tasted it, nodded approval. The host poured it for us, speaking Spanish and laughing with Alain. When he left, Alain uncrossed his legs, leaned forward. Picked up his glass.

"Elle, a toast." He met my eyes. "To a fascinating woman. And to our time together. This night belongs to us." He took a long, slow sip, holding me with his gaze.

I flushed. Sipped quickly, felt naked. "Alain," I wasn't sure what I was about to say, but his mood had changed so abruptly that it disarmed me, and I felt the need to lighten the moment. But he stopped me.

"No—in a moment. First, I have something to say to you. I owe you an apology."

He did?

"I underestimated you, Elle. You know only a little about me. But one thing you do know is that although I am married, I am a lonely man. I sometimes stray."

I looked at my wineglass. Put a hand on the stem.

"I thought that you would be another of the women with whom I share—moments. I thought, this woman will be here for only a short time. Why not make that time memorable for her, and at the same time make my own nights less lonely? Nothing complicated. Win-win, as they say."

My face sizzled. And my neck. The people at the next table weren't talking. Were they listening in?

"Alain—"

Again, he stopped me. "But I was wrong. The incidents this week—the killing of Greta. The death of Claudia. The losses have hurt me badly—more than I would have anticipated. Nevertheless, I went on, proceeding as usual. Then, you were attacked. You nearly died, too. And I realized that, although I've known you for only a short time—although we haven't even become lovers yet, I was devastated. I spent the day in a stupor. The thought of something happening to you, of losing you, Elle, I couldn't bear it. It would be too much."

I looked at him. Saw the candlelight swimming in his pupils. Tears welling around his lids.

I didn't know what to say. Once again, I was doubtful. Were those tears real? For me? He didn't know me well enough to care that much. It just made no sense that this elegant, internationally known plastic surgeon who'd bedded wealthy world-class beauties would be smitten with a middle-class moderately attractive on good days second grade teacher from Philly.

He peeled my hand off my wineglass, held it in both of his. "I care about you, Elle, more than I expected to. More than I can explain."

I looked down at my lap.

The host came over again, asked a question. Got an answer. Alain released my hand, straightened up. "I ordered for us. I told him to make whatever was fresh. I hope that's okay with you."

I gulped wine. Glanced at Alain, the candles, the couple nearest to us. The sky.

"I've offended you? Frightened you?" He smirked. Amused at my discomfort?

"Maybe. Yes, a little." I sipped more wine.

"I want only to be honest with you. To me, this isn't just another affair."

How could he know that so soon? I thought of Becky, convinced after four days that Chichi was her soul mate. But Alain wasn't like Becky; he was worldly, seasoned. Accustomed to seducing women far more fetching than I. And to letting them go.

"Talk to me, Elle," he said. "Tell me what you're thinking."

I chewed my lip, fiddled with my wineglass. Stalled. "I'm thinking that it's exactly what you said. The trauma of the week. The pain of losing people. You're hurt and vulnerable. You need someone. I happen to be here. So you're turning to me."

He tilted his head. Raised his eyebrows. "Makes sense. But—"

"You said you want to be honest. Okay. I'll be honest, too. I'm attracted to you."

He nodded, eyes twinkling. "Good."

"But—honestly? Don't patronize or placate me. Because I have to admit I'm not sure why you're attracted to me. Your work—you're with stunning women. Every day, all day you're surrounded by women with perfect faces and bodies. Like Greta—you yourself said she was exquisitely beautiful."

He didn't patronize or placate. He watched me, waiting for me to finish.

"I'm not like those women."

"Okay, I understand." He nodded, looking me over. "You compare yourself to those other women and wonder what I see in you. Is that right? Well, I'll tell you what I see. I see a real person. Not a construct. Not a canvas that I've painted. Not a sculpture that I've molded. You aren't a work of art, Elle. You're a genuine, natural woman, complete with flaws and smile lines and, pardon me for saying it, an imperfect nose."

Again, blood rushed to my face. My hand rose to my cheek.

"You are not my creation. You are your own person. Frankly, I haven't met a woman of character like yours in years. You're resilient—refusing to be intimidated even by an attempt on your life. Brave enough to risk your own life trying to rescue a stranger. Loyal to your friends. You inspire my respect, rouse my curiosity. It isn't merely superficial physical beauty that draws me to you, my dear Elle—it's you. The person you are. The aura you radiate."

Wait. What? He could see my aura? Was it bloody and stained? Did he see spirits there?

"Your physical imperfections actually enhance your appeal. Your features are defined, but also slightly asymmetrical, making you uniquely, jarringly attractive."

My what? My physical imperfections? Had he just outright told me that I wasn't beautiful like his other women? And that my lack of beauty was what attracted him? I replayed his words. Yes. He had managed to say—to my flawed face—that my imperfect appearance was an asset. Wow. The man was slick.

Dinner arrived. Grilled fish again with some kind of spicy salsa. Fried bananas for dessert. Lots of wine. We talked as we ate. I mentioned going to the festival. He was relieved that I'd be away from the area, thought I'd be safer in the city. And he raved about Puerto Vallarta, the cathedral. The story about the Virgin Mary appearing to a peasant. I wandered, thinking about spending the night with him. Candlelight and wine influenced my thoughts, and his voice vibrated in my chest, steady and deep, rhythmic, with traces of far away places.

What's the point? part of me asked. You're leaving. You'll be just another one of his conquests.

Maybe, I answered. But also, he will be one of mine.

I considered going back to the suite. Lying in bed alone,

watching for a veiled night prowler. Waiting for dawn. Feeling dismal.

Even so, I knew I should go back, shouldn't leave Jen and Susan alone.

But Susan would bolt the door. They'd be fine. I hoped.

Because by the time we finished the fish, I'd decided. The rest of the meal was a matter of letting myself appreciate the light in Alain's eyes and the line of his jaw. I stopped resisting, stopped analyzing events before and after, savored the anticipation of the night ahead.

~

The radio was on, playing Latin rock. The cab driver wended his way through traffic, weaving, changing lanes. Susan and I sat in the back.

"So?" She sat sideways so she could see me better. Blinked impatiently.

"So what?"

"Really? That's how it's going to be?"

"How what's going to be?"

"Elle, please don't waste time playing dumb." She crossed her arms and looked out the window, harrumphing.

I tapped my foot to the music, watched the back of the driver's head.

"After you called, Jen went apeshit." Susan's tone was somewhere between scolding and tattling.

Her comment didn't surprise me. I'd assumed that Jen would not react well to news that I was spending the night at Alain's. "She didn't say anything about it this morning."

"She didn't speak to you this morning."

True. "So she was really mad?"

"I don't know. It's like you took something away from her. With Jen it's about pecking order. She doesn't want you to outrank her with him."

"Outrank? But she's just his patient."

"Just? We're talking Jen."

Right. Jen and her territory. I'd have to deal with it. "So, besides Jen's tantrum, the night went okay? No bad dreams or break-ins?"

"Of course not." She waited a beat, watching me. "Elle, are you seriously not going to tell me about it?"

Was I? "Why are you so curious? You don't bug Becky about her nights with Chichi."

"Becky tells us every detail, play by play. I never have to ask." She waited.

The driver braked suddenly, leaned on his horn. "This guy—is he crazy? Does he want me to hit him?" He sped up, swerved, cutting off the offending vehicle. Muttering in Spanish.

Susan was still waiting.

"It was nice," I told her. I turned away, looked out the window, avoiding her.

"Nice?"

"Yes." I supposed it had been, despite the awkwardness of all the firsts. First time being naked together. First time touching and exploring. First time being touched and explored. I'd felt self-conscious, like a "before" picture in a plastic surgery ad. I'd been the woman with too small a bust and a not tight enough butt. Alain had seemed not to notice. He'd been attentive, affectionate. Well acquainted with female anatomy. Skilled in manipulating it.

"So that's it?"

Why was she persisting? "Susan, there's nothing to tell. He's kind and thoughtful. And I spent the night with him. It's a fling."

She didn't look away. "You don't have flings, Elle."

Damn. Why did my friends know me so well? "So? Maybe I'm starting to."

"Okay. As long as you're okay about it. I've just never known you to be casual about relationships. And, since we're leaving in a few days—"

"I'll be fine. I know what I'm doing." I didn't, of course. I hadn't a clue. I knew that in Alain's life, I was one in a long line of women. In my life, he was only the second man who'd turned my head since Charlie. The first that I'd slept with. And sleeping with him had been complicated—not that Alain had done anything wrong. Physically, we'd been fine. Alain's body was attractive—compact and muscular. His hands were smooth and deft. His kisses deep. Our parts had fit together comfortably. The whole experience had been fine.

But emotionally, I'd had a disconnect. I hadn't wanted to, but the whole time, I'd kept thinking of Charlie. Missing Charlie. Telling myself that it had been a year, that it was time to have sex again. Time to be with a man who was still breathing. I told myself to enjoy Alain and the no-strings opportunity and get past the first time, end my celibacy. And so, I had. I'd had sex again. Mission accomplished.

Susan was still watching me.

"What?"

"You seem—I don't know. Different."

"It's been a crazy week. I haven't had much sleep."

She nodded. "Yes, it has been. How's your leg?"

"Healing. It doesn't hurt."

She put a hand on my arm. "Elle, I'm only asking questions because I care about you. But I'll stop interrogating. You know that if you want to talk about Alain or anything else that happened this week, you can."

Before I looked at her, I knew what expression was on her face. The concerned furrowed eyebrows, the softly intense stare. "Thanks, Susan. Yes. I know."

"Good." She sat up straight, smiling. "Now. Today we are leaving everything behind. Here's the deal: we won't talk about any of it. Not Jen, not your drowning or the dead women or Sergeant Perez or Becky and the love of her life. None of it. Today, it's just you and me and the Virgin of Guadalupe. We're on vacation. Agreed?"

"Agreed." It sounded glorious.

"Good. No exceptions. Unless you want to tell me about last night."

I snickered, shaking my head. Susan finally turned away, checking e-mail on her phone. The music played loudly, the bass so low that it vibrated our seats. Reminded me of Alain's body pounding against me. He'd been tender, appreciative. His eyes had been sad. And I'd wondered, while I was missing Charlie, if Alain were missing his wife. Probably he was; I'd felt them both, Charlie and Mrs. Du Bois, intruding on us, crowding the bed. A few times, I'd opened my eyes and looked around, almost certain I'd see one or both of them there. Even when I hadn't, I'd felt pathetic rolling around with Alain, as if we weren't really together but merely pretending. As if, having lost what we'd wanted, we were making do with what we had.

∿

The cab dropped us off near the boardwalk. It was long, crowded.

"It's called the *Malecón*." Susan had a guidebook with her. She practically skipped ahead, pulling me into a stream of strolling people. Some were foreigners like us, but most seemed to be Mexican families in town for the celebration. Girls in colorfully embroidered skirts or many-tiered festival dresses, boys in trousers and white shirts, intricately woven serapes draped over their shoulders or sombreros dangling on their backs. The joy around us was palpable—joy? When had I last felt joy? I tried to remember. Charlie popped to mind, of course. Our wedding. Had I felt joy that day? Did it count as real joy if it was later sullied by betrayal? Never mind. Joy was around me now, and I could sense it. Watch it. Marvel at it. People had gathered from all over. The city was decorated, vibrant. Hosting a party for the Virgin Mary. I wanted to blend in, lose myself in the celebrations.

But Susan had a different agenda. Consulting her travel book, she marched me along the *Malecón*, pointing out inanimate objects. Announcing that Puerto Vallarta was famous for sand sculptures. Indeed, the beach alongside the *Malecón* was covered with them, intricate and ornate. I stopped to stare at one, a sculpture of two men at a table playing cards and drinking beer. It was too realistic. Couldn't be made out of sand—had to be models in sand costumes. I watched, waiting for them to move. But, of course, being sand, they didn't.

When I looked up, Susan wasn't there. I looked ahead, across, behind. Saw throngs of people in every direction, but no Susan. I turned back toward the sculpture. Maybe she'd gone to get a closer look. Nope. I scanned the beach. Didn't see her.

Oh, great. We hadn't been in town for twenty minutes, and I'd already gotten lost. Faces flowed past me, families swarmed by. I waited for Susan's to emerge from the crowd. Wondered how long it would take her to figure out she'd left me behind. Watched the crowd. So many people, none of them Susan. Finally, thought I sensed her behind me and spun around, startling a sun-wrinkled woman with dyed blonde hair.

"Sorry," I said.

She kept moving.

I looked around. I'd been sure Susan had been there, that she'd been about to touch me.

"Elle?"

But she couldn't have been. She was calling from about ten yards up. I scurried to catch up. Listened to her scold me about getting separated, not paying attention.

We walked on. My stitches felt itchy and tender, but I didn't care. A man passed by in full Aztec: silver, black-and-red collar piece, scant loincloth, bracelets, and headdress. His thighs and shoulders glistened in the sun. I touched Susan's arm, laughed at her eyes traveling up and down, taking him in.

As we walked, Susan talked about Puerto Vallarta's art, pointed out famous statues. Elongated half-human, half-alien figures, facing out to sea. A boy riding a seahorse. Three leaping dolphins. A ladder leading up to the sky, being climbed by squat, robed figures with outstretched arms and wide triangular heads. Susan narrated the name of each piece, recited the artists' names. I didn't pay attention. There was too much else to focus on. Children with wide brown eyes. Musicians. Vendors. Living statues—people coated in makeup textured like golden sand, standing motionless along the beach: A Santa Claus. Flamenco dancers. A fisherman.

And no guardrail. No fences. One side of the *Malecón* simply dropped off to the sand; the other was lined with shops, clubs, and restaurants. According to Susan, it went on for fifteen blocks. Apparently, she intended to walk all of it.

Every few blocks, though, I had to stop.

"Your leg?" Susan looked up from the guidebook.

It had begun to throb. The doctor had said to stay off it for a few days; I'd managed one. I sat on a cement wall around a cluster of palm trees, elevating my leg while Susan stood beside me, searching her guidebook for festival details.

"I can't remember what time the actual parade starts." She rifled through pages. A little boy dressed like a gaucho ran into her, grabbed onto her leg so he wouldn't fall. She didn't react, accustomed to children. "I think it's three. Maybe four. We have time to wander. If you're up to it."

We wandered. For hours. Despite the complaints of my leg, we explored souvenir shops and art galleries. We looked at paintings, carvings, jewelry, ceramics. Susan bought an abstract alpaca weaving for her den. It was bulky, but they wrapped it with a strap so she could carry it like a shoulder bag. In one shop, women were gluing tiny colored beads onto ceramic pieces in Aztec patterns. I bought a small jaguar mask with beads of orange, red, yellow, and green. The shopkeeper said that the jaguar was the most powerful of all animals, that the mask would protect me.

We walked past an amphitheater and a row of historic arches into El Centro. I moved carefully, watching the ground;

the streets were speckled with gaping potholes. I was avoiding one when Susan grabbed my arm and pointed ahead.

I looked up, stopped walking. The orange brick and terra-cotta of the Our Lady of Guadalupe cathedral towered over us, its famous golden crown shining in the sun. Susan resumed her role as tour guide, reviewing the history of this place, the meaning of that. I tuned her out as she dragged me up the steps and shoved me through the crowd toward the door. I pressed against others, squeezing my way through, bumping a fleshy bosom, a sweaty arm. Feeling that I didn't belong there—what business did I have shoving my way into a church? I was hot and tired and wanted to sit down. But Susan was behind me, her hand on my back. Pushing. People were on all sides of me, surrounding me, closing me in. I couldn't breathe, couldn't move in any direction. But Susan kept the pressure on, moving me forward and, finally, we crossed the threshold, entering the cathedral right in the middle of a Mass.

I slowed down, startled. The commotion was gone. I looked around. The air glowed. Light filtered in through stained-glass windows, glittered on a gilt-trimmed altar. There were white and gold statues of Jesus and images of Mary. Festive wreaths and icons. Burning candles. Stations of the cross. A throng of people crammed together, cushioned against each other like a single massive being. I felt its heart beating around me—inside me, and when I looked up, I saw golden light under the arches, felt its steady warmth beckoning. I imagined floating up weightlessly into that light, looking down at the people calmly wedged together, breathing together, praying together. The voices blended, cushioned, and comforting.

Susan grabbed my arm, ready to move on. Bumping people with her alpaca bundle, she tugged me out of the cathedral, down the steps, and onto a nearby plaza filled with booths selling everything. Cakes. Costume jewelry. Cotton candy. Pies. Purses. Baskets. Blouses. Trinkets. Toys. The opposite of the cathedral, the bazaar erupted with commerce, smells, and noise.

I had to get off my leg. Saw no place to sit. Just booth after booth.

Susan found a fountain across from the plaza and planted me there with her alpaca. I sat, hoping my leg would stop throbbing. Thinking about the feeling I'd had in the cathedral. I wasn't Catholic, wasn't even religious. So what had happened in there? Maybe the architecture had affected me. The height of the domed ceiling. Or the light.

Madam Therese shook her head. "Don't pretend you don't know. You were unburdened in the church. You felt calm and light because no dark spirits clung to you there. They couldn't go in."

Really? Where had that thought come from? Besides, how could spirits—if there were such things—how could they burden someone? Weren't they weightless? Did they even have mass? Why was I even thinking about this? I wasn't going to; I refused to let thoughts of spirits intrude upon my day. I reached into my bag, took out the jaguar mask. Admired the beadwork, the colors, and patterns. Felt someone behind me, also looking at it. A shadow hovered over me. Lingered.

Ignore it, it's nothing, I told myself. Just a passerby. Don't be so jittery. Stop taking it personally just because someone is standing behind you—it's mobbed here. People stand behind everyone.

Still, I was uneasy. I rewrapped the jaguar and placed it in my bag and slowly turned as if casually looking around.

The moment I turned, someone darted off into the crowd. I didn't see who it was, just a ripple of bodies reacting to it, a disturbance like a pebble dropping into water. I watched the crowd close in again, absorbing the newcomer. And I rubbed my arms, feeling chilled, even though the day was hot. Even though the shadow had disappeared.

～

Already that day, I'd felt someone watching me twice. Twice, I'd felt alarmed.

I was too nervous. Oversensitive. Imagining things. And I'd

been that way for a while. Even at Alain's house, I'd had the feeling someone was slinking around in the shadows. I was too on edge. Needed to get over my jitters and have fun.

Fine. I would get over my jitters. I sat, getting over them, studying the spot where I'd seen the crowd ripple. Still getting over them, I picked up my bag and Susan's alpaca and headed over there.

"Señora, take a look. I have good deals for you." A vendor leaned out of a booth at the edge of the marketplace, holding up a pair of wool gloves.

"No, gracias." I turned away, then back. "Can you tell me— just now, a minute ago—did you see someone go by? Maybe running?"

The man shrugged. "I see many people, señora." He waved the gloves at me. "These are hand knitted with an authentic Aztec pattern. A very good value. Or maybe you'd like something else?" He put the gloves down, held up a scarf.

I kept going, entering the crowd in the marketplace, looking over people's heads, up and down each aisle. I passed one booth, another. My leg nagged at me, Susan's alpaca was heavy, and I didn't know who I was looking for. Probably not that heavyset woman buying a tablecloth. Or the one with a little girl, trying on necklaces. Maybe that man? He wasn't buying anything, just standing next to a booth with his arms crossed. What was he doing there? Had I ever seen him before? I moved closer, trying to remember. He seemed oblivious to his surroundings, bored. A woman came up to him, held up a baby dress for his approval.

Not him.

Of course it wasn't him. It wasn't anyone else either. I'd probably imagined the whole thing. No one had been following me here or watching me at Alain's. People were here to celebrate. Their actions—standing near me, running into a crowd— had nothing to do with me.

I went back and sat at the fountain, watching for Susan. As-sessing people who walked by. Trying in vain to regain the sense of peace I'd found in the cathedral. Telling myself to be calm. Reminding myself that we were far from the hotel and safe from whatever dangers might lurk there. Nobody here knew us; no one had reason to follow or harm us. But when Susan showed up with lunch—enchiladas, pie slices, drinks, and fruit salad—I was still on guard, searching for a shadow. She approached from behind. And I wheeled around swinging, almost slapping the food out of her arms.

～

"What the hell?" She juggled tortillas and drinks, barely catching them before they dropped.

"Sorry." I helped her gather up the food. "I thought you were somebody else."

She cocked her head. "You what?"

"I mean I thought someone was sneaking up on me."

"You thought someone was sneaking up on you?" Coming from her, the words sounded ridiculous. She unwrapped an enchilada.

"Never mind. I was wrong. It was just you." I opened a bottle of lemon soda. I was thirsty and hot. And I didn't want to annoy Susan by referring to events of the week.

"Elle, why would anyone sneak up on you?" She took a bite, talked with her mouth full. "Nobody even knows you're here. We're miles from the hotel. And besides, we agreed to leave all that—"

"I know. I shouldn't have said anything. Leave it alone."

"Relax, Elle. Nobody here is going to follow you or harm you."

I nodded. Drank. Thought about Sergeant Perez, warning us not to go anywhere alone.

As if she could read my mind, Susan said, "What Sergeant Perez said about our safety applies in Nuevo Vallarta, not here. Here we're anonymous tourists. Nobody knows or cares what happened there."

I nodded again.

She passed me an enchilada, bit off another chunk of hers. "So, what happened? Why did you think someone was following you?"

Really?

"Forget it, Susan. It was just my imagination. Nerves."

Susan chewed. And she talked. She went on about how beautiful the cathedral was. How she couldn't wait for the parade. How there were a lot of potholes in the streets and we'd have to be careful to avoid them later, in the dark. How glad she was to be away from the hotel and, oops, how she was sorry for mentioning it and breaking her own rule.

Susan chattered, almost giddily, all through lunch. I rested my leg until Susan proposed visiting some more art galleries until the parade, and we set off, following her guidebook, winding through narrow streets that led away from the festival.

"Thank goodness," she said. "It's great to be away from the crowds, isn't it? I can finally breathe."

Really? The farther we got from the center of town, the more exposed I felt and the tighter my chest got. Breathing was an effort.

But Susan was unfazed. She talked about the exciting art in the area. The symbolism, the variety of media and traditions. I half listened, noting that the sun was getting lower in the sky, thinking that we should return to the crowded plaza. Picturing sheep wandering from the herd, becoming prey for wolves. But I didn't say anything. I tagged along with Susan but, like a stranded ewe, I watched for predators. An hour later, I didn't care if I never entered another art gallery in Mexico or any other country.

"I need to go back," I told her.

"Why? Your leg?"

Fine. I'd blame it on my leg. "I shouldn't be standing as much as I have been."

"Sorry. I lost track of time."

We finally headed back toward the plaza. I hurried, not sure why. Except that the winter sun would soon set and it would be harder to recognize danger in the dark.

~

An endless stream of torches and candles flowed through the darkness. Banners identified each section of the procession: families, neighborhoods, villages, organizations, businesses. They wove through the streets and ended up at the cathedral, paying homage to the Virgin of Guadalupe, singing, reciting prayers. Elaborately decorated floats portrayed the Virgin and her appearance to the peasant Juan Diego. Pickup trucks carried bands or DJs playing music, or overflowed with family members of all ages. Some groups were composed by gender. Men reading prayers or carrying placards. Women dressed in splendor, singing as they marched.

People paid homage to Aztec traditions, too. They dressed as jaguars and deer. One man wore feathers, head to toe, might have been an owl. There were people with faces painted gold, wearing white robes and metallic headdresses, rayed like the sun.

Susan and I didn't talk—we couldn't. There was too much noise, too many people, too much movement. We stood on a street corner near the cathedral, pedestrians swarming by or straining to see over each others' heads. Torch flames flowed past, glowing like burning lava.

Charlie whispered, "Remember, Elle? Torches on the beach?"

I turned toward his voice even though I knew he wasn't there. And despite myself, I saw the beach and the torches. In Negril. A band played reggae, and people danced—hell, *we* danced, couldn't help it. The night pulsed with music and life and rum and ganja. Charlie's tanned face glimmered in the torchlight, his body radiated heat.

"This is how life should be." His voice penetrated the music, and he pulled me close. Spoke into my ear. "We need to stress less, celebrate more. Are you happy, Elf? Because right now, here with you, I'm the happiest man alive."

We stepped away from the others, into the dark. Beside the

ocean, under the open sky, to the rhythm of steel drums, just outside the light of torches. Charlie and me.

Yes, I remembered.

But Charlie was gone. And the memory was useless. Why did everything always revert to Charlie and the past? Why couldn't I spend even one lousy evening without him intruding and spoiling it? Hell, he'd shown up even when I'd been in bed with Alain.

"But the parade is better with me here," he spoke into my ear.

"Go away," I said.

"Come on, Elf. It's a parade. What fun is it if you're solo?"

"I'm not solo. I'm with Susan. And what are you doing here? Why aren't you with that woman on the beach?"

"What woman?"

"I saw you."

"It wasn't me."

"Señora?" A man standing beside me tried to move away, but the crowd closed him in. He watched me warily.

Of course he did. I'd been talking to myself. Who would want to stand next to a woman who talked to herself?

I needed to move. Felt closed in. Couldn't stand there anymore. Maybe the crowd would be less dense farther from the cathedral. Besides, I was thirsty, wanted a bottle of water. I turned to Susan to tell her. But the person I faced wasn't Susan. I looked behind me, saw a gray-haired woman with a wide nose. Turned to the other side. Faced the man who was still watching me, pretending not to. Beyond him was a woman with a young boy. His wife and son? Maybe. But no Susan.

I rotated, looking behind me, diagonally, to the side. Saw dozens of strangers in every direction. How had I gotten lost again? We'd agreed not to separate. So where was Susan? She'd been standing right next to me. She wouldn't have simply walked away, would have brought me along with her. Or, at least, told me where she was going.

Unless, maybe she had and I hadn't heard her. Maybe I'd

been traveling with Charlie in Jamaica, not paying attention. That must have been what happened. Susan had probably needed to go to the bathroom. Had probably said so. Would probably be right back.

With difficulty, I reached into my bag, found my phone. Sent Susan a text. "Where are you?" If her phone was on, and if she was paying attention to it, she'd get the message and answer. But with all the commotion, she might not notice it. I watched my phone for a reply. Finally, I dropped it back into my bag.

I waited. I stood where I was, watching the parade, but not really seeing it anymore. The parade rumbled ahead like a landslide, unstoppable, powered by its own momentum. Bystanders teemed moblike, dense, sweaty, passionate. Ignitable. I was closed in, breathless. I stood on tiptoe, looking for Susan. She'd be back any moment. Probably she'd come from behind and startle me again, and I'd swing around, almost knocking her down the way I had earlier. Probably, she'd say that she'd told me where she was going. "Didn't you hear me? Were you 'pulling an Elle' again? I swear, you miss half of everything around you. It's a wonder you can function."

We'd laugh and take in the parade for a while. Stop someplace for dinner. Find a taxi to go back to Nuevo Vallarta.

Except that I was doing it again. Wandering in my mind. I looked around again. Didn't see Susan.

Obviously, she'd come back here, to this spot. So I couldn't leave. I waited, watched.

Susan didn't come.

Maybe she was lost? I rotated, scanning faces. Not seeing her. The crowd rippled and swayed. A throng of women paraded by, carrying candles and singing hymns. A low, unnamable fear rumbled in my belly, insisting that something was wrong.

No. Nothing was wrong. I was overly sensitive, still jumpy from the trauma of my near—or actual—death. Susan and I had simply gotten separated. She'd show up. I kept searching the crowd. In the dim light of sunset, I saw couples, families with young children, young men dressed as gauchos. Guys with Aztec masks, guys with their faces painted silver. No one familiar.

So where was she? What was keeping her? She could have found a bathroom and been back twenty times.

Unless she was waiting in line for a toilet somewhere. I needed to be patient. My leg grumbled. The old woman next to me leaned her body against mine. I felt her dampness, smelled stale sweat, tried to step away. Bumped into the man who'd been warily eyeing me. Apologized. I had to move, couldn't stand there any longer. I turned, edging away from the curb. The crowd shifted, spongelike, letting me press my way through. Finally, I emerged from the mass of flesh and leaned against the darkened window of a shop. Took a breath. Smeared sweat across my forehead. Looked around again for Susan. And came face-to-face with a demon. Not a real demon, just a demon mask. The kind worn by Mexican wrestlers, made of black-and-white Spandex. Just another guy in costume for the fiesta.

But even in the dark, I could tell that this demon's eyes were fixed on me.

⁀

Adrenaline jolted through me. But I didn't panic right away. I broke eye contact and turned the other way. Probably the mask was no big deal. People wore all kinds of costumes to the parade, even if a demonic wrestler seemed out of place at a festival for the Virgin Mary.

Damn. Where was Susan? And why had a masked stranger been giving me the evil eye? Maybe he hadn't been. Maybe I'd inadvertently bumped into him. Maybe he hadn't even been looking at me, and I'd just been in his line of sight while he'd been looking at someone behind me. I turned to see who that someone might have been, saw the empty windows of a closed shop. Okay. So maybe he had been looking at me. I might have overreacted to his glare. Slowly, trying to look casual, I glanced back at the wrestler.

He was still watching me. Openly staring. Except for the white parts of the mask, he was dressed all in black, his back to the parade. I looked away again as if I hadn't noticed him. After all, he had no reason to bother me. And it wasn't as if he could with so many people around. A chain of chattering women snaked past me, holding hands, making their way through the crowd, talking in Spanish. When they'd moved on, I looked up, didn't see the wrestler. He was gone.

I searched the area where he'd been. Looked right and left. No wrestler. How could he have disappeared in just a few seconds? He couldn't be far. I could feel him watching me, hovering like a cloud. Like a fist aimed at my head. With my back against the shop windows, I inched toward the cathedral. I'd felt safe there earlier, protected by its warm stained glass and golden crown. Maybe I'd be safe there again. The parade ended up there; there would be security officers. Police. And no one would harm anyone right in front of the cathedral, not with the icon of the Virgin of Guadalupe watching. Not on her festival day. Would they?

Not that I was really in danger of being harmed. I knew better. It was just my nerves. Just Susan's unexplained absence. Just the mobs of people in the darkness and the endless stream of torches that reminded me of those carried by the frenzied peasants storming Frankenstein's castle.

Just my overactive imagination.

Still, I was alone. Unsure what to do. And I knew I'd feel better close to the cathedral with its gleaming golden crown. I kept edging my way along the shop window, looking over my shoulder. Worrying about Susan, wondering where the hell she was. Watching people around me. Nearing the end of the building, looking around for a wrestling mask. Seeing none.

Approaching the jam-packed intersection, I stepped forward, away from the building toward the curb.

"Stop!" The voice was urgent, not more than a whisper. Was it Susan? No—a deeper voice. Charlie? I hesitated, and before I could figure out who was stopping me, I saw movement around the corner of the building. Glimpsed a black-and-white mask. And a glint of metal, reflected in torchlight. Before I could register the images, the blade whipped around the corner of the shop, aimed at my heart.

~

I leaned back, dodging. The thing swiped at my tank top, grazed my collarbone. I spun around, diving into the crowd, pushing arms, shoving shoulders, darting through tiny spaces. I divided couples, separated little children from their moms. Stepped on feet without apology. I kept moving, tearing ahead, driven by instinct. What was it called? The fight or flight response? I'd chosen the latter, was doing my best to fly. Once or twice, people pushed back, resisting, and I had to veer left or right. But I kept going, not pausing to look behind me, not daring to stop.

I don't know how long I charged through the choking crowd, opposite the clamoring, swelling parade. But at one corner, it occurred to me that I'd move faster if I turned off the main street, away from the congestion. At the next intersection, I turned up a side street. People gathered there, but not as densely. I had room to move, time to catch my breath. I stood in a shadowy doorway near a streetlight, looking out. Saw no sign of the man in the mask.

Who was he? Why had he tried to stab me? I was panting, my leg felt battered. My tank top clung to me, soaked. Was I sweating that much? I looked down. My white tank top was wet, but not with sweat. Damn. A dark stain had streamed down my chest. I put a hand over my collarbone, felt a raw sting. And sticky, oozing skin. Whoever he was, the masked creep had cut me. The bleeding wasn't bad, but I had to stop it. I reached into my bag, found a pack of tissues. Wadded them up, stuffed them under my bra strap. Told myself to be calm. I'd be all right. It was just a minor flesh wound. But what if I hadn't heard that warning and hesitated? The knife would have plunged deeper, aimed better. Would have sliced my throat.

What the hell? The fact slowly sunk in. I'd been stabbed. Again. That made twice. First in my leg and now this. Somebody was trying to kill me. But why?

My jaw tightened. My hands clenched into fists. Rage bubbled up from my belly, surged through my chest.

And then it hit me: What about Susan? Oh God, had this maniac done something to her?

In the street, a dozen faces turned toward me. My mouth was open. Had I let out a sound? A curse or a wail? Could they see the bloodstains on my once white tank top, the drops on my khaki Capris? I put up a hand, reassuring them, and when they looked away, I sunk down in the shadows, holding in a howl.

❦

Think. Just think. Figure this out. Do not panic. Think. Just think.

I repeated this as a mantra, a rhythm to breathe by.

My mind was a scrambled mess, hopping in circles, not completing thoughts. I heard snippets of garbled sound—trumpets and drums, singers praising the Virgin. I crouched in a shadowy doorway, smelling heat and sweat. Was the sweat mine? Was the heat the smell of blood? And, oh God, where was Susan? Was she all right? I closed my eyes. Of course she was all right. She was probably looking for me. Annoyed that I'd wandered off. I saw her, standing with her hands on her hips, scolding. Felt a pang, a slash of fear. Opened my eyes.

Think. Just think. Get control. My leg screamed at me, angry that I'd run on it. Never mind. It could wait. I had to focus, prioritize. People strolled by. Didn't notice me. None of them wore masks. I peered out of the doorway, looking up and down the street. Who was the guy with the mask? Was he still chasing me? Had I lost him? Was I safe?

I waited, watching. Wadded fresh tissues against my wound, replaying what had just happened. Someone had tried to kill me. Would have, if someone hadn't—Oh God. Someone had warned me. I heard it again: "Stop!" Recognized the voice.

Could it really have been Charlie? Had Charlie saved my life?

Had I really just asked that question? Charlie was dead, couldn't warn me about anything. He was a figment of my imagination, part of my grieving process.

So, then who had told me to stop? It must have been my own mind, sensing danger. Again, I saw the glimmer of steel in torchlight, heard the whoosh of a blade slicing through air, felt a stab of fear: Where was Susan? Was she okay? How was I going to find her?

"Get up." The voice again.

Charlie? I gazed into the dark street. Tried to find him. Saw strangers in fiesta clothing.

"Get moving. You're a sitting duck here."

A sitting duck? Really? I'd never in all our years together heard Charlie use that phrase. I was tired. My sore leg didn't want to support me. My chest stung. I didn't want to wander around lost in the dark. And then I remembered: I had a phone. I'd call Susan, find out where she was. We'd arrange a place to meet and get the hell out of there.

I almost giggled with glee, delighted with myself and my clever solution. I opened my bag, rooted around, found my phone caught in a rip in the lining. Took it out. Punched in Susan's number and, waiting for the call to go through, looked into the street.

As if on cue, a guy wearing a wrestler's mask was heading in my direction. And he was looking right at me.

∿

I ran. I didn't remember getting to my feet or how long ago I'd done that or how many corners I'd turned. I just ran. My lungs were raw, my breath ragged. The last time I'd looked around, I'd seen the mask glowing in the dark, maybe twenty yards behind me. How far was twenty yards? I wasn't sure. Maybe it had only been ten yards. Damn. That was pretty close. My legs pounded cement, wanted to explode. I tore ahead, dodged potholes, ducked into narrow streets, crossed a footbridge, veered to the left at a corner and then left again, doubled back. The streets were empty here, deserted. Everyone was at the cathedral. I ran.

Crossing a street, I thought I heard violins. Kept running. They got louder. And it wasn't just violins—I heard a cello, too. Or wait—a string quartet? Clearly, I was imagining it—hearing a mirage. Could you hear a mirage? Or maybe I'd passed out and was dreaming. Or the guy had caught me and killed me, and I was hearing music in heaven. But in heaven, would my leg still hurt? Would my chest? I ran on. The music got louder. And I heard voices, too. At the end of the block, around the corner, I saw clusters of people dressed all in white. Like angels.

My throat was dry. I had no strength. I headed for them—maybe there were fifty. Maybe more. The musicians performed on a platform set up in the middle of the street. I dashed behind it, crouched low beneath the cellist and peered out. No one took notice of me. Waiters in white passed out hors d'oeuvres to guests also in white. There were carts offering food and drinks. People mingled and laughed. Where the hell was I?

I wondered if I could blend in. The khaki of my Capris was light, even if not quite white. And, except for the blood, my tank top was—no, obviously, I was underdressed. Couldn't fit in there. But maybe someone would help me.

"*Por favor*," I said, but no one looked my way. Didn't they see me?

Could I really be dead?

"You're not dead," Charlie assured me.

He ought to know. The last time I'd been dead, he'd come to get me. I remembered him holding me, lying beside me. He'd been wearing white.

I was panting. And painfully thirsty. I eyed a waiter, thought about grabbing a drink off his tray. What would he do? Would he chase me away? I couldn't run anymore.

"*Por favor*," I tried again, louder, motioning to him.

He glanced at me, seemed surprised to see me. Did a double take. I must have looked ghastly.

"*Agua?*" My voice was rough. Dry.

He must have pitied me because he walked over to a cart and returned with a bottle of water.

"*Gracias*," I grabbed it. Opened it. Was drinking before he could say, "*De nada*."

He asked me something in Spanish. I didn't understand. Maybe he wanted to know what I was doing there, crouched behind the musicians' platform. Or why I was wearing a blood-stained top. Or if I needed help or a doctor. Or the police.

Of course. "*Por favor*," I asked him. "Do you speak English?"

He shook his head, no.

But surely, someone there would. Someone would get help for me.

The waiter pointed to my shirt, said something else. A white-clad guest motioned to him and, gesturing to me that he'd be back, he moved away, attending to the party.

Gradually, my breath evened out, my pulse slowed. I looked around and saw, beside the bandstand, a sign in Spanish: "Fiesta Blanca." White Party. What was a white party? Was it only for Caucasians? Or was white just the color of the week, among a series of blue, yellow, and red? Did they have purple parties? Mauve? I didn't get it, didn't know who these people were, what drew them together. Had no idea what they were celebrating. But since they were all in white, anyone wearing a color or pattern would stand out. I hunkered behind the platform, alert. Watching for someone in black, wearing a wrestling mask.

～

I was still holding my phone. Oh God—Susan—I'd been calling her when I'd started running. Had she answered? Could she have been hanging on all this time, hearing the frantic soundtrack of my chase? I put the phone to my ear, covered the other so I could listen.

"Susan?"

Nothing. Not a sound except the party voices and energetic music vibrating the platform, shaking the air.

Okay. It was okay. It didn't mean anything that she wasn't there. I'd probably disconnected the call as I ran. I'd call again. Pressed redial. Strained to hear the ringing of the phone.

And then, amazingly, Susan's voice. "Elle? Where the hell are you?"

For a few seconds, I couldn't speak. I was choked with relief. Susan was alive. She'd answered her phone.

"I've been looking all over for you," she went on. "I told you I'd be back in a minute."

She had?

"What in God's name possessed you to wander off? I've missed half the parade trying to find you."

Even with my ear covered, the music interfered. I couldn't hear everything she said, but it didn't matter. Hearing her voice, knowing that nothing had happened to her was more important than whatever she was saying.

"Susan," I began. "I'm not at the parade—"

"I can hardly hear you," she said. "Just tell me where you're standing, and I'll come get you."

I tried to explain, had to huddle under the bandstand and shout to hear myself over the quartet. Couldn't take the time to tell everything, but told her about the attack.

"A wrestling mask? What, like the Green Hornet?"

The Green Hornet? I had no idea. "It's Spandex. Black and white, and it glows in the dark."

"So what makes you think he's coming after you?"

Was she kidding? "Susan, he's following me. He has a knife. He cut me."

"He cut you? Why didn't you say so? Are you all right?"

"For now—as long as he doesn't find me."

She was silent for a moment. "Where are you? I'll get the cops. We'll come get you."

The cops? "Susan, the police will keep us here all night, asking questions. Once the mask is off, I won't be able to identify this guy. Please, no cops."

"But they can look for him. Spot the mask."

"I just want to get out of here."

I pictured her sputtering. "Just tell me where you are."

Where was I? I looked around. Tried to see a street sign, a landmark. Saw glowing faces, white gowns, sparkling smiles, the glitter of liquor bottles. The backside of the platform.

I didn't know.

"Ask somebody."

Okay. Good idea. I'd ask. Cautiously, I got to my feet, looked around for the masked attacker, and, not seeing him, approached a young couple.

"Excuse me," I put a hand up. "Do you speak English?"

They nodded, yes. Didn't seem alarmed to see a smudged woman with mussed hair wearing a bloodstained top. They told me where I was: Not far from some main roads, Ignacio L. Vallarta and Aquiles Serdán. I had to spell the names a few times as Susan couldn't hear me with the din of the parade.

And so, I stood up, inhaling. I'd survived. I was getting out of here, going back to Nuevo Vallarta. Time had passed since I'd seen the masked maniac. He'd lost me, must have given up. I was safe. All I had to do was go to a nearby corner of two main streets and wait.

I walked slowly, limping, trying to figure out who'd attacked me. Why someone wanted to hurt me. Probably, it was connected to Greta and Claudia. But how? Did I share some kind of profile with them? Or did I know something about their deaths?

The party went on behind me. The quartet played Vivaldi as I thought about Greta, revisiting what I'd overheard the night of her death. Luis had been there. And so had Alain. Had one of them killed her and now come after me? But if so, why here? They'd each had plenty of chances back in Nuevo, didn't have to come all the way to the parade, dress up in a costume, and chase me. I pictured the masked man. Had he been as wiry as Alain? As broad-shouldered as Luis? I wasn't sure. The light had been dim, and he'd been dressed in black. All I'd noticed was the mask. I hadn't focused on his size; I'd focused on my speed.

And now, just a block from the party, I was exposed again. Alone, in the open. My skin tingled, alert. What if he hadn't given up but had just waited at the perimeter of the party for me to emerge? The music flitted through shadows, and the shadows held me, asked me to dance. I spurned them, clinging to buildings, trying to fade into the darkness. I assured myself that no one was breathing on my neck, it was only the night air. I told myself that no knife was aimed at my spine, but I looked over my shoulder just to be sure. No one was behind me.

Madam Therese whispered, "You sense them, don't you? It's your aura. Spirits are all around you."

No. It was not my aura. It was my imagination. My dissociation. My mind travel. I had to get a grip. Susan would be here any minute. I looked over my shoulder again, checking. No one was there. Of course no one was. Just as no one was waiting at the corner with a knife. And no one lurked in the doorway of the building ahead. I moved on, left foot following right, the night air barely daring to enter my lungs. Susan was coming any minute. And I wasn't alone. A party was a block behind me. And a couple passed, heading that way. The woman turned to me, wishing me a good evening. *Buenas noches.* I smiled back, but when the streetlight shone on her face, it revealed skin dangling in shreds, and she raised a fist. "*Quiero la venganza!*"

I slammed my back against the wall of a building. Obviously, that hadn't happened. I'd imagined it. Oh my God. I was hallucinating. Having a psychotic break? This was more than just stress. I wasn't simply imagining or remembering or doing another "Elle." I was seeing things that weren't there. Had there even been a couple? Had I just changed her face? Or had I completely created them? I took a deep breath, made myself turn and look.

The couple was still there, walking, arms around each other, oblivious to everything but each other. The woman's white skirt swayed with her hips. If her face was in shreds, neither of them seemed to notice.

Okay. My imagination was affecting my perceptions. Distorting things. But I hadn't imagined the demon mask—I had the knife wound to prove it. Now, I had to stop picturing ghouls. Take control. Focus. Had just another half a block to go to get to Aquiles Serdán. Had to breathe. I was fine. Susan was on the way. I mumbled to myself, told myself soothing things. The night would be over. I'd be fine.

"Elle." Someone called from the corner ahead.

Thank God. "Susan?" I picked up my pace, didn't look where I was going, stepped into a pothole. Went down hard, twisting my ankle, sprawling at an angle, letting out a shriek as stitches in my leg strained.

Damn. I grimaced, pushing myself up off the ground. Assessing the damage.

"Are you okay?" Susan called. "Wait, I'm coming." There was something hungry in her voice.

Pain roared in my leg, my hip, my elbow. The palms of my hands stung. Blood trickled from my knife wound. But I clamped my jaws and answered. "I'm fine."

I climbed to my feet, started limping ahead as if to meet my friend, but at the narrow alleyway between us, I faked to the right, racing away from the dark figure who might or might not be wearing a mask, but who definitely wasn't Susan.

∾

In the darkness, I didn't see the dead end until I almost flattened my face against it. Even then, I had the absurd hope that I'd escape. That at the last moment, I'd find a skinny passageway between buildings. Or an open door. But no exit magically appeared. I was trapped in a dank, dark cul-de-sac. No time to think. No time to do anything except spin around and charge the person chasing me. Fine. I'd do that. I took a breath, counting to three before my counterattack. One—

I never got to two. Someone grabbed my hair, yanked my head back. Pulled me down. I reached behind me, trying to break my fall, hoping to rebound and come back up, but my attacker was too fast. He came around and shoved me, pouncing onto my midriff. Landing hard on top of me. Pushing the air out of my lungs. Did he plan to rape me before he killed me? I swung my fists, pummeling the masked head. He grabbed my wrists, pressing them down. I bucked and rolled, trying to knock him off, but he rode my ribcage like a rodeo champ. We struggled that way, with Vivaldi playing faintly in the background, until, finally, I wriggled an arm free, grabbed the mask and yanked it off of him.

Except that he wasn't a "him." Thick tresses of long hair burst out of Spandex, concealing the attacker's face. Even so, I could tell who it was.

"Melanie?" I croaked.

She pulled a knife from its sheath, aimed it at my face.

"Man, it was hot under that damned thing," she swung her hair. "Thanks for pulling it off."

What the hell? I tried to grasp what I was seeing: Melanie straddling my torso, waving a knife. So that meant that Melanie had been the one chasing me around Puerto Vallarta, wearing that bizarre wrestling mask? And Melanie had swung at me, cutting my collarbone, trying to cut my throat? Clearly, yes. She had. But why? Just two days ago, she'd rescued me from the ocean. She'd saved my life. So why was she brandishing a knife at me, trying to end it? And, just as puzzling, how had skinny, spindly Melanie bested me in a fight?

"Don't move, Elle. If you move even a pinkie, I'll stick this in your eye." She said this matter-of-factly, pointing out a simple if-then relationship.

I didn't have to think long; I decided not to move even a pinkie. I made my body go limp, hardly daring even to breathe. In the dimness of the alleyway, I watched her toy with the tip of her blade.

"You shouldn't have betrayed me, Elle." Her voice was lilting, almost singsong.

Betrayed her? "I never—"

"I took you into my confidence. I trusted you. And what did you do?"

I tried to remember. What had I done?

"You snuck behind my back and hooked up with Luis. Did you really think I wouldn't find out?"

Find out? "Melanie, I don't know what you're talking about."

"Well, it's obvious. You tried to steal him from me."

Steal him from her? I blinked, trying to make sense of what she was saying. "But you hate Luis—"

"I saw you with him, Elle." Her voice got lower, more urgent. Her knees tightened against my ribs. "Did you think I wouldn't see you? Did you think I'd sit by and passively watch you taunt and mock me? After everything I told you?"

"Melanie, but you told me that you—"

"Cut the bullshit, Elle. I know who you are and what you've done, you hypocritical, back-stabbing, lying, man-stealing whore."

The knife pressed against my cheek, silencing me. Was she going to slice it? Make ribbons of it like Greta's? Oh God—Greta. Greta had been involved with Luis. Is that why she'd died? Had Melanie found out and come after Greta, preventing her from seeing Luis? Making sure Luis wouldn't be attracted to her anymore? Oh man. I needed to get Melanie off of me, but I didn't dare move. I stared into the dark pebbles and dirt of the alley, saw my bag beside me, its contents spilled onto the ground, the beaded jaguar that was supposed to protect me. Melanie was still talking, leaning over me. Accusing me. Explaining why she was going to kill me. Why I deserved to be killed.

"I saw him kiss you. I saw you pressing yourself against him, whispering to him."

"But I never kissed him—"

"Stop lying, Elle." The tip of the knife dug into my skin.

I gasped. Thought back. Remembered taking Luis aside, talking to him privately. Oh God. "Melanie, wait. It wasn't what you thought—I talked to Luis. But I was trying to help you."

"Fucking pathetic liar." She looked down, her knife on my cheek, her hair dangling over my face.

"No, I swear. You said he'd been stalking you, so I told him to leave you alone or I'd go to his boss. That's what you saw."

"Were you jealous, Elle? Couldn't you stand it that a hot guy like Luis would choose me over you? Is that why you tried to take him from me? Well, guess what? You can't. I won't let you. This time, I'll make sure you're gone for good."

"But you don't have to, Melanie. I'm leaving in a couple of days. For good. You'll never see me again."

"I thought I'd gotten rid of you, Elle." She shook her head. "But you came back. Why wouldn't you stay dead?"

Dead? What? Oh Lord. She had to be talking about when I'd nearly drowned. But Melanie had been the one to pull me out of the water. She'd risked her own safety to save me.

Unless she hadn't.

Again, I saw the cloudy water. The floating figure with seaweed hair. Had that been Melanie? Had I kicked her away as she'd swung her knife? Had she held me under the water, bringing me to shore only after she'd thought I'd drowned?

Melanie's knife slid deeper into my cheek. Blood dribbled down my cheek, into my ear.

"I'm so sick of you, Elle. This time, no rescuers, no CPR. You're done. Good riddance."

She lifted the knife off my face and her arm arced upward above her head. Fury pulsed through me, adrenaline roared. Before she could bring the knife down, I freed my fist and swung it, slamming her wrist.

The knife went flying, clattered to the ground. Melanie climbed off of me, scrambling for it, but as she did, I rolled onto my knees, using my extra thirty-or-so pounds to thrust myself onto her legs. Her knees hit the ground, but she slithered ahead, dragging herself forward on her elbows, shoving me with her feet until she slid out from under me, skittering toward the knife. I struggled to my feet, hurried to hobble past her. As she reached for the knife, I put my weight on my sore leg, lifted the other, and stomped on the back of her hand.

Something crunched under my foot. Melanie howled and cursed, then reached around with her uninjured hand, grabbed my stitched leg and dug in her nails. Air rushed out of me; flashes of white pain blinded me. I fell facedown in the gravel, my left arm on a toppled trashcan while Melanie scuttled on her knees, still trying to get to the knife, her crushed hand useless. I pushed away from the trashcan, mustering the strength to propel myself forward. I landed just behind her legs, tugged on her ankles, pulled them out from under her. Melanie plopped flat onto her belly, and I used my last bit of energy to drag her body away from the knife.

Or I thought I did. In fact, I didn't. I was too late. I dragged her, but at the tip of her extended arm, beneath her grappling forefinger, the knife was hooked, scraping the ground right along with her. Melanie's unbroken hand reached out, struggling to grab hold of it and close around the hilt.

I wasn't aware, anymore, of pain or exhaustion. I had not the slightest bit of fear, no sense of time passing or of a need to hurry. Somehow, the night sky had become overly bright, improving my vision. Calm passed through me, as if I knew what was going to happen. As if all I had to do was go through the motions of acting it out. No—as if all I had to do was watch.

Melanie held onto the knife. I held onto Melanie. When I stopped pulling her legs, she twisted and reared, swinging her body at me, the knife in her fist, hurtling toward my chest.

I grabbed her arm and turned it downward, stopping the knife. She roared, jumped to her feet and rushed at me with so much force that I almost fell over. For a long moment, we stood pushing at each other, balanced like a human triangle. Melanie thrust herself at me; I countered with equal force, clinging to her wrist and leaning toward her.

"Melanie?" I panted. "Stop. Will you?"

She pressed harder, her body angled sharply to the ground. If I let go, she'd fall.

"Truce?" I was losing my strength. My leg was done, wouldn't hold me up much longer. Melanie snarled, yanked her arm out of my hand, and swung the knife.

I released my grip, jumped out of the way.

Melanie slid in the gravel and fell facedown, reaching out to break her fall.

I waited for her to get up. She didn't move.

I didn't go to her. Knew that she was waiting to grab and cut me again.

"Melanie?"

Melanie didn't answer. Didn't budge.

I watched her warily, braced for her to rise up and resume her attack. But she didn't. Finally, cautiously, I ventured over to her. Knelt, despite the angry protests of my leg. Touched her. Got no response.

"Melanie," I repeated until it became an unanswered question, no longer a name. And until, rolling her over, I saw the knife still clutched in her hand, its blade half buried in her chest.

∼

Susan, Jen, and Becky were sitting around my bed. They didn't notice that I was awake; they were too busy talking. The room wasn't familiar. The walls were green. Sunlight poured in through the window. I closed my eyes again, dozed, having a sense of déjà vu, lulled by their voices.

Until a man came into the room, greeting them. Even without opening my eyes, I recognized Sergeant Perez. "How is your friend doing?"

They all answered at once. Susan, of course, won out, insisting that I was sleeping and shouldn't be disturbed. That the police in Puerto Vallarta had interviewed me for most of the night. That I was the victim, that the woman's death was both accidental and in self-defense. She would have gone on, but Sergeant Perez interrupted.

"*Señora, por favor.* I asked only how your friend is doing. 'Fine' or 'not so well' would have been sufficient answers."

Susan didn't back down. "Her leg needed to be stitched again. Wounds on her collarbone and cheek needed to be closed as well. She has bruised ribs, abrasions all over her arms and legs and face. Her ankle is discolored and swollen. Is that a good enough answer?"

"You left out that she was filthy," Jen added. "Effing mud wrestlers are cleaner."

"Stop it, Jen." Becky bristled. "That's so not important. They bathed her. She's clean."

"Bullshit—of course it's important. Do you have any goddamned idea how many bacteria were on her? Crawling into her frickin' wounds? Contaminating her open wounds? She could have hundreds of horrible infections—"

"She's on antibiotics. She'll be fine."

"How do you know? Are you a damned microbiologist? Some bacteria are resistant to drugs. And, trust me, her leg? Even with these ace plastic surgeons, it's going to have a hell of a frickin' ugly nasty scar."

Really? It would?

"My friend Nan—" she went on. "You met her, Susan. She

had two C-sections and they used the same incision site for both, so they stitched up the same place twice. She showed me the scar."

"A C-section's different—"

"No, it's not. A scar is a scar. Now, it's three years later and she showed me the scar. It's disgusting. Thick and red. Ugly. And her skin buckles around it and she has these damned internal adhesions—"

"Señoras, if you don't mind." Thank God, Perez interrupted. "I came by with some news."

"News?" Susan's voice.

"The dead woman. We checked her room in the hotel. All over the walls, she had pinned up photos of this man."

What man?

I cracked open an eyelid. Perez took out a photo, held it up.

Becky gasped. "It's Luis."

"You know him?" Perez asked.

"Of course I know him. Everybody knows him. He works for the hotel, he's one of the activity directors—"

"Yes," Perez confirmed. "Do you know if this Luis had a relationship with the woman your friend killed?"

Killed? I winced, wanted to correct him. Make sure he knew it had been an accident. Did he think I'd killed her?

"How would we know about her relationships? We didn't know her." Susan again.

But I did. I knew. I could tell them about Melanie and Luis. Their relationship.

"Why don't you ask him?" Becky suggested.

"What a good idea, señora." Perez sniped. "If only we'd been clever enough to think of it."

"Okay, so if you've already talked to him, and he's told you, why are you asking us?" Jen sounded belligerent, was standing up for Becky, in a way.

"He wants to corroborate Luis's statement," Susan said.

"So? What did he say?"

"He denied having a relationship with her. He said he'd seen her only at the pool."

But made no mention of her breaking into his room or vandalizing it.

"You said she had pictures of him on her walls?" Susan asked.

"Many. Dozens. Candid ones, mostly of poor quality. Probably she took them with her phone camera and printed them in the computer room. But she had other things, as well. Official hotel shirts with his name embroidered on them. Other items of clothing and toiletries that he's identified. Also charge slips he's signed. Notes she'd written to him but apparently never sent. Some were quite—explicit."

Perez went on. I lay still, eyes closed again, replaying Melanie's visit to Luis's room. Seeing her climb in through his window. Waiting while she left her message to make him leave her alone. But now I understood: What she'd told me had been backward. Luis hadn't been stalking Melanie; Melanie had been stalking Luis. Had gone to his room to invade his space, pilfer his possessions. She'd been obsessed with him, had seen me talking to him. Had watched his sarcastic kiss good-bye and assumed we were having a relationship.

"You're trying to steal him from me," she'd hissed.

Melanie had tried to kill me to keep Luis for herself.

And if she'd tried to kill me just because she *suspected* that I was seeing Luis, what would she have done to women who'd been openly and unapologetically enjoying his company?

"What about Greta?" I sat up. "Melanie was jealous of anyone Luis paid attention to, and she used a knife to attack me, and Greta's face was cut—" I stopped, aware of four faces gawking at me.

For a few beats, there was silence. And then everybody spoke at once.

∾

Perez had already thought of the connection. But in the flurry and consternation that followed my comment, it took a while before he could say so.

"You're awake?" Becky asked.

"Obviously, she's awake," Jen took my hand. She looked battered; her eyes were still black, her nose bruised and swollen and taped. "Becky and I tried to bring you get well balloons—"

"Or a stuffed animal."

"But the stores weren't open yet."

"It was the middle of the night."

"How do you feel, Elle?"

I raised an arm, saw an IV tube attached to it. "Fine." My voice didn't work. I had to repeat myself.

"How long have you been awake?" Susan eyed me. "How much did you hear?"

I shook my head, didn't actually answer. Focused on Sergeant Perez, who, when he had a chance to speak, admitted that Melanie was indeed being considered a suspect in Greta's murder. In fact, now that the police were aware of Melanie's fixation on Luis, they wondered if she'd been involved somehow in Claudia's death as well.

"It seems that Luis also had romantic ties with Claudia Madison. In fact, he admits that he visited her on the very evening of her death."

"I told you," Becky said. "Chichi said that Luis gets around."

"Wait a frickin' minute," Jen put her hands up. "Was Melanie the maniac who got into our room? I bet she was. I bet she was looking for Elle that night. But instead of killing you, the bitch pulled off my effing bandages."

"That makes no sense, Jen," Becky folded her arms. "Why would she attack you if she was after Elle?"

"Why wouldn't she? She was a fucking lunatic."

"Señoras, we don't know everything that this woman did."

Perez put his hand up for quiet. "But we suspect that she made an attempt on your life at least once before, Señora Harrison." He looked at me.

"You mean in the water?" Susan looked from him to me.

I felt Melanie's weight pressing on my chest, heard her complain that I hadn't stayed dead.

Perez explained that Melanie's rescue had been a cover. He believed that she'd been the one who'd stabbed me, that she'd tried to drown me, and that she'd pulled me to shore only after she thought she'd succeeded.

"Well, that supports Elle's claim of self-defense." Susan gestured lawyerlike.

"Indeed, señora. You need not worry. There will be no charges, as far as I can tell."

A cell phone rang and Jen dug into her bag. Rolled her eyes. Mouthed, "Norm." Walked into the hall to take the call.

Susan thanked Sergeant Perez for coming by, walked him out of the room, asking questions in a muted voice.

Becky closed in on me. "I feel terrible, Elle. It's just like the other day. If I'd have been there, it never would have happened. She wouldn't have attacked us both."

"It's not your fault." I reached for the control button so I could sit up a little. Grunted because every part of me hurt.

She grabbed the control, handed it to me. "I know. Because somebody had to be here to help Jen. And besides, Chichi and I have only two more days together. I couldn't have gone with you. I couldn't bear to lose a single minute with him."

"I understand." The head of the bed came up. I could see her better now. Her hands fidgeted. Her round eyes were strained.

"Honestly, Elle. Just two more days? I don't know how I'll manage without him. It's not possible. How do you let go of someone you love?"

She asked me as if I'd know. I reached out, held her hand. She didn't wait for an answer, kept talking.

I closed my eyes. I think they'd given me pain medicine. Maybe I was just numb and exhausted. But I drifted, and fading, I saw Charlie in the distance. He called to me, held his arms out for me, and disappeared into haze.

~

It was sometime after lunch. I'd managed to feed myself some noodle soup and yogurt with the arm not connected to the tube. Left the rest untouched. Now I was alone in my room in the medical center, lying in a drugged daze. Drifting. Dropping in on my past. Visiting life with Charlie, our good times, when I'd still held happy illusions about life, about Charlie. We were in the den, sharing a bottle of Shiraz. Watching an old mystery movie— *Charade*? Or *Arsenic and Old Lace*? Something with Cary Grant. And chowing down on white pizza with spinach. Or maybe shrimp. Charlie flashed me a steamy smile, and my heart did a fluttery dance. Oh God, I missed him. The good Charlie. The one I'd thought I'd married. Picturing him, I could almost hear him breathing, smell his Old Spice. Or not Old Spice— something sharper. Wait—had Charlie changed his aftershave? Did men even shave after death? Never mind. I was losing the memory. Went back to it. We were in bed, now, lying side by side, staring into each other's eyes. Charlie put a hand gently on my cheek and ever so lightly placed his lips on my mouth.

Wait. I held my breath. The kiss felt real.

And the lips. Weren't. Charlie's.

I opened my eyes.

"Hey, there." Alain pushed a wisp of hair off my forehead, smiling. He pulled a chair up beside the bed. Sat. Took my hand. His teeth gleamed white against his tan. "You awake?"

"Hi." I tried to return his smile, felt my lips crack.

"You've been sleeping most of the day." He furrowed his brows, focusing like a doctor. "Do you have any pain?"

"No, no pain."

"I didn't think you would. We're giving you painkillers."

Yes. I was swimming in them. The IV tube was pumping them into my arm.

"You were in a sorry state last night." He studied me. I felt like a specimen in a lab. "You gave me a fright, Elle. But you look much better now."

I did? Oh. I hadn't thought about how I looked. I put a hand to my hair, felt tangles and frizz. Became aware of gauze patches on my hands and forearms. Touched my face. Felt another patch on my cheek. And one on my chin.

"Those will come off tonight. They're mostly for protection, to keep the wounds clean. A good deal of grit and dirt had worked their way in; it was a job cleaning them out. But the knife wounds shouldn't scar. And the abrasions were superficial; they'll heal well. I think you'll be pleased with your results."

My results?

"I sutured you myself." His voice was low, intimate. His head glowed, backlit by the window.

"Thank you." My mouth was dry. I licked my lips, tasted blood where they'd cracked.

"In a few months, I doubt you'll be even able to locate the spots where your cheek was cut. Or your clavicle, for that matter. Thank God, the blade struck where it did. Another few inches, she'd have cut your common carotid artery."

I saw the blade swing, felt the whoosh of air. A sting.

Alain took a breath, frowning. "Your leg, however, was a challenge. Tissue was damaged in and around the wound. Even so, I'm confident I minimized the scarring there. You'll have a mark, but over time, it should fade and become less noticeable."

He tried a smile. It didn't work.

I squeezed his hand, asked for some water. He held the glass for me, put an arm out to support my back. My ribs ached, my head felt heavy, and the distance seemed far from the pillow to the glass, but finally my mouth made contact with the rim. My fingers wrapped around Alain's, tilting the glass, trying to pour the water down my throat.

"Slowly, Elle. Just little sips."

I ignored him, gulping. Breaking into a spasm of coughs that made my ribs shriek.

"You need to be patient, Elle. It will take time to get your strength back."

I was still coughing, holding my sides. Couldn't respond.

"But there's no reason for you to remain in the clinic. You are being discharged and can leave as soon as you are ready."

Really? I looked around for my clothes. Didn't see them.

"Susan brought over some fresh clothes."

Was he reading my mind? He held up a plastic bag, laid it on the bed.

"So, you can go back to your hotel suite to rest. But I'd like to propose an alternative." He paused, eyes zeroed on mine. "Why don't you stay at my place? I can monitor you, make sure you have no infection or pain."

What? Stay at his place? I looked away. Didn't know what to say.

"As you know, I'm not a bad cook." Again, he attempted a smile.

"Thank you, Alain." I cleared my throat. Reached for the bag.

"Does that mean yes?"

I didn't meet his eyes. "It's generous of you to offer."

"Oh. It means no?" He tilted his head. "It's not a marriage proposal, Elle. It's a doctor friend, offering to care for you for a day or two."

"But I leave in two days."

"No. You're here for two days. You leave on the third."

How did he know that?

"I spoke to Susan."

Again, he answered my thoughts.

"I don't want to impose."

"It's no imposition. You can stay just tonight or as long as you want. You can come back to the hotel during the day if you feel up to it or rest all day beside my pool. Ana, my housekeeper, will assist you. It's up to you."

He smiled, but his eyes dug deep. He sat close to the bed. Again, I wondered about him. Why was Alain so interested in me? What did he really want?

"Alain, I should go back to my friends."

He let out a breath. "I understand. You should know, though, that I have already talked with them. My invitation was made with your friends' interests in mind. Becky wants to spend time with her lover, but she'll feel obligated to stay with you if you go back to the suite. Jen is still recovering from her procedures and doesn't feel capable of helping you. And Susan, well, quite frankly, she was very shaken by what happened to you. In my opinion, she needs rest. If you're there, she won't. She'll feel the need to mother you."

Oh.

I didn't say anything. Couldn't. My throat choked, and my eyes blurred. I blinked away tears. Alain had essentially told me that my friends didn't want me to come back to the suite. That I would be a burden.

I bit my lip. Felt a jab where it had split. Not only did they want me to stay out, Susan had even packed me a bag.

Alain waited, watching me. I felt cornered. How could I say no? But if I went to his house, would he expect me to sleep with him again? Once a man had sex with you, he expected it again, right? I couldn't even consider it. Didn't want anyone close to me, let alone touching me. I recoiled at the thought, closed my eyes. Maybe he'd disappear. Maybe I'd wake up in my own bed, back in Philadelphia. Maybe Charlie would be next to me.

"Elle, don't feel any pressure. You would be my guest, no strings. Just rest and recuperation. No obligations of any kind. Nothing physical, especially in your condition."

What was the deal with Alain and my thoughts? Was he probing my brain?

"How about you come just for tonight. You'll see how it goes, how you feel. We can take it one day at a time, okay?"

I reached for the bag of clothes, held my ribs, and sat up to get out of bed. Something plummeted inside my skull and the walls whirled. I lay back against the pillow.

"Take your time," Alain said. "You might feel dizzy."

Might? Maybe it was the drugs. When they wore off, I'd be steadier.

Then again, when they wore off, I'd probably hurt all over. Damn. I had bandages all over my body. Would I be able to change them myself? Bathe myself? Take my own medicine, make my own meals? I wanted to be with Susan and Becky and Jen. I belonged with them, would feel comfortable with them. But Alain was right, it wouldn't be fair. I shouldn't make them take care of me.

"Okay," I nodded. "I'll come for one night."

"Excellent." Alain called a nurse to remove my IV.

He waited outside as the nurse helped me put on the loose sundress and flip-flops Susan had sent. The nurse also helped me fix my hair. I didn't look in the mirror, didn't dare.

Alain took me out of the clinic in a wheelchair and helped me into his car. He put the top up, maybe to protect me from the wind. Maybe to hide me from public view. Either way, I didn't care. I felt far away, as if nothing happening was real. Or as if I were watching from the sky. Probably it was the trauma, the shock. The drugs. Probably I would be stronger in the morning and need to spend only one night at Alain's. No big deal. After all, how bad could one night be?

～

We listened to classical guitar. The sun had long since gone down, but Alain had lit a lot of candles. I lay beside his pool on a pillowed lounge chair, beside a half-empty glass of lemonade and a tray holding the remnants of dinner—tatters of tomato and rice. A few bites of chicken breast.

I tried to be comfortable. Earlier, Alain had gone inside for a moment, leaving me alone. I'd been safe, and had known he'd be right back. It hadn't mattered. As soon as Alain left, shadows had begun to dance, taking ominous forms, and unseen creatures had rustled in the foliage. Even the night air thickened, wrapping me in dampness and dark. I'd watched the candles, refusing to get rattled. Telling myself that that nothing was wrong. That Melanie was dead and no one else would hurt me. My senses, though, remained on alert, and I was palpably relieved when Alain came back outside. He was drinking something caramel colored. Whiskey?

"Feeling better?"

I was still woozy, but my bruised muscles were waking up and beginning to ache. My abrasions stung, and the places that had been cut and stitched were telling me about it. "Much better. And dinner was delicious. Thank you."

"If you have pain, let me know. I have your medication. Meantime, take this." He handed me a pill. "Antibiotic. You'll need to take them for the rest of the week."

I swallowed it with lemonade. Again, sensed movement behind me. Turned, saw only hedges lining the wall.

Alain sat facing me. Leaning on his knees. "So. Do you want to talk?"

Talk? We'd been talking for hours. All through dinner we'd talked about sailing, about whales and other endangered animals. About our childhoods, traveling, books. But Alain looked serious. Oh dear. "You mean about Melanie?"

He tilted his head. "Yes, if you want to. Or about anything else."

Anything else?

"Look, Elle. I understand you've been through a lot this week. You've had a lot on your mind besides what's happening with us."

Oh. *That* anything else.

"But when I saw you—Elle, honestly, when I responded to the call at the clinic and came in, I saw you lying there half-conscious covered with blood and, frankly, I wasn't prepared for my reaction. I've already told you how bad I felt when you nearly drowned. Well, this—" He paused. "It was more difficult than I can say."

Actually, it hadn't been a picnic for me either. But Alain's eyes shone in the candlelight. Teary.

Teary again? Was it a cultural thing to cry easily? Because in the last few days, I'd seen Alain almost cry twice, more often than any man I'd ever known. Hell, more often than any woman. Except Becky. So what was going on with him? Was he sensitive? Emotional? Melodramatic? Manipulative? Whatever it was, I felt bad for him. Took his hand. "Alain—"

"You don't need to reciprocate my feelings," he went on. "I don't expect you to. But I want you to know that you aren't merely a conquest or another affair. I've already told you that. Look, I don't know how it happened so fast. But already, in this short time, you've become—Elle, you're very dear to me." Slowly, he lifted my hand to his mouth, kissed it.

In his eyes, I saw sorrow. Deep, tortured, bleak. That sorrow couldn't possibly have to do with me; it was too old, too comfortable with its surroundings. Maybe caring for me—even just beginning to care—had reopened old wounds. Not the kind that could be stitched.

"Well." He blinked rapidly, looked at his watch. Took a breath. "It's late. You're tired, and I have to see patients in the morning." He stood, reached for my hand, helped me to my feet.

I leaned against him as I stood. Wasn't surprised that his arms closed gently around me. Or that, when I looked up, he was waiting with a kiss. I wasn't sure what I felt for Alain. And, even with his teary eyes, I wasn't sure that he was sincere, that he wasn't trifling with me, tossing out glib, manipulative lines.

But that night, while my body hurt and the bushes rustled and the shadows watched, I was glad to have his arms around me, walking me inside.

~

He asked if I'd prefer to sleep with him or alone. "You're welcome to stay with me. And, obviously, I'd like you to. But you need rest. I don't want to keep you awake."

I felt awkward about wanting to sleep alone. How should I phrase it? I hesitated.

"It's not a problem, Elle. Why don't you stay in the spare bedroom? It's right next to mine."

He opened a door, turned on a light. Revealed a room unlike the rest of the house. The walls were covered in baroque art and tapestries. A dark four-poster bed was draped with black lace. I stopped, didn't walk in.

"Whose room is this?" I already knew.

"No one's." He looked away.

We stood at the threshold, not moving.

"Alain, I don't think—" I began just as he said, "It was my wife's."

"Your wife's?" They'd had separate bedrooms?

"She wanted her own space. She decorated it to her own tastes, as you can see. Sometimes she retreated into it. But, look, if you're uncomfortable—"

"Where is she now?"

Alain let out a breath, withdrew his arm from my waist. "Why don't I give you my room? I can sleep on the sofa."

"No, it's okay. Really. This is silly. Let's both stay in your room."

And so, we did. We lay side by side, chastely. Politely leaving a few inches of empty space between us. I wore one of his t-shirts; he wore boxers. Before bed, Alain checked my wounds, reapplied ointments, replaced bandages, removed gauze. He made sure I had everything I needed—from a new toothbrush to a sponge bath to a pain pill. Finally, the light was out. My leg hurt, my ribs ached; I waited for the pill to kick in. Wanted to drift off.

"Alain — " I was going to thank him.

"At the clinic."

What?

"You asked where my wife is." His voice floated over me, disembodied in the dark. "She's been staying there. I've told you she's disabled. Sometimes it's worse than others. When she's well enough, she comes home. But caring for her has become — I can't manage it alone."

I reached across our no-man's land and found his hand, took it.

"It's not that she's completely incapacitated. She can walk on her own. She just needs a lot of care. She doesn't function."

"I'm sorry."

"I blame myself, Elle. The accident was my fault. Her condition is my doing."

"Alain, blaming yourself won't help her. It won't help either of you." In truth, I was simply placating him, saying what seemed appropriate. I had no idea what kind of accident had happened or what permanent injuries his wife had sustained. "You might have hurt her, but it wasn't intentional. Accidents happen. You're doing your best. And your best is all you can do." I'd have kept going, but ran out of clichés.

He didn't respond. I lay in the dark beside him, listening to him breathe, holding onto his hand. In a few minutes, sleep began to close in on me. Vaguely, I felt him lean over and kiss me good night. And then I heard — or maybe I imagined hearing him cry.

∿

"*Buenos dias, señora.*" Alain was buttoning his shirt when I opened my eyes.

I looked around. Light poked through the bedroom curtains.

"What time is it?"

"Not yet seven. Go back to sleep." He bent over, pecked my forehead. Smelled like soap and aftershave.

"You're leaving?"

"I have to see a patient at the clinic, and then I'll be back. My housekeeper will be here any minute. I won't be more than an hour. Coffee's made, and there are pastries. Your antibiotic is on the nightstand with some juice." He nodded to my left.

I turned my head. Saw the pill and the juice.

"Thank you." I started to get up, but stopped halfway. I was sore all over. None of my parts wanted to move.

"How are you feeling?"

"Spectacular." I winced as I reached for the juice.

"I expect you'll be stiff. Your bruises and muscle strains will probably bother you more than your stitches."

"Good to know." I took the pill, drank the juice. Fell back against the pillow.

"Sorry to run off. But you're safe here. Ana will take care of you until I get back. If you need anything—even your pain pills, just ask her."

I nodded, thanked him. He put a hand on my head, smoothed my hair. Looked at me for a moment before leaving. I closed my eyes, heard his footsteps on the tiled floor and the opening and closing of the outer door.

I tried to sleep again, but the house was too silent. Nothing moved. The place felt hollow. I strained to hear birds chirping or breezes rattling foliage. But the windows were closed, shutting out small sounds. The house sat still, empty, making no noise. I lay there, listening to nothing until it became a bellow. I rolled over, grateful for the rustling of the sheets. Aware that until Ana the housekeeper arrived, I would be alone.

～

Alain had said there was coffee. If I got up and moved around, I'd stop fixating on silence and solitude. I debated the proposition with my body and, finally, it wasn't relief from silence but the promise of pastries that won. I dragged myself out of bed, hobbled to the bathroom. Brushing my teeth, I glanced at the mirror. And gasped.

When had my face been scraped off? A patch of raw puffy red crust covered part of my chin and one cheek. The cheekbone was swollen and purple. Dried blood lined my nostrils. My tan had turned a frightening shade—was it ocher? Ocher came to mind, but I wasn't sure. This face was a horror—and forget the rat's nest on my head. No—not even a rat would tolerate that. No wonder Alain had kept his distance, not even trying to hold me in the night. I thought again of the beauties he treated, their perfect features. My face got hot, ocher became blotched with crimson, and I grabbed a washcloth, cleaned dried blood off my nose. Dabbed the rest of my face and neck. Wished I had a hairbrush. Some mascara.

Don't be stupid, I told myself. Who are you trying to impress? Alain? Why? You're leaving soon. And no matter how you fix yourself up, you can't compete with his perfect women. And he's married. Go have coffee. Eat pastries. Relax.

Fine. I tied my hair into a makeshift knot. Wandered through Alain's red, yellow, green, and blue house into his kitchen, poured a mug of coffee. I picked out a pastry of sweet flaky dough filled with custard. Sat and took a bite or two, a sip or two. Wondered if his wife had chosen the flower-patterned dishes. If he'd usually bought pastries for her breakfast as well.

I stopped eating. Looked around the house. The colors, fabrics. The décor. Were those her choices? I doubted it; her bedroom was all heavy brocades and darkness, in sharp contrast with the rest of the rooms. So had Alain chosen the tiles and furnishings? Had it bothered her that their house—even their dishes—reflected his taste, not hers? I wondered about her taste in clothing. Her personal style. Was she pretty? As pretty as Alain's patients?

What did I care? I was leaving, remember? Alain and his marriage were not my problem.

I took another bite of pastry. Another sip of coffee. And re-alized that, whether or not she'd selected the floor tiles and dishes, Alain's wife might have some makeup. Or at least a hair-brush. I should go look in her room.

No, wait. What was I thinking? I couldn't use her things. How would I have felt if some woman Charlie had bedded had come into my house and helped herself to my personal—

Oh, right. Some woman had.

I saw them yet again in the shower. Felt my heart freeze as if I was finding them for the first time.

But that was the point. I had been devastated. Still was, after all this time. I couldn't do to Alain's wife what had been done to me.

Except that I already had. I'd slept with a married man. I had become the Other Woman, the enemy. A lowlife, amoral, man-stealing, home-breaking piece of scum.

I bit my lip where it had cracked, made it hurt. Taking a breath, I told myself that I was leaving in a day and a half. That Alain wasn't a typical married man; he was alone because his wife was an invalid. That, even so, I wouldn't sleep with him again. But that, even if I did, Alain's marriage was his problem, not mine.

I felt crummy, took another bite of sweet chewy dough, washed it down with a gulp of bitter blackness.

I tried to imagine Alain's wife. Was she naturally beautiful? Or had he done surgeries on her, improving her looks? And after the accident, had she been disfigured? Had he done procedures to restore her beauty? Why weren't there any photographs of her? I thought about that. Maybe there were pictures in her room.

It was normal to be curious. That's what I told myself as I hobbled across the living room to her door. It wasn't as if I were snooping. After all, Alain had offered me her bedroom the night before. If I had slept in there, I'd have seen her things, wouldn't I? So I wasn't doing anything wrong by opening her door and stepping into her room, pausing to take in its dark textures.

Wasn't hurting anyone by going into her powder room and opening her medicine cabinet, trying to translate labels on medications and cosmetics, examining the creams and lotions covering the counter. Opening drawers filled with blushes, eye shadow and liner, compacts, mascara, gloss. Dozens of colors, sizes, brands.

No, I wasn't hurting anyone. I was only looking for a photo. Trying to learn about the woman. Jewelry covered her vanity. Earrings and bracelets, rings. Pendants. Ornate hair combs. In one drawer, I found scarves and shawls, neatly folded. In another, lingerie. Nightgowns. Bras.

Okay, enough. Now, I was crossing the line into snooping. Invading a person's privacy. I thought of Melanie, pictured her ransacking Luis's room. Lord, was I becoming like her? I shut the drawers, backed away. Knew I should get out of the room. Started to, but stopped at her nightstand and opened the drawer, still looking for even one photo. Surely, there had to be at least one? Inside, I found a hodgepodge: a sewing kit, more bottles of medicine and an almost empty one of tequila. Note-books with entries scribbled in Spanish. Pens. A book of word puzzles. Fashion magazines. And, deep in the bottom, finally, a photo. Well, half a photo—it had been ripped in half. Alain, grinning by the pool, was all that was left.

Oh my. Had she ripped herself out of the picture? Why would she do that? Unless it had been taken after the accident, after she'd been hurt. Maybe she hadn't wanted to be photographed that way. I could relate, wouldn't want my picture taken the way I looked, and her injuries must have been far worse.

But none of this was my business. I replaced everything. Looked around the room at its dark heavy furnishings, its walls heavy with somber art. My body ached, but not just from my injuries.

I started for the door. Stopped to consider using some mascara. Decided that it would be too creepy. On the way out, I casually opened the mahogany wardrobe. It was an impressive piece. Ornately carved. Dresses and skirts hung inside; shelves held shoes and sweaters. I almost closed the wardrobe, almost didn't notice the garment hanging on a hook inside the door.

But when I did, I stood, staring at it, unable to form a thought. Unable to move.

~

I felt wobbly, the kind of wobbly I'd felt on the balcony railing with Claudia. The kind of wobbly that, if I moved even a finger, I knew I'd lose my balance and drop into nothingness, falling forever.

So I didn't move. I held still, watching the garment with disbelief. It couldn't be there. A hotel maid's uniform? Why would there be a hotel maid's uniform in Alain's wife's wardrobe?

Images poured through my mind. A maid in the hallway, turning away, concealing her face. A maid in our room after Claudia died. A maid in Greta's room the night she was killed. Sergeant Perez showing us pictures, suspecting that our intruder might have been a maid.

Why did Alain's wife have a maid's uniform? I studied the thing. It was embroidered with the hotel name, made from the hotel staff's deep-maroon cotton.

I hugged myself, trying to think of a reasonable explanation. Maybe—no, probably, the uniform belonged to Alain's housekeeper. Of course. That had to be it. What was her name? Ana? Ana had probably worked for the hotel and Alain had met her while treating his patients there. Had hired her to work for him and help with his wife. She'd kept her uniform. Why shouldn't she? She'd probably change into it as soon as she arrived. I'd been frantic over nothing.

I shook my head, told myself to lighten up. I was way too on edge, still shaken by Melanie and the violence of the week. I needed to go finish my coffee and relax. Closing the wardrobe door, though, I stopped. What was that under the hem of that dress, half-hidden by the skirts? I reached out, moved the fabric aside. Uncovered a head of hair.

My hand jerked back reflexively, even as I realized it was just a wig.

The hair was chin length and black. I stared at it for a moment, then shut the wardrobe door, hurried out of the room, went back to my coffee. Sit down, I told myself. Finish your breakfast. None of what you've seen is your business.

I sat down, but I couldn't stop thinking. A maid's uniform. A wig. Lots of cosmetics and jewelry. Medicines. But, now that I thought about it, there were also lots of things that I hadn't found in Mrs. Du Bois's room. Like feminine supplies. No tampons or birth control. No razor or tweezers or hair curler or hair dryer. No deodorant, conditioner or shampoo.

So what? I asked myself. She probably had those things with her at the clinic.

If she really was at the clinic.

Wait. What was I thinking? That she didn't actually exist?

That she had died in the accident?

And Alain was in severe denial?

No way. I'd gone way too far. I was making things up based on nothing. Still, I was trembling. I gulped coffee to get warm, but it had cooled, tasted like watery mud. Maybe I'd pour a fresh cup from the pot. I stared at the pot. Wondered if I was drinking from a dead woman's mug.

Stop, I told myself. You've just had a series of traumas; your thinking is convoluted because of Melanie. And Greta and Claudia. And too many movies like *Psycho*. And being married to Charlie. Not everyone has dark evil secrets—certainly not Alain. Alain was a gentleman, an internationally renowned plastic surgeon. A decent guy.

But Alain was also a man who cheated on his wife. A doctor who slept with his patients. He was about my height, would probably fit into the maid's uniform. And if he wore a wig, no one would suspect he was in disguise, especially if he lowered his head or turned the other way.

I couldn't sit. I limped around in circles. Sat again. Held my head, chewed a fingernail. What I was thinking was bizarre. Why would Alain dress up like a maid, sneak around a hotel and kill two of his own patients? Women he'd had affairs with.

I had no answer, except that he wouldn't have. Absolutely not. The idea was preposterous. I dismissed it. Looked at the rest of the pastries. Thought about having another. Picked out one with nuts, but didn't take a bite.

Because I still had a question that wouldn't go away. If Alain hadn't disguised himself as a maid and killed his patients, why did he have the uniform and the wig?

~

My face hurt. My ribs hurt. Every part of me was sore. I rubbed my forehead. Remembered the veiled woman who'd appeared in the night and torn off Jen's bandages. She'd also been about my size. Had that been Alain dressed in his wife's clothes? Hiding under her shawl? If not for Susan and me, would Jen have been his third murder victim?

No. What was I thinking? Alain hadn't done any of those things. Couldn't have. I'd slept beside him, had sex with him. He'd been tender. Serial killers weren't tender, were they?

My head hurt. Snippets repeated themselves: Alain blaming himself for his wife's injuries. The bathroom lacking tampons. The house reflecting nothing of Mrs. Du Bois's taste. The wig and the uniform hanging in the wardrobe. The maid working in Greta's room. The veiled woman tearing at Jen. My mind went round and round, seeking connections.

But maybe there were no connections. The explanations I was imagining were far-fetched. For example, it wasn't believable that Alain's guilt and despair over his wife's accident had caused his personality to split into two. The first part was his persona as Dr. Du Bois; the second as his wife. And when his wife's was in charge, he'd disguised himself as a woman — internalizing his wife, expressing her pain, jealousy, and rage. Acting out her desires.

No. That scenario was unthinkable. Unimaginable. And yet, there I was, thinking and imagining it: Alain dressed as a woman, exacting his wife's revenge upon Greta and Claudia, murdering his own lovers.

I closed my eyes, saw a veiled woman raise her fists in the dark, crying out *"Quiero la venganza!"*

Ridiculous. I had to stop this far-fetched twisted thinking. The dress belonged to Ana. Probably the wig did, too. Not everything had diabolical significance.

I picked up the nutty pastry. Smelled almond paste. Scolded myself for eating so many sweets. And for doubting a man who'd been nothing but kind and affectionate to me. Who just the night before had fed me dinner and tended my wounds. And kissed me gently, telling me—what had his words been? Something like, "Already, Elle, you've become dear to me."

Oh, shit. I swallowed, nearly choked on almond paste.

I told myself that his words didn't mean anything. I wasn't like Claudia and Greta, wasn't one of his patients. Wasn't having an actual affair with him. And besides, he wasn't a psycho, killing his lovers for his wife's sake. No. I wasn't even going to consider it.

To prove it, I took another bite of my pastry. Chomped on it. Gulped cold coffee.

But what if being a patient didn't matter? What if the connection between the dead women was simply that they'd slept with Alain? Would that qualify me to be the next victim? Would the part of his mind that had snapped and become his wife—if indeed part of it had—would that part want to eliminate me as well? I touched my face, pictured Greta's.

Nonsense. Bull.

Alain didn't have a split personality—if there even was such a thing. This wasn't a Hollywood movie. Real people didn't simply divide into two personalities. The maid's uniform was simply for Ana, the housekeeper. The wig, like the dresses and shawls, probably belonged to his wife. Alain had nothing to do with either of the deaths at the hotel.

Fine. Enough. I put the topic to rest.

And then I rushed into his bedroom, pulled on my clothes, called a taxi, limped out to the street to wait. My leg throbbing and scrapes burning, I hid in a cluster of bushes so Ana wouldn't see me if she arrived before the cab came. I hunkered down, picturing Alain in a maid's dress, coming at me with a butcher knife. Or cutting ribbons in Greta's face or backing Claudia against the railing, shoving her over.

Of course, none of that was real. Alain was innocent. Even so, I counted seconds and minutes, waiting for the taxi, filling my head by counting time, shoving out images of wigs and uniforms and a man acting out the anger of his dead or incapacitated wife.

When the cab pulled up, after I'd counted six minutes fifty seconds, I darted into the backseat, my breath shallow and my body shaky. I told the driver the name of the hotel and then stared out the window, refusing to think, especially about Ana. An old pickup truck had dropped her off at Alain's as I'd watched from the bushes.

The housekeeper was a short, wide woman. Very round. Definitely too large to fit in the maid's uniform.

~

I heard Jen when I came in. "I can't wait to see you either, Honey Bear. I miss you so much."

They'd been married for what? Twelve years? Despite her normally foul language, she called Norm Cuddlesnooks. Sweetikins. I'd never called Charlie anything but Charlie. Not true. I think I called him a fucking wad of slime once or twice. But Honey Bear? Never.

Susan was on the balcony, sunning herself. She looked up when I opened the door. "You're back?" She looked me over, frowning. "I thought Alain was going to take care of you. What are you doing here?"

I sat on a chair next to her, deciding how to explain. Wondering how crazy I'd sound.

"Honestly, Elle, he promised you'd stay at his place today.

You look like hell. And you shouldn't be on your feet. And look at your face—is it infected? Because it looks slimy and, honestly, I'm not qualified to deal with it."

She went on. I waited for her to quiet down. But Jen came out before Susan stopped for a breath. Her eyes were less black and her nose less swollen.

"What's Elle doing here?" Her eyelashes batted at me.

"Not sure." Susan took a sip of lemonade.

"I couldn't stay there alone," I spoke up. "I took a taxi back."

"So Alain doesn't know you're here?"

I shook my head. Bit my lip.

"You look frickin' terrible. Do you hurt?" Jen eyed my face. Only everywhere. "I'm fine."

"Well, stay out of the sun," Jen squinted at my glossy abrasions. "You don't want scars."

"I thought sunlight helped healing," Susan said.

"Nope. Gives you wrinkles, scars, and cancer."

They discussed the effects of sunlight. A pelican swooped by the railing. I looked down at the people lying by the pool, absorbing large doses of wrinkles, scars, and cancer. Chichi and Becky canoodled near the waterslide. No sign of Luis. I hadn't seen him since Melanie's—

I pictured the wrestling mask. The knife sticking into her.

"Elle?"

"What?"

"I just asked you if you knew when Dr. Du Bois would be by. He's usually here by now."

Oh. Damn. Alain would come by any minute to check on Jen. What would I do? Hide in my room? Explain that I'd freaked out and run away? Ask if he was a cross-dressing killer?

"No, sorry. I don't know."

"Hungry?" Susan got up. "I'm getting some fruit." She opened the sliding door, headed into the suite, and we heard someone at the door, knocking.

Oh God. Was it Alain? I froze, facing the railing. Deciding

what I would say. Maybe I'd say that I'd needed to get something from the suite. Or that I'd been uncomfortable staying in his house by myself. Or just that I'd wanted to come back, and leave it at that. After all, I didn't owe him an explanation. Thinking of Alain made me queasy. Brought up gooseflesh on my arms. Had I made love to a murderer? A psycho serial murderer?

No. And anyway. I was here now, safe with my friends. I took a breath and stepped into the suite, ready to face him. But Susan was alone. She held out a plate of pineapple slices. "Want one?"

"Who was at the door?" I limped inside, wished I'd taken a pain pill.

"Nobody." She picked up a slice, bit into it. "Just the maid. I told her to come back later."

∿

"A maid?" My spine felt like ice.

"Were you expecting someone else?"

"Susan. Are you sure it was a maid?"

She stopped chewing, looked at me.

"Not just someone dressed like a maid?"

"Sorry. What?"

I went to the door, opened it slowly, checked the hallway. A maid's cart stood outside the suite across the hall.

Probably it was really a maid.

"Elle? What's going on?" Susan's cell phone rang and she grabbed it.

I closed the hallway door, felt her watching me.

"Yup, she's here."

Damn. Alain was calling.

"No, she's fine. Want to talk to her?"

I shook my head, no. Violently. But she held out the phone, scowling, and mouthed, "What's wrong with you?"

I put my hands up and backed away, refusing the phone, whispered, "Tell him I'm asleep."

She let out an exasperated breath. Mouthed, "Why?"

I kept shaking my head.

Susan glared at me. "Alain? I just peeked into her room and she's asleep. Want me to wake her?" Susan paused. "Okay. Sure. That'll be fine."

I stood motionless, listening. Feeling my face get hot.

When the call ended, Susan turned to me, hands on her hips. "Want to tell me what the hell's going on?"

We sat in the living room. Susan brought the pineapple slices and munched as I talked. I spoke in a hushed tone, didn't want to involve Jen if I could avoid it. Alain was her surgeon, after all. I told Susan about the maid's uniform and the wig. Reminded her about the maid in Greta's room.

"That's it?" She crossed her arms.

No. "Listen, Alain had had affairs with both Claudia and Greta. And his wife might have found out."

"But you said she's an invalid."

"Yes, and Alain blames himself for that. The accident was his fault, so he blames himself for her condition."

"Sorry." Susan shook her head. "I'm lost. What does that accident have to do with a maid's uniform?"

I explained my theory. That Alain himself might be punishing the women who attracted him, might be acting out his disabled wife's jealousy and anger. I told her about finding shawls and scarves, and reminded her of the intruder who'd ripped off Jen's bandages.

Susan blinked at me. "So you're saying Alain dressed up in shawls, broke in here, and attacked his own patient. Because— why? Are you saying he's attracted to Jen?"

"Maybe. Susan, I don't know. But I swear. Something was off at his house. There wasn't a single photo of his wife. She had no personal items like tweezers or nail files. And, come to think of it, there was no wheelchair. No hospital bed or bedpans. Nothing installed in the shower for someone—"

"Elle, what in God's name are you saying?"

Good question. For a moment, I couldn't articulate it. But I realized that the house gave no indication that a handicapped person actually lived there, even part time.

"What do we know about Alain's wife?" I asked. "Do we know anything about the accident? What happened to her?"

"All I know is what you've told me."

"Alain said she's been staying at the clinic. But what if it's not because she's disabled? What if it's worse? Like she's in a coma? A vegetable?"

Susan frowned, looking doubtful. "Elle, are you hearing yourself? When's the last time you met with your shrink?"

"What?"

"I think you might need some help. You've been through a lot, and with your disorder—"

"Susan. This has nothing to do with my disorder."

She leaned back against the sofa cushions. "Fine." She let out a sigh. "Then consider this. You don't know that anything you've just told me is based in fact. But if Alain's wife is indeed in a coma, which we have no reason to suspect, her condition might explain why there's no need for equipment for her at home. And it still wouldn't imply that Alain has been dressing up in women's clothing and committing murder."

She went on, but I didn't hear her. Charlie was standing in the kitchenette, munching discarded pineapple pieces, listening to us talk. I closed my eyes, but when I opened them, he hadn't gone away. What was he doing there? He didn't say anything, just stood there, watching me with a twinkle in his eyes. Except that, obviously, he wasn't watching me. Wasn't there at all. I was conjuring him up again. Why was I doing that? What was my mind trying to tell me? I stared at him, missing him, wishing that he weren't dead.

But he was.

Oh, wait. Was that it? Had Charlie shown up to indicate that Alain's wife was like him? Also dead? I remembered seeing Charlie on the beach with a woman. Had that woman been

Mrs. Du Bois? Had she been killed in the accident? Had it even been an accident?

Oh God. Had Alain deliberately killed her? Had his guilt about killing her driven him to incorporate her identity and kill women he cared about, depriving himself of love, punishing himself. And, in a way, avenging her death. Like our intruder had said: "*Quiero la venganza*."

Had that intruder been Alain?

Susan was still talking. Telling me that I'd had a traumatic week and it had affected my thinking. Advising me to see the therapist when I got home. Assuring me that not everything was as bizarrely awful as I seemed to think. That not everyone was a maniac like Melanie had been. That Alain was a decent, reputable guy who'd taken an interest in me, though God alone knew why.

I tried to listen. Susan stopped when Jen came in from the balcony. "What's going on?" she plopped onto the sofa beside me, smelling like coconuts. "You guys look deep."

Susan's eyes remained on me. "Alain called," she said.

I tensed, opened my mouth to stop her, but she went on. "He won't be by until this evening. Something came up at the clinic, and he's been delayed."

"Why'd he call your cell and not mine?" Jen pouted. "Does he think you're our fucking mother?"

Susan was still watching me. "Well, he wouldn't be far off. Someone needs to take care of you kids."

Jen picked up a pineapple slice. I leaned back against the cushions. Susan thought I was going crazy. Charlie winked from the kitchenette. Maybe I was.

᮫

Becky's eyes were red and swollen, her nose stuffed. She came into the bedroom while I was folding clothes to put in my suitcase.

"Want to talk?" I asked.

She shook her head, no. "I'll just cry more." Her chin wobbled.

I hobbled over to her, put my arms around her. Gently, she pushed me away.

"Don't be nice to me. It'll make me cry. I've got to stop. It's so stupid. All I do is cry." She turned away, opened a bureau drawer. Pulled out a souvenir t-shirt. Stared at it. "I can't do this." Tears spilled down her face. "I can't."

Oh Lord. Becky usually went through men like a shark through water. No, that was too harsh. More like a dolphin. Men were drawn to her and she liked them, at least until they got serious, and then she discarded them lightly. This time, though, she seemed smitten. Chichi, just as Madam Therese had predicted, had captured her heart.

I took her hand. "Can I do anything?"

She bit her lip. Shook her head. Looked at me and opened her mouth. "Elle, you look terrible."

I nodded. "You do, too."

We looked at each other, both disheveled, miserable messes. And even as tears dripped off her face, we burst out laughing. Neither of us could stop.

"What a vacation," she could hardly get words out. "I fell in love with—" She had to stop and catch her breath. "With the pool guy." She sat on the bed, convulsing as if she'd just said the funniest thing ever. "And you—"

"And I nearly—" This time I paused for breath. "—I nearly got killed."

"Twice." She held up her fingers because she was laughing too hard to talk.

Twice, yes. How hysterical. Uproarious. My ribs raged, but Becky and I rocked, howled, stopped only to inhale. We looked at each other and started laughing again. When the fits finally subsided, we lay side by side on Becky's bed, spent.

"What the hell was that?" Becky wiped her eyes. "A case of the opposites? I'm so unhappy that I laughed?"

"Catharsis." I stared at the ceiling. "A release of pent-up emotions."

"So we should feel better now?"

I didn't answer. My body throbbed and my head was empty.

"Because you know what? I kind of do."

She did?

"I do. Yes. It's not like I'm over Chichi or anything. It's just that I feel emptied out. Like I can't cry anymore, at least not right now." She looked at me. "How about you?"

Me?

"Do you feel better?"

I thought about it. Did I? Looked over at my half-filled suitcase. In one day, we were leaving. Going back to cold weather. Christmas. In a few weeks, my semester off would be over. I'd be back at work, teaching second graders. My leg would be healed, my scabs gone. This place and everything that happened here—love, adultery, obsession, murder, and attempted murder—would be just memories, shared among friends.

"I do," I told her. And I did.

We got up and packed. Aromas drifted in from the next room where Susan was cooking steak fajitas. The four of us would have dinner together. Life was beginning to feel normal again.

All we had to do was get through one more night.

～

We ate on the balcony, looking at the ocean. Jen was upset that she was still sore, and her swelling and bruises hadn't completely disappeared.

"You're healing fine," Becky said. "You'll look perfect in a couple weeks."

"A couple of weeks?" Jen pouted. "I want to be perfect tomorrow. When Norm sees me, I want him to be frickin' blown away."

"Oh, trust me. He will be," Susan said.

"What's that supposed to mean?"

"It means he'll be blown away. He'll think you were hit by a truck."

Jen sipped sangria. "Damn. I bet you're right. Especially if he sees Elle and me together."

Everyone made comments about what Norm might think if he saw us together: We'd been in a pileup on the alligator slide. We'd slammed into each other water skiing in opposite directions or been mistaken for piñatas. Bottom line: we both looked like escapees from a trauma ward. I looked a lot worse than Jen. As the day went on, the scabs on my cheeks and arms became darker and crustier. But at least my injuries had been free.

Becky chattered about Chichi, about saying good-bye. Jen and Susan gave her useless advice. She left us to be with him one last night.

The sun was setting, the air chilling. Alain was expected shortly. I told myself not to be nervous about it. Even if he'd murdered his wife—which he probably hadn't—it wasn't my problem. His wife, dead or alive, had nothing to do with me. And neither did he, really. I was leaving. Our relationship—if I could even call it that—was over. Susan had been right; I'd been traumatized, overly suspicious. I'd invented sinister motivations and exaggerated the significance of details when, in fact, I should simply have been flattered that Alain had been interested in me. Hell, because of Alain, my vacation hadn't been a complete wreck. He'd stitched my wounds after Melanie. And he'd been the first man I'd slept with after Charlie.

Charlie. I thought of him as I watched the ocean, the rosy glow of sunset. Recalled how he'd come to me when I was drowning, declaring his love. I drank sangria. Drifted. Saw Luis strolling near the pool, his arm around a matronly woman. He nuzzled her neck. A pelican flew overhead. At some point, someone knocked. Not Alain. A nurse, explaining that Alain had sent her. She went with Jen into the bedroom.

And then, while Susan made coffee, Alain finally arrived. He didn't ask for Jen. Didn't talk to Susan. He came directly to the balcony, carrying a couple of Coronas, looking for me.

~

"Are you all right?" He looked haggard.

"Of course." I leaned against the railing. "Don't you need to see Jen?"

"I will. She just needs a discharge signature." He opened a beer, handed it to me. "What happened, Elle? I got worried when Ana said you'd gone."

I didn't answer. Looked at the ocean. Swallowed some Corona.

"As it turns out, it was just as well you didn't wait for me. I had to be at the clinic all day." He moved closer, took my hand. Kissed me.

For a minisecond, I grimaced. Alain didn't seem to notice because I caught myself and covered my reaction, overdoing it, returning the kiss a little too enthusiastically. It didn't matter, though. It was just a kiss. I'd already kissed him dozens of times. One more wouldn't matter.

We stood at the railing, silent for a moment. He pulled on his beer.

"Elle—" he began just as I said, "Alain—"

We smiled, exchanging "you go first," and "no, it's okay, go ahead" until, finally, he began.

"Has Sergeant Perez been in touch?"

I grabbed the railing. "No. Why?"

He took a breath. "There was an incident at the clinic today. He thought there was a connection to what happened."

An incident? "Was someone killed?"

He waited a beat. "Someone was hurt. Actually, two people."

Two of his post-op patients had been attacked much the way Jen had. While they were sedated, their bandages had been ripped off, dressings messed with. He'd spent the day fixing the damage, calming patients, talking to Perez.

"Did the staff see who did it?"

"No one saw anyone who didn't belong there."

Of course they hadn't. Because they wouldn't be surprised to see Alain. Doctors would be expected to check in on sedated patients.

"It must have happened early this morning, after the night nurse made rounds."

Alain had gone in early. Stop it, I told myself. The man wouldn't attack his own patients. Even if he had, would he simply scrub up and fix them again? Would he be able to change so quickly from his wife's persona back to his own? Wouldn't he remember what he'd done? Wouldn't it frighten him? I eyed him, looking for signs of remorse or fear. Saw only exhaustion. A tired man drinking a beer.

"I found the maid's uniform." I hadn't planned to say that, it just came out.

"Sorry?"

"In your wife's room. There's a maid's outfit. From the hotel."

He seemed impatient. "Elle? I don't see what that—"

"Why would there be a maid's uniform in there?"

"I don't know." He paused. "Maybe it's Ana's."

Of course. Ana's.

"Tell me about her." I persisted, pushing to see if he'd snap.

"My wife? You want to know about Inez?" He cleared his throat. Stalling? Planning what to say? "Honestly, I've had quite a day. Can we just relax?"

"Her name is Inez?" I'd never heard it before.

Alain's eyes shifted, became flat and stony. "I—honestly, I don't like to talk about her. Okay, fine. What do you want to know?"

I faced him. "What's she like?"

He smiled, staring into air. "Beautiful. Inez was the most beautiful woman I'd ever seen."

Was? As in, she isn't anymore? Because she died in the crash?

Alain chugged his beer, finished it. Looked out at the water. "Elle, I'm going to tell you something I've never said to anyone." He paused. Reconsidering? About to confess? "The women I work on—the hundreds of noses, chins, cheeks, breasts, eyelids, lips—whatever. All of them are modeled after Inez. That's how beautiful she was. I take average women and turn them into copies of her."

What? "I don't understand." Didn't want to.

"I try to reproduce the perfect ratios and symmetry of her features. Or course, none of them end up comparable to her. They never get the whole package—not her bone structure or alignment. Most get only one or two of her elements."

I couldn't speak.

Alain's eyes were on me but he wasn't seeing me anymore. He smiled sadly, shook his head. "It's a terrible joke, isn't it? All the women I've treated. I've gotten rid of scars, erased wrinkles, improved figures, created exquisite faces. But when it came to the woman I cared about most, I could do nothing. I couldn't repair her."

He clutched his empty beer bottle, his jaw rippling. I took a step back. Had I been right? Had Alain been so devastated about his wife that he'd taken on her persona? Become frustrated with the women he'd molded to look like her?

"Where is Inez now?"

"Now?" It was almost dark, but I could see his blank eyes. "I told you. She stays at the clinic. In a private suite. She's not well."

"Is she conscious?"

The question seemed to surprise him. "Conscious? Why would you ask?"

Why? How should I explain? Because there were no tampons in your house? Because I didn't see a bedpan? Because I suspect that you might have killed her?

"I just wondered."

Alain looked at the horizon. "She has moments of clarity. In between, it's as if she's gone. Her skin was like flawless porce-lain. Her features were in perfect proportion, the epitome of the feminine aesthetic. But in a single instant—a mere moment of carelessness, it was gone."

Gone? So she was dead or comatose? I'd been right? I didn't know what to say, felt cruel for having opened the Pandora's box that was Alain's conscience.

"It's surprising," he talked to the distance, "how fragile we humans are. We can shatter so easily."

Was he talking about his wife or himself?

"Alain, I'm sorry. I shouldn't have asked—"

"No, no. I'm glad you did." He took a breath and his eyes came alive again. He set the beer bottle down and took my hand. "You have a right to know, given what's passed between us."

I stood still, not wanting to arouse the jealousy of his other self. Took a swig of beer.

"Here's the situation, Elle. My wife won't recover. I won't di-vorce her because, as I've said, her condition is my fault. I can't abandon her." He lifted my free hand to his mouth, kissed it.

I stiffened.

"I have no right to ask this. I can't offer you marriage or a future. But you're not like other women, Elle. You are a com-plete person, comfortable in your skin. You don't need me to fix or change you. You don't expect me to be God. You let me be who I am, flaws and all."

I held my breath, sensing where he was heading. Trying to figure out a neutral response. Something that would neither hurt him nor incite his alter ego. Wondering if he might transform into his wife's character right in front of my eyes. Picturing it. Would he use a falsetto? Pull a knife out of his pants' pocket? Oh God.

He was still talking. "Anyway, forgive me for sounding maudlin. But what I'm trying to say is that I'd like it if—Elle, can I see you again? I could come to the States in a few—"

Susan pulled the sliding door open. "Dr. Du Bois—it's Jen—"

Alain let go of my hand and rushed inside.

As I followed, I heard an ear-shattering scream.

~

"I think she's having a reaction to the salve." Susan hurried, sounded scared.

"Salve?"

"The scar-prevention stuff you sent. With your nurse."

Alain gaped at Susan. "My nurse?"

Susan looked around. "I think she left right before you got here."

We hurried, frenzied, while Jen screamed and Susan kept talking, saying that she couldn't remember the nurse's name. That the nurse had said Alain had sent her because he was running so late. That moments after Jen applied the salve as instructed, her skin had gotten red and burned.

We ran through the bedroom, into the bathroom where Jen stood in the shower, belting out a litany of curses. I stood in the doorway, helpless, chewing my lip.

"I didn't know what to do," Susan jabbered, "so I threw her into a cool shower."

"Get clean towels," Alain commanded. "And washcloths. And gauze. Let me see that salve."

Susan rushed around, assisting. Alain spoke calmly to Jen, trying to examine her, telling her not to stand directly under the spray. I felt useless. Confused. Couldn't understand what had happened. An allergic reaction? A pharmacy mistake?

And why didn't Alain remember sending the nurse over? Had he been so busy at the clinic that he'd forgotten? So busy that he'd even given her the wrong salve? Dammit. What if Alain had had another "moment of carelessness," making another mistake, causing an accident that harmed Jen the way he'd harmed his wife?

Jen wasn't cursing anymore, just whimpering. I couldn't bear to listen. I left the room, wandered uselessly across the living room, pacing. Worrying. Thinking about the nurse.

What if Alain hadn't forgotten about her, but hadn't sent her? What if the nurse's uniform had been a disguise like the maid's uniform?

Was it possible that Alain's other persona had dressed as a nurse, wearing a wig, keeping his face turned away so no one would recognize him? After all, she'd left moments before he'd arrived. He could have changed his clothes and come back. In fact, he might have worn the nurse's disguise and injured his other patients earlier, at the clinic.

Oh God. Was it possible? Could Alain be that sick?

I didn't want to think so. And in truth, I had no evidence that he was. All I had were possibilities and my imagination. But there had to be other possibilities.

I tried to think of some. Couldn't stop picturing Alain in a nurse's uniform, a maid's uniform. His features were refined; he wouldn't make a bad-looking woman. Except for his jaw. And the hair on his hands. And his prominent Adam's apple. Susan would probably have noticed. Jen definitely would have.

So the nurse couldn't have been Alain. And if she hadn't been Alain—

I stopped breathing, bit my lip. Maybe it had been Alain's wife all along. Maybe she was well enough to attack Alain's patients, seeking vengeance on the women who'd received her nose and lips.

My mind spun. One minute I was suspecting Alain, the next his disabled wife. For all I knew, Jen's reaction wasn't related to either of them. It might merely have been an allergy. But, deep down, I knew better. One of them, Alain or his wife, had gone too far, had hurt my friend. And I couldn't let that go. Had to find out.

The clinic was close to the hotel. Even limping, I could be there in ten minutes. I would pay a visit to Mrs. Du Bois and find out how badly disabled she was, how angry she was. And whether or not she was capable of doctoring Jen's medication or slicing Greta's face.

In the next room, Susan was soothing Jen. Speaking in mommy tones, saying that she'd be fine. Alain was telling Jen to lie still so he could apply cool compresses, then assuring her that the burns were superficial and wouldn't cause scarring. That, even so, she'd have to change the dressings twice a day, use antibiotic cream, apply aloe. He talked on.

I didn't tell them where I was going, didn't want Alain to object or try to stop me. Besides, I'd be back before they even knew I was gone. I hurried to my bedroom to get my shoes, so focused on what I was about to do and what I might learn that I didn't pay attention to anything else. So I didn't see the nurse hiding by the door, and I'm not sure which happened first, the flash of white light or Charlie's voice calling my name.

~

"Come here, Elf." Charlie sounded comforting. "Let me hold you."

Charlie was with me. Did that mean I was dead again? Damn.

"Charlie?" I tried to speak. I might have, wasn't sure. Thoughts and actions seemed to have merged. "Where are you?" I couldn't see him, couldn't open my eyes. But I felt his arms around me.

"Nobody else ever mattered to me. I compared every other woman to you. They never came close."

"Stop bullshitting," I told him, or thought I did. "It's too late. It doesn't matter any more."

"Of course it matters. We have the entire future."

He continued, but I didn't understand what he said next because it was in Spanish.

Wait. Spanish? Charlie didn't speak Spanish. And I was answering in Spanish, which I didn't speak either.

Damn. Did people speak new languages after death?

Even in my confused state, I realized that it made no sense.

If I were able to speak a language, I would also be able to understand it, wouldn't I?

I faded for a moment, resting in Charlie's arms. "It's okay," he whispered. "I'm here. You're not alone."

See that? I thought. He's speaking English again.

I listened as he'd told me to stay still.

Susan yelled. "What's going on? Oh God—Elle? What the hell—"

A man said, "Get out."

A woman yelled, "No, do not move. Stay right there."

So the man's voice hadn't been Charlie's. And the woman's hadn't been mine. So whose were they? Where was I?

"Charlie?" I tried again.

"What's happened to Elle?" Susan demanded. She sounded far away.

It was a good question. What had happened? Slowly, I took inventory, starting at the top. The back of my head hurt. Oh, and my eyes were closed. Cautiously, I opened one. Saw a broken lamp. And fabric—The hem of a bedspread. I closed the eye again. Reasoned that I must be on the floor beside Becky's bed. That my head hurt because someone had hit me with the lamp.

The man and woman kept arguing. Back-and-forth. Spanish and English, English and Spanish.

"*Ponga la cuchilla. Por favor. Venir aqui.*" The voice was Alain's.

"*No. Yo le voy a matar.*"

"You don't want to kill her. She's no one to me. Just a tourist."

"Don't you think I can see her face? Look at the wounds. I can see that you destroyed her, too."

"No, she's not a patient."

"Liar. She's one of your women. I can see your trademark in her scars. I can smell you on her skin."

"Please, Inez. *Te amo.*"

Inez? I opened my eyes, turned my head. A woman in a

nurse's uniform crouched over me. Holding a long, thin knife over my chest.

"*Te odio,*" she hissed. "You ruined me. You made me ugly, and now you spurn me."

"It's not true, Inez—"

"You think I'm not good enough for you. You go to other women instead. Women you've made beautiful. Well, no more. *Es terminado*. I'll finish them. Or I'll make them as ugly as I am—"

"Inez," I could see Alain's feet step closer to the bed. "You are my only love. *Solo le amo.*"

"Really? Then tell me: how come you help every woman but me? You take crows and make them swans. But me you leave ugly. Why didn't you just kill me? Then at least I wouldn't scare children and repulse everyone who sees me—"

"Don't say that, Inez. It's not like that. I'm trying to help you. Everyone at the clinic is trying." He tried to sound soothing, but his voice was unsteady.

"The clinic? Hah. You sent me there so you wouldn't have to look at me. Admit it."

"No. It's not true."

"Anyway, they can't help me. How are they going to take away my disfigurement and give me back my face?"

Alain sighed. His feet moved closer.

"No—stay back. And you—don't move."

"Okay. I'm not moving." Susan's voice came from outside the door.

I turned my head slightly, tested my fingers and toes. The knife was just a few inches above my breastbone. If I rolled over, she'd miss my heart, hit my side. Maybe puncture a lung—or was it a kidney. I couldn't remember anatomy. Couldn't think of parts of my body that hadn't been injured yet. My head buzzed. Inez's knife was inches from my heart. I didn't dare move, and yet I had to if I wanted to escape.

Alain kept talking, trying to calm her. Asking her to put

down the knife. Swearing his love for her. "You are still beautiful to me. *Mujer bella.*"

"Oh, yes. Very beautiful. Except, if I am so beautiful, why can't you make love to me anymore? When's the last time, Alain? You can't remember, can you?"

"I will, *mi amado.* I'll make love to you now. Let's go home. *Haga el amor conmigo.*" Alain stood near my head. "Come to me, Inez. You are the love of my life."

The love of his life? Charlie's exact words. Did all husbands say that to their wives? Or just all cheating husbands?

"*Lo siento. Es demasiado tarde.*" Inez turned, met his eyes with fire and raised the knife, ready to plunge it into me.

Reflexively, I thrust a hand onto her arm and a knee into her hip, surprising her, diverting her aim, unbalancing her. She glared, recovering, swinging the blade at me, shouting, "*Te matara,*" as Alain pounced, trying to disarm her. He reached for the hilt, missed, caught the blade, yowled. Dived onto her. Susan joined in, grabbing Inez's legs, pulling her away from me.

As they struggled, I managed to sit up, felt a bump on the back of my head. Inez turned and twisted, still wielding her knife. The light was on, so I could see pretty well. And as closely as I studied her face, I couldn't see the slightest trace of a scar.

～

Susan and Alain finally pinned her down. Inez panted and muttered in Spanish, spat when Alain spoke to her. But, finally, she stopped resisting and seemed to quiet down.

"Where's the knife?" Susan looked around.

She sat on Inez's knees; Alain's torso covered her shoulders.

Alain shifted his weight, peeking under the dresser. When he did, Inez wriggled her arm out from under him, raised her fist, stuck the blade into his side. Alain slumped on top of her. Air rushed out of his lungs. Susan screamed my name, telling me to do something. I grabbed hold of the bed, pulled myself up. Saw Inez pulling the knife up, ready to stab him again. I lunged at her wrist, took hold of it, and yanked. She spouted torrents of Spanish, fighting to get free, but I held on, squeezing and rotating it.

"Inez," Alain breathed. "What have you done?"

Inez ranted.

"What the fuck?" Jen stood in the doorway, gaping. She must have heard the struggle and come to investigate. Her nose was covered with a wide gauze patch, her robe hanging open, revealing other patches on her breasts and belly. "Holy fucking crap."

"Call," Susan was out of breath. She struggled to hold Inez down with her legs and grab a t-shirt from Becky's open suitcase. "Call for help." She pressed the shirt onto Alain's open wound.

"Jesus God," Jen stood frozen, gaping.

"Use the hotel phone," Susan barked. "Now!"

Jen left.

"Inez. You've killed me," Alain wheezed.

"No, she hasn't," Susan told him. "You're going to be fine." She looked at me with eyes full of shock and the heightened strength of adrenaline. And doubt.

My whole body hurt. I was tired of twisting Inez's wrist. I was just tired. With a final effort, I tugged her arm back and landed my full weight on it with the knee of my good leg. I heard a crack. She howled, dropping the knife to the floor. I pushed it out of reach, even though Inez wouldn't be able to pick it up. Then I grabbed a towel and helped Susan put pressure on Alain's still gushing wound. Everyone was making noise—Alain moaning. Susan soothing him. Jen calling that help was on the way. Inez ranting in Spanish.

"*Por favor, Señora.*" She moaned, looking at me.

Was she talking to me?

"I don't want them to see me."

She was looking at me. Urgently. Must be talking to me.

I pressed on Alain's ribcage. Wondered if he would die.

"Señora?" Inez persisted. "Please. When they come. Cover me?"

"What?"

"Can I have a scarf? A shawl? Even a towel? Something. Please. I can't let people see."

See what? "You're fine." My head hurt. I touched the place where she'd slammed my head. It was tender and lumpy.

She wouldn't stop. "I beg you, señora. If you have any humanity, a shred of kindness, understand my shame."

The shame of stabbing her husband? "You mean you're sorry?" I could understand that.

"Don't mock me, señora."

Mock her? Alain's moans were getting fainter. Susan grunted, pressing on his torso with bloodied hands, sitting on Inez's thighs.

"Don't make me show my face," Inez was still talking. "The scars. Please. Let me cover them."

"Mrs. Du Bois, honestly," my voice was flat, "I don't see any scars."

She kept talking. "Of course, you don't believe it, but I was once beautiful. My husband—he did this." She turned her head to show me a cheek. "Please don't make me display my disfigurement in public."

I stared at her cheek. It was smooth. Soft. The skin was unmarred.

"Please, out of pity. Lend me a towel. Anything."

I met her eyes. This woman had murdered both Greta and Claudia. She'd attacked others, including Jen and me, and she'd stabbed Alain. But her pleas were so despairing, her tone so mournful, that I stood up and went to my suitcase and took out a shawl I'd bought as a souvenir.

"*Gracias.*" She smiled, then grimaced in pain, trying to move her arm. "Please—tie it. Hide my face."

Susan watched me. Alain was silent. Was he dead? Unconscious?

Jen kept repeating, "Help's coming," until she looked at me, draping my shawl around Inez's head. "WTF, Elle? What are you doing?"

I shook my head, shrugging. I wasn't sure why I was doing it, but I draped the shawl around her face. As I did, I noticed a white mark the width of a hair and the length of a fingernail on the side of her chin.

Or did I? Maybe it was just a flicker of light.

∾

I was wary of knives. Done with them. When Susan began slicing limes, my leg, cheek, and collarbone tingled. I thought of Inez and Greta, and I couldn't watch. Couldn't be in the same room as the splitting of skin, the squirting of juice.

I backed away, but she stopped me.

"Don't be so queasy." She handed me three shot glasses and the tequila bottle.

It was late at night. Or, no, early in the morning, sometime before dawn. Alain had been taken to the clinic. Sergeant Perez's officers had taken Inez. Jen was sprawled on the living room sofa under compresses, no longer in pain. I'd been examined by one of Alain's colleagues, who said I had a bump on my head but no serious damage.

Susan, Jen, and I passed around the bottle and lime slices, downing shots.

"Take another." Susan commanded. We took tequila as if it were medicine.

Susan leaned back in her easy chair, let out a long breath. "You owe me, Jen."

Jen didn't move. "Fuck, I do."

"If I hadn't tossed your ass into the shower, you'd be a skinless wonder."

"What was it?" I asked. "Some kind of acid?" I hadn't been there for the explanation. I'd been in my bedroom, getting knocked out.

"Alain thought it was bleach or oven cleaner. She put it in

skin cream." For the nine hundredth time, Jen picked up her robe, peeked under a gauze pad. "Damn. Who knew bleach could burn like that?"

"Well, you're not supposed to rub it onto fresh wounds."

Jen swallowed another shot.

Susan picked at her fingernails. "I feel like Lady Macbeth. I've got blood permanently under my nails. It soaked into my cuticles."

"Bleach gets blood out," Jen suggested. "Use some of my skin cream."

"Maybe I'll just paint my nails red."

We sat silent for a while. Jen asked if it would be worth it to go to bed. Susan said no way. She wasn't going to close her eyes until the plane landed in Philly. I said we wouldn't be able to sleep anyhow with all the adrenaline in our blood.

We put on the television and watched programs in a language we didn't understand. We talked about what we'd do when we got home. Susan cringed, dreading all the Christmas shopping she'd have to do. She asked Jen if she'd bought Norm's gift yet.

"You bet I did. I got him a flat tummy and new boobs."

"How very Neanderthal," Susan said. "After all your years of marriage, you still think he loves you for your body?"

Oh, here we go, I thought. I poured another shot of tequila and curled into the cushions.

"Why are you such a bitch, Susan? Norm loves me for me, and part of me is my body—"

"But he'll love you more if your boobs are perky?"

"I never said that he'll love me more. But who knows? Maybe he will."

Susan smirked, shook her head.

"Damn, Susan. What the hell's wrong with you? Are you jealous? That's it, isn't it? You're frickin' jealous that I improved myself."

"Improved yourself? Really? If you want to improve yourself, learn Italian. Or read a book—"

"You wish you had the guts to get your boobs done. Or some liposuction on your thighs and butt."

"You're saying my thighs and butt are fat?"

"I'm saying you've had three kids. And if you got your body back the way it was when he married you, Tim would love it."

"Tim wouldn't notice."

"Of course he would. Don't be embarrassed, Susan. There's no shame in maintenance. We maintain our houses and cars, why not our bodies? I can hook you up with a great doctor."

"Unless he dies," I blurted.

They turned to me, startled, as if they'd forgotten I was there.

"He's not going to die," Jen said. "Is he?"

"Of course not." Susan set her jaw.

For a long time, nobody said anything. The silence was full of worries and doubts, but at least no one was bickering. And soon it would be morning, and we would go home.

≈

Sergeant Perez came by while we were having coffee. He'd stopped at the desk and retrieved our passports.

"Have a safe trip home, señoras." He laid the passports on the kitchen table.

Susan offered him coffee. He accepted, took a seat beside Jen.

"It's been a long night." He sucked his coffee with a loud slurp.

"For all of us," Jen flinched at the sound.

"You've had quite a difficult week here," he noted. "I hope you won't think badly of Nuevo. It's generally a very peaceful place. I hope you will come back again."

Really?

"Oh, we will," Jen promised. "In fact, Susan's thinking of getting some work done when Dr. Du Bois recovers."

Susan glared. "Isn't it time for your aloe treatment?"

"How is he?" I asked.

"He was sleeping when I was there. But I had a long talk with his wife." Another loud slow slurp.

We sat watching him, waiting for him to say more. He didn't.

"So did she tell you anything?" Susan prodded.

"It's confidential, part of the investigation."

Susan nodded, offered him a pastry.

"Gracias, Señora." He eyed them, selected a large one with cheese. "You know, since you are leaving, I suppose there is no harm in me telling you just a little bit." He took a bite, washed it down with a noisy swig of coffee. "Señora Du Bois was quite adamant. She denies having anything to do with the deaths of her husband's patients. In fact, she insists the killer was the doctor himself, dressed as a woman, impersonating her."

I swallowed. Saw the maid's uniform hanging in her closet. A chill slithered up my back, encircled my skull.

"Obviously, the woman is *loca*—I mean she needs psychiatric care."

"What else did she say?" My voice was unsteady.

Perez hesitated. He set his cup on the table, blinked at it. "*Tonterias*—it's nonsense."

We waited. My skin tingled.

"I try to make sense of it, señora. She says her husband caused her to be—*fea*—ugly. Disforme. Your word is 'deformed'? But she is a beautiful woman. Truthfully, I see no deformity. But she insists that Dr. Du Bois ruined her and then became determined to re-create her as she'd been before her injuries—"

"So he did work on her," Jen said. "That explains why she looks so good."

"No, señora. The work wasn't on his wife. He tried to re-create her beauty by making his patients into likenesses of her."

Jen's eyelashes flapped. She touched her nose.

Susan said, "That's crazy."

"*Sí*," Perez chewed the sweet roll. "But, according to Señora

Du Bois, these patients were never exact re-creations. They never met his expectations. So, like an artist unsatisfied with his work, he destroyed them."

"What?" Jen set her coffee mug down.

"Ridiculous," Susan said.

"Indeed," Perez agreed. "Nevertheless, she says she was only trying to stop her husband from hurting more of his patients. She insists that he is the only person she harmed—except, unintentionally, you, señora, when you discovered her." He looked my way.

"What about me?" Jen asked. "She pretended to be a nurse and brought me salve that almost burned my skin off."

"Oh, yes, the salve. I almost forgot. She insists that she picked it up from Dr. Du Bois's office when she checked his schedule. He had made up the cream and the prescription bottle had your name on it, so she brought it along. She said she had no idea anything was wrong with it."

Susan and I exchanged doubtful glances.

"Inez Du Bois will be charged with the murders, of course. But clearly, the woman is *loca*." Perez pointed to his head.

"Insane," Susan said.

"*Sí*. Insane."

Or was she? Inez's story was detailed and consistent. Could an insane person create such details and consistency? I repeated her version of the facts in my mind, trying to find a discrepancy. But I couldn't. Maybe Inez had misinterpreted events. Or projected her own guilt onto Alain or twisted facts to fit her distorted perceptions.

Or maybe she was simply stating unbearable but nevertheless actual truth. After all, hadn't I already considered the possibility that Alain had murdered Claudia and Greta? Hadn't I imagined that he'd impersonated Inez, wreaking her vengeance on women he'd had affairs with? I'd discounted these suspicions, discarded them. But what-if? Was it possible that I'd been right?

No. It wasn't. I hadn't been. When it came down to it, I

couldn't imagine Alain's wiry male body stepping into a maid's uniform. Or any other woman's clothing. And even if he did, he wouldn't pass for a woman. Didn't move like one. No, he hadn't posed as a woman to kill his patients. At worst, he was guilty of hiding evidence that would incriminate his wife.

Even so, I shuddered at Inez's vehemence. The woman was determined to ruin Alain by blaming him for her own crimes. Punishing him for whatever harm—real or imagined—that he'd caused her. But Alain could not be a murderer. I would have sensed murder in his touch, wouldn't I?

But then again, had I sensed Charlie's cheating in his kiss? Or seen his lies in his eyes? Nope. I hadn't had a clue. Had been deceived and naïve. So, if I hadn't sensed treachery in my own husband, how could I be sure of a man I'd met only a week ago?

Perez's hand extended before me, a foot or two from my chest. Oh dear. I hadn't noticed it. How long had it been there, waiting for me to shake it?

"Señora?"

I grabbed it in both of mine, met his eyes. Hoped he hadn't noticed me drifting. "Thank you for all you've done, Sergeant." I started to get up to say good-bye.

"No, sit. You need to rest." He moved on, shook Jen's hand, then Susan's. Wished us all well and said that he hoped we'd return. "*Hasta la proxima!*"

Susan showed him to the door, pushed her hair behind her ear. Taking a deep breath, she gave us each our passports.

≈

Our suitcases were packed. A doctor dropped by with Jen's discharge papers.

Becky still wasn't back when I limped over to the clinic to see Alain. He was hooked up to IVs and looked ashen.

"Elle." His eyes brightened when I came in. "I thought you'd left without saying good-bye."

"No. I wouldn't."

"Your face is healing nicely."

I shook my head, smiling. "In the last week, I've had more injuries than I had in my whole life."

"Well, at least nothing was life threatening." He paused. "And I hope the week wasn't all bad."

"No. It wasn't all bad." I went to the bed, kissed him, felt no murderous emanations. "How are you, Alain?"

"An inch deeper, I wouldn't be here to answer you."

"So you'll live?"

"It looks that way." He smiled, but the light faded from his eyes. "She isn't responsible, you know."

"Alain, your wife tried to kill you. And she blames everything on you."

"Yes. Sergeant Perez just came by. She told him the deaths were all my fault, not hers." He reached for his cup of water, but had trouble lifting his arm.

I held the cup for him while he drank. When he finished, I sat on the chair beside the bed. "Tell me, Alain." I needed to hear him explain. "Why is your wife accusing you?"

"Because I'm at fault." He sighed. "Inez is a passionate woman. And jealous. And possessive. She wants me to suffer the way she has suffered."

I shook my head.

"She suspected I was having affairs with my patients."

"And you were."

"Yes, a few. But, since the accident, Inez felt unattractive. She would have suspected me of being unfaithful even if I hadn't been. After I had her admitted to the clinic, she decided to punish me by eliminating the women she thought were my paramours. She was quite clever about gaining access to them. She dressed as a maid and asked Claudia to help her change a light on the balcony. When Claudia stood on a chair to hand her the lightbulb, Inez shoved her over the balcony. As you know, Claudia caught the railing, and Inez would have forced her to let go, but she heard you on the other side of the wall and ran inside. In fact, she came to your suite next, pretending to be working, watching to see what would happen. Obviously, she was relieved when Claudia fell." He paused, wheezing a little.

"More water?"

He shook his head. "She got into my office at the clinic and looked up my schedule. Found my patients." His eyes became empty. "She dressed as a nurse to visit Greta. Greta's face—I'd made it exquisite—practically identical to Inez's. When Inez saw her, she became enraged. She destroyed it."

I stiffened. Alain had made Greta's face almost identical to Inez's, just as Inez had said. What else had Inez been right about? I didn't dare find out. I started to stand. "I ought to go."

"Wait. I want you to understand, Elle."

"What's there to understand, Alain? Inez is a murderer. She tried to kill you."

"She was on a rampage, avenging her wounds. Protecting herself. Preventing me from finding happiness with another woman."

"So she's not at fault because?"

"Because of the crash—I caused it. A shard of glass cut her face."

"So?" What did that have to do with murder?

He met my eyes. His lips formed a smile, but his eyes remained dour. "She believes she's disfigured. I treated her after the accident. She thinks I damaged her."

"But her face is fine."

"She believes she's terribly scarred. Her self-perceptions are—not accurate."

Wait. His wife had that disorder? The one that distorted self-perceptions?

"Inez has body dysmorphic disorder. She sees any small imperfection as grossly catastrophic. The scar on her face—"

"I saw it. It's barely noticeable."

"It was her undoing. In the years after the accident, she sunk into depression. Cut off contact with her friends. Refused to appear in public. Railed at me for deforming her. Confined herself to her bedroom. I gave her antidepressants, but they didn't work. About a month ago, I finally moved her into the clinic for in-patient psychiatric treatment."

"That's sad. But it doesn't mean she isn't at fault. Lots of people are depressed, and some think they're ugly. But they don't go around killing people."

He didn't move. "Inez is not well. Her thinking is—skewed."

Skewed, yet well organized and capable of complicated planning. Able to disguise herself as a maid and get into Claudia's suite. Able to construct a way to push her over the railing. And able to get out of the clinic into the hotel.

"How did she do it, Alain?"

He tilted his head, not understanding the question.

"If she was here in the clinic, how did she kill people in the hotel?"

"She was a patient, not a prisoner. Inez came and went freely. She took her medications and participated in therapy sessions. She wasn't confined. No one suspected that she'd hurt anyone."

I eyed him. "Not even you?"

His eyes shifted slightly. "Of course not."

"Come on, Alain." I leaned close to him, lowered my voice. "You knew how angry she was. And how jealous. And how unstable. When women you'd had affairs with began dying, you must have suspected your wife."

He looked at the window. Didn't answer.

I sat in silence until I understood that he wasn't going to say anything else.

"Well. I'm glad you'll be all right. Good luck, Alain." I stood to go.

"Elle, please—" He turned to me, his eyes haunted. "Have you ever loved someone deeply?"

I didn't answer.

"I mean so deeply that they became everything to you? So deeply that you lost yourself in them, that your own essence faded into theirs?"

What?

"Have you been so close to a person that you actually see the world through their eyes? Feel their joys or pains or sorrows as your own? Overlook their failings? Forgive them anything, no matter how heinous?"

I didn't move. Charlie appeared beside the window, winked at me.

"That's how deeply I've loved Inez. Sometimes it's as if she and I are one being, two halves of the same soul. Whatever she says, whatever she does, becomes part of me. I can't judge her."

What was he trying to say? That he'd known she'd committed the murders? That he hadn't tried to stop her?

"I know it sounds crazy, Elle. But Inez owned me. Even when I was with other women, it was only because when I looked at them, I saw her."

What? No way. He couldn't have seen her in me.

"Except once. You."

My face got hot. I didn't move.

"I meant what I said, Elle. I didn't think of Inez when I was with you. I reemerged, the person I used to be. Before." He tried to smile at me. Failed. "You are the only woman I've been myself with. The only one I haven't tried to change or felt I had to lie to."

Again, I wondered why, out of all the women he knew, he'd picked me.

"There's something about you, Elle. I've tried to figure it out. It might sound crazy, but I think it's your energy. Or—what do they call it? Your aura? Something. It attracts me to you, pulls me in like a magnet."

Oh God. Madam Therese laughed in my ear. "I told you so. You believe me now?"

I glanced at the window. Charlie was gone.

I leaned over, kissed Alain good-bye. "Good luck, Alain," I said. It seemed inadequate, but I couldn't think of anything else.

I hurried out of his room, past the front desk. On the way

out, I noticed a woman sitting in the corner of the lobby, her face covered with a scarf.

I stopped, spun around, went back into Alain's room.

~

"Just tell me," I burst through the door. "No bullshit this time."

"Elle?" Alain's eyes widened. He pressed against the pillows as if he thought I'd strike him.

"Were you there when Claudia died?"

"What?"

"Your story about how Inez lured Claudia onto a chair and pushed her off the balcony. How can you possibly know that?"

"What?" He seemed unable to say anything else.

"How do know what happened to Claudia? Unless you were there?"

"What? You think I was there?" He coughed, held his chest. "You think I stood by and watched?"

"Did you?"

"Why don't you just ask if I killed her myself?"

"All right. Did you?"

He looked away, slumping in the bed, shaking his head. "You think that little of me?"

"Answer me, Alain."

He looked up. His eyes were dull, hopeless. "I know what happened to Claudia because Inez told me."

I didn't know what to say. How should I know if he was telling the truth? "Okay. I needed to hear it."

"No. You're right. I'm guilty."

What?

"I didn't push her, but I'm just as much to blame as Inez. Maybe more. In a way, I killed Claudia. And Greta, too."

I stood perfectly still.

"If I hadn't been unfaithful, if I hadn't molded women to look like Inez, if I hadn't crashed our car and scarred my wife, no one would have died. But I did all those things. I did them even though I knew Inez and the fire of her passion and the possessiveness of her love. Inez and I are as one, and we are both to blame. I lit the fuse. Inez had no choice but to explode."

~

Waiting for our plane to take off, we sat at a bar at the airport, having a last drink to toast our trip.

Becky was tearful. "Chichi wouldn't let go of me. Did you see how he held onto my hand? He didn't want me to get into the taxi."

Jen rolled her eyes.

"You can come back." Susan downed a shot of tequila. "Christmas break starts in a week."

"He's going to try to get time off and come up to Philly, but it's tourist season. He might have to wait until summer."

"You'll have to pay for the tickets, right?" Jen examined her nail polish.

"What's that supposed to mean?"

"It means Jen needs to back off," Susan warned. "You have your own stuff to worry about, Jen. Like how you'll explain your swollen black-and-blue marks to Norm."

Jen swallowed. "I'll tell him that they're a surprise for Christmas, like I said."

"Uh-huh. Never mind that you lied to him—"

"Susan, back off. Norm'll be fine. In fact, he'll be fucking deliriously happy. He's been like a lost puppy without me."

"Yeah. Tim's been a mess, too. "

"I get it," Becky sniffed. "I've been away from Chichi for only an hour, and look at me. I can't stop crying. It's so hard to be away from the person you love."

Really? They had no idea.

"It's harder for them than for us. Men are more dependent. Norm can barely function when I'm not there."

"Tim either. I had to leave him a list for each day I was gone. When to put the recycling out. Which dinners to defrost—I prepared their meals in advance. What time the girls have to leave for school or get picked up, which shirt goes with which tie. I almost had to remind him to breathe."

"Norm's not that bad. He just works late and eats every meal out. He can't stand to be in the house when I'm not there."

They went on like that, talking about their men. About the strain of being apart for an hour or a week. I downed my Bloody Mary, aware that they were just novices. Newbies. Not like me. Me? I was an authority on being apart. I was a pro—a master of apartness. For me, being apart was a lifestyle. Permanent. Forever. But what if Charlie hadn't died? Our divorce would have been finalized, and then what? Would I have still have missed him? Or would I have gotten sick of him and moved on? Started dating? Fallen in love? I'd never know because Charlie was still in my head, unfinished, undead. I saw him in our den, the last evening we'd spent together. He opened a bottle of my favorite Syrah, his smile dazzling as he handed me a glass. His skin still warm, his eyes still shining and unaware of impending death. How was it that we hadn't sensed it closing in on us? What would we have done differently if we'd known? I started over, watched him pouring wine again. Offering me the glass. He stepped close to me—I could smell him, could feel his heat— and he lifted his glass, toasting our divorce, calling it "just the next phase" of our relationship. Claiming that we weren't over, that we never would be. "No matter what, you're the only one for me, Elf. The love of my life." I heard his throaty whisper. Felt his breath on my neck. I choked up. My eyes misted.

Damn it, Charlie. Was I falling for his act, even now? "The love of his life"? Really? I saw him again, soaping that infernal woman—

No, I had to stop. Charlie was over. Charlie was dead. I listened to Susan, Jen, and Becky and felt his absence, a hollow spot in my chest. Missing Charlie wasn't like missing Tim or Norm or even Chichi. Missing Charlie was a constant state of confusion and contradiction, inconsolable and as continuous as breathing.

A hand was waving in front of my face.

"She's pulling an Elle." Becky blew her nose.

"Yoo-hoo," Jen waved the hand some more. "Anybody home?"

I pushed her hand away.

"Well? Are you going to tell us?"

I'd missed what they'd said, had no idea what they were waiting to hear.

"They want to know about Alain," Susan explained. "Whether you're going to see him again."

"Alain?" I looked at Jen's nose. The swelling was going down; it was beginning to resemble Inez's. "No. That's over." I pictured a maid's uniform, his wife clutching a knife.

"Never mind." Becky said. "We'll see what she says."

What who says?

"Balderdash. Bunk. Don't waste your money." Susan put some cash on the bar. "Let's go. Time to board." She picked up her carry-on and walked off with Jen.

I reached into my bag for some cash, found my beaded jaguar head. I should take it back for a refund. The thing was supposed to have protected me. I shoved it aside, reached beneath it for my wallet.

Becky and I headed for the gate. "Never mind what Susan says. We're going back."

"Back where?"

She looked exasperated. "You didn't hear anything we said?"

I readjusted my shoulder bag.

"Madam Therese."

"You're not serious."

"Of course I am. Everything she said was spot-on. Both of us traveled and met men this week, didn't we? We have to go back. I want to find out more about Chichi. So it's you and me, Wednesday after school."

I kept walking. No way I was going back there. Becky yammered about Chichi all the way to the gate. She was still talking as we boarded the plane. I tuned her out. Didn't want to hear about Chichi or Madam Therese. Or to think about the alleged stains in my aura or the dead spirits I supposedly drew close. I wanted peace and solitude. I wanted quiet and rest.

I wanted to go home. And in just a few hours, I would be there. Back to real life, cold weather, and Christmas shopping. Back to teaching in three weeks. Ready to let go of the past and start the New Year fresh.

Jen and Susan sat together, Becky and I behind them. As I shoved my bag into the overhead bin, I glanced around the plane. It was almost full.

Charlie sat in the back row, between Claudia and a woman whose face was covered by a dull red scarf. When he saw me looking at him, he winked.

I took my seat, not really surprised.